Perfect Match: Book One

Mildred Gail Digby

Yellow Rose Books
by Regal Crest

ISBN 978-1-61929-414-1

First Edition 2019

9 8 7 6 5 4 3 2 1

Cover design by AcornGraphics

Published by:

Regal Crest Enterprises

Find us on the World Wide Web at
http://www.regalcrest.biz

Published in the United States of America

Acknowledgments

I'd like to thank the great people at RCE for their patience and support. Cathy, for always getting the job done even when life happens, Patty who helped me hone my writing technique even though my bad habits have a way of popping up like Whack-a-Mole, and Micheala for her tireless efforts to promote RCE authors.

Dedication

This book is dedicated to my wife.

You are my inspiration and my driving force, my best friend and my biggest fan. Thank you for always being there.

Preface

Itchi is a term used in medicine and forensics to indicate when a sample meets all the conditions of a pre-determined data set. When the result of itchi is highly desired, the possibility increases that the data may be misinterpreted, or certain outlying evidence dismissed as extraneous in order to skew the results to indicate a perfect match when in reality, it is anything but.

Chapter One

HER FINGERS SHOOK as she gently palpated the child's abdomen. Behind the hygienic mask, Megan clamped her teeth down on her lower lip.

"Hold still, Nikky honey," Megan said. Her voice threatened to shake and she forced the next words out. "That's a good boy."

"I'm a girl."

"Oh, I'm sorry." Megan concentrated on keeping her eyes down and her breathing even as her chest tightened. "I must have misread the chart."

"No you didn't." This time it was Nikky's mother Fabia Okamoto who spoke. She dropped her voice to a hiss and whispered, "Nikolaus, how many times have I told you to stop this nonsense?"

"My name is Nikky and I'm a girl!"

Megan blinked. She had misread the situation, not the chart.

"Hold still, please," Megan said. She silently begged the tears she saw welling up in Nikky's eyes not to spill.

"My tummy hurts."

"I know, Nikky," Megan said. "We'll make it better soon, okay princess?" She tacked the last bit on and didn't care about the way Nikky's mother let out an angry sigh and crossed her arms. The wishes of the patient took priority.

She ran down the mental checklist of steps she used in order to make her diagnosis. She prayed it wasn't what she thought it was. The child on the table gave a little whimper and turned to her. Megan's breath came faster, the tunnel vision crowded her. Megan couldn't give in. Not now. She fought the despair that came close on the heels of the panic. It had been a while since she'd wrestled with this particular demon and she'd hoped her battle with it was over. Apparently not. She was desperate for something to do. She grabbed the stethoscope from around her neck and twisted the cord around her fingers, cutting off the circulation.

"How did this happen?" Megan asked. "Really."

"I already told you." Fabia's voice was sharp. Her movements and expression became severe as she grew more agitated. The tension in the room spiked. Megan's heart kicked into high gear. She clenched her hands together and prayed to hold it together long enough to get through the exam. Fabia said, "Nikky was standing on the dining room table and fell on a chair."

"I really did," Nikky said. Dark brown liquid eyes looked up at Megan with all the hope and trust a child could give. "I'm clumsy."

The memory came to her like she was standing outside a window, watching a drama unfold without being able to change it. Crying filled her ears, never-ending and desolate. Shaking hands clutched at a tear-streaked child's face that was already bruising. The whispered words were harsh.

You slipped on the wet floor and fell. That's all you have to say. Do you understand? Mama loves you and wants to protect you. Remember that.

"Okay, okay, let's see," Megan said more to herself than anyone else. Her ears buzzed with static and her chest felt tight. She had at most a minute of control left unless she got out of there. "It doesn't look like anything's ruptured and the urine sample's clear so I'm going to pre-prescribe —" Megan ran out of breath. Her vision narrowed to a pinpoint.

"Are you okay?" Fabia asked. She leaned forward. Her long painted nails dug into the expensive leather of her handbag. Megan's attention got stuck on their shiny beige-ness.

"Yes, I'm fine," Megan gasped as she staggered to her feet. The nurse who was hovering behind the curtain darted forward. Megan made a few circles on the scribbled notes and thrust the page at the nurse. Her own part in the transaction could end there. She had almost made it. "Mrs. Okamoto, I've written Nikky a prescription for the pain. The follow-up appointment's at ten thirty next Thursday, but please come in if there's any change like fever or loss of appetite." She mustered her calmest voice as she said the words automatically, wishing for the patient to take care, "*Odaijini.*"

She didn't wait for an answer. She couldn't. Megan threw herself past the curtains and lurched through the narrow service hallway that connected the examination rooms. Her chest constricted, her throat closed. She couldn't breathe. With a quick jerk, she ripped off the mask and stuffed it into a pocket of her white coat as she forced her trembling legs to carry her—just one more step. And one more after that. The aisle was crowded with boxes. Her foot connected with the corner of one and she nearly tripped but managed to save herself at the last moment. The characteristic double T of Teitel Medical Supplies swam in Megan's vision. Pastel-smocked forms passed by her. Megan knew the nurses were glancing at her and the whispers were soon to follow. She had been fighting to block them out in the week she'd been at the Ruth Kurtz Jewish Hospital, and was doing it well too. Until a six-year-old with abdominal blunt force trauma sent her over the edge. Megan knew what they said about her. She'd heard the rumors, the truncated stories hovering on the edge of her hearing.

She's been out of practice for a year. I heard she hasn't worked since she lost her husband.

Motorcycle accident, dangerous things.

In Thailand, of all places! I'd hate to get injured there. So filthy!

I'm not surprised, it's chaos over there.

I heard he didn't stand a chance. Dead on the table before they even brought him in.

He deserved it, living in a place like that.

It certainly threw her for a loop. Such a pity something like that had to happen to someone so young. Such a promising career too! I hope she can get past it.

Her back landed hard against the cold bathroom wall. Her legs gave out and Megan sank to the floor. Fumbling and clumsy, she groped at her pockets. Finally she came up with a small bottle. Megan didn't open it, but clutched it to her forehead as if trying to inject the pills clattering around the bottom of it directly into her brain. Just holding the bottle helped. The shaking breaths slowed. She could do this. Megan held her bottle and let it anchor her. She didn't need to take a pill, but the weight of the object in her hand reminded her of the half-alive hell she'd lived while on them, solidifying her decision to wean herself off the medication over the past ten months. Her current therapist agreed with Megan that she wasn't in need of chemical remedies, just a kind ear and a forgiving point of view. Megan took the last dose two weeks ago. It was barely anything, only a bit of dust and the tiniest chip of a single tablet.

Her previous therapist never understood her reluctance to rely on the pills, only prescribing her more drugs, urging her to try a new this or that. Maybe he should have prescribed more bottles. In spite of herself, Megan found a wry smile on her lips.

"It's not an illness to be sad," Megan breathed the words. She squeezed her eyes shut. It wasn't an illness to make a mistake either. She had done both more than enough and hated the claw marks they'd left on her soul.

Her inner turmoil was interrupted by a patter of feet that stopped right outside the door, followed by a flurry of knocking.

"Meguuuu!" The singsong voice rang out from the other side of the door. "Are you all right in there, sweetheart? If you don't answer in five seconds I'm coming in, and I don't care if it's the ladies' or not. I'm cute enough to pass, so there."

"I'm all right, hang on a minute, Luka," Megan said. She took an experimental breath and was relieved to find the tightness in her chest easing. She lurched to her feet. Somewhere along the way, she'd lost her elastic hair band. For a moment, golden brown waves obscured her vision. Megan brushed her hair back so it fell over her shoulders instead of into her face, and in the process she snagged the two sparkly butterfly barrettes she wore to please and distract her little patients. Automatically, Megan shoved them into her pocket and glanced down at herself. Her starchy-new white coat was rumpled, the slim-fitting skirt was twisted around and her blouse was untucked. A glimpse in the mirror showed Megan she looked as if she'd just had a quickie. By herself.

If the person on the other side of the door had been anyone else but Luka Carmichael Goto, Megan would have been mortified.

"A minute's up, honey buns, hope you're decent!"

The door swung open and a long, lithe young man slipped in. His skin was a glowing brown, courtesy of his Nigerian mother and his build was slender and delicate from his Japanese father. He was the cutest thing Megan had ever seen and she was certain most of the people who met Luka fell hard for his sweet, sassy charm. For some reason, he'd taken a big-sisterly attitude with her, which amused Megan to no end when she was in a calm state of mind. He was seven years junior to her own twenty-nine, but Megan was already helpless in the face of his affectionate domination.

Luka exhibited that domination as he leaned one hip against the sink and crossed his arms over his light blue nurse's smock.

"You don't look all right," he said. "Come on, Megu-chan. I'll get you a nice cup of tea. Naomi and Arisa went to Osaka a couple days ago and if you're lucky there are some of the cookies they brought back left to go with it."

Megan protested weakly; however, she let herself be led out of the bathroom and down the hallway. She ended up on the elderly sofa that dominated the nurses' call room with a hot cup in her hands and the promised cookie in her mouth.

"I shouldn't be here, messing up your room," Megan said. She swallowed the cookie and shifted against the worn cushions. This was nurse territory and she didn't want to get caught in a turf war.

"Don't worry, honey," Luka said as he swished around the room. "I'm the queen bitch around here. If anybody has issues with you then they are gonna have issues with *a-ta-shi!*" Luka used the feminine form of address for himself and Megan found it uniquely endearing. He plopped down on the armchair across from her and leaned his chin on his clasped hands. "Now, tell me honestly, are you are all right? You ran out of that room like you'd seen a ghost."

"I'm fine," Megan said. She looked into the depths of her cup and studied the ebbs of the dark green powder at the bottom of her tea. The ghosts that haunted her weren't only in that exam room. She dredged up a cleansing breath and said, "Just first week nerves, I guess."

"Well, those are some pretty mean nerves then," Luka said. "Here's a little something to cheer you up!" He leapt up and started dancing. He shook his hips and pirouetted like a pro, adding all the flourishes in the right places. Megan had to cover her mouth to keep the laugh from escaping as he broke into song.

"Let's go, Megu-chan! You are A-okay! You are a fireball of medical know-how and you kick butt! Woo woo! Yay!"

The first real smile Megan had in what seemed like a lifetime broke over her face, then a portly, white-suited figure bustled into the lounge. She stopped in her tracks and demanded Megan's name with a curt, "*Anta, dare?*"

Guiltily, Megan leaped up. The cookie wrapper tumbled from her lap to the floor.

The nurse twitched as she got a better look at Megan. Her frown vanished and she stammered out a hasty apology.

"Please don't worry about it," Megan said. She tried to read the nurse's nametag without making it obvious she was doing so. "Nurse Murase, I was just leaving."

She was halfway down the hallway when Luka's scrambling footsteps caught up with her.

"Megu-chaaaan!" He slung an arm around her shoulders. "I didn't get a chance to tell you I've wrangled a seat at your table tonight. I hope you don't mind."

"Of course not," Megan said. Her shoulders slumped in relief. "You're an angel, Luka. You don't know how much I was dreading having to put up with the pretense this formal dinner thing was to welcome us freshies."

"Uh huh," Luka said. "We all know it's just to booze and schmooze the old-boy crowd. To tell you the truth, the Brockman family needs all the help they can get. Lots of us still prefer the way things used to get done around here."

"Really," Megan said with a chill. The hospital wasn't very large and if there was dissention in the ranks, there wouldn't be any place to hide from the fallout.

"But don't let that get you down, sweetheart," Luka said. "There are plenty of good people to balance out the few boring and stolid ones. For example, Setsuko and Emmy in the cafeteria, they're just the sweetest things you could ever meet and there's our groundskeeper Mr. Yamamoto and of course the entire burn center staff is a real hoot. Oh, and I absolutely adore..."

As they walked, Megan did her best to keep up with Luka's stream of excited talking. She nodded and made appropriate noises in response.

Suddenly, everything went silent as Megan's ears disconnected from her brain. She froze in mid-step and gazed down the hallway, stunned. Her already jangled nerves tingled and her heart pounded. The single most striking person Megan had ever seen was talking to a young couple. She swallowed hard as a spear of heat stabbed her in the belly. While she was at once viscerally aware of the other's undeniable femininity, the object of Megan's scrutiny carried herself with easy, elegant poise and confidence that defied gender.

Swathed in blue-green scrubs, the surgeon stood with her

arms crossed loosely over her chest, bare feet in Crocs placed farther apart than Megan was used to seeing women stand. She looked to be in her mid-thirties and her body was long and slender like a track athlete. Her stance was relaxed as she talked and joked with the couple. Her hair was a single length, just long enough to be tied back with a plain rubber band into a short, spiky tail that stuck out from the nape of her neck. A few strands had slipped free and hung over her brow.

Megan couldn't move her eyes from the tall surgeon, and she didn't want to. The other's face was classic with sculpted cheeks and a fine, strong gaze. Delicate but sweetly full lips that looked as if they could either laugh or scowl in an instant sealed her beauty in Megan's mind. Her stunning androgynous looks were unconventional and while she could never be called pretty, she radiated an allure that sent a needle of light past all of Megan's defenses and struck her hard, right in the chest. Megan was aware there were people who would judge her and dislike her at a glance just as certainly as Megan had been captivated.

Around her feet, a matching set of twin girls tumbled and the surgeon bent down as one of them grabbed onto her leg. Strong arms hoisted the little girl and the woman easily balanced her on one hip, surprising Megan as most Japanese people preferred the front-holding *dakko* way of carrying little ones.

"Earth to Megan!" Luka warbled in her ear.

"Who is she?" Megan asked and cringed at her breathless, almost longing tone. She'd wanted the question to come out much more nonchalantly than it had. She clenched her hands in the pockets of her lab coat as she unconsciously squeezed her pill bottle.

"Oh, that's Syler Terada," Luka said blithely. "I'm not surprised you haven't met her yet. She's got the most patients of anyone here and is always running off somewhere."

"So that's Doctor Terada," Megan said, too stunned to even blink. "She's beautiful," Megan whispered before she could help herself.

Luka hummed thoughtfully as he gazed at Megan.

Of course Megan recognized the name Syler Terada from the pediatrics department roster, and she knew the surgeon specialized in gastrointestinal issues but she'd been preoccupied with trying to get her own stuff in order. She hadn't had a chance to meet more than the nurses in the department, let alone make the trip to the office down the hall from hers where the surgeons and other specialists had their desks. In fact, Megan had barely even met Dr. Charles Brockman, her own department head. Their only communication was his self-important, extremely stolid and boring semi-speech in the office on Megan's first day. He was the son of the hospital's president and she wasn't exactly in a hurry to become friendly with him.

Doctor Terada looked up. Across the hallway their eyes locked. She gave Megan a quick, radiant smile that lit up her face and ignited something warm and tight in Megan's entire body. Her dark eyes held Megan's as if they were the only people in the entire world. Megan's cheeks flamed and she felt instantly foolish as she gave a shy nod in return before she hurried back to her abandoned exam room.

The nurse was waiting for her with a grumpy expression; however, the paperwork was done and on the table. Nikky Okamoto was Megan's last patient of the day and she let her shoulders sag with relief as she sat down on the wheelie chair. However, the day's work was far from finished. Megan tapped a finger on the pile of documents.

"Red flag this file," Megan said in a low voice to the nurse. "Let me know if either Nikky or Fabia Okamoto comes back with any kind of injury, all right?"

"Of course," the nurse said with a drawn look. She knew the drill.

"And I'd like to see the rest of this file, all of it from the very beginning. Oh, and we need to change this from male to female, just make a note here."

"Certainly. Everything will be on your desk by tomorrow morning." The nurse hesitated before she said, "Unless you'd rather wait until after Shabbos. The prohibitions on writing..."

"No, I want to do this as soon as possible."

As Megan went through her notes in preparation to head back to her desk in one of the open-plan offices the hospital allocated to the staff, the nurse took pity on her and placed a paper cup of weak tea by her elbow.

More than her near-panic attack, Megan was shocked at her own wayward thoughts—and actions. She'd been caught giving one of the senior surgeons in her department a thorough once-over, and a female one at that. Megan hugged the thick file folder to herself. There were already enough rumors flying around about herself without Megan adding to them.

She spent the rest of the afternoon at her desk, hiding from people under the guise of being buried in paperwork. The truth was, Megan felt frazzled but alive. More alive than she'd felt in a long time. She reached out with her left hand to grab a pen and inadvertently caught a glimpse of the gold band on her finger. Stung, Megan dropped the pen and cradled her hand. She was so used to seeing the ring she'd almost forgotten it was there.

It had been a non-negotiable part of her since Yasu gave it to her two and a half years ago. Megan let her eyes rest on the slim band for a moment longer. She wondered at the recent breath of life into her heart—and if she had to be honest with herself, a bit lower than that. Yasu was her first lover, her first everything. While Megan still felt the loss, it was no longer the aching void that had threatened to suck her soul into oblivion. It hadn't been for some time, Megan admitted. Was this new rush of feelings an indication she was returning to normal and ready to begin living her life again, or was this just her subconscious throwing a monkey wrench into her already overburdened mind?

Sick with indecision and guilt, Megan pushed herself away from her desk. The attendance-mandatory dinner was three hours away and Megan needed to get home, freshen up a bit, and change into something more formal. Her path to the exit took her past the small but well-appointed chapel on the first floor. Instinct slowed her steps. Megan paused outside the open wooden doors.

"Going home?"

The words made her jump and Megan whirled to see a small, sturdy woman with a prayer shawl draped over her modest suit. Her eyes were kind behind her wire-rimmed glasses.

"Rabbi Sharon," Megan blurted out. She patted herself on the chest as she tried to calm down. "Yes, but I'll be back for the dinner tonight." She hadn't meant to make a face, but her lips twisted as she spoke.

The rabbi reached out a hand and lightly touched Megan's arm. "Are you all right to take part in such a big event? Do you need more time alone to think about things?"

"No, I've been alone long enough," Megan said. The words

rang true on a number of levels.

"That's good to hear. You're coming to shul tomorrow, then?"

"Of course."

"Very good. Service starts at nine o'clock."

"Um, I don't have to read or anything, do I?" Megan shifted from one foot to the other. "It's been a while since I've been to a formal service."

"Don't worry," Rabbi Sharon said. "We are fairly informal, but I don't ask people to read on the spur of the moment. When you do feel ready, just let me know. I try to include as many members of the congregation as possible and it would be lovely to have you read for us."

Megan shook her head. She couldn't imagine standing up in front of the small congregation and raising her voice to God for a while yet. She thought about her attack earlier and felt sick.

"Are you all right? Would you care to sit down for a moment?"

She couldn't speak past the tightness in her throat, so Megan just nodded. Soon she sat down on the comfortable armchair in the rabbi's small office. A cup of tea was pressed into her hands and Megan savored the warmth of it. Tea really did soothe a number of troubles.

"Anything on your mind?" Rabbi Sharon asked in a gentle voice.

Megan looked into the calming, green depths of her cup and said, "I don't feel like a very good Jew. Or a good doctor either."

"Oh pshaw!" Rabbi Sharon slapped her hand down lightly on the desk. "First, what's a good doctor? People hurting and sick come to you and you do what you can and don't kill anyone."

Megan flinched.

"People die, yes, but that's not your fault." Rabbi Sharon paused before she said, "Second, you were born to a Jewish mother and a Jewish father. Being a Jew is not a choice for you. And what's a good Jew? Only God knows that for sure. Do you think you know better than Him? In the end, that's a personal understanding between you and Him. You are doing your best, Meirav and that's enough." She gently called Megan by her Hebrew name.

The rabbi's words eased the worry that plagued Megan since

she'd restarted her professional life and the rocky journey back to observance. She gave Rabbi Sharon a smile before she finished her tea. In addition to the mid-sized private hospital's reputation as having one of the best pediatrics units in the country, which Megan had been invited to join, Rabbi Sharon Kleiner played a key part in Megan's decision to choose that particular institution. While she'd let her own Judaism lapse in recent years, the discussions with the rabbi during her application and interview process helped Megan a great deal. Even more than the months she'd spent under the thumb of her first therapist, who seemed to take an "onion" approach to therapy as he relished peeling back Megan's layers and watching her cry more with each one.

After she took her leave from the rabbi, Megan continued her way to the exit, dodging clumps of in-patients and hurrying nurses. The brief conversation took a weight from her mind and Megan didn't dread the welcome dinner anymore—especially if it gave her another chance to see the elusive Syler Terada. However Megan wanted more than just to see her. She wanted to talk to her, reach out to her and see if she was welcomed. Megan wanted to see those maddeningly tempting lips blossom into a smile.

Shaken, Megan put an end to that line of thought. She didn't know a single thing about the surgeon outside of her name and title. She could very well be married with a bunch of kids at home, no matter how she looked and carried herself.

The doors slid open in front of her. The artificial bubble of jolly international modernity broke and the ancient, unchanged air of Japan embraced her. She closed her eyes as she breathed in the sweet scent of the cherry blossoms that flanked the hospital. The buds had just opened, but they'd be gone in a week and a half—less if one of the sudden, hard rains that area of Gifu Prefecture tended to get in the spring blew in. Suito City got them particularly badly, being at the base of the mountains. Megan feasted her eyes on the pinkish-white blossom-laden boughs as she headed back to her apartment. The wide, squat building was only a five-minute walk from the hospital and while her room wasn't gorgeous, it was comfortable and Megan liked being on her own again. Her parents were lovely people and Megan got along with them fine, but after living with them for the past six months, Megan was more than ready for her own space. While she still felt the emptiness keenly, she was grateful the simple rooms were free of memories.

On her way, Megan passed an ancient little shrine and with a shrug, she decided to stop by for a visit. The gentle Shinto beliefs had been with her since birth and Megan couldn't imagine herself without them even as she tried to reacquaint herself with her own neglected Jewish faith. Plus, it never hurt to cover your bases, she reasoned as she carefully poured the cold water from the brass ladle over her hands, then cupped a small measure of water in one palm and brought it up to rinse her mouth.

She had forgotten a hand towel and Megan glanced about before she wiped her hands on her skirt. She approached the offerings box. She threw in a five-yen coin and rang the clanking bells before she clapped twice and pressed her hands together. Instead of her usual prayer for her family's health, Megan could only think of of Syler Terada's brilliant smile and couldn't help but wish to be the cause of it again.

Chapter Two

"YOU LITTLE *LOBUS*," Megan shot the words in a tight whisper to Luka. She stared dumbly at the table. It was set for six people, located toward the front of the hospital's banquet hall. However, it was neither the expensive crystal glasses nor the opulent flower arrangement that had caught her attention. "You did this on purpose, didn't you?"

"*Konna atashi*?" Luka pressed a hand to his chest as he gave Megan his best *who me?* defense. He acted just a little too innocent for Megan's peace of mind. "I may have knocked a few of them off when I first came in, but I'm certain I put everyone's name card back in the same place. Honest!"

Luka batted his eyes and clasped his hands under his chin, the gesture made even more endearing given the powder-blue ruffled shirt he wore under the light green suit only he could pull off. With a toss of his head, Luka pulled out a chair and shooed Megan toward it. She half-sat, half-fell, still unable to believe the name card that had appeared next to hers. The given name was written with the character for star paired with another one that meant orchid.

"I know what you're thinking, with those characters it should actually be Sei-ra and not Sai-ra."

The words came from behind her. Megan squeezed her eyes shut. Syler Terada's voice was as beautiful as her smile. She had a sexy, languid way of speaking, and drew her vowels out in an accent Megan couldn't place.

"Call it poetic license on my parents' part. They were at the forefront of the so-called *kira-kira* naming trend that's making it hell to be an elementary school teacher these days."

Megan twisted around. Syler Terada stood with her hands casually tucked into the pockets of her charcoal grey dress slacks. She was breathtakingly handsome in a black silk shirt and deep red jacket that was classic in cut and flattered her slender build. Her hair was loose and brushed her collar. In a single touch of femininity, small silver rings shone at her lobes. She had a delicate silver chain around her neck that many of the staff wore, including Megan. However, unlike most, hers didn't bear the Star of David. Megan's own peeked out from under the collar of the light jacket she wore as a nod to modesty over her sleeveless navy dress. Even as her heart sped up at Syler's formal look, Megan couldn't help but recall the enthralling sight of Syler in her comfortably wrinkled scrubs and the aura of professional expertise she radiated.

"Shabbat shalom, honey!" Luka jumped up with a wide grin. "Funny thing we all ended up at this same table!"

"Shabbat shalom," Syler returned the traditional greeting with a smooth familiarity. "I was expecting to be over there with the other surgeons. Not that I'm complaining. The company here seems to be much more interesting." She slung herself into her chair and gave Megan a conspiratorial wink. Still with her eyes on Megan, Syler leaned her elbows on the table for an instant before taking them off with an apologetic look. Megan bit her lip to keep from laughing. As the silence stretched out, Megan couldn't think of anything other than how much she ached to reach out and brush the errant strand of hair back from Syler's brow.

A kick under the table startled Megan out of her fugue and she looked around, confused. Luka gestured with a nod of his head and gave a pointed cough.

Megan jolted forward in her seat and said, "It's nice to meet you, Doctor Terada. I'm Megan Maier."

"I know," she said. "And just Syler is fine."

"Okay, me too. I mean, wait that's not it," Megan said. She wished she could stop stammering and actually speak like an intelligent human, but she was reeling from the effect the other woman was having on her. Words formed in Megan's brain and tumbled out of her mouth. "You can call me Megan or whatever you want."

"How about Meg?" The question was accompanied by an arch of one brow and a quirk of delicately sculpted lips that completely undid Megan.

"Sure," the newly-nicknamed Meg croaked. She realized she really liked it when Syler called her that. Megan cleared her throat and straightened her back. "But just don't call me Megatron."

"I promise I won't," Syler said with a quick laugh.

The other members of their table arrived, an elderly couple along with a bookish-looking young man with glasses and curly chestnut hair that stuck out from under his dark blue yarmulke. They all joined in a lively round of introductions. The couple consisted of Harold Miller, one of the radiologists and his wife Edith, who worked as a clerk for the hospital until she retired a year previously. The young man was Jacob Hartman, a friendly new doctor working in their orthopedics department. Fresh off the plane from the States, he was at that point where he still did things like exclaim over the recycling bins in the train stations. Luka paid particular attention to him and Megan wondered if Syler's name card wasn't the only one that had "accidentally" ended up at their table.

Just as Luka was getting ready to launch into a long personal history, the room fell silent. Rabbi Sharon stood at the front of the room and led the blessing. Megan was pleased to note that both Syler and Luka bowed their heads respectfully and joined in on the "Amen." Then children of the various attendees were called up to perform their part in the ritual.

After the wine and bread, the meal service started. The food was served buffet-style and all of it looked and smelled amazing. As opposed to making up a plate for herself, Megan fell into the friendly practice of collecting an assortment of things for everyone so they could share at their table. To that end, each person had their own smaller dish and chopsticks as well as silverware for their own use.

"Thank goodness for these," Luka declared. He brandished his own chopsticks as they got settled down to eat. "I always choose the wrong fork and end up having to improvise by the end."

"Start from the outside and work in," Edith, who insisted on being called Edie, said.

"Oh, good advice from the eminent Lady Miller. Thank you," Luka sang. He helped himself to some salad from the plate Megan made up and piled on a generous load of gefilte fish. He chewed with a blissful look on his face for a moment before he said, "This is soooo yummy! I want these people to cater my funeral."

"But how will you enjoy it then?" Syler leaned across Megan to better address the young man, which caused Megan's heart to almost leap out of her chest.

"I won't," he said. "But I'll have so many guests seeing me off."

Megan got an uncomfortable jolt but forced a laugh and said, "I'd go for this potato kugel alone, but honestly, I'd rather go to your birthday party than your funeral. I've been to more than enough of those."

The table went quiet at that. Megan clenched her hands around her napkin and uneasily wondered what rumors everyone had heard about herself. She felt Syler's gaze on her.

"But the big question," Syler said, "is which team are you on: *takenoko-no-sato* or *kinoko-no-yama*?"

"What are those?" Jacob asked.

"Two yummy kinds of chocolate snacks, Takenoko are shaped like bamboo shoots and kinoko are like mushrooms," Luka said. He pulled out his phone and intercepted Syler's glare with an impish wink. He jumped up and draped himself over the other young man as he eagerly showed him something on the phone's screen. After a moment, Luka straightened up and said with a toss of his head, "Just so everyone knows, I'm on the kinoko team." He pinched the air with the fingers of his free hand. "They've got that little stem on them so I don't get melted chocolate on me."

"You are such a prima donna, Lukie. How about you, Meg?" Syler asked. Megan's cheeks burned under the direct attention and the irrational pleasure from hearing the nickname in Syler's rich voice.

"Takenoko of course," Megan said. She ignored Luka who pouted and stuck his tongue out at her from across the table. "There's more chocolate and I feel it's a better value."

"There you have it," Syler said. She leaned back in her chair and folded her hands behind her head. "The cookie middle's good too. Better than that silly little stick, I have to admit."

"Syyyyler! Don't tell me you actually agree with Megu-chan?" Luka spat as he flounced back to his seat. Across from them, the elderly couple laughed at the exchange. Luka turned up his nose and said, "For that, I'm not going to be your boyfriend."

"That's fine with me," Syler answered with easy grace. "It would never work out between us anyway. You're far too young and cute. You'd make me look like a lecherous old woman."

"That's because you are one," Luka said with a wave of one hand. He bolted upright and leapt out of his chair as Syler grabbed the empty bread basket and made a move as if to chuck it at his head.

"I'm not old," Syler said in a grouchy voice. Megan fought the laughter that bubbled up from her belly.

"She's thirty-five," Luka announced to the table and surreptitiously nudged Megan under the tablecloth. "Thirty-six in July. A good age, don't you think?"

After she gave Luka an incredulous look, Syler raised her eyes to the ceiling and shook her head as if appealing to God above to save her from the bubbly young man. Giddiness surrounded Megan. She took a deep breath and looked around the table. She felt nothing other than happy for the first time in far too long.

As they were finishing dessert, a shadow fell over the table. Megan glanced up from her fruit salad to see a sandy-haired man loom over them — Dr. Charles Brockman. Solid and well-dressed in what was obviously an order-made suit, he wasn't bad-looking, but there was a forced nature to his smile that Megan didn't find appealing, especially up close. He had a habit of glancing around the room and not looking directly at anyone that also put Megan off, but she guessed it was a side-effect of being the second-in-command of the hospital and co-host of the event.

"I thought I'd instructed Doctor Maier to be seated at the head table, as befitting one of tonight's guests of honor," he said. He had a bottle of wine in his hand and used it in order to insinuate himself at the table.

"Doctor Brockman," Megan said in a formal tone. She felt as if he was accusing her of something.

"I will have to have a word with the catering staff," he said as he leaned forward to fill the glasses of everyone at the table. He looked down at Megan directly for the first time, and said, "I trust you are enjoying your evening?"

"Yes, it's very nice, and I appreciate the chance to be introduced to everyone," Megan said. For some reason, she felt as if she had to speak as if she were performing in one of those boring old-fashioned TV dramas. She wanted nothing more than for him to go away, but he was her boss and his father ran the place, so she sat there and desperately tried to think of something non-stupid to say.

"Well then, how about we make those introductions?"

He didn't wait for her reply before he barreled off. Megan unwillingly followed in his wake. At the long head table, she made mindless small talk until she cleared through the bulk of the senior staff, including President Brockman and his wife, both of whom were much warmer and nicer than Megan feared they'd be. By the time she got through meeting old and grey fellows she was certain forgot her face as soon as she'd passed, the dinner part of the event was over and everybody stood around in conversational clumps.

Even when Megan ran out of people to greet, Doctor Brockman stuck stubbornly by her side. Megan felt trapped and awkward. She glanced around and wished for some way to leave that didn't seem like she was escaping from his dour presence. Her savior appeared in the form of a waving Luka and Megan was able to extricate herself from the vicinity of the head table. Luka was with Syler and Megan's heart gave a funny thump as Syler turned to greet her.

"What do you want to drink?" Syler indicated Megan's empty hands. "They've got wine and cocktails over there, plus soft drinks too."

Her face grew hot, but Megan managed to answer, "Wine would be great."

A few moments later, Megan sipped a lovely sweet red and watched Syler and Luka having a mostly friendly debate, which went on for several minutes.

"The purpose of the entire process is to return the bread to its original, fresh-baked state as much as possible." Syler waved her glass around to punctuate her argument. "That's why you need to preheat your toaster oven."

"No it isn't," Luka declared. "It's so your butter melts and it's all nice and crispy. And to use as a spoon for when you eat stuff like curry and cream stew."

With a deep, long-suffering sigh, Syler turned to Megan and said, "That boy gets the wildest ideas sometimes."

Megan laughed. "I don't know who is right, but you're making me want toast."

Syler looked as if she was about to reply when she twitched violently and turned away from them. Her fingers clenched over her glass. Her shoulders went up in a defensive posture. Megan scanned the room, curious about who or what had precipitated such a reaction. The end of the formal dinner brought a number of guests in to join the cocktail part of the evening, mostly staff members who didn't have the seniority to be invited to the first event.

"Oh God, oh God," Syler muttered to herself, still facing the wall. "I did *not* expect to run into them tonight."

With an uncomfortable heaviness in her gut, Megan watched Syler step away from them and put on a fake smile as she greeted one of the younger physicians who had arrived with a woman on his arm. Megan assumed the woman with him was his wife or at least a serious enough girlfriend to be invited as his partner to the official event. As for the doctor, Megan had met him almost by accident in the physician's office earlier that day when he'd hovered over her desk. She found out his move a few months ago to a hospital up north in the Tohoku area opened up the job that allowed Megan to be hired. He mentioned he'd been invited back for the event. His name was Kobayashi something or other and he was bland and not extremely gregarious, but seemed steady and serious.

"What's wrong?" Megan asked. "Why is Syler so upset?" She had the almost undeniable urge to charge up to Doctor Kobayashi and nail him in the nuts with her uncomfortable high-heeled shoe for whatever he'd done.

"That's her ex," Luka aimed his mouth sideways and said in a stage whisper. "Plus one."

Megan stifled the uncharitable thought that the stolid doctor didn't seem like the type of person Syler would want to associate intimately with.

"Syler dated Doctor Kobayashi?" Megan asked, at once she got a strange rush of relief tinged with disappointment.

"Not exactly," Luka said. He extended a long finger and drew a lazy circle in the air. "Her ex is the new Mrs. Yukina Kobayashi."

"Oh!" All the blood in Megan's body rushed into her head.

She swayed as if she were being buffeted by a strong wind. Under the pretense of sipping at her wine, Megan studied the interplay between Syler, who looked as if she was in the non-medicated throes of appendicitis, and the woman named Yukina, who smiled and chatted as if there was nothing odd with the situation. For some reason she couldn't explain, Megan wanted her to be tacky and trashy, an obvious gold-digger draped in crap jewelry who flaunted herself about in an inappropriate dress. Instead, Yukina was small and cute, with a stylish haircut and tasteful accessories. She deferred to her husband, but in a respectful way rather than as a subordinate. Neither of them seemed to be bad people, Megan had to admit.

However, there was no doubt that something had happened between Syler and Yukina in the past and only one of them seemed to be over it. Megan ruminated fiercely before she decided she didn't like Yukina Kobayashi very much.

But Syler had loved her. Syler had made love to her. The images exploded in Megan's mind. Syler's lips meeting soft, feminine ones. Syler's long body moving against yielding curves, her hands stroking over bare skin. Megan clamped her lip between her teeth. She willed the pain to bring her back to the present but she was only inundated with more mental interference. Was Syler demanding or was she tender? Would she dominate or would she allow her lover to please her as well? A shock of raw arousal ripped through Megan and she gasped. She had not felt anything like that for so long she thought her body had forgotten how.

The room spun away from her and Megan came back to herself with an uncomfortable lurch as Syler rejoined their little group. Both anxious and guilty, Megan gulped at her wine. She desperately hoped Syler wasn't aware of how hard her heart pounded in her chest.

The fake smile was still there, only wider and stiffer than before. Syler's lips didn't move from their Joker-like rictus as she said, "I have to get out of here."

"I know just the place," Luka said, at once all business. "I think we should move this party to Ken-mama's."

"That's the best idea I've ever heard, Lukie," Syler said. "Let's go. Now."

"Why don't you come along too, Megu-chan?" Luka linked his arm through Megan's and she looked down in alarm. "Don't worry, Ken-mama doesn't hate women, and straight couples go there all the time. Have you ever been to a gay bar?"

"No, I haven't," Megan said with a shy flutter in her chest. She suddenly remembered when and where she was. She blurted out, "But it's Shabbos. I'm not carrying any money."

"I'm not either," Syler said. She looked a lot better now they had an escape route planned. She shrugged and said, "It might be a bit in the Shabbos grey-zone, but I keep a tab there for times like these."

"Are you sure it's all right? I'm not imposing?" Megan asked.

"Not at all," Luka crooned. "Let's go, kids."

He ushered them both toward the exit on a course that put the maximum distance between the Kobayashis and themselves. Along the way, Luka snagged Jacob and convinced him to join them as well. Once through the doors, Luka led the small group away from the hospital in the direction of the train station. The clear night sky held the lingering fragrance of cherry blossoms and Megan filled her lungs with the cool air.

AFTER A FEW blocks, Luka stopped walking and directed them to a small door. Their destination was on the second floor of a time-worn building, accessed by climbing up a narrow stairway to a dimly lit hallway. The bar was located between two nondescript doors with small backlit signs that gave the name of the establishment but no other real information. Badly-sung karaoke could be heard yowling out from behind one of them. Megan hung back as Luka pushed open one of the doors and stuck his head inside. His cheerful greeting was echoed from the inside of the bar. Megan felt a soft pressure on the small of her back as Syler guided her with unassuming gentility. Warmth radiated through Megan's entire body from the slight touch.

"Ken-mama's a real hoot," Syler said in a low voice. "Come on, nobody's going to bite you."

"That's good to know," Megan said as a wide, silly grin took over her face. She could hardly believe what she was doing but it felt good and right to be there.

The bar was tiny, with a shiny, black-topped counter that faced a row of ancient green-velvet upholstered chairs. A cozy booth filled one side of the room, equipped with a semicircular sofa that looked as if it could seat six if they were friendly. Two monitors from the karaoke system loomed over the bar. They displayed the titles of various recommended songs: a mix of traditional *enka* tunes, oldies, and karaoke standbys, plus a few trendy new ones that Megan only knew by name.

Behind the counter, a neatly bearded man of about forty stood. He beamed and welcomed them with a cheerful "*Irasshaimase*" as they came in. He didn't seem particularly flamboyant, but since he was the only person working there, Megan assumed he was the mama-san. One other patron, an older fellow, sat at the far end of the counter with a bottle and a flask of something that looked like tea in front of him. He turned as they entered and appeared to recognize the two regulars. He gave them a bow before he moved over to open up more seats at the bar.

While Luka called out cheerful greetings and flitted around, Syler asked, "What's everyone having? How about a round of beer to start?" She leaned on the bar, her pose relaxed and easy. "Since I dragged you all out here, this is on me."

Syler spoke in her native tongue. It was no less exquisite than her flawless English. Megan noticed Syler referred to herself in the soft-masculine form of *boku*. It fit her. But first Megan needed to deal with the business details.

"I'll give you my share of the bill on Monday," she said. "Just let me know how much."

"Me too," Jacob said. He bobbed his head in an affable way.

"I can't be bothered with all that." Syler waved her hand at them. "One of these days you can buy me a coffee or something. After all, you two haven't gotten your first paycheck yet and Luka's too cute to pay for his own drinks."

"Thank you Syler," Luka crowed.

He pulled out the chair beside Syler and ushered Megan into it with a courtly bow before he plopped down on her other side. Jacob looked around at the tasteful black and crystal decorations before he sat next to Luka. Ken-mama got busy at the bar and soon everyone, including the master of the bar himself, joined in on a rousing chorus of *Kampai*! as they made a toast.

They chatted for a while before Ken-mama drifted off to take care of the lone patron. Jacob followed along with the rapid-fire conversation admirably well. While the hospital didn't require its employees to be bilingual, they were recommended to be fairly proficient in both English and Japanese in order to keep up with their daily tasks and the needs of their patients. As the small talk lagged, Luka was the first to break the karaoke barrier. He commandeered the remote and selected a cute pop song. He threw himself into the lively tune and Ken-mama nonchalantly danced along behind the bar, in perfect sync with the video on the twin screens.

"You're next," Luka sang as he plunked the remote down on the counter in front of Syler. She just shook her head and pushed it back toward the young men. Jacob proved his mettle and jumped into an enthusiastic rendition of the *Evangelion* theme song. Megan joined with the impressed applause afterward.

Both Ken-mama and Luka cajoled Syler until she entered a song for herself. Megan's eyes grew misty at the bittersweet ballad and Syler's sultry, low voice. Megan was too shy to sing by herself, so she entered a medley that featured not-exactly-new tunes she thought most of them would know. While Jayco, as he had come to be known, needed to share the microphone with Luka in order to get through most of his turns, they had a great time singing through the roaring finale. After that, Syler suggested they move over to the booth.

"Grab my bottle, would you? Thanks Mama."

"*Kashikomarimashita,* Saira-sensei!" Ken-mama gave his answer of *certainly* in a bright voice.

As Ken-mama shuffled through the numbered bottles, Luka and Jayco got settled on one side of the table and Megan took her place next to Syler on the other. She had an uncomfortably excited moment when she realized they looked like two couples on a double date—but who was with who? Megan glanced across at the guys, who happily pawed through the never-ending basket of snacks that was included in their table charge.

Ken-mama stepped out from behind the bar with a laden tray. He set a slim blue bottle down and followed it closely by a quartet of glasses. He leaned one hip against the table.

"And what would you like for a mixer?"

"Is jasmine tea all right?" Syler asked. Her attention was only on Megan. "They have green tea or soda water if you'd rather go with that."

"Jasmine tea sounds fine," Megan said.

"Good call," Luka piped up in agreement. "Not too many bars serve it."

"Really?" Megan asked. "That's interesting to know, and another reason to enjoy coming here."

"It's just part of what makes Ken-mama's bar special," Syler told her with a long look. Megan blushed, glad the lights in the bar were so low. "How strong do you like it?" She reached over and put ice cubes into one of the glasses, tacitly offering to make up Megan's drink.

"Medium-strong," Megan said. She couldn't take her eyes from Syler's graceful hands as she poured a generous amount of the clear liquor over the cubes.

They both spoke Japanese as if it was the most natural thing in the world. Megan was born in Saitama and attended mainstream schools until she went to an international university in Tokyo to study medicine. She was, in truth, more Japanese than American, but she was regularly greeted by the typical, "Oh shit I don't speak English", look of terror when she entered somewhere for the first time. There were also those who looked only at the color of her hair and eyes and asked placidly if she could use chopsticks and were astonished when they discovered she could not only speak the local language, but also read it. To be accepted without hesitation or ceremony was gratifying.

Megan sipped at her drink and watched as Syler made up one for herself with practiced ease. She leaned back and prodded Luka until he poured for Jayco.

"Question time!" Luka sang out after they'd all tasted their drinks. He clasped his hands on the table and looked around. "What are two things you always have in your fridge?"

"Cheese and vegemite," Jayco answered at once. As everyone looked at him with surprise, he said, "What? In med school I roomed with an Aussie and got addicted."

"And the ladies?"

Syler she gazed up at the ceiling. She swirled the ice in her glass with an impatient motion. She said, "Wasabi and non-alcohol beer. The first because the delivery sushi place never puts enough on and the second because I can't drink when I'm on call." She glanced over at Megan, who knit her brow as she mentally catalogued the contents of her kitchen.

Megan rolled the slender glass in her hands before she said, "Miso because it's miso and okra. I like to mix the okra with canned tuna and tomatoes for a good, quick snack. It's also great on rice if I don't want to cook."

"Oooh, I like that too," Luka said. He jumped up and down in his seat. "Drizzle a little sesame oil and sprinkle on some salt and you're gold. Oh, and I live with my mama and papa so I'm exempt from answering this one, just so you know."

"Convenient," Syler muttered. She gave Megan a gentle poke and rolled her eyes.

"Next question." Unfazed, Luka appeared immune to Syler's half-joking glare of annoyance. He lowered his long lashes and purred, "Kiss on the first date—yes or no? How about you, Syler?"

"That depends." She scooted over to sling an arm around Luka's slender shoulders. "Would tonight count as our first date or just our first double date?"

"Oh you!" Luka brushed her hand off with the air of offended majesty. "If you don't want to answer the question you have to do a dare."

"Fine. And the answer is," Syler paused and smirked before she said, "you'll have to take me on a date and find out for yourself."

"I don't think so." Luka preened. "Nice try, but I'm quite out of your league. Plus you don't have that certain *something* that is essential if you want to even have a chance to date me."

"Yeah, as you can see, I'm devastated. I guess I'll just have to give up on that dream and settle for crying into my pillow," Syler said, although she didn't look bereft in the least. "How about you, Jayco?"

"The first date?" The earnest young man rubbed a hand through his hair and stirred up a bunch of curls. "If things go well, I wouldn't be against a kiss on the cheek. But it depends a lot on how long we've known each other. I wouldn't want to rush things."

"Uh huh," Luka said as he selected a cookie from the snack basket. "We believe that too, don't we gals? Jayco, honey, you can be honest. Say you'd drop your pants and lunge, tongue extended after the first five minutes. Alone or not."

"Hey no way! I'm a gentleman," Jayco protested as Megan and Luka hooted and pelted him with snacks. "Uh, thanks for the treats, anyway." He grinned and plucked a sugar cookie from his shoulder and popped it into his mouth.

Syler laughed, then raised her glass and took a sip. Megan watched, transfixed as Syler slowly licked her bottom lip. More than anything else in the world, Megan wanted to know how those supple lips tasted. She ached for them with a hunger that took her breath away.

"How about Megu-chan? Do you kiss on the first date?"

With a guilty twitch, Megan tried to pretend she wasn't thinking about kissing Syler just a moment before. "I don't know. I never," she gulped then continued, "I never really had a first date."

"But you were married," Luka blurted out, looking upset. "How did that happen without a first date?"

"We were matched up online. Everything was arranged," Megan said quietly. She remembered the interview that substituted for anything resembling courtship, scheduled in among her preparations to finish her medical training and launch her clinic in Thailand. There hadn't been any time or need for formal dating. Once the agreement was hammered out, Megan had a ring on her finger and a second name on her mailbox. That was what she'd wanted. She registered with the agency and paid the not-insignificant fees with only one goal in mind. The rumor-mill painted her as a grieving widow. However, Megan needed to be honest with them on one point at least.

"We were together, but, um, we weren't exactly married. Not legally," she mumbled.

An uncomfortable beat of silence settled on the table. Megan wondered if she'd inadvertently ruined the evening. The awkwardness was broken by Syler.

"Lukie honey, you have to answer this one," Syler said as tapped Luka on the arm. "No wriggling out of it."

"Or so you thought! I'm going to take the dare."

"And that would be?"

"Getting eats," Luka said and leaped to his feet. "And I know the best yakitori place around. It's just down the street. But it's dangerous for a sweet young thing like me to go alone, so Megu-chan's coming with me. What do you all want?"

"Um, what do they have?" Jayco asked with a confused look.

"Let me choose for you," Luka said and patted him on the shoulder. "Don't worry, I won't get anything strange."

"Thanks."

"And for you, sweets?"

"Since you're buying," Syler said, "I'll have *bonjiri, shishito,* and *momo-gushi,* two each, salt not sauce."

"Gottit," Luka sang. He looped his arm around Megan's and led her out to the cool night. Once they were under the silent sky, Luka leaned close to Megan and said, "Nice call on the dress. Classy, but short enough to be interesting."

"What?" Megan choked.

"Syler can't keep her eyes off you. Especially when you cross your legs and your hem rides up over your knees."

"You're reading too much into things," Megan said. Her face flamed in the darkness. "I'm not doing it on purpose. These are all hand-me-downs from my mother's friend — her daughter actually, who is shorter than me. They're supposed to be frumpy and businesslike."

"Don't worry, I believe you. But I do have to admit, you have lovely legs. Do you work out?"

"I used to swim three or four times a week, and I love walking and hiking," Megan said in an automatic rush. "When things calm down a bit I'd like to get back into a regular fitness routine."

"There you go. You got it, you flaunt it, girl," Luka said. He leveled his piercing gaze on her for a moment before he spoke again, "You're interested in her, yes?"

"I don't know." She took a deep breath. "Maybe." Both sounded like a lie. They stopped in front of a shop with blackened wooden paneling and a half-curtain over the door.

Luka fixed her with another long, calculating look and Megan tensed, ready for him to say something, but he just ducked under the half-curtain into the shop. Megan followed close behind. They were welcomed by a raucously shouted chorus of *Irrasshai!* from the staff. The inside of the tiny restaurant was close and noisy, full of customers who were squeezed shoulder-to-shoulder at the narrow counter and filling the row of tables pushed against the wall. The air was thick with charcoal smoke and the heady scent of burnt sauce.

Two empty stools sat at the end of the counter, which Luka and Megan claimed before Luka leaned over the counter to place a long and complicated order. As the shorn-headed master placed a row of skewers over the coals, Luka ordered beers for both of them to sip while they waited. As one of the staff brought over two frosted glasses, a group of customers got up to pay, which elicited another round of thanks called out by the staff. Megan started to relax and settle into the atmosphere when Luka's words jolted her back.

"Talk to me honey. There's something going on here, right?"

"No, of course not," Megan replied. She looked into the depths of her frosted glass. She took a long gulp and tried to drown the uncertainty in a tide of beer, even though it was probably counterproductive to do so. She couldn't tell Luka about how one look had shattered the prison she'd shut herself into for the past year. And she certainly couldn't say how she wanted to take Syler home, listen to her troubles, and kiss her until both of them had forgotten whatever was worrying them.

"How about Jayco?" Megan asked as she gave Luka a poke. "I saw how you were hovering around him. Do you think he's, you know, playing for the same team?"

"I'm getting a certain vibe, but I want to play it cool. He hasn't said anything about having a girlfriend." Luka examined his nails. "But that doesn't mean much. I know how busy you doctor people are. It kind of makes having a personal life tough— for the first few years anyway."

Megan had to agree with that. She'd gone to school on a full-ride scholarship and hadn't seen the light of day for years. There hadn't been time to even keep up on popular culture, let alone embark on any kind of romantic adventures. For the first time in her life, Megan was thankful for the fact that she had hardly any friends, and none of those were good enough to feel bereft by the lack of her presence in their lives. When Megan finally finished her studies and internship, she'd felt like a time-traveler stepping into a world that had progressed without her. Even after all that time, she was still struggling to catch up. The year and a half she'd spent in Thailand hadn't helped keep her pop-culture knowledge updated either.

"Still, he's a sweet boy and I wouldn't mind finding out his first date policies firsthand," Luka said, glancing at her with a smirk before polishing off the last of his beer.

"Isn't there some kind of rule about relationships between staff members?" Megan asked. She knit her brow. The alcohol caught up to her and made her thoughts fuzzy and drifting.

"Oh honey," Luka told her with a typically gay hand-wave. "There is a policy but if they actually enforced it, there'd be like, only three people left on staff. And those would be the boring and surly ones who love tattling on others. Just keep things quiet and you're home free."

"That's good to hear," Megan said, although she wondered if it really was. She'd been hoping for an external reason to convince her to banish the wayward thoughts and newly-awakened desires.

Megan downed the last of her beer when their order arrived in a plastic takeout pack and once again she followed Luka onto the deserted street. Ken-mama welcomed them back with a big smile. They arrived in time to catch Syler in mid-monologue with Jayco leaning on his elbows as he listened intently.

"I have to say I'm a big fan of the Old Testament God." Syler didn't pause, just scooted over to let Megan have the spot on the sofa seat near the aisle. Fascinated, Megan picked up Syler's mostly-empty glass and made up a fresh drink for her. She didn't miss the approving look Luka threw in her direction. Syler leaned over the table and said, "Jesus is like, all my precious children, I love you and forgive you, but the Big Old Guy's like the parent of teenagers. His policy is, if you little shits don't behave I'm driving this car over the nearest cliff. And then he goes ahead and totally does it. He makes the rules and enforces them. You gotta respect balls like that." Syler sat back with a satisfied expression on her face. She found her newly-refilled glass and picked it up with a look of happy surprise that made a shy smile blossom on Megan's face.

"Amen," Jayco said.

"All right, time for chicken," Luka said. He opened the plastic pack with a flourish and briefly explained the selection. Ken-mama came over with small dishes and received a nicely grilled skewer of quail eggs for his trouble. The regular at the counter also got a few skewers as well, courtesy of Luka's bubbly generosity.

They snacked on the chicken, which Megan thought was the most delicious she'd ever tasted and chatted some more until Jayco listed over to one side and Ken-mama began to wash the glasses and straighten up the rows of bottles on the mirrored shelf behind the bar. Syler put the cap on what was left of her own bottle and bid their host goodnight before she led the group down the stairs and out to the deserted street below.

"Jayco's apartment's over on the other side of the station," Luka said with a sleepy Jayco on his arm. He looked at Syler and said, "I'll make sure this fine young gentleman gets home all right if you take responsibility for Megu-chan."

"Of course," Syler said in a calm voice that belied no signs of inebriation. She turned to Megan. "Where do you live? I'll walk you home."

"Sangi-cho," Megan said. The next morning, she would either kiss Luka or throttle him.

"That's not far from me," Syler said as they walked in the opposite direction to the pair of young men. Luka's bright laugh faded into the distance. "I'm just across the river from you in Kanade-cho. Probably close enough to flash you from my window if I forget to close the curtains."

Megan didn't really know what to make of that and so simply nodded. She was slightly overwhelmed in Syler's presence now that they were free from the comforting buffer of other people. As they walked under the wide night sky, Megan dredged up the nerve to ask, "Why don't you come up for a moment? I think you might like to talk to someone who understands."

There. She'd said it. Megan held her breath.

Syler paused, hands in her pockets. "All right," she said in a soft voice. Syler raised her head and their eyes met and Megan lost her breath at both the pain and promise in the depths of Syler's gaze.

The apartment Megan rented was shabby and ill-looking in the moonlight and Megan quailed for an instant as they neared it. Syler had been working as a full-fledged surgeon at the hospital for several years already. Wherever she was living had to be many grades above what the remainder of Megan's dwindling personal savings could secure. The gentle pressure of Syler's hand on the small of her back gave Megan the strength to continue and she unselfconsciously led Syler into the small lobby. While Syler studied the tattered announcements and garbage schedule on the bulletin board, Megan twirled the dial on her mailbox. She shoved aside the pile of envelopes and withdrew the key she'd hidden in the bottom of it.

"I'm on the second floor," Megan said. She led Syler up the

short flight of concrete stairs to her room. She lived in the corner apartment closest to the stairs and the balcony overlooked the narrow river, which glittered in the streetlights. The banks burgeoned with cherry trees. Their boughs were heavy with snow-like blossoms.

Megan unlocked the ancient steel door and eased it open before she ushered Syler into the cramped entrance hall, which was the only tiled area in the small two-room apartment. The rest of the flooring was hardwood, as the owner had redone it from the original tatami. The other room was the sleeping area. It was separated from the main room by a sliding frosted glass door and the kitchen was nothing more than a counter set into a recess in the wall. The bath and restroom were separate and that had been the deciding factor for Megan.

She inherited a sofa from a friend of Rabbi Sharon and it took up most of the space in the room, parked in the middle of the floor. It faced a small and scarred wooden table with a heater that doubled as a kotatsu in the winter. While the sofa itself was large and comfortable, the upholstery was threadbare and had more than a few stains on it. Megan hid the worst of them under a cheerful herd of cushions she bought from a nearby odds-and-ends shop. The room looked out onto the balcony and, except for the sofa, was quite bare, with most of Megan's home-decorations in the collection of still-unpacked boxes stashed in the other room. The room was already bathed in the gentle glow of the free-standing bamboo-shaded floor lamp Megan picked up second-hand.

"How about a drink?" Megan asked as she hovered in the kitchen nook. She opened the fridge and peered inside. With the automatic light disabled, she squinted to make out the writing on the cans. "I've got some grapefruit and lemon Chu-Hi. Do you have a preference?"

"Either would be great," Syler said. She took off her jacket and draped it over the armrest of the sofa before she settled down on it.

Megan tried to still her racing heartbeat as she crossed the small distance between them with a tray in her hands. She set out two ice-filled glasses, along with a chilled can of the fruit juice spirits and a dish of takenoko snacks she grabbed on a whim.

"Sorry my place is so small and crappy," Megan felt

the need to say.

"Why? It's fine," Syler said. She gave Megan a lingering, warm glance. Megan's heart thudded anew. Syler leaned forward and cracked open the drink can. As she filled their glasses, Syler said, "The location's excellent. It's difficult to find a good place around here, especially at this time of year when everybody's moving around, starting new jobs and school and everything. I like your taste in decorating too." Syler indicated the Takarazuka poster Megan had stuck to the wall beside the TV.

Megan gulped and her face flamed into a flush for what felt like the millionth time that night. In order to cover her discomfiture, she tossed her head and said in a prim voice, "I got that for free with the magazine. Which I hope you know I only bought for the articles. Not that I actually enjoy ogling women in tuxes. Nothing Freudian there at all. It's covering a stain on the wall that's shaped like Miriam the prophetess."

Syler let out a laugh and Megan relaxed as her doubts melted. Megan picked up her glass and gave a quick stir with the straw before she sipped her drink, enjoying the fizziness in her nose.

"Oh no, I forgot coasters," Megan said. She jumped up but was stilled by a hand on her own. Her heart bounded in a great thump as she looked down to where Syler held her.

"Hey it's all right." Syler gave Megan's hand a gentle tug that caused her to tumble back down onto the sofa. "I lived in Michigan for most of my life. I don't need any of that fussiness. All I need is you here next to me." With that, they both froze. "Wait! I didn't mean to have it come out like that. It's just nice being here that's all." Syler blurted out. Her sudden awkwardness captivated Megan and she cherished the moment of raw, human connection.

"It's okay," Megan said. She sipped her drink and savored the comfortable silence for a moment longer. It was nice to have Syler's presence beside her, but Megan hadn't asked Syler in to just sit there and stare at each other.

Even though she wasn't quite ready to end the contact, Megan dropped her eyes. She clasped her hands together and rubbed the coldness of the glass from them. She kept her voice calm as she started to speak. "So when did that all happen? With Yukina."

Syler studied the depths of her drink with a long sigh before she said, "I guess it'll be a year in May."

"So we've both been single for the same amount of time." Megan's face went hot and she added in a rush, "That is, assuming you're single. I'm sorry, it's really none of my business actually." Something black and horrible woke up inside of Megan as she considered Syler with someone else.

"No, you're right. I don't have anyone in my life, and I haven't since Yukina. Not for any real reason, I just kind of gave up on ever finding someone. There wasn't any point in looking anyway," Syler said in a soft voice. With a quick glance into Megan's face, Syler gave a slight wince as if she'd just remembered something. She knit her brow and pressed her lips together as she leaned over and put a hand over Megan's. "Oh God, I'm so sorry. Here I am moaning about a breakup when you've been through something so much worse."

So Syler had heard the rumors. Megan shook her head even as she basked in the warmth of another person near her and the feeling of skin-against-skin. It had been a long time since anyone had touched her with more than clinical or motherly intentions. Far too long. Megan didn't want Syler to move her hand, ever.

Megan said, "Bad is bad, it's not a contest. What happened is part of my life and I don't want it to be a taboo subject. I've been through counseling and I know the worst is over." She swallowed hard. The worst where Yasu was concerned, anyway. Megan looked into Syler's eyes. She saw sympathy tinged with something else she couldn't quite name. Megan continued, "I want to be your safe place where you can talk about anything. But I don't want you to feel obligated. I know we just met today but you can trust me to keep anything you say private. I'm not digging for gossip, I just thought you could use an ear." Megan reached out her other hand and clasped Syler's in both of hers. She tried to disregard the frisson of heat that raced from where they touched. "I know I wasn't ready for things to end when they did, and I think you weren't either."

"You're right about that," Syler said. She gave Megan a gentle pat on the back of her hand and drew away a little, only enough to sit back against the cushions. Her voice was low and soft as she said, "And thanks. I do feel safe here."

With Syler's movement, Megan followed automatically. She

settled back and crossed one leg over the other. The flash of Syler's eyes downward, followed by a slight flush on her cheeks made Megan acutely aware of exactly how much leg she was showing. She leaped to her feet.

"Hold that thought," Megan said. "I need to get out of this monkey suit before I spill something on it."

She heard Syler's good-humored answer behind her as she eased the sliding door open and threw herself into her room.

Her futon was still spread out on the floor, crumpled and comfortable amid the small herd of boxes that held all of Megan's worldly possessions. Megan grabbed a pair of loose cotton pants and a T-shirt from the pile of clean laundry she hadn't gotten around to folding yet.

For an instant, Megan thought of the one sexy piece of lingerie she had owned, a satin and lace nightgown she'd worn on her proverbial "wedding night" almost half a year after she and Yasu got together. It was one of the first things Megan threw out after the accident, and while she would never have worn the same one with anyone else, she spared a moment to imagine what would happen if she happened to have a similar item in her wardrobe. However, at that point in time, Megan had only comfy basics, resulting in a lack of temptation now that a dangerously alluring surgeon was sitting on her sofa. And that was a good thing.

After exchanging her dress for sleepwear, Megan shook out her ponytail and rubbed both hands through her hair. She briefly wondered what on earth had come over her before she trotted back out and plunked down next to Syler. Megan pulled her feet up and sat cross-legged on the sofa in order to face Syler squarely. She didn't miss the slow, appreciative look Syler greeted her with, but her own inner insecurity chalked it up to a natural reaction at the change from Megan's usual put-together professional outfits.

Without the business-like façade she'd learned to hide behind, Megan felt raw and exposed. She grabbed one of the cushions from behind her and hugged it for support as she began, "Do you want to talk about what upset you tonight? Was it seeing your ex with her new, um, person?"

"No, that wasn't it," Syler said with a shake of her head and a crooked smile that tugged at Megan's heart. It seemed like Syler was in the mood to talk. For once, Megan was on the listening and advice-giving side and she liked it. "I don't begrudge Yukina her happiness and I've had a good long time to get used to them together. Hell, I even went to the second reception at their wedding, which wasn't as strange as you'd think. It's just—" Syler let out a long sigh and sat forward. She buried her face in her hands for an instant. She straightened up and raked a hand back through her hair before she continued, "Seeing her so suddenly brought back something I thought I was over and all the insecurity came back and kind of kicked me in the face. The reason things didn't work out wasn't her, it was me." Syler knit her brow and squeezed her eyes shut. She opened them after a beat. "I gave her everything I had, Meg. Everything I was and everything I did was hers and it wasn't enough. At the end of the day, I couldn't give her what she wanted."

Syler's admission gave Megan an unpleasant jolt of uneasiness. She fought it down. Syler had begun to open up and it was up to her to keep the conversation going. "What did she want, then?"

"More than what she could have if she chose a life with me," Syler said. Her voice was hollow, her eyes empty. "She wanted to hit every rung on the ladder. Fancy wedding, house, kids, little designer dog, grandkids. She wanted to be on the PTA and make those lunchboxes that look like Hello Kitty and do stuff like take flower-arranging classes and meet up with her mommy-friends for fancy lunches. She wanted to go to the get-togethers with her old high school club members and have all the same milestones as they did. More than that, she wanted a safe, secure future where things like life insurance, inheritance, and pensions are automatic. Where every step in life isn't an exception to standard procedure—complete with the hassle that goes along with trying to color outside the lines in this bureaucratic nightmare of a country." Syler paused and took a sip of her drink before she said, "I get it, and I don't blame Yukina for choosing the path she did. I just wish she'd figured out what she wanted before we'd started to make a life together."

Megan gulped. It felt like a shard of ice was caught in her throat. She couldn't think of anything to say, but Syler continued on her own.

"In the end, I think she didn't want to come out. She never

told her parents about me. She never told anyone. We became a thing, we lived together, and then it all ended. There were no more milestones left for her to hit without going public about us." A wave of sick guilt swam through Megan's gut at Syler's words. With a self-deprecating smile that broke Megan's heart, Syler said, "I mean, what's the use of being partnered with a surgeon if you can't crow about it and lord it over your friends and everyone else you know?"

"Oh yeah, I'm sure that's the only reason she was with you. Syler, you are not responsible for her decision to take the easy road. I know in our line of work we get this complex where we think we've got to fix everything and be perfect all the time but it's bullshit!" Megan stirred her straw and nodded. She rode high on a wave of Chu-Hi and the words spilled out straight from her heart, "I mean, who the hell would choose a lack of paperwork over seeing your gorgeous smile every day? I know which one I'd choose and it's not the one with Hello Kitty lunchboxes, sheesh!" With a gasp, Megan cut herself off. She probably should keep that information to herself.

"Really?" Syler said. She fixed Megan with a piercing look that Megan felt saw right through her. They were very close to each other. Too close. Megan could feel the warmth from Syler's body. Every breath was tinged with the light scent of Syler's cologne.

To cover up her sudden attack of discomfiture, Megan picked up the cushion she'd been hugging and playfully smacked Syler with it. "Of course! You're such a catch. I'm sure the real reason was she didn't want to have to compete with all the cute nurses at work. Like Nurse Murase." Megan came up with the name of the elderly nurse who confronted her so grumpily in the lounge earlier.

"You got me!" Syler gave a guileless laugh. She collapsed onto the armrest with a fake injury. "Oh no, you've just fractured my humerus!"

"Physician, heal thyself," Megan replied archly as she tucked the cushion behind herself once more.

"I caaaaan't, I forgot my doctor-thingy in my other pants," Syler moaned and Megan broke into a fit of giggles.

"How unfortunate. I'll give you something for the pain anyway," Megan said. She leaned over the table and grabbed a takenoko before she chucked it in Syler's direction. Her toss missed by a mile and the treat rolled under the table. "Three second rule," Megan cried out as she dropped to her knees and peered around on the floor. Unable to locate anything other than something that looked like a forgotten bread-tag, Megan put on a miffed face and straightened up enough to prop herself up against the sofa. She was still on her knees, but in her search, she'd moved so the distance between them had vanished and she was almost in Syler's lap.

"It's five seconds," Syler told her. "But I think that little guy's gone to the great convenience store in the sky. Here's a fresh one for you, though."

Content in the position she'd found herself in, Megan studied the takenoko that Syler held in front of her face. She couldn't think about anything else other than those lovely long fingers a hairsbreadth from her lips. Megan raised her head and her mind went blank as Syler's eyes locked with hers. The only thing Megan wanted in the entire world was that sweet morsel and she leaned forward to take it. She slowly opened her mouth and held in a moan of pleasure as the rich chocolate met her tongue. With Syler watching her every move, Megan drew her bottom lip into her mouth and licked the trace of sweetness from it. Her chest rose and her breaths quickened with a surge of anticipation as Syler's hands drifted to Megan's face and cupped her cheeks. Syler leaned forward, her entire body focused on Megan. One thumb brushed over Megan's lip with a gentleness that was almost a kiss and Megan closed her eyes. She parted her lips and prayed for the real thing.

It didn't come.

As suddenly as it had started, the moment was over. Megan blinked. She was alone. Syler froze against the sofa cushions with both hands held up.

"I should go," Syler said. Her face flushed and she breathed heavily as if she'd just sprinted from somewhere. "We've both got an early morning tomorrow."

"That's right," Megan said with her mouth full of chocolate and cookie.

Megan scooted backward and stood up with a tremor in her knees. She felt quite foolish as she plopped back onto the sofa. Megan shifted uneasily and wondered if she should apologize or if she should just let what had almost happened die without mention. As Syler rose and stuffed her arms into her jacket, Megan scrambled to her feet and gulped at her drink in order to wash down the hastily chewed snack.

"Thanks for listening," Syler said over her shoulder as she made her way to the tiled entrance hall. Megan followed after a beat and met her guest at the door. Syler had one hand braced against the wall and the narrowness of the hallway brought Megan close enough so she had to almost stand under Syler's arm. With a brush of fire in her chest, Megan realized that if Syler lowered her arm just a fraction, Megan would be in her embrace. Syler swayed a bit as she shuffled into her shoes and Megan realized how tipsy she actually was. How tipsy they both were.

"Um, thanks for coming over," Megan said. She ached to say more, but had no idea what. She couldn't explain what had nearly happened and she didn't want to cheapen the moment that had passed between them by turning it into a joke. Syler paused. Their eyes met once more and Megan wanted to blurt out several things, most of which were along the lines of: "don't go" and "kiss me you sexy thing" which, even under the influence of several different kinds of alcohol, she knew were not appropriate to say to someone she'd just met that day, and would most likely have the exact opposite of the desired effect.

Syler was still looking at her and Megan met that look with her own. A low heat slowly breathed into life within her. The air between them hummed as if an electric current was passing through it. Megan caught her lower lip between her teeth and took a step forward. Only a hairsbreadth separated them. The warmth of Syler's body radiated through the thin material of her T-shirt. A deep pounding rhythm started up in Megan's belly. It echoed her heartbeat and brought a rush of desire that grew with every passing second. Megan had never been this affected by anyone before. She trembled with the desire to touch Syler. She studied Syler's face for the slightest amount of hesitation. There was none.

With a bolt of liquid fire that ignited everything from her chest to her toes, Megan leaned forward and closed the small distance.

"Let me kiss you goodnight," Megan whispered in a hoarse voice. "If that's okay."

"Please, Meg," Syler's answer was barely more than a sigh, but it was enough.

Megan reached up and twined her arms around Syler's neck, urging her to lower her head. With a soft groan, Syler did. In a slow, inexorable motion, Megan pressed her body up against Syler's. She heard a quick intake of breath at the first brush of resilient, firm flesh against hers. Megan rose up to deliver the promised kiss, but lost her nerve at the last instant and instead pressed her lips to the supple skin of Syler's cheek. Even so, the first contact was blinding and Megan had no choice but to close her eyes as their bodies came even more firmly together.

They fit so well, nestled against each other. The firmness of Syler's breasts against her own, the softness over steel of a woman's body hijacked Megan's consciousness and a wordless hunger howled through her. Then Syler's arms came around her waist and pulled her close. Megan's knees nearly gave out. A liquid shock of need sprung into life between her thighs. Megan let out a breath in a small whimper as she tangled her fingers in Syler's hair. The strands were silken against her skin. A rising tide of arousal threatened to bowl Megan over.

She never wanted to be anywhere else other than in Syler's arms. She lowered her head and dropped another soft kiss on the side Syler's neck. She had never kissed anyone there before and had no idea how erotic it could be. Syler's racing pulse thundered under her lips and Megan gave into the urge to open her mouth and ever so gently tease the fragile skin with her teeth and tongue as the heated whisper of her name reached her ears.

She felt more than heard the hum of Syler's voice as she murmured, "My God, Megan, do you have any idea what you're doing to me?"

Unable to come up with an answer to that, Megan settled for moving up to plant a kiss just under Syler's ear. The silver ring brushed over her lips. Megan's own heart raced, but she was too enthralled to care. One strong, searching hand came off her waist to trail up her back before making a slow detour over her shoulder. Megan's eyes flew open as gentle fingers cupped her chin and brought her lips to the same level as Syler's. For a long instant, Megan allowed herself to breathe into Syler's mouth. Their lips hovered the smallest distance apart before she realized she had Syler up against the wall and was leaning into her with the pressing intimacy of lovers instead of coworkers. This was Dr. Syler Terada, pediatric surgeon, technically her senior and supervisor in the vertically structured departmental chain of command. Sense flooded back into her. Megan snapped her arms back to her sides and stepped away. The loss of contact sent Megan's gut into a plummet before she collected herself enough to speak.

"Goodnight Syler," Megan stammered. She didn't know what else to say.

"Goodnight Megan," Syler replied. She blinked and looked just as stunned as Megan felt.

The door closed before Megan broke free from her brain-stall. She sagged back against the wall and knocked over the umbrella stand. Megan cradled her head in her hands as if she could physically keep her whirling thoughts in check. She locked the door and stumbled over scattered umbrellas into the kitchen where she forced herself to swallow two large glasses of water before she rolled into her futon.

Chapter Three

"IS THIS ALL of it?" Megan asked as she glanced into the folder the nurse had passed her.

"Yes, that's right," she said. "Do you need anything else, Doctor Maier?"

"No, I don't, thanks."

The nurse left and Megan flipped through x-ray films and scanned the documents, which were written in a number of different languages; English for the diagnoses and physician's reports, Japanese from the pharmacy and even a few notes in German from the time a surgeon assisted on a consult when Nikky came down with tonsillitis. While Megan didn't like the practice of using German in the OR, many surgeons did it in order to prevent the patients from overhearing.

Megan flipped back to the beginning of the records. Nikky had been born at that very hospital and nothing stood out about her history until a few months previously when the accidents started. Megan knew children often injured themselves in the course of being kids and doing normal kid-things, but the sum of the information in the file kicked Megan's intuition in a dark direction. The pattern was so subtle, the hint so faint but Megan knew something was wrong. It wasn't the first time she'd seen that kind of trend. Her heart pounded as her chest started the familiar squeeze. She closed her eyes and pressed the palms of her hands against her lids. Megan twitched to grab her pill bottle, but managed to resist until the shaking in her hands calmed.

She raised her head and took a deep breath. It wasn't the time to indulge her demons. In only a few moments, Megan finished her hungry perusal and shuffled the file back together. Her thoughts whirling, Megan got up and put the file on the trolley to be returned to their records room. Before she left the safety of the office, Megan took a moment to check the lace cap on her hair was straight and the pockets of her modest, dark green dress were empty. She didn't want to accidentally carry around a pen which would violate the prohibition against non-worship activities placed on Jews during their holy day. She checked her wristwatch. Service wouldn't start for another half hour and Megan needed to complete her rounds. She didn't have many patients under her care yet, but she wanted to familiarize herself with the staff and layout as much as possible.

Megan climbed the stairs to the pediatrics ward on the third floor with a strange, fluttery feeling in her belly. It was inevitable she would run into Syler and Megan trembled with the decision she'd come to in the early hours of the morning. An instant passed where Megan feared she wouldn't have the strength to carry through. That morning, she stood in the kitchen and recited the daily physician's prayer as had become her habit over the years. Megan's voice rang out strong and clear, and she got through it without needing to glance at the framed print on the wall. The habit was so ingrained that Megan could use it to gauge her own mental state. Following the accident, she stumbled and the words were choked by anxiety but that morning, she'd been in top form even after the late night and heavy drinking. If that wasn't a sign she'd made the right decision, Megan wasn't sure what was.

That meeting happened sooner rather than later. Megan passed through a few rooms when a shadow fell across her path and she found herself face-to-face with Syler, who looked rakishly elegant with a lab coat thrown on over a button-down shirt and charcoal slacks.

"Good morning! I'm just doing rounds, and see you are as well." Megan kept a smile plastered on her face even as she cringed from the blurted-out words. A bead of sweat worked its way through the hair at one temple and she tried to ignore it.

"That's right," Syler said and fell into step with her. She gave Megan a quick glance and said, "How about coming around with me? I can introduce you to some of our special patients."

"Yes, I'd appreciate that," Megan answered.

She drew in a breath, in awe of Syler's calm professional manner. She acted as if the previous night had never happened. She was giving her the chance to erase the event. If she didn't mention it, what they'd shared and what Megan had nearly done would fade from existence. For an instant, Megan wondered if the incident had really not meant anything to Syler, however her keen gaze detected a slight flush to Syler's cheeks and noted the slightly elevated rate of respiration that Megan herself echoed.

Together they walked down the hallway. Syler had a greeting or quick smile for everyone they passed. Everyone seemed to know her as well, which Megan understood. Syler had a presence that was difficult to ignore or forget.

Megan followed Syler as she paused to rub disinfectant on her hands outside one of the rooms. They both pulled hygienic masks over their faces before they went in. The room had four beds, but only one was occupied by a little figure in pink pajamas. Her tiny body was dwarfed even further by the hordes of machines and tubes all around her. She seemed to have been there a long time, given the lived-in look of the corner where her bed was, which was filled with stuffed animals and the walls were decorated with Hiroshima Carp memorabilia. Her parents, who Syler called Chiho and Toshi in a casually friendly way, sat on either side of the bed and they stood to greet Syler with warm words. They were young, both of them looked barely into their twenties. They must have been little more than children themselves when their daughter was born, Megan reckoned. Not that any amount of years could make what they were dealing with any easier.

Megan suppressed the ache she could never train herself out of as she approached the family. She didn't have to look at the chart at the end of the bed to know the small patient would most likely not see the outside of the hospital for a long time. Possibly ever.

"Saira-sensei!" The little girl looked up from the picture she was drawing with a bright smile that crinkled up her eyes. She was the only one in the room not masked and Megan felt for the child who spent every day surrounded by faceless adults. She saw Megan for the first time and shrank away. She shyly tucked her head under her mother's arm.

"Sakura-chan, this is Megan-sensei," Syler spoke in her usual elegant Japanese. "Megan, this is our most special patient, Yamane Sakura."

"Pleased to meet you," Megan said as she held out a hand for Sakura to shake. The girl hid her face again then lifted her head to peek up at Megan.

"Sakura-chan," Chiho said. She gave her daughter a nudge.

Obediently, Sakura uncurled herself and reached out one

hand, which Megan very gently took. The little fingers in hers were fragile and cold. Sluggish circulation, very little muscle tone, Megan noted. She was like a baby bird. Sakura drew away from Megan and put her head under Syler's hand, mewing like a kitten.

"Nyaaaa!"

"Ko-neko-chan." Syler said the nickname with obvious affection. She gave the girl a few pats before she smoothed the tousled hair away from her face. "What are you drawing, little one?" Syler asked. She leaned over the tray to get a better look at the picture.

"It's a horsey," Sakura told her, pointing. "And that's me. Mama is there and Papa is there. Saira-sensei is climbing in the tree and Nurse Emi and Nurse Luka are watching. We're having a tea party with potato chips and curry and apple pie!" Big eyes turned to Syler and she said, "When I get better I wanna eat lots and lots of things." She made a move as if to fret with the tube coming out of one nostril but was expertly blocked by Chiho.

Megan didn't miss the stricken looks in Sakura's parents' eyes.

"How about some tea?" Toshi jumped to his feet.

He was already halfway to the door when Syler said, "Thanks but we can't stay for long." She took out her stethoscope and gave Sakura a quick check-up, all the while she chatted about normal things. She slipped in subtle questions to gauge the little girl's condition. Megan allowed herself to gaze at the scene and appreciated Syler's poise and skill anew. As the exam wound down, Sakura reached out and grabbed Syler by the cuff of her lab coat. She gave a tug, which urged the tall surgeon to bend her head.

"Megan-sensei's pretty," Sakura whispered.

"She's more than just pretty," Syler said with a quick glance over her shoulder that caught Megan in mid-flush. Even though she was masked, her eyes told Megan she had a devilish grin that Megan found impossible not to return. Serious once more, Syler stepped away from the bed and slung her stethoscope around her neck. She gave Sakura's parents a nod before she said, "Everything looks good, but I'll have a nurse come around every shift just to keep an eye on things here. Don't hesitate to call if anything changes."

After another short round of greetings, they left the room. With a heavy feeling in her chest she tried to swallow, Megan followed Syler into the brightly-painted hallway.

Syler yanked her mask off and stuffed it into her pocket as she said in a low voice. "Sakura-chan was born here and hasn't been out for more than a week. She's never eaten curry and most likely never will. Her immune system is attacking her internal organs, particularly her digestive system. If this were the States, she'd be in line for multi-organ transplants, but not here. She's too young."

"How long does she have left?" Megan asked. She followed suit with her own mask. She wanted Syler to see her full expression without anything between them.

Syler rubbed a hand over her face and replied, "When she was born, we only gave her a year, two, tops. She's four now so she's already beaten the odds. She's scheduled for a procedure on Thursday and I'm attending. We'll have a briefing about it so you can get all the details then."

"I'll be there," Megan said. She fell into step with Syler. "This hospital must be a great one if people are coming here all the way from Hiroshima."

Syler didn't break stride as she flashed a grin at Megan. "Actually, they're from here. For some unknown reason Sakura-chan's a huge Carp fan. It's really fun watching her and Toshi-san when there's a Carp versus Dragons game on TV. They fight like cats and inevitably one of them ends up strutting around in victory while the other one sulks."

Megan's worried mood evaporated as she basked in Syler's smile. Her own bloomed in response.

"And where do your baseball loyalties lie?" Megan asked.

"Not where you think they do," Syler said.

"What's that supposed to mean?" Megan pelted after Syler who took off down the hall at a good clip. The only answer Megan got was an enigmatic look. "Okay so you're not going to answer that?"

Syler stopped and Megan nearly ran into her. She ended up practically pressed up against Syler. Instead of pulling away, Syler lowered her head and purred, "That's the idea. I need to keep a bit of mystery around you, Meg. You have a way of making me spill my secrets."

The way she said the words was teasing, not as if she regretted anything. Megan nearly laughed as she countered, "You know I'm not going to let this go so easily. You only *think* you're an international woman of mystery."

"If anyone can figure me out I'd put money on it being you," Syler answered. She stepped back and continued walking. Megan followed, her heart alight with how easy it was to talk to Syler. How fun. A tiny whisper prodded Megan. It was almost as if Syler was flirting with her. And Megan was doing something resembling flirting back.

As they continued with the morning rounds, a child started wailing. The cries went on and on and got louder as they moved from room to room. The sound was hopeless and never-ending. It sawed at Megan's nerves and caused her hands to shake. She wanted to clap her hands over her ears and shut out the noise, but she couldn't. She had a job to do.

She felt Syler's eyes on her and struggled to calm herself even as the old familiar tightness in her chest started up. Megan felt like cursing. The last thing she wanted to do was have a panic attack in front of Syler, not to mention all of the nurses and patients in the ward. Her near-miss the other day was bad enough. She focused on her breathing and concentrated on blocking the sound.

They passed a small cubby that held a number of vending machines and, under the pretense of getting a cup of coffee, Syler pulled Megan into it. "What is it?" Syler asked her in a whisper.

"The crying, it never ends, it's ringing in my head," Megan said. She hugged her arms to her chest. She was used to dealing with crying, but the unending misery of that particular timbre of wail hit Megan right in the most painful part of her psyche.

"Hang in there, I've got an idea," Syler said. She reached out a hand and looked as if she was an instant away from patting Megan on the shoulder, but at the last moment, she curled her fingers and turned away. Her lab coat flapped about her long legs as Syler swept over to the nurses' station where she briefly spoke to the nurse on duty. On her way back, Syler dug out her hospital-issue PHS and Megan looked on in confusion as Syler punched in a few numbers. She spoke into the phone and the page echoed over the in-house PA system.

"Who's Mr. Mori?" Megan asked.

"Come and see," Syler answered with a tilt of her head. She fixed Megan with a searching gaze that stripped all of her defenses. "Are you going to be okay for a few more minutes?"

"I think so," Megan said. She followed Syler out to the hallway just in time to see a balding and rather portly elderly man rush from the elevator. He held out his arms in an automatic gesture as two nurses swooped down on him with a paper gown. He put a hygienic mask over his face and hurried into the room where the crying came from. Only an instant after he'd passed through the doorway, the crying stopped. Megan fixed Syler with an incredulous look.

"Is Mr. Mori some kind of wizard?" she asked.

"Something like that," Syler said. She reached out again. This time she completed the motion as she put her hand on the small of Megan's back in an unconscious gesture that sent a thrill through Megan's body. "Come over and see."

Curious, Megan poked her head into the room and saw the gowned man standing by the window with a red-faced and sweaty-haired toddler sleeping in his arms. Two frazzled-looking nurses watched him with relieved expressions on their faces. Syler stood close behind her.

"Mr. Mori," Syler whispered in Megan's ear, "is a retired truck driver. Never married, no kids, but he has the unparalleled ability to calm crying children. He volunteers here just about every day to hold the little ones whose parents can't be here twenty-four-seven. He's usually in neonatal, but we can call him over here if the need arises."

Her entire body lit up like a Roman Candle with Syler so near. Megan held her breath until Syler stepped away from her.

"So that's what an angel looks like," Megan said.

Syler didn't reply, just gave her a quick, sideways glance before she ducked out of the room. Megan followed and caught up to Syler on the landing of the stairwell. It was removed from the bustle of the hospital and deserted as most people used the elevators. That gave Megan the strength to act. Before she could change her mind, Megan reached out and stopped Syler with a hand on one sleeve of her white coat. Her heart thudded. She had to get the words out right that instant or she'd never get the chance or the nerve to again.

At Megan's light touch, Syler stopped and turned. Her

expression was open and her eyebrows were raised in a questioning look as she waited for Megan to speak.

"Syler, um about last night. I want you to know I didn't ask you to my place with the intention of," Megan faltered but plowed on, "making a move on you."

Syler's eyes went to the floor and she worried at her lower lip with her teeth for an instant before her head came back up and she met Megan's look with a careless shrug. "I didn't go with that intention either."

"Just so you know," Megan said, "I don't usually do that kind of thing."

"What kind of thing?" Syler's quirky grin and quick humor were back. "Seducing women you've just met?" She paused and leaned against the handrail. Her voice lowered as she continued, "Or just seducing women?"

Megan gulped and croaked, "Both."

"Don't worry about it." Syler was at once cool and professional. "We were both Purim-level shickered last night and these things happen. I'm fine with chalking the whole thing up to temporarily losing the ability to tell the difference between 'cursed be Haman' and 'blessed be Mordechai'."

For an instant Megan quailed. She worried that Syler hadn't felt the connection or the hunger Megan had tasted. But she must have. Something like that couldn't be faked. She made up her mind and threw herself to fate. Life is short and you only get one shot. She wasn't going to leave with any regrets.

"I know I was drunk. I hope that didn't give you the wrong impression." Megan looked into Syler's deep hazel eyes and felt calm, strong, and in control for the first time in a very long time. "The impression that I wasn't serious."

"Wait, what?" Syler jerked away from the wall and nearly tripped on the step behind her. One hand grabbed onto the railing and she collapsed onto it. "You were serious?"

"I was then. I still am." Megan rubbed her sweaty palms on the sides of her skirt. "I know we barely know each other, but I'd like to get to know you better. Unless, of course you'd rather not. We still have to work together and if you think things might get awkward, in that case, nothing more will ever be said of last night. The temporary insanity defense can come in handy, just say the word." Even though she was willing to never mention it again, Megan would not offer to forget what had happened the night before. She couldn't. Even if nothing more ever happened between them, she would always remember that moment where her entire universe had been contained in the arms of the surgeon standing before her.

"Actually..." Syler drew a hand through her hair, which left it adorably tousled. "I think I'll pass on the insanity. I'd like to get to know you better too," she said.

Megan let out a breath in half a laugh. Was it really that simple?

"But I just want to know one thing." Syler fixed Megan with a long, low look that sent a thrill through her. "In what way do you mean you were being serious? You know I'm gay. I date and have relationships with women, and I need to know right now where I stand with you. I don't want to be your experiment. I'm not going to pressure you, but I want something more than friendship." Syler's gaze bore into Megan's.

"Don't worry," Megan said. She swallowed and continued, "I'm not going to run away or make this into some kind of game. I'm going into this with my eyes open."

"That's good to hear," Syler said with the easy grace Megan had come to expect from her. She crossed her arms and leaned back against the wall. "When's your next day off?"

"Tuesday," Megan said. She hoped her blush didn't showing.

"Do you have any plans?"

"No," Megan said. She tilted her head and gave Syler a long look before she said, "Not yet, anyway."

"All right, then. I have a gastroschisis procedure in the morning," Syler said, "But I'll be done by noon. How about I swing by your place and pick you up? We can do lunch." She gave Megan a grin and continued, "One person drinking in the park is a bum, but two is a picnic. I'll take care of the food and we can do the whole cherry blossom viewing thing. I know a great spot that is not so crowded and bonus, is walking distance from our places."

"I'd like that," Megan said, breathless with happiness and wonder. "What should I bring?"

"Just yourself," Syler told her.

"If you're sure," Megan said. "I don't want you to think you have to treat me all the time."

"Of course not, it's no big deal."

"All right, I'm looking forward to it," Megan said. She took a long look at Syler and made a decision to trust her. Megan said, "I want you to know I have a previous commitment in the evening. I've got an overnight shift at a walk-in clinic in downtown Nagoya, near Hanamura Park." The area she'd named was smack in the middle of the nightclub district, and not the mainstream one either. She waited a beat to see a spark of recognition in Syler's face before she said, "But I have the entire day free until then."

"Hanamura Park would mean the Angel Hand Clinic, right?" At Megan's nod, Syler continued, "I know that clinic. They do good work there. Is Dr. Junji Tonosaki still in charge?"

"Yes, but it's Junko now. Officially," Megan said. A knowing look dawned on Syler's face. The significance of the change to the feminine "ko" suffix was not lost on Syler.

"That's great," Syler said with a brilliant smile. "It's been a while since I went up there. I'll have to drop by and pay my respects sometime soon."

"She's usually in during the day," Megan said. "I've spoken to her quite a bit on the phone."

"All right. Anyway, don't worry, I'll make sure our picnic doesn't go on too long before your all-nighter," Syler said.

"Could I ask you to keep this between us?" Megan asked. At the guarded look on Syler's face, she hastened to add, "I mean my extra work at the clinic. It's kind of a personal project and I haven't told anybody here."

"Of course. I will be the epitome of discretion."

"Is this our first date, then?"

"It sure is," Syler said. With her usual easy grace, Syler tipped an invisible hat before she walked backward out of the stairwell. "Now go and hang out with your God, woman."

MEGAN ARRIVED AT the chapel just as the service began. She slipped into the room as quietly as she could. She picked up a pair of prayer books from the shelf but eschewed the prayer shawl. The hospital-run synagogue was progressive, so women were encouraged to wear shawls during the services, but Megan was not accustomed to the ritual of putting one on and decided to leave that for another day. Doctor Brockman the younger sat at the front with his parents and, while he turned around and gave her a nod, she didn't go over to join them. Megan slipped into a seat at the back of the room.

The service progressed and Megan joined in with the prayers. The words came back easily even after her years of non-observance. Her jittering nerves and thrill in her chest calmed down; however, her mind would suddenly generate an image of Syler and Megan would get the fluttery feeling all over again. She was doubly glad she had cleared up the issue of not having to read because Megan was certain she would not be able to concentrate well enough to get through even the simplest prayer. As usual, people came and went during the service and about halfway through a somewhat green around the gills Jayco stumbled in. With an internal smile, Megan waved him over to the unoccupied seat beside her. She felt quite naughty and young as she amused herself by poking him during the service and received a few pokes in return. While they teased each other, Megan fought the odd feeling that Jayco was the younger brother she'd never had.

Before long, they raised their voices in the final prayer and the service ended. Megan followed the crowd as they went out to the hall where the Kiddush and lunch would take place. She wanted to talk to Jayco and find out how his evening went, but they got separated in the crowd. That was fine, Megan decided as she waited to leave the chapel. It might be better to have that conversation in private, away from the massive gossip-festival of the synagogue-going crowd.

"How are you adjusting?" Doctor Brockman asked. His sudden question startled Megan as she gazed off into the distance with an irrational craving for yakitori.

"Very well, Doctor Brockman," Megan said. The rest of the congregation flowed around them and Megan ended up quite close to him. He ushered her through the crowd with one meaty hand planted on her lower back. Megan squirmed. Her skin buzzed with an annoyed itch. She hastened her steps to reach the open hall.

"Charles, please," he said. "And I would be pleased to call you Megan, at least outside of our professional duties." He hit the last syllable of her name in a way that made Megan cringe. It sounded just as stiff and formal as her title. She didn't like him using it. At least he wasn't going to try and call her Meirav. That was reserved for only people close to her heart.

"Yes, that is acceptable, Charles."

Megan hated the starchy way her own words sounded. The man made her feel like she was playing a role. In a way she was, pretending to be a professional with no dubious anxiety hang-ups. The crowd eased and Megan gratefully stepped away from him. She got a jolt in her chest when she saw Syler standing behind the long table, setting out a generous tray of blintzes as she chatted with a few members of the congregation. Without another word, Megan escaped from Charles's dour presence and went over to the table.

"Don't worry," Syler said as Megan came over, "I didn't make anything here. I'm just helping out so I can justify getting a free lunch. I recommend you try the cheesecake. Stan Cohen made it and it's ohhh so good." She closed her eyes as she said the last words.

"Really?" Megan wanted to laugh, but controlled herself.

"Really. He and his wife Midori-san run a bakery in the city. It tends to go pretty fast, so I took the liberty of putting aside a piece for you."

"Thanks," Megan said. She leaned closer and said, "I guess it pays to know someone on the inside, then."

"Yup," Syler said with a conspiratorial nod.

After the blessing, the casual lunch began. Before she could get herself anything other than a sip of wine and a small piece of bread, Megan found herself seized by the elbow and led around by Charles, forced into making awkward conversation with the rest of the congregation. All the while she was very aware of Syler's presence, even across the room and separated by a large number of people. As soon as Megan escaped from Charles's hold, Edie Miller came over and greeted Megan.

"I didn't want to say anything in front of the others, but I was so sorry to hear about your bereavement," Edie said. She patted Megan on the arm in a maternal way. "I lost my first husband quite early too, so please let me know if you need to talk."

"Thank you," Megan said.

"It does get better, you know."

"Yes, it does." She took a breath and said, "At first I thought I'd never smile again and the first time I laughed I felt so guilty."

"They wouldn't want to see us grieving forever. It's all right to be happy, never feel guilt for that."

Edie patted her again and Megan felt the kindness radiating through the motherly touch. Megan had thought it would be difficult to have conversations like that, but she found the connection soothing. She was grateful she was excused from giving details, much different from the soul-wrenching torture of prodding questions that her old therapist had liked to pelt her with. Often the only reason Megan could see for him doing that was to get a sordid thrill from getting her to reveal her deepest secrets and confidences. She fought a sudden wince as an unpleasant memory resurfaced.

Her old therapist had been particularly vicious when going after sexual details, not believing Megan's frank admission that there hadn't been much to tell. Yasu was over forty when they'd first met and had been respectful of Megan's shyness and deep insecurity about physical intimacy. Megan spent a decade immersing herself in learning the innermost details of the workings of the human body, but she had to admit she was sorely lacking in knowledge of her own. Their relations was standard from start to finish, nothing wild, nothing dangerous, exciting, or crazy. Megan had been well taken care of, even if she'd had to fake a few to get things over with.

After her late introduction to intimacy, Megan eventually harbored a secret curiosity about more inventive acts. She never revealed her desires, being somewhat ashamed of them as well as priding herself on being practical more than anything else. Her therapist tried to convince her otherwise but Megan was satisfied with the physical aspect of their relationship.

The reason why romance novels were so popular was they provided something that didn't exist in real life — at least Megan believed it didn't exist. As she reflected on the thrilling electric kick she got from being close to Syler, Megan began to reevaluate her opinion and it was exciting and unnerving in equal parts.

While Megan still had faith in counseling, she was glad she'd left that particular therapist behind. She hadn't had much of a choice, being way out in a tiny village several hours' drive over unpaved roads from Bangkok. He'd been the only English-speaking one in the country who would agree to Skype after the initial in-person consultation. While Megan's Thai was good enough to get by in daily situations, she thought therapy would be easier in her first language. She still wasn't sure if that was the correct decision.

At times, Megan felt she should have just stuck to drinking the sweet fruit juice that was sold in plastic bags at the roadside stand across the street from her clinic and ruminating on the meaning of life with the local elders and random monks who wandered by. Those rambling chats healed her soul more than any session with the so-called professional. At least she'd found a better therapist when she'd come back to live with her parents in Saitama. Megan was currently down to monthly visits and her most recent session was more of a check-in than actual counseling. Megan fought a smile as she wondered what her current therapist would have to say about the new development in her life.

Finally, Megan left her social duties and found Syler, who was with Jayco. Syler was in the middle of pounding him on the back and chortling as he nearly fell over. They both looked up with smiles as Megan came over, a rather sickly one in Jayco's case, but welcoming just the same.

"Here, I didn't think you'd have time to get lunch, with all the meeting and greeting you have to do," Syler said to Megan. She handed over a nicely made-up plate as soon as Megan was in range. "So I got this for you. I hope there's nothing you don't like. If there is, I guess you can just feed it to Jayco here."

"Urgh," the young man in question said as he turned a bit green.

"Thanks, it looks great," Megan said. "I'm sure I'll love everything. I'm really hungry and not picky." With her plate in one hand and a plastic fork in the other, she gratefully collapsed onto the chair Syler pulled over. Megan hadn't been to the supermarket in a while and her breakfast consisted of only a few leftover takenoko. She happily shoveled in her food as Syler and Jayco chatted.

"You get home all right last night?" Syler asked with a grin.

"I think so. I woke up in my bed with a bottle of water and something called Pokari Sweat on my table," Jayco said. "Remind me to thank Luka, it was just what I needed. You should have seen me this morning."

"Lukie's a good person. He takes care of all us here." Syler looked down at Megan as she savored her first creamy bite of cheesecake. "Good, huh?" Syler said with a satisfied smirk.

Mouth full, Megan just nodded. On a whim, Megan speared another morsel of cheesecake and held out her fork, offering it to Syler. Without hesitating, Syler leaned down and took the bite of cake. She finished by delicately licking her lips. A hungry buzz woke up in Megan's stomach that had absolutely nothing to do with food.

"Now that's good cheesecake," Syler declared. "I could eat a whole one. Drizzle on loads of chocolate sauce, maybe top it with a handful of juicy strawberries and I'd marry it!"

"Oh no," Jayco moaned and held his head.

"If you want, I can set you up with an IV upstairs," Syler said. She prodded the young man. "Get you rehydrated and take the edge off."

"No, I did this to myself. I'll suffer through it," Jayco told her with a wry grin. He excused himself and wandered off.

"So, did you get any juicy details?" Megan asked after Jayco was out of earshot.

"Not really," Syler said. "I guess the issue of which side of the fence Jayco's on is still up for speculation." She paused and fixed Megan with a warm look that made the recipient feel young and giddy. "Would it be all right to ask you for your number?" Syler shoved her hands into her pockets in the casual way she seemed to favor. "After Shabbos of course. I didn't bring my phone or a pen or anything today and while my memory's pretty good, it's not *that* good."

"Definitely," Megan said, a little taken aback at herself. She'd had Syler in her room, nearly kissed her, had declared she wanted to "be serious" with her, and had even arranged a first date but hadn't actually exchanged any digital information. "Are you coming in tomorrow?"

"Yes, I've got a shift in after-hours admissions starting midnight, but I'll be doing rounds in the morning as usual."

"Okay, there's no examinations tomorrow, so I've only got rounds. How about I give it to you then?"

"I'll be waiting. And now I have to go and start the cleanup." Syler placed a hand on Megan's arm as she spoke. "Take your time finishing your lunch. It always takes ages with all the biddies gossiping about everything and everyone."

Megan lounged in her seat and watched as the congregation

gradually thinned as people left. She took a deep breath. She was feeling good. It really was all right to be happy again.

Chapter Four

SUNDAY PASSED IN a blur, punctuated by a short, casual visit with Syler that left Megan breathless and dizzy for the rest of the day. She checked her phone an irrational number of times to reassure herself the contact information she'd added wasn't just a dream. Monday morning, Megan came in early as usual and stopped in her tracks. Charles stood in front of her desk with a frown on his face.

"I heard you flagged Nikky Okamoto's file," he said without preamble.

"Yes, I did," Megan said. Her heart pounded and she got a bad feeling in the pit of her stomach.

"I'm sure it was just a misunderstanding," Charles said. He pushed himself away from her desk and tucked the pen he'd been using into his pocket. "Don't worry, I've removed the flag and everything has been put back in order."

"What? No, you can't do that," Megan spat, suddenly on guard. "What do you mean misunderstanding? Someone is hurting that little girl and I'm going to put a stop to it."

"Girl?" Charles wrinkled his brow.

"Nikky's transgender, I updated the file," Megan said. She looked at Charles and mentally dared him to say something.

"That's not a problem. Thank you for correcting our oversight." Charles spread his hands and said, "However, you may not be aware of this, but the Okamoto family is one of our largest sponsors. They were responsible for funding our new x-ray film viewer. I cannot allow you to besmirch the Okamoto name over something small and easily explained."

"Excuse me?" Megan's voice ratcheted up a notch. She stood, feet apart and arms crossed, unconsciously echoing Syler's characteristic stance. "What are you talking about, Doctor Brockman?" She used his formal title on purpose and spat it out in a biting tone.

"This matter has been settled," he said. He reached out as if to put a hand on Megan's arm but she jerked away. In a bland way, he continued, "I know you've just started here, so you may not understand the way things operate. I trust if you are going to continue in this hospital, you'll become more familiar with the patients and the guidelines."

"And that means turning a blind eye to child abuse?"

"I'm not saying that at all. However, you do need to be more prudent when making accusations. You need solid evidence before you go around flagging files. I trust this will not occur in the future. Is that understood?"

Megan bit the inside of her cheek before she said, "Yes, I understand." She held herself very still as Charles walked past her. She allowed her legs to buckle only after he'd left the room. Megan seethed as she threw herself into her work. She organized her files and wrote reports like a mad person before she did her morning rounds. Examination hours were filled with activity, including treating a cute and chatty German girl on holiday, who came in with unseasonable jellyfish stings. From her surgical training, Megan knew a fair amount of German, but it was mostly technical so she fell back into English.

"Where ever did you meet a jellyfish, Annika?" Megan asked as she wrapped a bandage over the medicated lotion and gauze dressing to cover the place where she'd extracted a number of spines. She waited for Annika's mother to translate before she continued, "There isn't an ocean anywhere near here."

"Fish zoo," Annika told her in halting English as she proudly examined her bandage. "I want Mister Jelly to be my pet."

"Don't touch the animals in the fish zoo," Megan said with a mock stern expression. Her tone was conveyed even through the hygienic mask she wore. "They aren't friendly and some of them want to eat curious little people like you."

"Listen to what the doctor lady says," Annika's father told her.

"Okay." Annika giggled and squirmed as her parents gave her tickles and hugs. For a moment, Megan allowed her gaze to soften and her mind wander as she looked at the family. Every child deserved to be protected and loved like that. A sudden pain in her chest brought her back to the present. Megan shook herself free of the lingering anxiety and guilt.

The rest of the day was a never-ending stream of patients and Megan was more than ready for the last one. Conscious of the stack of reports waiting for her, Megan forced her tired body to go around the hospital one more time. She took care to greet and speak to the nurses and patients she was beginning to get to know. Her legs ached. She needed a break. Megan collapsed onto a bench in a cubby near the vending machines. She slipped off her low-heeled pumps and slouched for the first time that day. She'd only been there for a moment when she heard familiar voices.

Megan looked up as Syler and Sakura's mother Chiho came into the cubby. On the bench, Megan hoisted herself upright and a happy flush came over her as Syler gave her a long look and a warm smile.

"Hey there Meg," Syler said. She put a bunch of coins into the machine and offered Megan a drink with a quick and casual, *"Nanika nomu?"*

"I'm fine, I just wanted to sit down." Megan answered in Japanese as well, aware of Chiho hovering nearby. She wanted to include the younger woman in the conversation as naturally as possible.

"Okay," Syler said. "How about you, Chiho? Are you feeling a bit better than this morning? Think you could stand a bit of juice?"

"Yes, I think so. Something fizzy and not so sweet. Thank you."

"Ryokai!" Quick and cheerful, Syler acknowledged the request. She handed a bottle of lemon soda over and got a can of coffee for herself. Syler opened her drink and sat down beside Megan.

"How's Sakura-chan doing today?" Megan asked.

"Just fine," Syler said. After she sipped her coffee, she gave a stretch and ended up with her long limbs sprawled out in an easy way. The can hung loosely from her long fingers. Chiho came over to them. She looked tired and a bit shy. Syler continued, "Things are looking up for the procedure."

"That's good to know," Megan said.

"Sakura-chan's a fighter," Syler said. "We're doing our best and so is she."

"Thank you Sensei," Chiho said. Just then, she seemed older than her years. Megan ached for her but kept a respectful distance. She wondered if Chiho was well herself as she recalled the solicitous way Syler had spoken to her earlier.

"Anyway," Syler's bright voice dispelled the tense atmosphere in an instant, "has Toshi-san told you where he's taking you on this month's date night?"

Suddenly transformed by a shy smile, Chiho shook her head. "He didn't say anything, but I saw a brochure for Hana-no-Sato in the car."

"Nice," Syler said. She glanced over at Megan, who had knit her brow in confusion. Syler leaned closer to her and said, "Hana-no-Sato's this giant flower garden that's got a bunch of lights and romantic corners. Great date spot." She turned back to Chiho and said, "You two have a good time."

"It's all because of you." Blushing and smiling, Chiho shifted from one foot to the other as she said, "I have to get back now. Toshi's at work and I don't want to leave Sakura-chan alone for too long."

"Take care," Syler said. She tipped her head back to drain the last dregs of coffee and chucked the can at the recycling bin where it clanked home. "Heh, two points," she said.

"What do you do for their date night?" Megan asked.

"Once a month I take a night off duty and have a sleepover with Sakura-chan so her parents can go out and do something together, like go out to eat or hang out at a hot spring," Syler said with a casual shrug. "You know, normal couple stuff."

"That's very generous of you," Megan said past the tightness in her throat.

"Yeah, it's a real chore to hang out with that little cutie," Syler said. "We break out the coloring books, watch silly videos on my phone, and have 'go fish' battles. Sometimes things get crazy and we play beauty salon. One time I ended up with rainbow toenails."

Megan let out a laugh at the mental picture.

"Why don't you drop by for a round of fish or something if you're in the neighborhood?"

"Maybe I will," Megan said. She glanced at her watch and stifled a sigh.

Syler fixed Megan with her long, searching gaze that left Megan pleased to be the object of it. "Long day?" Syler asked.

"Yes and it's not even half over," Megan said. "I've got a ton of stuff left to do. Things were never this, um, *detailed* in Thailand."

"You can say pain-in-the-ass level nitpicky. Japanese love paperwork, that's one truth you'll never escape here," Syler said with a grin. She dropped her hand to the worn plastic of the bench and casually brushed her long fingers over the back of Megan's hand. A thrill raced through Megan at the soft pressure of Syler's hand. She let her own fingers curl around Syler's for a moment. Syler's next words were softer, more intimate. "Let me know if there's anything I can help with."

"Thanks, but it's not difficult, just a lot of reports and that kind of thing," Megan said. "I'm sure I'll get faster at finishing as I get more used to the hospital's procedures."

While she knew the hospital was quite progressive compared to the rest of the country, Megan wasn't sure how open she should allow herself to be around Syler, at least in public. When she thought about what might happen in private, a dangerous, sultry heat started up deep within herself. Her heart kicked into a fast rhythm as Megan allowed herself the luxury of leaning against Syler's arm. The calm strength of Syler at her side was nice.

"How about your day?" Megan asked. She wanted to draw the quiet moment out as long as possible, not ready to let Syler go yet.

"It's not too bad," Syler said. She brushed a thumb over the back of Megan's hand as she spoke. "I'm almost done here, and then I'm off home for a bath and bed."

"Don't let me keep you here, then."

"You're not keeping me from anything," Syler told her. "My day just got a lot better now that I'm hanging with you. There's nothing else I'd rather be doing."

Megan thought she could come up with a few ideas, but things were still so new between them she kept quiet. After a few more moments of subtle intimacy, they were disturbed as a group of children barreled into the cubby. Syler pulled away from Megan and got down on the floor to exchange jokey greetings with them and dish out generous high-fives. Two of the children were wearing pajamas, while the rest seemed to be either friends or siblings. They crowded around Syler, all of them talked uninhibitedly. The topic changed so many times, Megan was hard-pressed to keep up. Megan watched as Syler paid attention to each and every one of them, and they, in turn, hung onto every word Syler said.

The little crowd moved on and Syler stood, hands tucked under her arms with a look of pure adoration on her face. Megan's chest ached at the expression.

Even though she was half afraid of the answer, Megan asked, "Do you think one day, you'd like to have your own?"

With a quick glance back over her shoulder, Syler met and held Megan's gaze with hers.

"I already do. They're all my kids," Syler said with quiet conviction. "But to be a parent in the traditional sense of the word? I don't think it's in the cards for me. Not in this country anyway. Five years ahead in fashion, ten in technology but fifty behind in social issues." She paused and her gaze focused inward. "I did think about it when I was younger, but I absolutely couldn't justify putting my work on hold for something as long as maternity leave."

Stunned, Megan couldn't stop herself from gaping.

"What? I'm not that butch, am I?" Syler answered with a careless grin. "Hey, I've got the equipment too, and I would never expect my partner to go through something so physically invasive and demanding when I could save her from it. How about you, Meg? Biological clock ticking?"

"Not in the least," Megan told her, still breathless from what Syler had just said. "I love the children I see in here, but I don't feel the need to create any more. Most of all, I consider my home my sanctuary. I need a quiet and safe place to shut out the outside world." A sharp pain speared her in the chest and Megan struggled to take a breath. She fought the usual stab of regret. She would never betray her own ideals. Never again. She glanced at her watch and said, "I'd love to stay a bit longer here with you, but if I don't get back downstairs to my desk, I'm going to be here all night with reports."

"Get to it, then," Syler said. She paused and spoke in a soft voice, "Text me when you get home tonight."

Megan brimmed with happiness as she nodded.

BACK AT HER desk, Megan stared off into space far too many times instead of working but managed to get her reports done by a decent hour. She was only interrupted twice, once to help a little boy with a pea up his nose the doctor on duty in the after-hours admissions didn't feel up to treating, and again to put in an IV for a fussy toddler with a hovering mother who tried the nurses' patience.

Her head ached and her body was limp with fatigue by the time she finally put the last thing away and shut down her computer. Luka came by with a cup of tea and a handful of rice snacks for her a few hours before and although Megan was grateful for the offering, its effectiveness had long since worn off and her stomach growled. She rolled one stiff shoulder under her hand and mentally reviewed the meager scraps she had in her fridge. As she got up, Megan debated trying her luck at the nearby convenience store or going out of her way to the small kosher grocery behind the hospital. She hadn't made up her mind yet as she went through the doors leading outside from the after-hours admissions entrance when something came out of the darkness and blocked her path. It was Charles.

Megan blinked. Had he skulked around outside in wait for her, or did she just have terrible timing?

"I believe we may have gotten off to a bad start this morning," he said. "I would like to make up for it. Allow me to drive you home."

"That's very kind of you but it's not necessary." Megan continued walking. She aimed for her familiar street but Charles fell into step with her. He crowded her with his faster strides and steered her into the parking lot. She stopped suddenly as a sleek black Toyota Crown loomed up in front of her, looking smug in its reserved parking spot.

"Here we are. Please get in, I assure you it's no trouble at all."

Megan bit the inside of her cheek to stop the annoyed sigh from escaping. As much as she didn't want to be stuck in a car with Charles, attempting to make awkward and stilted small talk, she really was tired and her feet were beyond painful. It seemed that neither the grocery nor the convenience store were on her agenda for the night. At least she still had her okra.

"Thank you," Megan said. She tried to shake the feeling she was trapped.

"You are most welcome," Charles said. "There is no need to give me directions as I took the liberty of programming your address into my navigation. From your file, of course."

The matter-of-fact words sent a shiver of apprehension through Megan. He opened the car door and Megan caught a whiff of lemon-scented air freshener and new-car smell. The seats had stark white lace covers and the interior was immaculate. She felt distinctly odd and a bit worried as she got into the car and wrestled with her bag and the seatbelt for a moment. The door slammed and Charles sat next to her. He started the engine and pulled into the scant evening traffic.

The streetlights drifting by outside were hypnotizing and Megan struggled to keep her eyes open. Only when Charles drove right by the turnoff to her apartment did Megan bolt upright.

"You missed the turn," she said. The gnawing feeling of worry in her belly got worse. "Doct—Charles, it's back there."

"Yes, that's correct," Charles said. In the harsh streetlights, his face looked like it was made of stone. "I thought you would have dinner with me."

"What?" Megan breathed.

"Just a simple courtesy in order to show my appreciation for your decision to work with me and my family. It's not often someone of your status and pedigree joins us, after all."

The car pulled into a parking lot and Megan faced the intimidating entrance to the most expensive restaurant she'd ever seen. Her parents ran a dental clinic in her hometown and Megan's family had always been well-off. Although, they never made a habit of flaunting their wealth. The restaurants Megan was brought up frequenting were small, family-run, and friendly, usually serving interesting international cuisine. It was obvious that Charles's tastes ran several ranks above what Megan was used to. She didn't have time to protest before the car door was opened and Megan was being led up the white marble steps, her elbow held in Charles's grip.

"Wait a moment," Megan said. She wrenched herself free just outside the looming cut-glass doors. "I don't think this is appropriate. I mean, the two of us, alone here."

"Are you accusing me of something?" Charles swooped down on her. His face was calm but his tone was steely. "I'd like to know if you are going to be that kind of person."

"What kind is that?" Megan clutched at her bag.

"The kind who takes an innocent gesture of welcome and

turns it into something sordid."

"No, I'm not like that."

"It seems you are," Charles said. He turned and started back down the stairway. "Apparently this was a mistake, at least in your opinion. Don't worry, we're leaving. It seems you are not open to the idea of kindness without some ulterior motive. I have to admit, I'm quite taken aback you have projected that image on me, even before you have given me a chance to prove otherwise."

Her chest constricted and Megan grabbed at the railing. She couldn't let the evening end like that, with her boss storming off insulted and angry. The repercussions of a failed business relationship at that point could cost her the job she'd just gotten, not to mention undermine her entire professional reputation, which was already not the best given the gap in her employment history. In addition, she had responsibilities and patients waiting for her and Megan couldn't throw everything away on nothing more than a most likely-unfounded wariness. Six thousand years of Jewish guilt crashed down on her head and Megan crumbled.

"Wait!" she cried out. "Charles, I'm sorry, I jumped to conclusions. Please stay. I would love to have dinner here with you." The words tasted sour in Megan's mouth.

"Oh no, you wouldn't want to be forced into doing something you don't want to," Charles said. "After all, my simple offer of a welcoming meal seems to be unacceptably boorish."

"No, that's not it at all, please come back," Megan said. She clasped her hands, wondering how she was protesting one moment and pleading the next. "I was being hasty, I never meant to accuse you of anything."

"If you insist." His face relaxed. Suddenly the image of gentility, he brushed past Megan and opened the door for her. "This way please, I have reserved my usual table and I guarantee you, it is the best in the house."

The inside of the restaurant glittered with crystal and the other diners were few and subdued. The restaurant was almost uncomfortably silent, with the only sounds being the odd clink of cutlery and rumbled conversations. A waiter showed them to a table and Megan felt herself shabby and crumpled after her long day at work. She stood and excused herself to use the restroom. She picked up her bag with the intention of sending a few stealth texts to Syler.

"Why are you taking that?" Charles inquired as he placidly looked up from the menu. "To put your mind at ease, how about I promise I will not paw through it in your absence?"

"I just, um," Megan couldn't think of anything to say that wouldn't sound blatantly false.

"However if you don't trust me, then go ahead."

For the second time that evening, Megan was left with no other option than to acquiesce to Charles's will to save her professional face. She stammered out a quick apology and put her bag down on her seat. She was sure everyone in the place looked at her as she walked the length of the room.

The ladies' powder room was huge and just as intimidating as the dining area but it had the advantage of being Charles-free. Megan stayed there as long as she dared, internally scolding herself for not being mentally quick enough to stop herself from being manipulated. Very aware of the passage of time, Megan pictured Charles sending a waitress in after her if she failed to reappear — or worse, coming to look for her himself. Spurred into action by the thought, Megan splashed water on her face, smoothed back her hair, and re-entered the restaurant.

He had her cell phone in his hand. Megan bristled and opened her mouth to say something. However Charles cut her off.

"I'm confiscating this for the duration of the meal," he said as he tucked it into the breast pocket of his custom-made shirt. "Some people allow themselves to ignore who is actually in front of them for electronic substitutes. I hope you are not that kind of airheaded follower."

"No, of course not," Megan said in a defeated tone.

"That's good to hear, and for the record, I didn't think you were that low-bred type." Charles studied the menu and said, "We will be having the grilled lamb tonight."

"Actually I'm not really in the mood for something heavy like that," Megan said. She opened her menu and ran her eyes over the list of entrees. "Ooh, listen to this: slow-oven roasted spring vegetables in basil sauce with home-made herb bread." As she said the words, Megan suddenly realized how hungry she was. Her stomach threatened to gurgle and she surreptitiously pressed a hand to her abdomen.

"Their grilled lamb is quite famous," Charles said. He looked at her over the top of his menu. "I'm sure you'll find it superb."

Megan wondered if he hadn't heard her and repeated, "But I was going to go with the roasted veggies."

"It's not the best dish here," Charles said. The way he folded his menu made Megan want to rip it out of his hands and smack him across the face with it. "In case you were wondering if I was attempting to undermine your religious observance as well as defile your reputation as a virtuous woman, this restaurant serves kosher-compliant meals. So why don't I order the lamb for the both of us?"

"That sounds nice, but I usually order vegetarian when I go out," Megan said.

"Oh really?" Charles looked across the table. "You are no longer in a third-world country so your concerns about health and safety are misplaced."

He already beckoned the waiter over so Megan swallowed her protests. Frustration formed a knot in her stomach. She didn't feel hungry anymore and the silence of the room put her nerves on edge. Refusing wine only got her faced with a full glass of it, along with a remark that she felt was rather condescending about insulting the chef's handiwork by drinking water. Dishes were placed in front of her, and Megan forced herself to eat from them.

The conversation lurched forward in awkward stops and starts as Megan wracked her brain for something intelligent to say. She settled for listening to Charles go on about several extremely boring topics related to taxes and politics and hoped her responses were at least somewhat appropriate. She started to feel queasy halfway through the meal and gulped at her wine just to get each mouthful down. She chased the wine with water even though that earned her more than a few contemptuous looks. Charles ate with maddening slowness. He didn't even seem to enjoy the rich fare, but he simply acted as if he had all the time in the world. As Megan twitched with impatience, he just chewed endlessly which reminded her of a cow with its cud.

After a dinner that felt a hundred hours long, Megan suffered through a dessert she didn't want and nearly ran for the door when Charles motioned for the check. She let him pay without a fuss. Her share alone was more money than she could squeeze out of her wallet without resorting to the platinum card provided by her parents.

They were back in the car when Charles said, "Next time I

hope you do me the courtesy of actually contributing to the conversation when I'm doing my best to entertain you. I don't believe you paid attention to a single thing I said."

"I'm sorry about that," Megan said. Her seatbelt felt too tight around her body. The roiling in her stomach got worse and Megan wondered if she was going to be sick. The back of her throat welled with bile and she swallowed hard.

"How about I give you a chance to make up for your behavior tonight?"

"Um, yes?" Megan stammered as her thoughts tumbled around in disarray. She didn't know what she had just agreed to but she hoped it didn't involve spending any more time alone with Charles.

"Good, then I will tell Rabbi Kleiner to expect you to join us for Passover Seder. It falls on a Friday night this year so it's a very auspicious occasion."

"Oh. Yes. Of course." Megan scanned the road and prayed for her apartment to come up soon.

Dinner with Rabbi Sharon and probably a number of others from the congregation didn't seem too bad, and as a bonus, was over two weeks away. She was glad Charles wasn't going to submit her to his presence one-on-one again. However that didn't help her current physical state much. The bilious churning was at the point where Megan was no longer wondering *if* but *when* she would have to find a bucket.

He pulled into the parking lot of Megan's building and made a great show of annoyance when Megan informed him that there was no visitor parking. Grateful to have avoided the awkwardness of Charles attempting to see her to her door, Megan thanked him as she stumbled out of the car and escaped into the stairwell. She dashed through her front door and barely made it into the washroom before the nausea caught up with her. The expensive dinner vanished into the swirling depths of the toilet and Megan lay on the cool tile floor for a while after that and wished for the room to stop spinning.

After a few minutes, she felt better. Megan got up and brushed her teeth, annoyed to discover a trail of vomit speckling the front of her dress. Muttering, Megan balled up the whole sorry mess and threw it into the hamper. She got into her comfortable sleeping clothes and flopped down onto her sofa. She stared at the phone in her hands, aching to talk to Syler. She swiped in her code, but a burst of paranoia stilled Megan's hands from sending a text until she'd done a check and sweep of her phone to confirm that Charles hadn't tampered with it in the time it had been in his custody.

Megan was worried about a number of things and decided a chat with Syler would help her a lot. She sent a short message.

```
Are you awake?
```

She only had to wait a minute before the reply came.

```
    I   am   now.   Thanks   for   your   message,   I   was
thinking  about  you  all  evening.  Did  you  get  bogged
down with paperwork?
```

Megan's face got warm. A lovely, humming feeling woke up in her chest just from reading the words Syler typed. Megan drew in a breath and went with the truth.

```
    No,  worse!  I  got  hijacked  by  Dr.  Brockman  and
had the worst time tonight!

Do you want to talk about it?

Please!

In person?
```

Yes yes yes! Megan thought with a wild conviction. Instead she just replied with a single stamp. It was a popular character, a googly-eyed anthropomorphic string bean named Mame-Mame that was making the "Ok" sign with both arms raised in a circle over his head.

```
I'll be there in five.
```

Megan got to her feet and wondered if she needed to tidy up. She'd just decided things were fine when there was a soft knock at the door. Megan tried to calm her racing heartbeat, but found it quite difficult as she opened the door and let Syler in. She'd obviously been in bed and was in sweats with a knee-length peacoat thrown over her shoulders.

They ended up side by side on the sofa. Megan hugged a cushion to her chest. She wished it was Syler.

"What happened?" The compassion in Syler's eyes undid all her defenses and Megan blurted out the whole sorry spiel of the disastrous dinner from hell including Charles's odd behavior with ordering the food and taking her phone like she was an irresponsible high-school student caught texting in class, all the way to with the explosively unpleasant ending. Syler listened and shook her head while Megan talked.

After she'd finished, Syler asked, "How are you feeling now? Do you think it was food poisoning?"

"No, just nerves probably," Megan admitted. She drew in a quick breath as Syler shifted to sit closer to her. With a concerned look, Syler reached out and laid a hand on her forehead, then moved to press her palm against the side of Megan's neck. Even though her touch was professional, Megan couldn't help but feel tingling warmth where Syler's skin met hers.

"No fever, glands are normal, no sign of hives or dehydration either," Syler said. "You're right, it probably was nerves." She paused and then asked, "Did he try and come up to your apartment?"

"I think he wanted to," Megan said. "But he didn't."

"Good," Syler said.

"There's something else," Megan said. She took a deep breath. In a few words, she told Syler about Nikky Okamoto's case and Charles's reaction to it. Syler's face went hard at the details and she crossed her arms over her chest.

"Has anything like that happened before?" Megan asked. "The hospital trying to cover up stuff."

"With Charles Brockman?" Syler bounced one knee. "He's one slippery specimen and I wouldn't put it past him to pull something like this. But I don't really know what he's capable of, he's only been in our department for a couple months. Before that he was in Nephrology. It was all very sudden, the change. There was an—incident and we lost a bunch of good people. It was awful, really tragic, and he was practically the only one to come out of it unscathed. Nothing sticks to that man, absolutely nothing. Watch your back, Meg."

"Oh I definitely will," she said and lifted her chin with a

proud tilt. "Don't worry, I ran my own clinic in Thailand, I get how these things work, especially the shadier aspects."

"I heard you worked overseas," Syler said. "It's great you had your own practice. What did you do there?"

"Everything," Megan said. She relaxed into a smile as she remembered back to the freedom and happiness she'd once had.

"So you weren't always a pediatrician?"

"No," Megan shifted against the sofa cushions. "I'm a general practitioner with training in family medicine and surgery, plus emergency care and a bit of obstetrics. They had an opening in pediatrics and I was invited to apply by the president. Our families kind of know each other, mostly by reputation. The Jewish medical community here is pretty small."

Syler went quiet for a long moment and Megan wondered uneasily if something was wrong. However, Syler just stood and held out a hand. "Come over here."

Megan happily put her hand in Syler's and followed her over to the glass balcony doors. Syler drew aside the curtains and pointed to the apartment building just across the river from them.

"See that room up there? The right-side corner room on the top floor."

"Yes, I see it. The one with the blue curtains and the classy lamp, right?"

"Yup." She released Megan's hand and moved to stand behind her. Syler gently placed both hands on Megan's shoulders and bent her head to speak softly into her ear. "That's my place."

The close contact ignited a gush of fire within Megan. She held herself still when all she wanted to do was arch back against Syler's slim body.

"I left the lamp on just to show you the line of sight." Syler paused before she spoke again in a low, urgent voice, "It's probably nothing, but if you ever feel like you're in trouble, maybe there's someone in your room you don't want to be there and can't use your phone, I want to work out a signal. Do you have any kind of small lamp or decoration that lights up?"

Megan thought for an instant before she nodded and ducked into her bedroom. After a quick rummage through one of the boxes, she came back with a string of tea-lights, each bulb held in a tiny ball of glass threads. Megan bought the lights in Thailand to use as seasonal decorations in her clinic. She never got the chance. Still, they were pretty and Megan wasn't sad to see them. In fact, they brought back a few good memories. A year out of sight had taken the sting from them and Megan allowed herself to cherish the moments that seemed a lifetime ago.

"They're beautiful," Syler breathed. Her long fingers stroked over one of the glass cages, her face soft. "And will do nicely." She went back over to the window and peered up at the curtain rods. "If we put them up around here, I can see them from my place and I'll come over the instant they're lit. Is that all right with you? I promise this isn't a weird stalking thing."

"I know that. And thanks," Megan said. She found some zip-ties she'd been using to organize her electric cords and together they put up the lights, hanging them from the inner curtain railing.

"I feel like we should be listening to Hanukkah songs," Syler said as they worked.

"How about singing one?" Megan said, feeling giddy. "Do you know that one they use to teach kids about Hanukkah?"

"The one about candles?" Syler paused. "That kind of goes like..." She sang with confidence and Megan clapped before happily joining in.

"The neighbors are going to think I've lost my mind," Megan said with a laugh that reset her entire mood.

"Let them," Syler replied. She stepped back and studied their work. "Would you mind if I did the honors?"

"Not at all."

With that, Syler knelt and plugged in the string of lights. They glowed like jeweled fireflies and Megan caught her breath at their delicacy.

"You know," Megan said in a conversational way, "I might just have these on all the time to keep you running over here from your place."

"That's fine with me," Syler said. She looked up with a wicked gleam in her eyes. "But there's no need to burn them out now." She unplugged the lights and pulled the curtains closed. "And I guess my job here is done," she said with a satisfied nod.

"No it isn't," Megan said. "You haven't hugged me yet." For an instant Megan wondered if she'd overstepped some boundary and wished to take the words back.

"You're right, I haven't. Get over here, then," Syler

murmured. She held out her arms and banished Megan's worry in an instant.

Megan tried not to move too fast but she could barely hold herself back as she crossed the few steps between them. Syler's arms came around her. In response, Megan wrapped her arms around Syler's waist. She heard a catch in Syler's breath as she did so. She melted into the soft heat of Syler's body. Megan buried her head against one strong shoulder. She let out a sigh she hadn't known she'd been holding for the past year.

"This is nice," Megan said as she breathed in Syler's scent. She smelled like sunshine and clean laundry and Megan didn't want to let go.

Syler didn't reply but her arms tightened around Megan and she dropped a quick kiss into Megan's hair. The contact was warm and firm, not exactly the lust-filled pressure that had gripped Megan the other night, but she felt safe and cherished. Megan was surprised at the sting of tears against her lids.

"Oh God, sorry," Megan hiccupped.

Syler drew back. "Are you all right?" Syler asked.

Their eyes met. Megan held her breath and waited. Her body trembled with the need to feel Syler's lips on hers. Nothing happened for a heartbeat, then Syler dropped her arms.

Released, Megan took a step back and rubbed a hand across her eyes. "I'll be fine. It's just been one hell of a day. One hell of a week actually."

"It sure has. Do you think you'll be able to sleep all right?"

"Yes, but," Megan felt very young as she continued, "would you stay for a bit longer? Like, um, until I'm asleep?"

"Of course," Syler said. "I'll be right here on the sofa and I'll wait for your monstrous snores to rock the building before I leave."

"I don't snore!" Megan huffed. "Here's the remote, feel free to watch anything you like."

"Sure thing," Syler said. She folded her long legs and got comfortable on the sofa. Soon the thin strands of a late-night variety show filled the small room. Megan hovered behind the sofa, more interested in Syler than the show. She leaned against the back of the sofa and propped her elbows up on it.

Syler didn't seem to mind Megan's hovering. She pointed to one of the guests on the panel. "He's gay, you know. They say his wife is too. And the host has never been married or even in a relationship that anyone's seen and doesn't seem like he ever wants to. Maybe ace, maybe gay and hiding it."

"My dad does that," Megan said. "Except he's always pointing out who's Jewish."

"That's your job now," Syler said with a laugh.

Comforted and warm, Megan wanted to stay there with Syler all night, but she straightened up and made herself step back.

To be quite honest, Megan wanted to invite Syler into the bedroom, but the thought of that long, slender body beside her on her narrow futon made Megan's heart race and her skin tingle in a way she knew would drive any chance of sleep from her mind and body. Instead she ducked into her closet and came back out with a spare blanket for Syler. Without hesitation, she dug into her bag and came up with the key to her apartment.

Megan put the blanket down on the end of the sofa and passed over the key. "This is so you can lock up when you leave."

"Thanks," Syler said. "I'll slip it back in through the mail slot. Anyway, you look beat, Meg. Go sleep and forget about all your worries. Tomorrow's a fresh new day."

"I'm sorry about dragging you out at this time of night," Megan said. She lingered in the doorway of her bedroom. "I know you've got surgery tomorrow. Maybe we should reschedule the picnic?"

"Not on your life," Syler said with a grin. She draped herself over the sofa and folded her hands behind her head.

Megan slipped into her room and was just snuggling down into her futon when she thought she heard Syler say, "I even dug out my tux and everything."

Chapter Five

THE NEXT MORNING, Megan rose late, refreshed and alert. She nearly sang the daily physician's prayer in her kitchen cubby. She ran a bath for herself and luxuriated in the fragrant water. After a light breakfast, she got in touch with her inner Audrey Hepburn and dressed in a simple but stylish knit top and slim-fitting capris. The silver Star of David at her throat gave the outfit a sleek and sophisticated air. She was just wondering about whether to go with a cardigan or a jacket when there was a knock at her door. A happy light came on within herself as she pulled the door open only to freeze with her mouth open.

Syler stood in the hallway, dressed in an immaculate tuxedo. From the tips of her polished boots to the silk hat, every line was perfect, her sweeping androgynous magnetism undeniable. She raised her head from the casual tilt and her gaze met Megan's.

Megan choked. Of course Syler had a tux. And she looked absolutely breathtaking in it.

"I'm a bit underdressed," Megan said. She hung onto the door knob for dear life as her knees didn't seem to want to work anymore.

"Not at all," Syler said. She doffed her hat and leaned against the doorframe. Humor danced in her eyes. "I got this for myself as a kind of 'now you're free' present and haven't had the chance to wear it yet. Just because I felt like it, I decided to take you on a super classy picnic. If you want to change, that's fine. But you look great in what you've got on. You're quite classy yourself."

Megan flushed and a warm wave rose from her belly at the frank complement.

"How about this? I'll be your butler. I would like to let you know," Syler dropped her voice to a purr, "I can buttle with the best of them."

"I'm sure you can," Megan said. She felt as if she was floating. Because it was closer at hand, she grabbed her cardigan and whirled it around her shoulders. "All right, my good butler, shall we be on our way?"

"Yes, of course. Right this way, miss."

Syler picked up a large bag she'd put down in the hallway and led the way out to the street. They arrived at the promised location, which was a rather secluded spot on the riverbank, only a few minutes' walk from their apartments. Syler stopped underneath a grouping of cherry trees. While the thick clusters of branches overhead provided a frothy white canopy, the blossoms were still young enough the petals weren't scattering too much. The fact that it was a weekday, added to the distance from the usual cherry blossom watching areas, which boasted food stalls and parking, ensured that they had almost complete privacy. A bicycle path passed beside them and a scatter of houses was nearby so Megan didn't plan on any large romantic advances—no matter how she burned for one. In a way it was something of a relief to have that artificial dampener there to keep things from happening too quickly, before either of them was ready.

With a theatrical groan, Syler put down the sturdy bag and massaged her lower back. She dug through the bag and came out with a blanket, which she spread over the ground. In true butler-like fashion she held out a hand to assist Megan as she kicked off her ballet flats and stepped onto the blanket. After rummaging around a bit more, Syler pulled a floor cushion from the bag and offered it to Megan with a courtly flourish. Megan quickly folded her legs and sat down primly with her feet tucked underneath herself.

"This is a great spot," Megan said from her princess-like perch. "It's so beautiful here."

"I'm glad the lady approves," Syler replied.

Once Megan was settled, Syler doffed her hat and took off her gloves. She started to unload the lunch items, which were in a number of boxes, jars, and one intriguing Tupperware container. Syler quickly and efficiently made a nice arrangement over on one side of the blanket.

Ensconced on her cushion, Megan surveyed the bounty and hoped her stomach didn't rumble because the sight and smells of the food made her suddenly hungry. Syler's long, slender form accented by the classic lines of the tux lit a flame to another kind of hunger.

"I went with the dairy options today. You didn't have any meat for breakfast, I hope," Syler said as she pulled out a jar that was filled with luscious-looking pickles.

"No, I just had some yogurt, so it's a dairy day for me."

"That's good." Syler looked up just as Megan was busy giving her a long once-over. She wasn't repentant in the least at being busted and just returned Syler's look with a small smile. With a sly, knowing grin of her own, Syler continued, "I made the blintzes as kosher as I could and everything else is from the shop by the hospital. Okay, not the takenoko, but I think those are sacred in their own way."

"Syler, this is wonderful," Megan said in amazement. For a moment, she wondered if she was hallucinating from the puked-up lamb the night before. "But this is the first time in my adult life I'm actually trying to be observant so I'm not being super-strict with it all until I've got a handle on the basics. Honestly, I don't expect you to go out of your way to accommodate me."

"That's all right," Syler said. "I've kind of gotten into the habit. After all I've been eating in the hospital's cafeteria for the last six years. And I've always had a healthy respect for the kosher laws. They make a lot of sense."

The words sent a pleasant jolt through Megan, but she only said, "You've got a lot more practice than me, that's for sure, especially if you've been doing Saturday lunch duty."

"It's mostly just setting out stuff people made the day before. The only hard part is getting the timing right." Syler said with an air of nonchalance, but a pleased smile quirked up the corners of her lips.

"And you don't have to be my butler anymore," Megan said. She picked up a paper plate and looked over the array of delicious things spread out in front of her, including a bottle of grape juice Syler had placed in a bucket of ice. Megan blathered on without thinking, "You can relax, enjoy the day, and just be my—" Megan froze. She cleared her throat and asked, "What would you be?"

"What do you want me to be?"

The words were low, husky, and sent a thrill through Megan's chest. She swallowed hard.

"Would the term 'girlfriend' be appropriate? I mean, well, maybe it's too early to stick labels on or I don't know if you even want a label, I mean I don't want to assume anything, how about we just go with something simple like—"

"I'd love to be your girlfriend," Syler interrupted, her voice easy and warm. "Either that or pet penguin."

Syler sat up and pretended to waddle like a penguin. The tense moment dissolved into laughter. While Megan snickered, Syler leaned over and started to dish out a good selection onto both of their plates.

Her girlfriend. A sweet, shy happiness come over her as she watched Syler serving with grace and her own casually dashing style. With a pleasant jolt, Megan realized that meant she was Syler's girlfriend too. She liked the sound of that.

"Your lunch, *O-jousan*," Syler said and handed over the plate with a princely air.

"Everything looks great," Megan said. She thought it was cute how Syler called her *lady* and treated her with such respect that didn't feel like play-acting.

"There's plenty for seconds if you want," Syler said. She clasped both hands together around her chopsticks and Megan followed suit. Both of them chorused, "*Itadakimasu!*"

Megan decided to try the blintzes Syler had made first. Several small jars of jam were in a friendly cluster in a basket and Megan selected a blackberry one for topping. Once her blintzes had been suitably doctored, Megan took a bite and the sweet-sour cottage cheese filling radiated into her mouth like a fragment of heaven.

She closed her eyes and moaned out, "Doctor Syler Terada, you make the most gorgeous blintzes, you save people's lives on a daily basis, and you rock a tuxedo." Megan opened her eyes and speared Syler with a stern look. "Is there anything you can't do?"

Busy with her own lunch, Syler had sprawled down onto the blanket, her long body stretched from one end to the other. She looked up with a wry grin. "I can't slurp noodles," she said. "They go up my nose and the sight of that is not something I would subject anybody to. The first time I went out with Yukina, she made us go get ramen and let me tell you, that was nearly the last date. I gave Cthulhu a run for his money."

"I can see how that might put a damper on a romantic evening out," Megan said. She let out a laugh, a bit surprised that she felt absolutely no sting from the casual mention of Syler's ex-girlfriend. The past was in the past and if Syler didn't have any animosity toward her, Megan decided she wouldn't either.

She was glad to give Syler the opportunity to share her life, both the bad and the good. There were probably only a few people at the hospital who Syler could talk to about personal things and Megan was glad to be one of them. She didn't know about Syler's life outside the hospital, but if she was anything like most of the surgeons Megan had known, Syler's life pretty much would be the hospital.

Megan continued, "I'm glad for your sake she didn't go running for the hills at your sudden transformation. Or would it be better to say reversion?" Megan gave Syler a gentle poke on one shoulder. "And don't worry, Ms. Lovecraftian creature, I can slurp well enough for the both of us."

"That's good to hear," Syler said. She reached over and pulled the bottle of juice from the bucket, then whipped out a white towel that was printed with the hospital's logo, apparently a commemorative item from some kind of event. She got to her knees and wiped drops of water from the bottle before she twisted the cap off. With a flourish, Syler picked up Megan's wine glass and poured with a steady hand that spoke of years of practice and control. As she was sipping her juice, Megan got an idea. She grabbed her bag and rummaged around in it before she came up with her phone.

"Photo time!" Megan said. "If that's all right?"

"Sure," Syler said. Glass still in one hand, she came over to sit beside Megan. Syler slipped an arm around Megan's waist which caused Megan's mind to go blank. For an instant, Megan stared at the phone and wondered what she was doing with it before she blinked herself back to reality and called up the camera function.

"Say cheese!" Megan said as she held the phone out. She hoped her hand wasn't shaking too badly as she snapped a quick photo. She tried not to think about how close they were. She was practically in Syler's arms. The soft heat where Syler's body was pressed against her back radiated through her and she imagined she could still feel it even after Syler pulled away. Megan gazed at the picture. They looked natural together, complementary but linked by some unseen force.

"How about I send this to you? Um, you know, just because," Megan said with her eyes on the screen.

"I'd like that a lot. Thanks."

She sent the pic and put her phone away. Still trembling and stunned from the photo, Megan finished the delicious lunch in a daze. Very aware of the potential people around them, Megan leaned back on her hands, which took her away from Syler's alluring presence, when she really wanted to be going the other way. She stretched her legs out and took a deep breath, content to bask in the slight chill of the early spring day, tempered by the heated gaze she felt raking over her body. She knew Syler was watching her and she didn't mind one bit. With a languid stretch and the decision to make the best of the situation, Megan pulled her cardigan off and folded it into a pile in her lap.

"Why don't you take a rest?" she asked and patted the cardigan. "You certainly deserve it. You worked so hard to make this truly the classiest picnic I have ever had in my entire life." Emotion overcame her and Megan whispered the last words, "Thank you."

"Only the best for you, Meg," Syler told her. With a quick motion, she stripped off her jacket and scooted over so she could lie back and place her head in the proffered lap. Megan drew in a reverent breath as Syler closed her eyes and clasped her hands over her middle. "Very nice," Syler murmured before she went quiet. Only her regular breathing marred the perfect stillness.

In repose, Syler's face was open and relaxed. Megan looked down at Syler and her heart filled with warmth. How could anyone toss this wonderful, sexy, and thoughtful person aside and choose another over her? Wanting a bureaucratically simple life was only an excuse. There were always workarounds. Insurance companies allowed people to choose their beneficiaries if they didn't want the settlement to automatically go to their biological families. Similarly, wills could be written and notarized at the local *Kosei-yakuba* office. In the absence of partnerships, the practice of adoption called *youshien-gumi* could serve to blend families that couldn't be any other way. Anything was possible, the key was to want it badly enough to find a way.

The wind rustled the branches above Megan's head and released a spray of delicately pink-stained blossoms over them both.

As if in slow motion, Megan reached out and picked up a stray petal that had fallen into Syler's hair. The contact unleashed a sultry heat in her chest. She marveled at the sensation. Megan trailed her fingers through the strands. She traced the delicate curve of Syler's ear down to the lobe. She'd replaced her usual rings with sparkling studs, two in her left and one in her right.

Megan wondered why Syler hadn't kissed her yet. There were a few moments when they'd been close, but Syler let them slip away. Then Megan understood. Syler was waiting for her. A kiss was a big step. After all, women friends hugged and even held hands all the time, but a kiss, especially the kind Megan yearned for, was not something that passed between friends. The timing was up to her. Until then, Megan was certain Syler would not cross that line. Megan alone had to be the first to breach that barrier, to claim those delicately sculpted lips with hers. For an instant, Megan wondered if she could be brave enough to make that first move before she admitted it was only a matter of time before she succumbed to the powerful force that was drawing her closer to the edge.

Every beat of her heart sent a jolt through her as Megan cupped Syler's face. Her thumb brushed over Syler's lower lip. Megan could barely believe how much she wanted to touch the woman who was lying across her lap. Eyes closed and breathing deeply, Syler didn't move and appeared to have fallen asleep. At the lack of resistance, Megan became bolder. She traced the clean lines of Syler's jaw before she dropped down to draw her fingers over the immaculate knot of the white bow tie. A wild thought flashed through Megan's mind and she envisioned loosening that snug collar and letting the tie flutter to the ground before she unbuttoned the crisply pleated shirt and slipped her hand inside.

An almost painful twinge gripped Megan and she shifted slightly, startled at the force of her desire. She brought her hand back up, away from temptation and gently cradled Syler's head once more. A slight smile came to Syler's face and she turned to press against Megan's hand.

She wasn't asleep after all. Megan caught her breath the instant Syler opened her eyes and looked up at her. There was no way Megan could hide the longing in her expression and only hoped Syler was tactful enough to ignore it.

Syler reached out and twined her fingers around Megan's before she sat up. She brought Megan's hand to her lips. The kiss was the barest brush of silk across her knuckles but it sent a tingling thrill up Megan's arm. It was her left hand, but Syler either didn't notice or didn't mind the ring. In that instant, the words of confession bubbled into Megan's mind and she almost opened her mouth to speak. At the last moment, her courage gave out and she remained silent. She couldn't open the floodgates of that dam. Not yet.

With a slow, deliberate stretch that made Megan flush and wonder where to look, Syler said, "Sorry about drifting off there. Occupational hazard and survival mechanism left over from my intern days."

"I know about that," Megan said, glad for the neutral subject as she tried to wrestle herself back under control. "I get comfortable enough, I can conk out anywhere. It's kind of a superpower at this point."

"Feel free to take advantage of that anytime," Syler told her with sincerity. "I'll keep an eye on you and wake you up if need be. Especially if we're on the train."

"Thanks," Megan said. "I'll return the favor for you, but hopefully both of us don't drift off at the same time and end up in Russia." She tried to calm the kick her heart gave at the thought of nestling into Syler's embrace and letting sleep take her. Her gaze softened, her mind wandered. Syler's voice brought her back to the present.

"So tell me about the good doctor, Megan Maier. You're from Kanto, right?" As she spoke, Syler flopped back down onto the cherry blossom-speckled blanket and lay on her side, looking casually gorgeous.

"Yes. I've always lived in Saitama but I've got American citizenship. My dad's from Maine and my mom's ethnically Polish but she was born and raised here just like me. They're dentists. They actually met in dental school."

"So the hassle with national health insurance runs in your blood, then."

"I guess so," Megan said. She gazed up at the canopy of blossoms waving over them. She didn't really feel like talking about herself or her family. She shifted so she could study Syler. Megan admired her lithe grace, even in repose. "Anyway, what were you doing in Michigan? Did you study there?"

"I was raised there, and did my undergrad there," Syler said. "My father has always been this hippy free-range dude and his only goal in life was to live in the States. He got a job in one of the auto parts factories around here with only that in mind. The minute he got his first assignment overseas he picked up and moved us all to this way out in the middle of nowhere town called Carrowville. I was about four at the time. As soon as we landed there, he renegotiated his contract to become a local worker, got his green card, and eventually started his own business selling lawn stuff. Things were a lot different in those days, but I think even now he'd have gotten what he wanted. My *oton* is pretty unstoppable when he puts his mind to something." She laughed, a pure, uninhibited sound. "That's why all of us — me and my three brothers — have anglicized names. He was planning his escape from day one."

"Really?" Megan was intrigued. She drew her knees up to her chest and hugged them. "What did your mother think of all that?"

"I don't know," Syler said. "She took off when Gene, that's my youngest bro, was just born. I was only two, so I don't even remember her. It's always been my dad and the four of us against the world."

"It sounds like you're close with your family."

"Sure, they're good guys," Syler said. "We email and talk a lot."

Megan wasn't surprised Syler's father had gotten custody of the children. It was common practice for the man to take the assets of the marriage when it dissolved, and the greatest of those were the offspring. It was very businesslike, but how many marriages, particularly in Japan, were more business arrangement than a love-match? Maybe it was the same with Syler's father. Megan couldn't fault anyone for that, particularly because she'd chosen that path herself. A sharp pain threatened to choke Megan and she shook it off as the urge to speak came over her.

"But you came back," Megan said.

"Yeah, I did." Syler looked up at Megan. "I mean, I could have changed my citizenship and become American, but I could never stop being Japanese. You know? No matter what my passport says, Japan is in *here*," She paused and pressed a hand to the starched front of her shirt. "And it's been that way since the day I was born. When I came back here in high school, I really noticed it. At first all I wanted to do was run away and go back to the States, but eventually I realized I'm part of this country and this country's part of me. I couldn't outrun twelve thousand years of history and every single one of my ancestors glaring down at me in an unbroken line right back to the dawn of civilization." Syler gave a wry smile that spoke of her past struggle and called up a spear of recognition within Megan. She said, "I didn't fit in back then, and I still don't, but at least I've made a place for myself where I'm doing the best I can." Syler reached out to Megan and touched her on the back of one hand. "I've never told this to anyone, but something tells me you get it."

"You're right. I do," Megan said. Her own chest got warm as if Syler's hand rested there instead. "I considered changing my nationality too, but the permanent resident visa is good enough. I've got freedom to live and work here without worrying about having a guarantor." Syler was close enough to Megan that she could give Syler's arm a nudge with her knee, "Plus I don't want to put up with a lifetime of incredulous looks if I introduced myself as Japanese."

"That's the trouble when a nationality is also a race," Syler said. She draped her arm over Megan's leg in a way that was intimate without making Megan feel trapped.

To distract herself from the soft pressure on her thigh, Megan asked, "Is that why you went to high school here?"

Syler got a sour look on her face. "No. My dad sent me and my younger brother Gene back to stay with his parents when we were in high school. Hal was working and George was in college so they got to stay. We, but mostly me, were having problems. You know, skipping school, mouthing off to the teachers and generally being entitled little shits. I guess he thought it was time for us to get back to our roots. They're all in the States now, but I ended up back here." Syler shifted as if getting into a more comfortable position and said, "I did two years of high school here and absolutely fucking hated it. I thought the uniform was a pervert-magnet and the whole after-school club activity stuff was a bullshit waste of time." She spat the curse words in English.

They'd fallen into the easy habit of speaking Japanese while outside of their workplace. Megan liked how Syler could switch lightning-fast between languages. She, like Megan, was a true bilingual. It didn't matter which language they were speaking. The connection was just as strong and true. With her usual careless grace, Syler rolled over and lay on her back, supporting her head on her folded arms. The contrast of her comfortable sprawl with the sleek formalwear only further charmed Megan.

Syler continued, "It didn't help that I'd missed out on a lifetime of shared culture. I could speak the language, but I couldn't speak *their* language. I didn't know the in-jokes. I couldn't finish sentences other people started and I always used the wrong word to describe things. I had no idea who the fuck those SMAP guys were and thought they were out of their minds when they tapped their hands onto the table and said, 'hey hey hey hey.' I was missing a bunch of stamps from my Bingo card and it was like we were standing on opposite sides of the Grand Canyon."

"Well I had all my stamps and it didn't make any difference," Megan said with a wince. "High school sucked for me too. Teens can be absolutely vicious to each other."

Syler glanced up with a look of raw pain on her face. "You weren't bullied or anything, were you?"

"No, nothing so dramatic," Megan said. "It was like once the novelty wore off, I just didn't exist. You know when you see a bunch of girls and they all burst into wild giggles the second you walk past them? That was basically my life. I didn't really have any friends until I was in university and even then I always felt like I was on the outside looking in." She shrugged. Those scars had long since faded, the past hurt dwarfed by the more recent wallops life had blasted her way.

"You must have been a late bloomer then," Syler rolled over onto her front and leaned her cheek on one hand as she gazed up at Megan. "I can't imagine anyone being able to ignore the swan you are now."

"Flattery will get you nowhere, my pet penguin," Megan said. She reached out to give Syler a playful slap on the shoulder. It never landed.

Syler reacted with catlike grace as she caught Megan's hand in mid-air and pulled. The action resulted in Megan falling forward and being caught in Syler's arms. Their faces were inches apart and Megan sucked in a breath. She knew exactly where she wanted to the moment go next. Nerves froze Megan into place as she doubted her ability to carry through. A cheerful chorus of ringing bells shattered the mood and Megan wrenched herself upright just in time for a posse of uniformed students to fly by on their bicycles.

"Now that I've talked your ear off about myself, how about we call it a day?" Syler said. She got to her feet and put on her chunky-heeled demi boots by the time Megan realized what was going on. "I know you've got to go into the city tonight."

"Yes, that's right," Megan said, both relieved and disappointed. She helped gather up the remains of their picnic lunch and soon they were in front of Megan's apartment building.

"I hope it's okay if I don't see you to your door," Syler said as she hoisted the large bag over her shoulder. "This thing is heavy and I don't want to leave it lying out in the open."

"That's fine," Megan said. On an impulse, she reached out and touched the hand that was holding onto the straps of the bag. Syler smiled at the hesitant caress. Megan said, "Thanks for a wonderful afternoon."

"The pleasure was all mine. I'll see you tomorrow at the hospital. Until then, you'll be in my thoughts and my dreams," Syler said. She stepped back and broke the contact. She tipped her silk hat before she turned and strode off.

Megan trembled from the burst of emotion Syler's parting words had brought as she watched Syler walk away until the passing cars blocked her lean form. With a reluctant last glance over her shoulder, Megan ducked into her building. She let out a sigh as she unlocked her front door. It seemed she'd discovered Syler's first date kissing policy.

AFTER SHE TOOK a power nap to prepare herself for the long night, Megan spent the remaining daylight hanging around her room, absently vacuuming with the TV on in the background for company. She thought about what Syler had said about not fitting in and ached for the lonely pasts they'd both had. That loneliness was over, Megan decided with fierce conviction. She had only known Syler for a few days, but already Syler's presence filled a void within herself. Megan could only hope she did the same for Syler.

The time to go loomed. Megan got her medical bag ready and boarded the rapid train for Nagoya. The mountainous landscape of Gifu prefecture gave way to the coastline of Aichi. Megan leaned her chin on one hand and watched as the train crossed bridge after bridge and the city came upon her. Even though she'd only been there for a week, Megan had grown used to her own little town and sighed as more neon lights flashed past.

Megan was raised in the sprawling grey urban landscape of Saitama and Suito City's countryside charm appealed to her right away. After her father passed the letter of invitation on to her, Megan researched the area to help with her decision. Because of the hospital, the town was home to a substantial Jewish community. Megan was immediately captivated by the thought of a small, backwoods town in the middle of Japan that was overrun by Jews. It fascinated her enough to spur Megan to leave the black rut she'd been stuck in and re-start her professional life.

She'd never been to Nagoya before except to travel through it on the bullet train. After she popped up from the nearest sub-way station, she relied on the printout of the map to the Angel Hand Clinic in her hand as she navigated the increasingly narrow streets. It was still too early for the nightclubs and bars to be open and Megan was faced with closed shutters on either side of the street. After she found the tiny triangle of scrub that was Hanamura Park, the clinic came into view. It was housed in a two-story glass-fronted building opposite a flamboyant shop that sold fancy dresses for the club-working girls.

And boys, Megan observed as she sidestepped a few suspiciously large-sized dresses displayed in all their fluttering tulle and sequined glory on liberal-minded mannequins. She tucked the map into her bag and entered the clinic. The small reception area boasted a single padded bench and a counter that separated the lobby from the inner office. The receptionist-nurse behind the counter jumped up at her approach and rounded the counter at a fast trot.

"Maier-sensei," the nurse greeted her. "Thanks for coming. I'm Kawasaki Keiko."

"Nice to meet you, Keiko-san," Megan replied as she returned Keiko's bow.

"You too," she said. She waited as Megan shook out her lab coat and shrugged into it. When Megan was ready, Keiko said, "It's not much, but I'll give you a tour of the facility."

"Thanks," Megan said. She quickly looped her stethoscope

around her neck as she followed Keiko's trim figure down the worn linoleum-tiled hallway. Keiko pointed out the small break room with a sturdy but battered cot flanked by an ancient fridge and microwave, before she led Megan to the second floor with its locked stockroom that held drugs and equipment as well as the tiny OR for minor surgical procedures. There was also a room with two curtained-off beds for any patients who couldn't be moved but weren't in serious enough condition to be passed onto one of the nearby hospitals. Keiko informed her those types were mostly drunks.

As Megan followed Keiko back to the examination room where Megan would spend most of her shift, Keiko asked, "Are you all right with, um, special patients?"

"Of course," Megan said. "I wouldn't turn anyone away, if that's what you mean."

"Good. We don't ask people for their health insurance cards. If they have them, great. If not, don't pressure."

"That's fine, I get it," Megan said. She knew there would be patients she'd need to be careful with—undocumented workers and overstayers, in addition to people whose names and appearance didn't match the ones on their official identification. They reached the examination room and Keiko ushered Megan inside.

"We have a lot of people coming in for hormone shots," Keiko said in a rush. "You don't have a problem with things like that, do you?"

"Of course not." Megan paused, one hand on the curtain that separated the exam room from the hallway. "That's why I'm here. My education is just beginning but I want to learn more."

"That's great," Keiko said. "There was this one guy who came here and we found out he was trying to talk people out of transitioning."

"Why would anyone even think about doing that?" Megan gaped. "What an idiot. Ethics aside, by the time people are getting needles in the butt, they're well decided."

"Agreed. He didn't last long, Tonosaki-*incho* booted him out the second someone complained and spread the word. He was a *yabu-isha*," Keiko spat the term for "quack" with a satisfied smirk. "Anyway, while you're waiting, you can stay here, or you can lie down in the break room in back. Things are usually pretty slow

on weeknights. We have Wi-Fi if you want to surf the net or
something." Her face got a sly look and she said, "We have a
rather nice gaming setup too. It's in the room we used to use for
physical therapy."

"Ooh," Megan said, unable to contain her excitement. "Can I
bring in my own games?"

"Yes, we encourage it."

"Nice," Megan said. She made a mental note to slip *Zenith of
the Undead* into her bag in preparation for her next shift at the
Angel Hand Clinic. "Oh, and about my salary."

"It's not much I know —"

"I want it funneled back here," Megan said. "I don't need it.
Let it help cover anyone who can't pay."

"Understood," Keiko said. "Well, that's it. We've only got
one appointment tonight so you can hang out here or wherever
you like. I'll buzz you when we have a walk-in."

"Sure, thanks."

Megan closed the curtain and sat down at the desk.

She felt better, more at home in the small clinic. The sterile,
high-class atmosphere of the hospital grated on her. In Thailand,
Megan got used to being the master of her own place, rundown
and makeshift as it was. She opened the top drawer and glanced
at the admission form. She was gratified but not surprised to see a
number of choices in the section for the patient's sex. The
washrooms in the lobby had also lacked designation.

After the accident, she'd spent half a year in Thailand, tying
up loose ends and training her replacement to take over her
former clinic. She seesawed from bloodless professional to broken
down survivor, from regretting her unfinished work to wanting
to get as far away as she could. The violent flip-flop left Megan
with mental whiplash. In the half year following her return when
she'd been living with her parents, slowly coming back to herself,
Megan did a lot of research and the Angel Hand Clinic ticked a
number of boxes for her. She wondered when she could start
introducing some small changes to the Ruth Kurtz hospital.

Satisfied, Megan stowed the papers and straightened up as
the intercom rang. Keiko-san introduced her first patient, a Thai
woman with her infant who was suffering from a lingering rash.
She greeted Megan in halting Japanese and looked surprised but
grateful when Megan replied in her own gently accented Thai.

Megan was pleased to use her language skills and after she examined the baby and handed over a generous handful of sample ointments from their stock room, she chatted with the young mother for a while, asking about her son and commiserating on the taciturn nature of Japanese men. Megan didn't even ask, but the young woman told her she was waiting, without much optimism, for the father of their son to acknowledge him.

"He doesn't want his wife to find out," she said, jiggling the boy on her lap as he started to get fussy.

"Keep at it, for the little one's sake," Megan told her. Without acknowledgement, the child wouldn't legally exist. He wouldn't be able to go to school or even work when he got older. There was no question about voting, not even Megan could do that without giving up her nationality.

She bent down and made a funny face at the little boy. He turned, attention caught, and she pulled a set of keys from her pocket and jingled them at him. The little boy forgot whatever it had been occupying his mind as he reached out in fascination. Megan kept the keys just out of his reach and he squirmed and giggled.

While Megan never understood the attraction they held for kids, she kept that set of keys for no other reason than to distract little ones.

Megan walked out to the lobby to see them off and turned from the door to find Keiko staring at her.

"How many languages do you speak?" Keiko asked from her perch at the reception desk.

"Fluently? Two," Megan said with a shrug. "My Thai's only passable and my Hebrew's a bit rusty. I can curse pretty well in Yiddish though."

"Teach me English!" Keiko blurted out.

Megan just fixed her with an odd look and said, "Um, no."

For the majority of the rest of her shift, Megan hung out at the reception desk with Keiko. She enjoyed watching various people walk by outside and greeted the drop-ins. Apparently news of the new "foreign" doctor had spread and the clinic saw a steady stream of traffic from locals who came by to introduce themselves to curious passers-by who were lured over by the little crowd gathered on the sidewalk. Megan met a mixed bunch of small business owners, street callers, and random customers from the nearby bars and shadier establishments. A couple of grizzled curmudgeons came in with a bottle of *shochu* between them and helped themselves to free cold tea from the machine in the lobby before they mixed it with generous dollops from their bottle. Megan turned down a strong cup of it before they took up court in the waiting room and sermonized at length about the state of the world to anyone who would listen.

Around two a.m. a pleasantly drunk mama-san from a nearby *okama* style gay bar came in for nothing more than a chat with a pack of takeout sushi to share. Megan was pleased to have an excuse not to eat the rather flat aluminum-foil wrapped rice ball in her bag. The mama-san was swathed in a kimono and wig, immaculately made-up and Megan enjoyed the lively conversation. She had missed that. The friendly drop-ins, the casual outreach that brought people into the clinic, blurring the lines between untouchable doctor and lowly patient.

Megan saw a few more people come in for various odd reasons and ended her shift by patching up a trio of hosts who had gotten into a scuffle outside their club.

"Fight with words, not your fists," Megan told them in her best schoolmarm voice. She ignored the hiss of pain as she swabbed a jagged cut on one young man's brow in preparation for stitches. "Remember, you can always just walk away. It saves on cleanup and you won't have to answer all those questions tomorrow night at work. Understood?"

"Yeah, understood," they muttered in a chorus.

The relief doctor came in at four and since the first train wasn't for another two hours, Megan sprawled out on the narrow cot in the crash room and exhibited her superpower by falling into a deep, dreamless sleep.

Chapter Six

ONCE THE TRAINS were running, Megan slipped out into the gently waking streets and made her way to the station. On the train ride back, Megan slouched in the seat between clumps of uniformed students and suited businesspeople on their way to work. She felt good. She hadn't done a lot, but she was doing something positive. The guilt that constantly hovered over her head didn't feel quite so heavy. She absently twisted the ring on her finger as she gazed out of the window, lulled into a half-asleep daze by the rocking of the train.

Megan finally relaxed as she walked down the store-lined street on the way from the station to her apartment. She couldn't help but glance over to Syler's window once she was back in her room. The curtains were drawn and, with a slight stir of anticipation, Megan wondered what she was doing. Was she already awake or was she still lying in bed? Did she glance over at Megan's window and think about her as well? The thought brought a slight warmth to her cheeks.

However, she didn't have time to ponder things like that. Megan sloughed off the night's grime with a quick shower and changed.

She was early for the briefing and idly hung out in the hallway in front of the pediatric department's event board. It was decorated with a poster of photos from the hospital's Purim costume party the previous month. Megan looked them over with a smile on her face. She found a shot of Sakura in a wheelchair, her little face peering out from a pile of pajamas and mismatched scrubs with a bottle of detergent clutched in one hand. One picture in particular caught Megan's eye. It was of Syler standing in the middle of a bunch of cheerfully-costumed children, most of whom seemed to be variations on the theme of pirate with one child wearing a box and apparently being a wall, complete with bulletin board and light switch. Syler looked tall and regal in the colorful group. She made a cape from what looked to be a blue bed sheet and was in a long robe with a gold foil crown on her head. She also sported a magnificent grey beard that fell to her waist.

"Of course Syler would go in drag for Purim," Luka said in Megan's ear, startling her.

Megan patted herself on the chest as she answered, "I'm not surprised. Syler makes a great Mordechai. I mean, I would expect no less from anyone who owns a tux."

"Wait a minute, you know about her tux?" Luka peered into Megan's face. "Okay, honey, there's something going on here that I do not know about."

"There's nothing going on," Megan said. She batted at Luka as he danced around her.

"Uh huh. I don't believe you. Spill it."

"We just went on a picnic, that's all."

"And she told you about it then?"

"No, she wore it."

Luka froze in place with his mouth hanging open. He recovered and gave Megan a brilliant smile as he took both her hands in his. "You lucky thing! I bet she looked drop-dead gorgeous."

"Yeah, she did," Megan said. She glanced around in case anyone else was around, but at that early hour the hallway was deserted. She felt a shy smile on her face and didn't fight it. There was no need to hide anything from Luka. He had been nothing but kind to her and was a friend and ally of Syler's as well.

Luka gave her a good-humored shove with one shoulder and turned back to the board. "I went as Queen Esther. See, that's me there."

"Very lovely," Megan said. She studied the cluster of photos featuring an elegantly decked-out Luka. "But isn't that dress Queen Elsa's?"

"Shush," Luka said with another shove. "A queen is a queen, my dear."

"You can say that again," Megan said with a laugh. She glanced at her watch. "I should be going. The briefing is about to start. Luka, are you coming too?"

"Of course," he said. "I think pretty much everybody who can is going to be there." He looked sad, but continued, "Sakura-chan's practically family to all of us here."

By the time they got to the briefing room, most of the free

medical staff was already there and Syler was at the front of the room in scrubs and sprawled out over her chair. She was sitting next to Paul Bleaker, the physician in charge of Sakura's case. Megan forced her face into a neutral expression and tried to keep her gaze from lingering but it was difficult as Syler turned and gave her a quicksilver grin, complete with a wink. The rest of the world vanished with the slight but undeniable connection and Megan's legs gave out. She half-fell into one of the last free chairs and ignored Luka's knowing looks in her direction. Instead, she focused her attention on the display of x-rays and the projected CT scans that were on the screen behind the podium.

At precisely the hour, Charles barreled into the room with Gerald Hayashi, the chief surgical resident and the briefing began. Megan listened as a little girl's life was explained in technical terms and diagrams.

"Thank you, Doctor Hayashi," Charles said. He clicked at the laptop on the podium and called up a new slide. "As you can see, I will be the surgeon in charge with the following support team I have personally selected."

Megan blinked in surprise, not pleased with what she was seeing.

Apparently Syler wasn't either because she jerked upright in her seat and interrupted him with a spat, "Excuse me?" She got to her feet amid murmurs and rustling. "As patient Yamane's primary surgeon, Doctor Brockman, I'd prefer to take the lead here with my usual team to assist me. You're welcome to observe, but I am not going to let you touch her." Her face was dark with anger. Megan winced. There were better ways to question authority. But this was Syler's way. It was impossible to imagine her bowing her head in submission to anyone.

Charles glared at her and said, "I do not recall needing your permission for assignments in this department. And I wish to get first-hand experience using the new pediatric gastroscope we have recently acquired."

Syler looked at him with disbelief. "That's no reason to highjack my patient. This is a person's life we're talking about here, not some kind of exercise for your benefit."

He cut her off with a practiced and curt, "If you would let me finish."

Syler let out a long breath and crossed her arms over her

chest as she listened with a scowl.

"The decision has been made. You have two choices, accept the fact that I am in charge here and my decisions are not to be questioned or overruled, or you can find another place to practice surgery. I hope I have made myself clear."

He leaned back on his heels and looked satisfied with himself. Megan wanted to charge up to Charles and smash the smug expression from his face. Her hands trembled with barely-controlled violence and Megan clenched them to stifle the sudden urge. Syler was still on her feet. She didn't appear particularly surprised or impressed at the threat, indicative that she and their department head had clashed in the past.

"This is a very delicate operation on a patient who I have been responsible for her entire life. She's barely got anything left for us to work with and this has to be done with the utmost precision," Syler said through clenched teeth. "And I am aware that daddy is still in charge here, not you. You fuck my patient up and I will take you down." With that, she took a step toward Charles. Her menacing charge caused him to back up and bang his elbow on the podium. She continued in a dangerously calm tone, "Make a note of that, Doctor Brockman."

"I will," he said in a sour voice. "And my decision stands. Now please sit down unless you have anything else to add?"

Syler remained standing and looked ready to do battle but a calm voice suddenly rang out.

"Actually I'd like to say something." The voice came from the side of the room and, along with the rest of the people in attendance, Megan turned to look. Munehiro Takahashi, the anesthesiologist for Syler's surgical team, stood up. He was the eldest member of the team and had thick, wavy grey hair that made him look like a Japanese Beethoven. "While I understand your reasoning, Department Head Brockman, I think switching up the team at this point would be counterproductive. If you'd like to see the new gastroscope in action, there is a procedure scheduled for the day after tomorrow on a first-time patient who is older and will provide a better opportunity for study."

As he sat back down, Megan wanted to applaud. Most of the people in the room nodded and the other four members of Syler's team all wore the same stern expression.

Syler's scrub tech, a compact woman named Daniela Sato,

stood up and added, "I agree with Takahashi-sensei, and I have to say I'm not comfortable with a new team taking over a case that has had the same surgical team for four years."

Charles looked around the room with an expression as if he smelled something nasty. He settled his glare on Syler, who just cocked a brow in reply. He tucked his tie into his jacket and said, "It seems you win this time, Doctor Terada. I will bow out. I only hope for your sake, that nothing like this occurs in the future." He looked over the assembled personnel and said, "Dismissed."

After she gave her team a nod from across the room, Syler pushed past Charles. She was the first one out the door. Charles stalked out as well and as soon as the door closed behind him, the room buzzed with excited voices. Megan twisted in her seat. She wanted to follow Syler, but she wasn't certain her presence would be welcomed.

"She usually goes up to the roof when she needs to cool off," Luka told her. "Just so you know."

Megan didn't even pause to thank Luka for the information before she raced up the broad stairwell. The fire door was still easing closed when she got there. Megan braced her shoulder against the heavy door and pushed through it. She paused. Almost hidden by the towering water tank, Syler leaned on the railing, eyes closed and head back, her face raised to the sky. Megan had to catch her breath as Syler's unique beauty once again struck her like a bolt of lightning.

A few steps took Megan to the middle of the roof and she stopped in uncertainty. Her doubts vanished as Syler turned to look at her with a brilliant smile.

"Hey," Syler said and rubbed a hand through her hair, looking a bit sheepish. "Sorry about going off like that in the meeting. It's just that man is so aggravating."

"Has Ch—Doctor Brockman always been that way?"

"What, a blowhard control-freak? Probably. It wasn't so bad when he was in another department but now I have to see his smug face every day. Ugh. So many times I just want to punt that stupid head off his shoulders." Syler let out a sigh and her shoulders dropped. She turned back to look out over the sprawling town. "I know mouthing off at the boss wasn't the smartest thing to do, but I will not allow him to take over my patients and mess up all my team's hard work. Taka-chan and

Dani standing up for me really saved my ass, though."

"You were right to argue," Megan said. She came over to stand beside Syler and casually draped her arms over the railing. She gave Syler a sideways glance. "Not very tactful, but right just the same. And if anyone can pull off that procedure, you and your team can. I've seen your file and the work you do is exemplary."

"Thanks," Syler said. "Your support means a lot to me."

"You have more than just my support," Megan said. Her heart gave a kick. She reached out and wrapped her fingers around Syler's, loving the strength in them as Syler gave her a squeeze in return. As she savored the moment and the intimacy of the small gesture, Megan kept her eyes on the view before them. The morning sunlight turned the river into a carpet of diamonds and the wind carried the scent of cherry blossoms. She took a deep breath and said, "It's nice up here. I can see why you come here sometimes. It's like I'm at the center of the universe."

Syler turned to face her fully, and Megan drew in a breath at the heat of Syler's gaze.

"You are," she breathed.

They were so close, the lapels of Megan's lab coat almost brushed Syler's scrub top. The tension in Syler's stance radiated across the tiny distance that separated them. Megan couldn't look away. Her heart thundered and her body trembled with the need to feel Syler against her. Just as Megan thought she would not be able to contain herself any more, Syler let go of her hand and stepped back.

"Thanks for coming up here. I think I needed to talk to someone," Syler said. She turned and started back across the roof toward the door.

Stunned, Megan could only stare before she fell forward a step and blurted out, "Syler wait!"

At her words, Syler turned with a look of surprise, which changed to something warmer as Megan came up to her one more time. Megan reached up and took Syler's face in her hands, guiding her to bend down. Syler came willingly. Her lips came ever closer but stopped just short of touching Megan's. This was the last step, and Megan was going to have to take it. Megan's heart nearly stopped. She would prove she was indeed ready and willing to back up her words with actions.

Without hesitation, Megan rose up and pressed her lips to Syler's. They met in a kiss that shook Megan to her toes with the sweet, immediate rush of desire and completion. The kiss was brief and innocent and only lasted an instant but it still stole her breath. Megan had not expected the spark of electric heat the simple touch ignited. Her hands were still twined in Syler's hair as they drifted apart. Megan's body thrilled with the feeling of Syler's breath on her skin, the taste of Syler on her lips. She wanted more. She craved it. Once more, Megan leaned forward and closed her eyes as she pressed ever so gently on the back of Syler's neck.

That was the last thing Megan had to do. In a single swoop, Syler met Megan's kiss with undeniable hunger. A wave of desire hit her square in the chest and Megan let out a low moan. Megan thought she would melt as Syler's arms came around her and pulled their bodies together. Instead of submitting, Megan opened her mouth and claimed Syler's. Megan was responsive and bolder than she'd ever been before. She cupped the back of Syler's head in a silent plea for more. She got it. Megan's body ached from the soft pressure of Syler's hands on her waist. Against hers, Syler's lips were demanding but tender. She drew out every motion and responded deeply to Megan's own exploration. Megan had never been kissed like that in her life.

The heady rush from Syler in her arms threatened to overwhelm her. Megan relaxed the grip she had on Syler and allowed the kiss to end. She sagged as Syler's hold on her loosened, and Megan dropped her head to rest on Syler's chest. Megan could hardly believe what she'd just done. She knew she should be feeling at least guilty, but she was soaring. Megan was shocked at how she had responded. That kiss had shaken the foundation of her world and had opened up a cosmos of new possibilities she had never imagined. Megan trembled and gasped as Syler took her face in her hands and brought Megan's eyes back to hers. A gentle thumb brushed over Megan's lower lip.

"I knew this would be fireworks," Syler whispered. "But my God, Meg. I never expected the Fourth of July."

"Really?" Megan couldn't stop the incredulous expression. With a guilty cringe, Megan said, "You're not just saying that to make me feel better, are you? I know I'm not really very good at all this. I—I've been told I kiss like a dying fish."

Syler raised her eyebrows as she said, "Really? If that's how fish kiss, then I need to re-think my sexual orientation. Seriously though, whoever said that was mistaken. You are incredible." Syler got a wicked light in her eyes as she bent her head, brought her lips close to Megan's, and whispered, "Kiss me again and you'll have your proof."

Her mind exploded into happy squiggles as Megan drew Syler to her once more. Their lips met with a sweet softness that soon heated up. Hungry for more and needing Syler's entire length against herself, Megan let Syler guide her to press her back up against the water tank. Through her lab coat, the metal was cool and a line of bolts dug into her spine but Megan didn't care. She loved the position it put them in, with Megan supported from behind and Syler pressed hard against her front. Her mind was full of nothing but Syler. While Syler had both hands braced against the water tank, Megan's were wrapped around Syler's waist, holding her close. Syler's breathing quickened in her mouth as Megan dropped her hands to the supple curve of Syler's backside. Urging a more intimate contact, Megan pressed Syler to her and she slipped one thigh between Syler's legs. The move was rewarded by a gasp and a tremor as Syler's hips rocked under her hands.

Megan lifted her chin and let her head fall back as Syler's lips found her neck. It didn't even occur to Megan that someone could come through the door at any moment. Her body was on fire. Megan arched back. She bit off a whimper as the movement caused her rock-hard nipples to rub against the softness of Syler's breasts. She wished Syler's hands were on her and didn't even try to be scandalized at the depth and strength of her own desire. She wanted to touch Syler and taste her, she wanted to give everything of herself and accept everything in return. Megan had never been allowed such freedom and she was drunk with it.

"We need to stop," Syler panted against her skin.

"I know," Megan said.

She fought the rush of loss as Syler drew away from her. For a long moment, Megan regarded the woman standing in front of her and tried to get her heart back to its normal speed. They were both rumpled and breathing hard as they stared at each other. Megan was pretty sure her hair was a mess and her lips felt swollen. Her entire body tingled. She'd never felt as good in her life as she did at that moment.

"I hope I didn't scare you or anything," Syler said. She looked uncomfortable. "I didn't mean for it to get that hot so quickly."

Megan shook her head and reached out to take Syler's hand in hers. "Don't worry, please. You didn't do anything I didn't want." She glanced up into Syler's face and continued, "And I really liked it getting hot."

"That's good," Syler said with her usual casual cheer. "For the record, I did too, but I'm sure you already knew that."

"Yeah, I could kind of tell," Megan said and gave Syler a nudge. "Anyway, I have to do rounds before examination hours."

"I do too. Let's go then."

Syler reached over Megan's head to hold the fire door open for her. As they passed through the long-term care ward, Megan caught a glimpse of a giant man hovering around behind the nurse's station. He was swarthy and bearded and his massive body was clad in a worn-looking coverall. The front pocket was embroidered with the name of a local small-parts manufacturing company nearby. Megan had passed the small factory a number of times and recalled it clanking away at all hours of the day and night. He had a bouquet of wildflowers in one hand and was in the middle of changing out the wilted arrangement in a vase on the desk.

"Is he supposed to be here?" Megan whispered to Syler.

"Yup, he's kind of a fixture around here," Syler said. She changed direction and walked over to the big man. He looked up and greeted them with a smile. Syler said, "Hi there Paulo. Have you met our new pediatrician, Megan Maier, yet?"

"I have not," he answered in heavily-accented English. He put the vase down and offered Megan his hand. He gave her a gentle, warm handshake before he returned to his task. "I am Paulo Gomes."

"How is Gabriela?" Syler asked. She leaned one elbow on the desk in a comfortable way.

He said, "I read the newspaper to her and I think she listened. I read that story about the panda. My Gabriela likes pandas. I saw her blinking. It was more than yesterday."

"That's good to hear," Syler said. "And are you all right

Paulo? Not working too hard?"

"Working hard is good," he said. "I work nights, come here days, do my garden in between. All is good."

"Take care of yourself," Syler said. She patted him on one shoulder and continued on her way. As they went down the stairs to the pediatric ward, Syler said in a quiet voice, "Paulo's case is not one of the hospital's finer stories. About a year ago, his wife came in for a routine surgery, something went wrong in the OR and she's been in a vegetative state ever since." Syler paused, hand on the railing. She shook her head. "I don't know what happened, but everyone who was on that surgical team is now no longer here. Everyone except one and he's the new head of our department."

Syler paused to knit her brow and scowl before she continued, "Paulo is a good guy, he's always doing stuff for the nurses but he's got reasons of his own to stay under the radar. Paulo and Gabriela are both overstayers. I've offered to help him out with his visa, like if he needs a sponsor or something. Even after all this time, I think he's got a good reason to get special permission to stay, but he's scared." Syler glanced at Megan. "So if you see any police or immigration people coming around here, use your PHS to page Doctor Johji Yazawa from neurology. It's code for 'lay low.' There's more than just Paolo who doesn't want to attract attention."

"Okay, got it," Megan said as she filed the name away in her mind. "But if they're illegal, they won't be able to get *kogaku-iryou hoken*." She referenced the public insurance that put a cap on necessary medical costs. "Paolo must be paying a fortune just to keep his wife here."

"No, the hospital pays for everything."

"Why?"

"The hospital has always had a few subsidized cases," Syler said. "When Saul and Libby Silverman were in charge, thing were much more transparent. Now, let's just say it doesn't pay to look too closely at the way things are done. I often wonder about the criteria they use to pick who gets the golden treatment. There's no real pattern, except they all have some kind of...complication about them."

Megan got an unpleasant jolt and asked in a whisper, "You don't think this is a cover-up for a mistake on the hospital's part?"

"All I know is that anytime anyone starts getting too curious about Gabriela Gomes's case, they either get transferred or fired or they suddenly change their mind about finding answers. Meanwhile, Paolo's in almost every day to read to her and count her blinks."

"That's terrible," Megan said. She didn't mean to let it get to her, but the situation hit her hard. She bit her lip and tried to keep her calm mask in place. "Paolo seems like such a good guy."

"Sometimes terrible things happen to good people." Syler reached out and brushed back a strand of hair from Megan's forehead with a gentle touch before she started walking again.

While Megan managed to keep her mind focused on her patients during examination hours, she was tired from her late night and still reeling from what happened on the roof. Megan drifted into daydreams at inopportune moments and often had a dreamy smile on her face when she really shouldn't. When public examination hours finished at noon, Megan wandered into the cafeteria in a happy daze. She got herself a couscous salad and a generous cup of minestrone soup from the pareve section and found a table by the window.

"Mind if I join you?" Luka's cheerful voice broke Megan's reverie and she looked up to see the young man standing in front of her with a tray of his own in his hands. He tilted his head and continued, "Or is this seat saved for someone?"

"Not at all, please sit down," Megan said. She jumped to gather the spread-out bits of her lunch and consolidated them on her tray.

"Okay!" Luka plopped down across from her. He had sea-weed-wrapped sushi rolls on his plate and drizzled soy-sauce over them as he spoke, "I was just talking to Jayco the other day and he said there's a pottery market in Tokobe City that he wants to go to the Sunday after Passover's finished. He asked me to go with him too and I was wondering if you'd like to tag along. Don't worry, it's not a third wheel type of thing. What do you say, honey?"

"Sure. That sounds fun," Megan said, then froze as she saw Syler entering the cafeteria. Their eyes met across the room and Megan couldn't help the rush of fire that filled her like a dazzling fountain of glitter. She came back to herself as Luka regarded her with one eyebrow raised. "What?" Megan hissed. She fiddled with one of her butterfly barrettes and attempted to look nonchalant.

Luka didn't say anything, but he jumped up once more and waved Syler over.

"What are you doing?" Megan asked in a whisper even as her heart thudded with happiness and excitement.

"Simply inviting our good friend over to join us for lunch," Luka said. He took a delicate bite of his roll and regarded Megan through his lashes. As Syler appeared with her tray, Luka nodded to the empty chair next to Megan. "Have a sit, stranger. How are things with our favorite shit-disturber? Get into any more fights since this morning?"

"No," Syler said with a sigh. She met Megan's eyes in a sideways glance and they exchanged twin looks of exasperation.

"Uh huh," Luka said.

"*Itadakimasu,*" Syler murmured before she picked up her rice bowl and started to eat her lunch. Megan noticed she held her chopsticks in her left hand, even though Megan was sure Syler was right-handed. At Megan's puzzled look, Syler held up her hand and showed the rubber band around her wrist.

"I switch hands a couple days a week," she said. "Keeps my dexterity up for surgery."

"Oh yes," Luka piped up in a gleefully sarcastic tone, "For *surgery*, sure we get it, don't we, Megu? Hmmmm."

As Syler just smirked to herself, Megan fought a flush.

"Anyway!" Luka fixed Syler with his dark gaze and perched his chin on his clasped hands. "Syler are you free two Sundays from now? Me and Jayco and Megan are going to the Tokobe pottery festival. Why don't you join us? It can be a double date—" He stopped short as Syler gave him a warning look. Luka leaned forward and whispered, "Well it is a date, isn't it? For you two anyway. Or am I seeing something that is not there? Some kind of romantic energy is not flowing then? Come on, you can tell me!"

"Not here, Lukie," Syler said and lowered her eyes to her plate.

Silence fell and Megan got a shiver of worry. It looked like she and Syler needed to clear up a number of issues before things got complicated. Still, Megan didn't regret anything that had happened, heartened when Syler used Luka's distraction as Jayco came into the cafeteria to slip her hand under the table and give Megan's a quick squeeze.

"We were just talking about Tokobe," Luka said. He ushered Jayco into the last remaining chair. "And I think I've found our driver."

"So that's the real reason you asked me," Syler said in a grumpy voice. "All right, I might as well ferry the lot of you around. I don't have anything else to do on that Sunday and I need dishes too."

"Great!" Luka clapped his hands together. "So, what time should we all meet up? I was thinking get an early start, get shopping over with in the morning, do lunch, and then go our separate ways after that. Sounds good, hm?"

Megan, along with the other two, nodded in agreement. They discussed the mundane details of the plan and the topic meandered to other things. Megan curled her fingers around her after-lunch mug of coffee and looked around at the others at the table. She couldn't imagine a more mismatched group, but there was a common current uniting them. While she'd had acquaintances throughout her life, Megan had never felt that kind of harmony with anyone before. Anyone except Yasu.

They finished their lunch and the young men hurried off to their respective duties. Megan lingered in the hallway with Syler, aware of the waves of passing patients and hospital staff around them.

"What time are you finishing today?" Megan asked.

"I'm done now," Syler said. "I just have a bunch of things to do tomorrow before the big day on Thursday."

"That's right," Megan said. "It's a big day for both you and Sakura-chan."

While Megan wanted to spend more time with Syler and iron out the details of their relationship, she wondered if it was wise to throw complications into Syler's life at such a crucial time, but then was there really a non-crucial time in the life of a pediatric surgeon?

"How about you?" Syler leaned one hand on the wall, casually relaxed. "If you have stuff to do, I can hang out here and walk you home when you're finished."

"I'd like that," Megan said as her face broke into a smile. It seemed as if Syler was open to spending time with her as well, and maybe Megan could convince her to come up for a chat—and something more than just talking, if she was lucky. Her cheeks grew warm and Megan hurriedly glanced at her watch. "I'll probably be done in half an hour or so. I'm actually getting the hang of the paperwork here."

"Great. I'll swing by your office then." With that, Syler stepped back and loped off down the hall. Megan watched her for as long as she dared, then went back to her desk and buried herself in reports.

MEGAN WAS LEANING back in her chair for a stretch when Syler came in.

Mindful of the small cluster of nurses in one corner, Megan kept her greeting casual. However she couldn't help but give Syler a long look of appreciation. She'd apparently availed herself of the shower in their prep area and her hair hung damp and spiky around her face. She looked comfortably dressy in her usual work wear, minus the white coat.

"Good timing, I was just finishing up," Megan said. She pushed herself away from the desk and stood. If she left with Syler, it invited more rumors to fly, but Megan didn't particularly care. The gossipy nurses could talk about something other than how they pitied her personal tragedy.

Outside, the afternoon sun was warm and golden. The cherry blossoms were in full bloom and the wind was full of swirling petals.

"It's a pity they'll be gone in a week," Megan said as they passed under a white arch.

"Nah, it would be weird if they were always like this. Trees need leaves. You know, for all that photosynthesis stuff they do," Syler said. She took a deep breath and raised her head. "The blossoms don't last long, but that just makes the time they're here more precious."

"True," Megan said, inwardly moved by Syler's answer. As they walked down the street, she wished she could take Syler's hand. Megan had never wanted to be publicly demonstrative before and she was intrigued by the change in herself. Was it just because she knew she shouldn't? No, that wasn't it. She simply enjoyed being with Syler and loved the feeling when they were close. With a nervous thrill, Megan asked Syler to see her to her front door, and Syler agreed with casual gentility.

They stood at Megan's door and she paused just before she opened it. Megan leaned back against the frame and looked up at Syler who was gazing at her.

A light went on in Megan's mind. She breathed, "The day of our picnic, you didn't walk me up on purpose."

With the wry half-grin Megan was beginning to love seeing, Syler answered. "Busted."

"Why?"

"You know why."

Megan arched a brow. "First date policy?"

"Among other things."

"This isn't our first date anymore," Megan said. Her heart thundered when Syler met her eyes and didn't look away. "What would you have done?"

"Do you really want me to tell you?"

"No. I want you to show me."

"Here?"

"Sure, nobody's looking."

Just to confirm, Megan glanced around. There were six other apartments on her floor, but they were all facing the same direction with nothing directly across from them except an ancient fire extinguisher that was most likely not interested in the goings-on between humans, and even if it was, it wasn't going to talk.

Megan drew in a deep breath as Syler stepped forward and brought her hands up to cup Megan's face. As she had before, Syler gently brushed her thumb over Megan's lower lip. The caress ignited a wave of fire that burned through Megan. The pressure increased until the very tip of Syler's thumb pushed past her lips and entered her mouth. Megan stilled her breath and accepted the intrusion with a soft touch of her tongue. She closed her lips and sucked gently, very aware of the way Syler drew in a sharp breath in response. Megan's body came alive anew as Syler slipped free and trailed her wet digit over Megan's lower lip. Megan let Syler lift her chin and she closed her eyes in sweet anticipation. The first contact was heartbreakingly gentle. Syler's lips against hers were reverent. She didn't demand a deeper kiss, but held her and welcomed her. Megan had never felt as cherished as she did in that moment. She bit back a groan of regret as the kiss ended.

With sweaty palms, Megan reached behind herself and twisted the doorknob. "Um, would you like to come in for a minute? I think there are some things we need to talk about."

Syler just nodded and followed Megan into her apartment. Once inside, Megan put on the hot water pot for tea and pulled the curtains back but left the sheer lace ones in place. Megan was glad she didn't have anything more than a few towels hanging on her clothesline outside. The lights they'd put up the other night glistened in the sunlight. With her usual easy grace, Syler sprawled out on the sofa, one foot propped up on her knee. As Megan clinked around in the kitchen corner, she watched Syler pick up the remote and flip through channels. She looked so at home Megan had to fight a wave of emotion that was crowding out her reason. It was nice having someone in her room, in her life.

Not someone. Syler.

Megan came over with steaming cups of tea and set them down on the table. The tea was too hot to drink so she just held the cup in her hands.

"What did you want to talk about?" Syler asked. She rubbed a hand through her hair and shifted on the sofa.

"I just wanted to know how open we should be at the hospital."

"That's up to you. How open do you want to be?" Syler leaned back against the cushions and waited.

"I'm not sure," Megan admitted. "I mean, even if we were a straight couple, we should probably be discreet, you know, because of the whole workplace thing. But you know what, I don't think I mind certain people knowing."

"There are some people who I trust." Syler put both feet flat on the floor and hunched herself forward. She rested her elbows on her knees. "Luka's fine. In fact, he's probably already planning our wedding. I swear, I hold the door open for a woman between the age of eighteen and seventy and he's got us paired off." She glanced over at Megan and a smile tugged at her lips. "Although in this case, he's correct. There are a few others on staff who are cool, and of course there's nobody I trust more than my team. Most people already know about me, though. The whole bullshit mess with Yukina and Doctor Kobayashi kind of blew me out of the closet. I was an idiot and confronted him at work, made it personal, and things just snowballed from there. Still, most people in this country don't really understand the concept of gay as something that exists outside of TV shows and dirty comics. Pretty much everyone who thought badly of me after that whole load of crap went down did so more on the principle that they thought I was messing up a couple, when it was actually the other way around."

"Yukina cheated on you?" Megan gasped. She immediately revised her opinion of Syler's ex-girlfriend sharply downward.

"It's not as simple as that," Syler said. She was silent for a while before she said, "We were together for three and a half years, pretty much all of those we were living together. Looking back, I know we rushed things. We didn't have enough spark for the relationship to survive for long. Somewhere along the way we stopped being lovers and ended up as nothing more than roommates. For Yukina, we were over a long time before she actually told me she was having a thing with him. To her credit, she wasn't fucking both of us at the same time."

"I'm sorry," Megan said. It was the only thing she could think of. The words hit her hard. While she and Yasu had grown to love each other, there had never been any spark to begin with. Maybe it had something to do with the clinical way they'd met. From the start, their relationship had been clear-cut, hassle-free, and comfortable. Even after they'd become physically intimate, things stayed that way. Megan couldn't miss what she'd never had.

"It stung for a while," Syler said. She raised her head and speared Megan with a heated look as she said, "But I got over her."

"I'm glad." Megan put her mug down and rose up onto her knees. "Because you're mine now." The words came out before she could stop them.

"Yes, I am," Syler breathed and Megan's heart jumped.

Syler looked at her, eyes bright with need. Her own body hummed with burgeoning desire. Megan slipped one knee over Syler's legs and settled down on her lap. She reached out and grabbed the back of the sofa, corralling Syler in place. For an instant, Megan hesitated. Then Syler leaned her head back and let out a low moan as her eyes fluttered closed. She reached out and put her hands lightly on Megan's hips. From that moment, stopping was no longer an option in Megan's mind.

"Is this too much?" Megan asked. Her body ached to move and even as she spoke, she let her hips roll gently under Syler's hold. The action was met with a sound of approval from deep in Syler's throat.

"Not yet."

"You'll let me stop before this goes too far, right?" Megan spread her knees a bit more and settled down. Their bodies fit snugly together and Megan was aware of a throbbing heat pressing against where she was spread over Syler. Megan's skirt rode up dangerously but she didn't care.

"How far do you want to go?" Syler's voice was breathy and tight.

"Not all the way, but close," Megan said. "I'm probably going to leave you frustrated. No, I am *definitely* going to leave you frustrated. Is that all right?"

"That's fine," Syler said. She let out a low chuckle and said, "I happen to know a cure for that. And you can trust me. Just say the word and I'll stop, no pressure. I won't let things go too far."

"Thank you," Megan breathed.

Her words were met with a murmured acknowledgement. For the first time in Megan's life, someone wanted to give her as much as she could take, more even, and Megan hungered for it. She felt like she was holding a live grenade in her hands. A wave of arousal burned through her at Syler's touch. The hands on Megan's hips tightened as she continued to move, rocking herself gently against Syler. Megan lowered her head and pressed a kiss to Syler's neck. She felt the taut tendons under her lips.

"Oh God Meg, that feels so good. Keep doing that."

Encouraged, Megan continued to kiss Syler's neck. She reveled in the heartbeat thundering in her ears and rode high on the sound of Syler's harsh breaths. The hands on her hips moved up to her waist and Megan hungered for their warmth on her bare skin. She rose up against Syler and met her in a greedy kiss. She welcomed Syler into her mouth and responded with her own entrance. Megan didn't break the contact as she ripped the blouse from the waistband of her skirt. She reached down to guide Syler to her.

As Syler's hands met her skin, Megan arched against her. She wanted more.

She pulled her lips from Syler's and whispered, "Higher."

Her words were met by a low purr of pleasure as Syler complied. She delved under Megan's blouse and stroked her hands up and down Megan's bare back. Megan pressed her breasts against Syler's. She used the motion to rub up against her. Already her nipples were hard, begging for attention and the indirect contact only made them worse.

Talented fingers found the clasp of her bra and Syler whispered against her mouth, "Give me permission to undo this. I want to touch you."

The pounding heat between her legs throbbed and Megan nodded.

"Say it," Syler commanded.

"Please," Megan said. The pressure building within herself was almost unbearable. She was in heaven but only an inch from hell. "I want to feel your hands on my skin. Syler, please touch me."

The next instant, her bra gave way. Megan dragged in a long, shuddering breath as Syler's hands came up and cupped her breasts, still hidden under her blouse. Megan bit off the moan that rose up from her chest as a knot of tension clamped down in her groin. Syler bent her head and nuzzled Megan's neck.

"Is this okay?" Syler asked, her words hot against Megan's skin.

"Yes," Megan said and arched in pleasure as Syler's thumbs teased her hardened nipples.

Syler's kisses on her neck and the feeling of her hands made Megan whimper with need. She would have to give the word to stop soon or else risk losing the last tenuous hold on her control. Megan heard Syler's quickened breathing, felt the trembling in the long, slender body against her own and knew that Syler was just as aroused. She wasn't touching Megan out of duty or because she wanted Megan in a good mood for something. She wasn't even doing it because Megan had asked her to. Syler *wanted* to touch her and be close to her. Megan pulled back enough to take Syler's face in her hands. She gazed down into deep sun-flecked eyes and wondered at the desire she saw mirrored in them. The hands on Megan stilled and stroked down to take her around the waist once more.

"Enough?" Syler asked.

Megan swallowed and nodded. She let out a long breath as she eased herself off of Syler's lap. Her bra hung loose under her blouse. Megan wriggled around a bit and pulled the somewhat fussy and ruffled garment out of one sleeve. She didn't miss the euphoric look on Syler's face.

"Oh my God, I love it when women do that," Syler groaned.

"You make it sound like you get to see that a lot," Megan said, only half-teasing.

"Every day if I want," Syler said, relaxing back against the cushions. "I've got *Flashdance* on my phone and I've bookmarked that part. Don't worry, I don't have a team of bra-shedding ladies on my speed dial. You're the only one."

Megan shook her head and laughed softly, secretly pleased at Syler's assurance. The arousal that had gripped her twisted into an uneasy tension. It knotted the muscles of her thighs and cramped deep in her belly. Her nipples were still painfully erect and Megan didn't dare look down, knowing they were probably quite visible through the silky material of her blouse. She remembered what Syler had hinted at before they'd started and Megan's mind wandered down a dangerous path as she wondered how Syler would relieve the pent-up sexual energy Megan had stuck her with. In fact, if she didn't get herself calmed down soon, Megan was going to have to take matters into her own hands as well.

With some effort, Megan squashed the naughty thoughts and tucked her feet underneath herself. She couldn't help but ask, "So you're the sports bra type then?"

"That's for me to know," Syler replied with an enigmatic look, "And you to find out."

"Don't tempt me," Megan said. She quickly covered her blushing cheeks with her hands. "That's two mysteries you've dangled in front of me now."

"Sorry about that. I'll behave, no more mysteries," Syler said with a cocky grin. She lost the grin and studied Megan's face with a calm and intense expression before she said, "It's a bit early, but I just wanted to let you know that I've kept up with my testing and I'm clean."

"Me too," Megan said. "But for the record, I wasn't worried

about you. This hospital has the strictest health regulations I've ever seen. Some of the things I had to get tested for I wouldn't even think are relevant to our work, but I did it anyway."

"What do you mean?" Syler's brows came together.

"The pre-hiring health screening. You know, where we have to provide results for a whole battery of tests. Not just HIV, but also pretty much everything that can be tested for including malaria and if I'm a genetic carrier for things like PKU and fragile X syndrome, which is kind of odd but I guess that's standard for the hospital."

"No it isn't," Syler looked at Megan in a way that made a jolt of worry go through her. "Who made the request? HR?"

"No, Charles handled that part of the deal personally," Megan said. She jumped to her feet as an odd feeling of unease gripped her. "I guess it's new policy, then. How about I get some cookies to go with the tea?"

Syler got up as well. She ran one hand through her hair and looked a bit uncomfortable as she shifted her weight from one foot to the other. "Actually, I have some stuff to do today, so I should probably go." She gave Megan a quicksilver grin that banished the slight awkwardness. "Sorry to kiss and run."

"Don't worry about it," Megan said. "I wouldn't want to keep you from what you've got to do." She held out a hand and drew Syler to her. Syler came willingly. Very gently, she put her hands on Megan's hips. Megan reached up and twined her fingers in Syler's hair. She asked in a soft voice, "You don't mind taking things slow?"

"Not at all," Syler said. Her arms came around Megan and enfolded her in a warm, full-body hug. "I feel like I'm your first."

"In many ways, you are," Megan said into Syler's shoulder.

For an instant, her hands tightened on Syler's shirt. She held onto the sturdy material before she forced herself to let go and step away. The loose hold on her hips drifted away as well. They lingered in the entrance hall and Syler gave Megan a chaste but nonetheless tender kiss on the cheek before she left.

Alone again, Megan flopped down onto the sofa and hugged a cushion to her chest. Her heart thundered and she felt like she was flying. It was with more than a slight twinge of guilt that Megan at last acknowledged as absolute truth that she had never felt that way before. She had never felt the all-encompassing need for anyone the way she needed Syler.

Chapter Seven

AS SCHEDULUED, NIKKY came in the next day with Fabia for her follow-up appointment and Megan found the child in perfect health. However, she scheduled another appointment for the next week, just to keep an eye on things. After the appointment, Megan noticed a subdued and rather sad-looking Nikky leaning against the wall as she watched a group of children who were playing and cavorting with Luka. With a kind word, Luka invited Nikky to join the group and soon a shy smile bloomed on her face.

Megan smiled as she watched them. She was too preoccupied with her own demons to notice during that first appointment, but there was something so cute and elfin about Nikky. That day, her shaggy hair was clipped back with a plain bobby pin and she was wearing a purple sweatshirt with a sparkly unicorn on it over patched and embroidered jeans. Instead of running, she seemed to skip, and she was quite expressive with her hands and face. Megan could see her easily growing up to become a dancer or even a *rakugo* comedic storyteller.

Nikky took a break from playing and trotted over.

"Hi Doctor Megan! Thanks for making my tummy better."

"That's all right. It was nice to see you again today," Megan said. She crouched down to Nikky's level. "Where's your mommy?"

"She's getting something from the shop."

"Okay," Megan said. She glanced over her shoulder and hoped that Charles wasn't anywhere around. She reached out and gave the sparkly unicorn a poke which elicited a giggle. "That's a very pretty top. Is purple your favorite color?"

"Yup!" Nikky held the shirt out proudly and beamed. Just as quickly, the expression vanished. "But Mama doesn't like it. She says I can't wear stuff like this. Too girly."

"What's wrong with being girly?"

"I dunno."

"Do you want all of us here to use female pronouns for you?"

"What's that mean?"

"It means, do you want to be called things like she and her."

"Yeah," Nikky said with a big grin. "Cause I am a girl!"

"All right then," Megan said. She returned the grin. "I apologize for using the wrong ones before."

"That's okay. I wish Mama would too."

"She will," Megan said. "Sometimes adults are stubborn about stuff they don't understand." She got an idea and pulled one of the sparkly butterfly barrettes from her hair. "Here, you can have this. It matches your sweatshirt."

Megan had just finished securing the barrette on Nikky when a sharp voice rang out behind her. "Nikky! Stop bothering Doctor Maier. Go and play with your friends."

As Nikky ran off with a haunted look, Megan stood and straightened her lab coat. Fabia came through the lobby at a good clip. She looked put-together and sophisticated as usual, immaculately made up with her long professionally-streaked hair twisted and held with a gold comb that was studded with a slim line of sparkling stones. In an instant, Megan felt her single remaining paste-jewel butterfly was cheap and gaudy.

"May I speak to you for a moment?" Megan asked. "About Nikky."

"I guess if it's quick. I thought you said nothing's wrong," Fabia said. She had a small bag with the hospital's snack stand logo on it and she slipped it into her Louis Vuitton handbag. Her hands worried at the clasp. Her eyes flicked down to the cigarette case inside before she shut the bag with a snap.

"How about we go out for some fresh air?" Megan suggested in an easy manner. She glanced over to where Luka and Nikky held hands and pranced around in a circle while singing some kind of pop-sounding song. "Nikky's all right here and won't even notice you're taking a quick break."

The other patients and nurses wandering around looked at the scene with nothing more than indulgent smiles. Megan was grateful that Japan, for all its backward ideas, had never adopted the odious Western practice of equating "gay" with "pedophile."

Fabia hesitated for a second before she said, "Okay."

Megan led the way out to the unofficial smoking area behind the hospital. It was a small corner off the parking lot, surrounded on three sides by chest-high concrete planters. They were filled with some kind of round-leafed bush that had seen better days. One fellow in a wheelchair was already there, but he stubbed out his cigarette and dropped it into the storm drain grating as they approached. By the time they arrived, he was already wheeling back toward the main building.

The hospital responded to the illicit nicotine gatherings by playing a looped recording about the dangers of tobacco. While the calm female voice spoke about increased risk of lung cancer and reduced birth weight, Fabia dug into her bag and came out with the slim cigarette case. Like everything else she owned, it looked expensive. She must have noticed Megan's slightly wistful gaze before she held out the case with her sculpted brows raised in a question.

"Want one?" Fabia asked. "If you're okay with menthol."

"I really shouldn't." Megan fidgeted for a moment before she said, "Oh well, one won't kill me." She reached out and took a cigarette while sharing a conspiratorial look with Fabia. She let the other woman light her up with a gold-plated lighter bearing the Gucci logo and took a quick drag. At that point in Megan's life, she found more comfort in the action than the actual nicotine. With her eyes closed, Megan slowly breathed out a long stream of smoke. Once her lungs were empty, Megan came back to reality and tapped her ash into the portable ashtray Fabia generously left open on the ledge of the planter.

"That's very nice," Megan said as she bent her head to inspect the ashtray. "Everything you have is really nice. Brand name too."

"Yeah," Fabia said. "It's from the shop I manage."

"You're a manager? That's great," Megan gushed.

"I'm not a parasite," Fabia said, suddenly guarded. "What? Did you expect I was working in some bar? That I trapped Junichiro-san with a shotgun wedding for the visa?"

"Of course not," Megan said. She hastened to add, "Fabia, I would never think that of you or anyone else here. I actually would really like to go to your store."

"Here's my card," Fabia said. She dug into her purse and handed over a pink and white business card.

"Thanks," Megan said as she tucked the card into her pocket.

"So what did you want to talk about?" Fabia asked. Her eyes were fixed on the glowing tip of the cigarette in her hand.

"Nothing much," Megan began in a carefully casual voice. "Just wanted to know how things are at home."

"Fine," Fabia said. Her lips thinned as she pressed them together before she turned her head and took another long drag.

"Are you all right?" Megan asked. "Your husband isn't— unkind to you?"

"He doesn't touch me," she said. Her words came out along with bursts of expelled smoke. "He doesn't look at me. Maybe he regrets what his life has become." She finished by pursing her lips and blowing the rest of the smoke away from them.

"So he doesn't hurt you? Does he argue with you? Does he try to keep you from contacting your family or going out with your friends?"

Fabia propped her elbow on the planter, cigarette pointed at the sky. She brought it to her lips one more time before she replied, "He doesn't care what I do. For him, it's all work work work. His job is all he cares about and all he does."

"That's got to be difficult," Megan said. Her heart ached with the next few questions she was going to have to ask. The acrid smoke burned her throat and Megan remembered why she quit. She asked in a gentle voice, "How is his relationship with Nikky?"

Suddenly Fabia hunched her shoulders and looked away. She sucked hard at her cigarette. "Nikky disappoints him. I try to hide it, try to get Nikky to act different, but it never works. Nikky doesn't listen. I tell him Papa will be angry but he doesn't stop. He's not—boyish, you know? He screams when I try to cut his hair and he hates the toys and clothes we buy for him. He won't answer to his real name either. We've been calling him Nikky instead of Nikolaus for about a year and he won't give up. He'd rather play house with the girls than mini cars with the boys."

"That doesn't sound bad at all. There's absolutely nothing wrong with Nikky," Megan said. Her voice came out harder than she'd intended and Megan paused to take in one more lungful of smoke before she stubbed the cigarette out. She ground the glowing tip off with a practiced twist. "Fabia, be honest with me," Megan said. She kept her voice low and her gaze steady. "Does your husband hit Nikky?"

Fabia flinched. She threw her own cigarette down and crushed it under one slim high heeled foot. "I can't talk to you anymore." She grabbed her ashtray and shoved it into her bag before she whirled and walked away at a fair clip. Megan bit back a curse as she dashed after her.

"If you or Nikky are in danger, I can help you get out," Megan said as she caught up to the fleeing woman. She frantically dug though the pockets in her lab coat. "Look, I'll give you my card and you can call me anytime."

"No, it's okay. Papa's away now. He's in Tokyo on business for the next couple of months." Fabia pushed Megan's proffered card away as she spoke. "I can't have this in the house. Papa wouldn't like it."

She pushed past Megan with a look on her face that declared the discussion was over. Megan was left weak and shaky. She took a few deep breaths and stuck her hand in her pocket. She wrapped cold fingers around the pill bottle, gripping it with all her strength. It was a while before Megan could get her feet to take her back into the hospital. She made it to her desk and fell limply into her chair, not paying attention to the scattered papers in front of her.

"And what were you doing out there with Mrs. Okamoto?"

Megan jumped at the words aimed at her back. She twisted in her chair and looked up at Charles, who glowered down at her.

Her heart pounded, but Megan forced a guilty smile. She said, "Oops! I know the hospital has a no-smoking policy, but Fabia offered and you know how it is. Sometimes you just get a craving." She didn't like how close Charles was to her and she eased her chair away.

"And what were you discussing?" Charles asked. He didn't move.

"Girl stuff," Megan said with a manufactured titter. "Fabia always has such nice things, you know, brand stuff. I was just talking to her about where she gets them and you know what, she actually has her own shop. Isn't that just the best?"

Charles looked as if he didn't believe her, but only said, "You should not be smoking. Think of the damage you're doing to your future children."

"That's true, if I wanted to have any," Megan said as a flash of anger filled her. She lowered her gaze to the work on her desk and shuffled through her papers. She hoped Charles would take the hint and go away. He didn't.

"One day you'll change your mind," Charles told her. He had his hands in his trouser pockets and didn't seem in any hurry to leave. "You don't have any siblings. You don't want to deny your parents the joy of having grandchildren now, do you? Every woman wants to give her husband a child. You owe it to him. And you know, Megan, babies sometimes have a way of just happening."

They would not be happening to Megan. Her face got warm. She didn't like how Charles just dropped the information he knew about her that she hadn't told him, as if reminding her he'd read her file. And she really didn't want to discuss her personal reproductive choices with him.

"You're wonderful with children," Charles continued. Megan wished she could shut his voice out of her ears, "And I'm sure the day you hold your own, you'll understand what true love is. There is no bond like the one a mother shares with her child."

"Doctor Brockman," Megan said as she fought a wave of nausea, "I'm not comfortable having this discussion."

"But you have no trouble sharing 'girl stuff' with Mrs. Okamoto."

"That was different," Megan said. "It was just a friendly chat over a ciggy."

"It would be prudent if you refrained from doing so in the future. The matter we have discussed before still stands. Is that understood?"

"Yes, I understand. But really, nothing was going on."

"For your sake, I hope that's true." Charles was silent for a beat and Megan was ready to breathe again as she thought he was about to leave. Her hope was shattered as he spoke again. "I will pick you up at a quarter to five next Friday."

For an instant, Megan just looked at him, then it came back to her with a sick thud. "That's very kind of you, but I can find my own way to Rabbi Sharon's. I was thinking of going with the Millers, as they live quite close to me and it would be a pleasant walk."

"That is inappropriate due to the fact you are coming as my guest," Charles said in a placid way, however his eyes were steely. "Although I have been informed the gathering will be somewhat informal, you are an employee of this hospital in addition to being my guest, which makes you a representative of my family, so I expect you to be suitably attired. That means your skirt is to cover your knees. I will contact you if there is any additional information."

"All right," Megan said in a stunned voice. She felt as if she'd just been run over by a steamroller. She was at once very aware of her current skirt, which was shorter than Charles's stern order specified. As Charles finally removed himself from her presence, Megan was puzzled that he hadn't asked for her number. She made a face. Of course he'd helped himself to her contact information. It was in her file along with the few personal details she'd seen fit to share with the hospital. Megan was glad she'd been deliberately vague about a number of things, mostly about her clinic and her life in Thailand.

MEGAN GAVE UP on her work and pushed herself away from her desk. She left her office and clambered up the stairs to the roof. She draped her arms over the railing and let out a long sigh. She would have to tread carefully, but she wasn't giving up on Nikky. Megan clutched at the railing to stop her hands from shaking. Maybe she was reading too much into the matter. Maybe her own history made her oversensitive and biased.

Megan hadn't allowed herself to think of those days clearly for a while and the memory hit her hard. She concentrated on keeping her breaths even as she fought the waves of anxiety. She almost reached for her pill bottle, but stopped herself. She wouldn't give in. Not this time.

She was involved in her own inner struggle and didn't notice she wasn't alone on the roof until Syler's long frame settled down beside her.

"You weren't at your desk and I was wondering if I'd find you here," Syler said in a low voice. "Is everything okay?"

"It is now," Megan said. She turned around and leaned back against the railing. Her dark mood vanished in an instant as she looked at Syler. She ached for Syler's touch, but didn't feel ready to reach out. Instead she said, "I talked to Nikky Okamoto today and confirmed it—we need to change pronouns. She's transgender."

"Okay," Syler said in her usual easy way.

"The family doesn't seem supportive. And I suspect Nikky's

father is abusing her. I talked to her mother today and she seems scared. Luckily he's away on a business trip or something so they're safe for the moment."

"That's one small mercy at least," Syler said. "Have you reported this?"

"I can't. Not until I have some real proof. Doctor Brockman saw me and warned me off. It seems Nikky's family is rich and influential and apparently that takes precedence over protecting a defenseless child from being beaten at home," Megan said. She bit her lip and gazed out over the town. "But I'm not going to back down. I'm not going to let this go until both Nikky and Mrs. Okamoto are away from that violent bastard and safe."

"Good, don't let him intimidate you," Syler said. "You know I'm behind you one hundred percent, so if Charles wants a fight, he's got one."

"Thanks, but I hope it doesn't come to that." Megan turned around and leaned back against Syler. A happy thrill started up in her belly as Syler wrapped her arms around her and pulled Megan close. Megan enjoyed the intimacy of Syler's warmth at her back for a few heartbeats. She remembered the afternoon's events and gave a shy laugh.

"He caught me bumming a smoke from Fabia and gave me a health lecture with bonus guilt-trips about not giving my future husband the children he deserves."

Syler snorted and said, "That sounds like Charles. Always knowing better than everybody else. You won't catch *him* with any bad habits."

"Oh no, not mister perfect," Megan said. She nestled a little deeper into Syler's arms and said softly, "And I wish I could have told him in no uncertain terms there is never going to be any husband in my life."

Syler didn't answer, but Megan felt her drop a swift kiss into her hair.

"Anyway, I quit smoking years ago," Megan babbled. "I should really have known better than to even start, but the nicotine rush helped me get through med school when I didn't have time to eat or sleep. I hope you don't think worse of me because of that."

"Not at all. We all do things that aren't great for us. Still, I've never really seen the appeal of tobacco." Syler paused before she said, "Meg, how do you feel about, ahem, medicinal herbs?"

"I don't have first-hand knowledge, but I believe they've got a lot of benefits," Megan said. "And they're far less harmful to the body than cigarettes or alcohol. Honestly, I have no problem with the use of certain less-than-orthodox herbal remedies for either medical or recreational purposes. There are a lot of people who could really benefit. I wish Japan wasn't so strict about them."

Syler didn't say anything more but she gave a little chuckle. Megan snuggled back into Syler's arms, content to bask in the moment. The comfortable silence unfolded. The muted noises of traffic and rustling leaves were the only sounds that wafted over the rooftop. Megan was very aware of the rise and fall of Syler's chest against her back, the supple strength of the arms around her.

"How about Sakura's operation tomorrow?" Megan broke the silence to ask. "Is everything set to go?"

Syler was quiet for a moment before she said, "No, it looks like we're going to postpone it a week. She's a bit feverish and might be coming down with a cold."

"That's too bad," Megan said with a pang of worry.

"It'll be okay."

Syler bent her head and gave Megan a slow, soft kiss just behind her ear. She trailed her lips over Megan's skin as if sampling an exquisite sweet. The action sparked a host of desires into life. Megan leaned back against Syler. She savored the resilience of her long body and the softness of her breasts and grew hungry for more. Megan remembered what happened on that rooftop not very long ago and her breath quickened along with her heartbeat. If someone walked in on them at that moment, it would look suspicious. Anything more than that would be a complete guilty conviction. Megan wished she dared to turn around and give in to the need to taste Syler's lips, but it was the middle of the afternoon instead of early in the morning and the ground outside, not to mention the hallways of the hospital, teemed with people going about their business.

Still, the fire building in Megan's belly wouldn't die and she whispered, "Syler, you don't know how much I want to kiss you right now."

"Actually, I think I do," Syler answered. She lowered her head to nuzzle the side of Megan's neck as she held Megan to her more firmly. Syler's heartbeat pounded against her back. Megan got an almost overwhelming urge to do something that would certainly get them both into trouble. The arms around Megan dropped and Syler stepped away from her. She had a sly smile on her face. She held both of Megan's hands in hers and took another step backward. "Come on," she said in a low voice, "I believe I have some important documents or files or whatever that I need to show you. To collaborate on something."

"Really?" Megan arched a brow, intrigued. "As I am a great believer in the benefits of collaboration, I believe such an undertaking would be most beneficial. Lead on, Doctor Terada."

Syler led the way down the stairs and breezed through the surgeons' office, which was much messier and more chaotic than the one Megan was in. Someone was sprawled out under an old blanket on the sofa in the corner, but the rest of the office was empty. Syler grabbed an armful of files from a desk that Megan assumed was hers and was just as quickly back in the hallway.

"As you can see here, the patient's CO2 levels are holding stable," Syler said as they walked. She flipped through a few files. Megan made an interested expression even as her heart thundered in her ears. "We're recommending a comprehensive round of antibiotics, perhaps amputation and, oh yes, here we are."

With the characteristic preoccupied shove of a busy doctor, Syler opened the door to an unused private exam room and flipped on the lights before she ushered Megan inside. The door eased shut behind her and Megan fought the growing frisson of arousal for a split second before she decided there was no need to resist any more.

The files hit the small desk next to the examination table. The next instant Syler had Megan up against the wall and kissed her with a hunger that nearly stole the little restraint Megan had left. There was no need for words as Megan cradled Syler's head. She gave all of herself to their kiss. Syler responded with a low moan in her throat and stroked her hands down to hold Megan around the hips. A thigh pressed between her own. Megan reached down to yank up her skirt. She hissed in a breath as Syler urged their bodies together. The pressure was gentle but   definitely there. Megan was in heaven, knowing Syler could feel the heat between her legs, that she could understand in a visceral way how much Megan wanted her. Under Syler's hands, Megan rocked her hips and ground against Syler's firmness. She couldn't believe what she was doing, but she couldn't stop.

Megan wanted Syler's lips on her neck. She lifted her head in invitation and wasn't disappointed. Between hungry kisses, Syler gave her a light nip that caused Megan to arch her back as the small pain set off a chain reaction of pleasure that blazed through her.

"My God, Megan," Syler gasped and Megan could barely contain herself at the raw need in her voice. "You feel so good."

"So do you," Megan said.

Syler replied with a low chuckle and continued kissing Megan. She pulled Megan's blouse open enough to expose the lace edge of Megan's camisole and the swells of her breasts underneath. With a reverent moan deep in her throat, Syler paused, her breath hot on Megan's skin. Megan stilled herself as well. She trembled with the willpower it took.

"You sweet thing," Syler murmured as she dropped a kiss onto the soft fullness of Megan's breast. Syler continued to speak between hot kisses, breathing the words against Megan's skin, "You taste so good, Meg. I can't get enough of having my mouth on you. I want to suck you dry."

The shock of the words, plus the pressure of Syler's lips, separated by a layer of lace, sent a tremor through Megan. Syler must have felt it, because she raised her head with an apologetic look.

"Why did you stop?" Megan whispered the question. Her mouth was dry with need.

"I thought I offended you," Syler said. "You know, um, by the dirty talk. I felt inspired and it just slipped out. I don't usually say stuff like that out loud. Say the word and I'll behave."

"In that case," Megan said in a low purr, "please continue to misbehave."

Megan rolled her shoulders so the strap of her camisole came down. The action was met by a feral light in Syler's eyes. Megan's skirt was riding up enough that she could bend one knee and wrap her leg around Syler's body. Both of Syler's hands went down to cradle Megan's backside. The pressure against her was immense and so was the wave of pleasure that hit Megan right where they met. Syler bent her head to resume her greedy kisses.

She whispered, "God, Meg you have such a sweet ass. And I

like you right there."

Her entire being responded to the gentle movements of Syler's body against hers. Megan let out a gasp of desire. She loved the way Syler was speaking to her. Megan was so involved in holding Syler to her that she didn't realize where she'd gotten her hand until she felt the resilient softness of a breast against her palm. Startled, she jerked her hand away and banged her elbow painfully on the door.

"I didn't mean to do that! I'm sorry!" Megan said. Her heart pounded. What had she done? She braced herself for the brusque rebuff and couldn't meet Syler's eyes.

"Why are you sorry?" Syler's voice was soft. "You didn't do anything wrong." Syler paused. "Was it weird, touching me?"

"No, not at all," Megan said, still with her head down. "I just didn't think you'd be okay with it."

With a murmur of understanding and the softest touch, Syler took Megan's face in her hands. Finally Megan got the nerve to look up.

"For the record," Syler said, "I'm *riba*. Do you know what that means?"

Megan drew in a shaky breath before she answered, "You don't mind being touched?"

"That's right," Syler said. She dropped her hands to Megan's shoulders and pulled her into a hug. She rested her cheek against Megan's hair and said, "I don't only not mind it, I really like it. And I'd love to have your hands—and more—on me, but only if you feel it's something you want to do."

Megan swallowed hard. This was another big step for her. Even as she trembled with apprehension, Megan ached with the need to touch Syler and know her body intimately, and it seemed Syler was open to the idea. Megan's body buzzed with wondrous feelings that had lain dormant for too long.

"Would you really let me?" Megan asked. Her mind whirled and her skin prickled with the electric need to feel Syler in her hands.

"Come over here," Syler said. She stepped back and led Megan over to the exam table. She patted the paper-covered foam padding. "Have a sit up here."

As Megan hoisted herself onto the table, she wondered what Syler had in mind. However, she wasn't uneasy at all. She trusted

Syler implicitly and knew she was safe. Syler turned around and leaned back against her. Megan shifted. She tucked up her skirt a bit as Syler's long body nestled between her knees.

"Put your arms around me. From now, I belong to you," Syler told her in a quiet voice. "I'm not going to move unless you ask me to. And I'm not going to get angry, okay? You're in charge." With that, Syler let out a breath, dropped her shoulders, and closed her eyes.

Megan could scarcely believe the gift Syler had given her. She reached out and pulled Syler into a loose hug. She kept her arms wrapped around Syler's middle and simply held her for a moment. The gentle rhythm of Syler's breathing lulled her. The long, graceful line of Syler's neck was too tempting and Megan left a trail of kisses as she let her lips move down from behind Syler's ear to the juncture of her shoulder. Syler's breath caught as Megan drew her teeth very lightly over the silken skin. Encouraged, Megan tightened her arms around Syler's body. She spread her hands and gently stroked over Syler's midriff. As she began the journey upward again, Megan's own breaths roughened. Megan punctuated the movement of her hands with kisses until she once again felt that wonderful softness in her hands.

A low groan and slight shift in Syler's stance welcomed Megan's exploration. Bolder now, Megan stroked her fingers over the swells of Syler's breasts. The hardening nipples strained against the layers of her clothing.

Syler's body pushed back between Megan's legs. Her thighs trembled and her arousal grew with every heartbeat.

"So you *are* the sports bra type," Megan whispered.

"Uh huh," Syler said eloquently. She threw her head back and said in a tight voice, "Don't stop, Meg. I love your hands on me."

Her mind and heart were full of emotions she'd never experienced before. Megan was about to take the plunge and delve under Syler's top when the door banged open. Megan looked up in panic as she met the eyes of a very surprised-looking nurse.

"OW!" Syler shouted out, which startled both Megan and the nurse.

Syler grabbed her shoulder and rotated it. She swung her elbow in a wide radius as she stepped forward. At the same time Syler neatly distanced herself from Megan while shielding her from being seen from the hallway.

"Oh shit, that hurt," Syler said. "Actually, you know what? The last shove popped that sonofabitch right back into the socket. Thanks!"

Megan was grateful for Syler covering her as half of the buttons of her blouse were undone and she'd pulled her skirt up to a degree that could only be explained if Syler were a gynecologist. Megan hurriedly refastened her buttons as Syler addressed the nurse, who stood frozen in the doorway.

"Old sports injury acting up," Syler said. "Doctor Maier was just assisting me in reversing an anterior dislocation of the humerus."

"I told you that ladder was unstable." Megan played along as she jumped off the table. She used the motion to hide the fact she was also yanking her skirt back down. "The next time you go ass-over-teakettle and need me to pop you back into place, it's going to cost you a coffee. And not the machine stuff either, Doctor Terada. I want Starbucks."

"I'll make a note of that," Syler said. She turned back to the nurse. "Sorry, did you need to use this room? We were just leaving."

"Yes, thanks," the nurse said.

Her eyes followed the two of them as they edged out of the room. Syler paused on her way out to scoop up her files. Megan managed to keep a straight face until they were back in the surgeons' office. The guy on the sofa had gone off somewhere and the room was deserted. She met Syler's eyes and they both burst into fits of giggles.

"We were so busted," Syler gasped as she wiped at her eyes.

"Quick thinking with the shoulder injury," Megan said.

"That was the easy part. I actually did dislocate it when I took aikido in college and every couple of years I do something stupid and bust it again."

"Do you think the nurse bought it?"

Syler gave a careless shrug and unleashed a megawatt grin. "Who cares, at least she's got the official story and if she's got any sense, she'll stick with that."

"That's good," Megan said with a stir of unease. Syler was already on Charles's bad side and Megan didn't want to think about what might happen to her if he found out about them. Her disquiet didn't last long, though, and Megan gazed about in wonder. She felt as if she'd been burned to ashes and reborn.

With a stretch and a sigh, Syler sat down. She offered Megan a chair, but Megan declined. She preferred to perch on the edge of Syler's desk.

"Thank you," Megan said in a soft voice. Wary from their near-miss earlier, Megan just reached out and brushed back a trailing strand of hair that had fallen across Syler's brow.

"For what?" Syler replied. She caught Megan's hand in hers. With a smirk, she pressed a lightning-fast kiss to the inside of Megan's wrist before releasing her. "I liked what you did just as much as you liked doing it. More maybe, since I could feel everything behind me too."

"That's good," Megan said. She fought the habitual flash of shyness. Still, she was proud of the way she'd been able to please Syler, even if it was over far too soon. She tilted her head and said, "Next time I hope there won't be any interruption."

"Pleeeease yes," Syler said. She closed her eyes and rolled her head back.

"Have you ever done anything like that before?" Megan asked in a hesitant voice.

"Fooled around at work?" Syler looked up at her, one brow raised. "No way. When I was playing the field I would never have brought a date here and Yukina would have slapped my face off if I had even joked about it." Syler rested her elbows on her desk and fixed Megan with her deep gaze. "I've never had the experience of being with someone as an equal partner. While I can go both ways, I've always been expected to take the *tachi* role to the point where I can safely say I was a *bari-tachi*. Untouchable. Maybe I looked the part." Syler gave her a grin and held her hair back away from her face. "This is the longest I've ever had it. Once I gave up on the whole finding a special someone thing, I just left it alone. What do you think, should I go pay a visit to the local barber?"

"Only if that's what you want. I like it the way you have it now," Megan said. While she still harbored some residual anger at the events and person who had caused Syler to turn her back on finding love, she was fiercely glad she had found Syler. Glad they had found each other. Megan straightened up and added, "That's not just because I want to keep you off the market, but it's mostly because I don't care about roles people make up and enforce on others. I just want you as you are." She flushed as she said the words.

"You're the first one." Syler met her flush with a calm gaze. "The rules of the gay community here are strict, more old-fashioned than with straights even," Syler spoke softly, as if more to herself than Megan. "The moment you step into any kind of singles event or dyke bar or whatever, the first thing they ask, even before your name is your *seku*. Your sexuality, as if it's any of their business at that point. Usually the *neko* is femme, the *tachi* is boyish but not always. There's a whole subset of in-between but the important thing is you have a label and you stick the hell to it in the bedroom. The *neko* is pleased, the *tachi* does the pleasing. It's not reciprocal in any way. It's old school, but that's the way it's always been. I went along with it because nobody willing to date me wanted a reversible partner and I didn't want to be alone."

Megan chewed her lip as she thought about what Syler was telling her.

"I get the whole *neko-tachi* thing, I do," Syler said after a moment of silence. "It's an incredible gift to be trusted like that. Being in charge, knowing everything is up to you is really powerful. Some people love to be taken care of, and others genuinely don't like being touched. Some, especially people who identify as *boi-tachi*, are uncomfortable with sharing their bodies, and that's fine if everyone's satisfied."

"But you weren't," Megan said.

"Hey, like I said," Syler gave a shrug, "I'm *riba*."

"Maybe I am too," Megan said in a small voice.

With a low, sultry look, Syler reached out and brushed her thumb over Megan's lower lip. "That you are. And I like it."

"I'm glad," Megan said. She struggled with herself briefly before she said, "I guess I've always been put on the receiving side. But now, the things you do to me, the things I want to do to you, I can barely believe what's come over me."

"You're not the only one," Syler dropped her voice and said, "I think we could be incredible together, Meg. And not just, you know, physically. I feel complete with you."

Megan took in the information, but didn't reply. She could only hold Syler's gaze with her own and bask in the promise of Syler's words.

Talking in the hallway preceded the entrance of a group of surgical interns and Megan scooted away just in time. She stood at a judicious distance and said a businesslike goodbye to Syler before she returned to her own desk. As Megan waded through her paperwork, she mulled over the day's events and got a giddy smile on her face that remained until she went home and fell into her futon.

Chapter Eight

RAIN SCATTERED THE cherry blossoms and the bare branches grew lush with green leaves. The new academic year began. New workers starting company jobs with their resulting welcome drinking parties and hazing kept everyone in the hospital busy. In pediatrics, Megan was inundated with sniffling children who brought home colds from their classmates. She drank a strong lemon and black sugar draught with a generous helping of raw ginger every morning and evening to keep herself from getting sick as well.

She did her second shift at the downtown clinic and dealt with a number of patients, mostly inebriated bar patrons who only needed fluids and a place with access to a bucket. During a lull in the action, Megan was just getting into her game of *Zenith of the Undead* when Keiko burst into the room.

"Sensei," she said, "We've got an emergency. Come quickly."

Immediately Megan abandoned her game and barreled down the hallway with Keiko at her heels.

"Twenty-four year old FTM, gave his name as Leo. Pre-op top and bottom but his friend said he's been on T for about a year."

Megan nodded. She wasn't sure all of that was relevant, but Keiko continued on.

"Penetrating trauma to the right anterior abdomen. He fell off a fire escape and onto the corner of a dumpster. His friend brought him in and he's refusing to be examined."

"Let me see if I can change his mind," Megan said. She grabbed a mask and gloves from the dispenser outside the exam room. She had just snapped them into place when she cleared the curtained doorway Keiko held open for her. A young man was already on the table. He was curled up, shaking and sweating as he clutched his stomach. His clothes were bloody but not terribly so, due to the location of the injury. The friend was standing by the bed with his hands shoved into his pockets.

"We were just messing around." He looked at Megan with

desperation in his eyes. "Leo's going to be okay, right?"

"Of course," Megan said. "Thanks for bringing him here. Keiko-san's going to take you to the waiting room and I'll have a look at Leo." As the friend was led out of the room, Megan bent low over her patient. He was hovering on the edge of consciousness. "Leo, can you hear me? I'm Doctor Megan Maier and I'm going to take care of you. I need to see your injury. Can you take your hands away for me?" She dropped her voice and said, "It's all right, I understand and I promise you will get proper and respectful care here."

With that, he nodded and relaxed just enough for Megan to make a physical examination. She drew in a slow breath, trying not to make it obvious how worried she was.

"Leo, you're going to need surgery," she said. She hated herself for subjecting him to such an ordeal but she had no other choice. "You're going to have to go to a larger hospital. I don't have the staff to take care of you here. I'll write you a letter of introduction and —"

"Not going," he gritted out. Leo made a move as if to sit up and Megan jumped to hold him down. With one bloody arm, he pushed her off.

"Keiko-san!" Megan cried out. Even injured, Leo had a stubborn strength that was hard for her to overpower.

Keiko rushed over to help.

"You can't leave," she said. "Sensei, what happened?"

"I'm not going, you can't make me!" Leo collapsed onto the bed once more. "I want to see Tonosaki-sensei or I'm going home."

"I understand, please calm down," Megan said, then asked in a soft voice, "Would you allow me to operate on you?"

He closed his eyes for an instant, then looked up at Megan with such trust that she realized once more how young he really was. He nodded his assent.

"I'll do the procedure here. Keiko, will you assist me?"

"No, not alone! We need help. Doctor Tonosaki's in Yokohama this week and the on-call doctor's two hours away. Can we wait that long?"

"No, we can't. We can still do this. I know someone who can be here faster," Megan said. She pulled off her gloves. "Get his blood workup done and start him on replacement fluids. I also want an abdominal CT and prep the ultrasound kit. Also, get the paperwork out and signed STAT."

"Yes Sensei," Keiko said, fully in professional mode.

Megan barreled into the break room and picked up her cell phone. She switched on her Bluetooth and tied her hair back before slipping on the earpiece. With shaking fingers, she called Syler's number and breathed a prayer under her breath.

Syler picked up right away. "Hey Meg, slow night?"

"Just the opposite, in fact. I need your help," Megan said. She briefly outlined the situation. "I think we need to do a laparotomy and I can't do it alone. Syler, this patient needs special consideration and he absolutely won't go to a larger hospital. He's transgender and I'm guessing he's had a bad experience and doesn't want to go somewhere where he'll be disrespected or forced to explain things that should be obvious."

"Pre-op?"

"Yes," Megan replied tightly. She knew Syler had a reason for asking, but she couldn't think of one.

"Okay, I'll take the next rapid. I can be at the clinic in forty minutes," Syler said without a second of hesitation. In the background, Megan could hear footsteps and knew Syler was in motion. "Do you have enough staff? I can rustle up my team if you need. I'm pretty sure most of them are around."

"That would really help us out," Megan said. "Especially if you could get Dr. Takahashi up here. We don't have an anesthesiologist and I was going to go with an epidural or a local and valium like I used to do in Thailand."

"No problem. Meg, I need you to prep the patient for the procedure."

"Thanks Syler, you really saved us here," Megan said, feeling a jolt of weakness hit her in the knees.

"No problem. By the way, this is your show," Syler said. "My team and I will assist you." She paused. "How many times have you done this kind of procedure?"

"More than I can count," Megan said. She gave a wry smile as she said, "The people in my village were constantly getting slashed up and impaled on things. Once I had to remove a stop sign from an unlucky farmer who rolled his tractor in our only intersection."

"Ooh, ouch," Syler said. "I'm going to call my team and I'll let you know our ETA."

After a quick goodbye, Megan shoved her phone into her pocket and dashed back into the exam room. Keiko ministered to Leo. Megan was pleased to see the IV was already in place and the equipment she'd requested set up with the laptop   showing the results of the tests Keiko had done.

"Leo, you're going to be all right," Megan said. She bent over the young man and pressed a hand to his shoulder. "I've called in someone who can help. Doctor Syler Terada and her team are going to assist me. She's an excellent surgeon. She's also my girlfriend."

Atsuko Igarashi and Munehiro Takahashi arrived in short succession and Megan ushered them into the prep area. They got ready in record time, showing their true professional colors. Megan was still scrubbing up at their narrow scrub sink when Syler burst into the prep area. She was in the purple scrubs they kept at the clinic, masked and capped, and Megan had never wanted to hug anyone more than at that moment.

"Sorry to keep you waiting," Syler said. She grabbed a brush from the holder and ripped the package open. She used her elbow to get a good dollop of the antibacterial soap and started in on her nails.

"Thanks for coming," Megan said. It was exhilarating to stand next to Syler, knowing they were going to be facing the enemy of time and injury as a team. "Nurse Igarashi and Doctor Takahashi are already in the OR."

"Great," Syler said.

Megan rinsed her hands and elbowed the water off. She turned to meet Atsuko, who held out a gown for her. Once properly attired, Megan stood across from Syler with her hands held up in front of herself. Between them, Leo's prone body lay draped and packed with heating pads.

"Nurse Igarashi, Takahashi-sensei," Megan greeted the two who were already there.

"Atsuko and Taka-chan, please," the anesthesiologist said. His eyes twinkled at her over his mask. "You're family."

"All right, Atsuko and Taka-chan it is," Megan said. She got a concerned jolt as she wondered exactly what he'd meant by *family*. She met Syler's eyes and said, "First things first: the playlist. I know you like rocking with the oldies, but I prefer to keep things a bit more classic."

As Syler raised her eyebrows in interest, Megan nodded over to where Atsuko stood next to the plastic-draped stereo in the corner with the remote in her hand. She acknowledged the signal and started the music.

"We will be accompanied by a selection including Ishikawa Sayuri and Misora Hibari," Megan said. She turned to address everyone equally, "Singing is allowed, but only if you know all the words and dancing is to be limited to only the choruses. Now, let's get this show on the road."

Behind her, Taka-chan's calm voice read out the vitals as the anesthetic took effect.

"All right, let's have a look," Megan said. She bent over the patient and held her hand out for forceps, which Atsuko handed her with smooth efficiency. As she inserted packing into the wound, Megan delicately explored the organs for any damage. Syler hovered with her and clipped back the edges of the wound.

Megan continued, "Disfiguration of the wound is minimal and so is swelling. He was wearing a *nabe-shatsu* that kept everything compressed nicely until we had to cut it off him."

"That's good," Syler said, her eyes meeting Megan's. "But too bad it had to get wrecked."

"Yeah, it is," Megan said. She broke the contact and focused on her task once more, her entire world narrowed to the small area bathed in harsh white light in front of herself. The words came out automatically. "Those things are expensive."

"For sure," Syler said. She bent her head to watch Megan start to work. "That's why I asked you that question on the phone. I brought in a *nabe-shatsu* I got myself as kind of an experiment way back when and never got around to wearing. I figured Leo might miss the one he had. The receptionist's hanging onto it."

Megan raised her eyebrows, impressed. She didn't comment as she delved into the opened cavity. "Okay, here we've got a small laceration."

The operation progressed smoothly and Megan moved as one with Syler. They breathed in harmony and their movements perfectly matched. Atsuko and Taka-chan worked tirelessly alongside them. Megan once more appreciated the skill and ease with which they supported her and Syler. Megan never had much help in the OR and the teamwork freed her to concentrate on the patient.

Still, Megan had not done surgery for nearly a year and the long-unused muscles, both mental and physical, were stiff and everything took much more effort than she remembered at the peak of her skill. By the time Syler closed the wound with the tiny stitches only a trained pediatric surgeon could execute, Megan was lightheaded and reeling with exhaustion.

"Looks like we're done here. I just want to thank you all one more time," Megan said. She looked around the small OR and met everyone's eyes in turn. "I appreciate this and I owe every-one here a huge favor, so feel free to call it in anytime."

She left the others to finish up and stumbled out of the OR. After tearing off her paper gown and gloves, Megan collapsed onto the bench in the break room and draped an arm over her face. She felt Syler sit down next to her and heaved herself upright.

"Good work in there," Syler said. "Hey, are you okay?"

"Yeah," Megan said. She raised a hand to her face and her fingers came away wet with tears. "It's been a while since I was in an OR." She clenched her hands together as she tried to stop them from shaking. Reality caught up to her and the emotions she'd locked up buffeted her mercilessly. "The last patient I operated on died."

"My God," Syler breathed. "Don't tell me, it was your—"

"Yes, it was." Megan leaned back against the wall and closed her eyes. She fought to speak through the fist of tears that clenched in her throat. "My clinic was the only hospital for miles, and even so, Yasu gave everyone specific instructions to be brought to me if—anything happened. Three of them were injured in the accident, but I could only save two." Megan bowed her head and buried her face in her hands. Her voice was muffled as she continued, "I used to think that maybe if I had better equipment, or more help I could have saved them all, but after I reviewed the case, I knew it was impossible. There was no hope from the start. I understood that with my head." As if a great weight pressed down on her, Megan looked up at Syler and said, "But my soul and my heart never believed it."

"In this case you should listen to your head," Syler said. "Believe the facts. It wasn't your fault. You did all you could, you are a skilled physician. I know, I've just seen you in action."

"Thanks, that means a lot," Megan said. She gave a squeak as Syler's arms came around her and held her tight. The tension drained from her as she melted into the embrace.

"Sorry about the sweatiness," Syler murmured into her hair.

"That's okay, we're both pretty soaked," Megan said. She was glad she always brought a change of underwear with her in case she ended up in the OR. And that night she had, with Syler beside her. It felt right to be there with her. Megan let out a long breath and snuggled closer. "It was really good working with you." She paused under the weight of the words. "It was an honor. We make a good team."

"Yeah, we make a *great* team," Syler said. "And it was good for me too. Very educational. I can tell you're used to being more on your own. You have an unconventional way of doing things, but you get the job done. Like the way you hold a bunch of instruments in your left hand and switch back and forth lightning fast. I've never seen that done before."

"That's just a habit I picked up in Thailand," Megan said, "I probably have a bunch of bad habits that could get me in trouble here. But I'm glad I spent that time overseas. I was over there for a number of reasons, but mainly I was learning how the medical establishment deals with transgender patients. Not only the medical details but paperwork and things like triage protocols."

"That explains a lot, actually. I've read some of your articles," Syler said. Her hands trailed absently up and down Megan's back. "You're doing an exceptional thing, Megan."

"Not really," Megan said with a tired shrug. "Every person, no matter what their demographic is, should be able to get reliable and respectful medical care. I worked with a lot of really good people in Thailand, but I never had the opportunity to work with someone of your caliber."

"Hopefully we can do it again," Syler's voice was warm and rippled through Megan. "Without the crisis situation."

"Definitely. I'd like that."

"Hey, is this standard post-op procedure here?" A voice interrupted and Megan straightened up in a hurry. Atsuko stood in front of them. She had a bunch of towels in her arms and looked down with a slightly amused expression. "Does this mean I get a hug too?"

"This isn't what it looks like," Megan said with a burst of worry. "I was just—oh damn, I didn't mean to—"

"It's okay," Syler said. She reached out and twined her fingers around Megan's. "Atchan already knows. I told all of my team and they're cool with it. After all, you're the best thing that's happened to me in, well, ever. I hope you don't mind."

"No, not at all," Megan said. Syler had told her team. That was a big step. A warm burst of pleasure filled Megan. She gave Atsuko a smile and said, "I really appreciate you coming out here at such short notice. You and Taka-chan made a huge difference."

"No problem," Atsuko said. She put the towels down on the bench next to Megan. "Keiko-san sent me in with these. I guess both of you are going to want to take a shower." She paused and continued deadpan, "Together."

Megan blushed madly but Syler just stood up. She poked Atsuko on the shoulder and said, "Sure, why not? And you're welcome to join us, Atchan. It's a good way to save time and water."

The words broke the tension that held Megan captive. She stretched her arms over her head and said, "That sounds like a plan. I'm all for helping the environment and the more the merrier, especially in the shower. The one here's more like an upright coffin, but I'm sure we can all fit if we perform a bit of real-life Tetris."

While Syler sputtered in laughter, Atsuko raised an eyebrow. She returned Syler's poke and said, "Good taste in tunes, smart, *and* funny. This one's a keeper. Anyway, thanks but no thanks to your offer. I'm gonna hit the road. Thanks for the party tonight."

Syler nodded with a pleased look on her face. Atsuko held out one fist and Syler gave her a casual bump before Atsuko turned to leave.

The reminder of duty prickled at Megan. She straightened up and said, "The relief doctor should be in before long and I want to do another check on Leo before I go."

"Good idea," Syler said.

"Just so you know, I was joking about the showering together part," Megan said. She stood and shook out her hands, which were feeling a bit sore and cramped. "I hope you're not disappointed."

"That's all right, I'll survive" Syler said. She leaned back against the wall and fixed Megan with a long, calm gaze.

"Anyway, what's on your schedule?"

"Nothing," Syler said. "I've got two procedures scheduled tomorrow so I'm taking it easy today. Unless there's an emergency, I'm just going to hang out at home. You?"

"Same," Megan said. "I arranged things so the I'm off duty the day after I work here." She reached out, seized with an undeniable urge, "Why don't you come home with me? We can hang out at my place together. I'll make you breakfast."

"I'd like that," Syler said. She stood and cupped Megan's face, then bent down to lightly touch foreheads. "Now go take your shower so I can get one too. The trains will be running soon."

"Aye aye sir!" Megan said. Syler released her and Megan trotted off.

THE RAPID FROM Nagoya Station had double-seats instead of long benches and Megan, sitting in the window seat, felt like she and Syler were in their own private world, one tinted red-gold from the morning sun. Megan rested her head on Syler's shoulder and dozed on the way back. Syler made good on her promise and prodded Megan awake as their train arrived at Suito Station. The sun cast long shadows over the cracked and grassy sidewalk as they headed down the still-sleeping streets. Megan was lightheaded and not just from exhaustion. She had revisited her own personal hell and the pain lurking there no longer had the power to incapacitate her. The guilt still haunted her, but it was no longer in control.

When they got to Megan's apartment, Syler took up her usual place on the sofa. She sprawled out and looked rather deflated. Megan went into her kitchen corner and threw together a simple breakfast of yogurt and fruit, which Syler appreciated with such genuine words of gratitude that Megan flushed with shy pleasure.

"I'm going to be a terrible guest," Syler said through a yawn as Megan cleaned up. "But could I ask if it's okay to crash out on your sofa for a few hours."

"It's not okay," Megan said. She plopped down on the end of the sofa and caught Syler's surprised glance. Megan's heartbeat jumped. "I have a very nice futon in the other room that is much more comfortable."

Syler raised one brow. "Really? And would you be volunteering to keep me company?"

"Yes," Megan said. She leaned forward and said, "Just for sleeping, though."

"That's fine. Actually, that's more than fine. I don't think I have the energy for anything else."

Megan's face heated up at the thought of what Syler meant by *anything else*. Like Megan, Syler kept extra clothes and a small toiletry kit in her bag, a side-effect of the job that required suddenly having to work at any time of the day or night. While Syler brushed her teeth, Megan ducked into her room, grateful she had thought to straighten up before she left. She was just rummaging around in her dresser when Syler came in.

"Do you want to borrow some pajamas or anything?" Megan asked.

"Nah, I'm fine," Syler said. "I always sleep in the nude."

Megan whirled and fixed Syler with an incredulous look. Syler let out a laugh.

"Sorry, Meg, I was just joking. The look on your face right now is priceless." Syler shoved her hands into her pockets and leaned back in her easy stance. "I'll just strip down to my T-shirt. Is that okay?"

"As long as you're comfortable," Megan said. She turned back to her dresser and as she took out a sleep shirt for herself, she heard the rustling of Syler getting undressed. Megan yanked the shirt over her head, then Syler's arms came around her from behind. The bare skin of Syler's legs brushed her own, and the sensation jolted her body alive.

"Kiss me goodnight now," Syler said in a mint-flavored murmur. She lowered her head to press her lips to the side of Megan's neck. "Because if you do it when we're lying in each other's arms, we might not get any sleep."

"Good idea."

Megan's heart pounded. She turned around and slipped her arms around Syler's waist. She let out a soft breath as their bodies came together. Megan closed her eyes and gave Syler a kiss on one cheek, then settled more intimately against her as Syler's arms drew her close. Megan couldn't help herself and pressed her lips to the side of Syler's neck. She moved to nuzzle behind one ear, just as she had the first night Syler came up to her room. Megan caught her breath as the memory hit her hard and drove a spike of arousal through her. She didn't mean to let things go further, but the soft groan Syler gave deep in her throat set Megan on fire and she moved to catch Syler's mouth in a devouring kiss she hadn't been able to do that first night.

Syler responded to Megan's kiss with a passion that belied her earlier admission of exhaustion. Warm, strong hands trailed up and down Megan's back and she arched into the caress. Her legs trembled and she drank Syler in as deep as she could. Her body started to move. She undulated against Syler as she craved a more intimate contact. A thigh slipped between hers and Megan let go with a breathy moan. Megan ground against Syler. She dropped her hands to Syler's hips and pulled them together. The yielding surface of her closet doors was behind her and even though the handle dug into her backside, Megan didn't care. She knew she should stop but her resistance was worn into dust from physical and emotional exhaustion. Her body screamed to be touched, her breasts tingled and the throbbing need between her legs was almost unbearable.

It was Syler who was the first to put on the brakes. With a gentle reluctance, Syler ended the kiss and moved back a fraction. Megan followed unconsciously. Her lips sought Syler's even as her reason told her it wasn't the time. Soft hands cupped Megan's face and brought her back to the present. Syler's breath was harsh in her ears and hot on her skin, separated by the smallest distance.

"Now that's what I call a goodnight kiss," Syler said as she gently brushed her thumb over Megan's lower lip.

"Oh God, sorry," Megan gasped. She let go of the death-grip she had on Syler and stifled the sigh of regret as Syler eased out of their embrace. "I didn't mean to let things go like that."

"Don't worry about it," Syler said. "It takes two to tango."

She sank down onto the futon. Megan crawled under the covers. Her body brushed up against Syler, and she was scarcely able to believe what was happening. Megan cast about herself in confusion. She didn't know where to put her feet and her arms were awkward and in the way.

"What's wrong Meg?" Syler propped herself up on one

elbow. "If you're uncomfortable having me here, I'm fine with the sofa."

"No, that's not it," Megan said. She swallowed a fist of embarrassment and said, "I've never slept with anyone before." As she heard the words and realized what she'd just said, Megan flapped around. She continued in a rush, "I mean, I've always had my own bed, not that I don't want you right here, I do very much, but you'll have to kind of, um, be patient with me while I get the logistics sorted."

"That's all right, Meg. Just turn around and let me know if anything's not all right."

With some maneuvering, Megan managed to get into a comfortable position. Syler draped her arm over Megan's hip, her hand rested ever-so-lightly on Megan's belly. Syler's quiet breaths were warm on the back of Megan's neck. She was also very aware of the softness rising up against her with each of those breaths, in contrast with the resilient feel of Syler's long legs and the heat radiating from the pressure of Syler's body curled against her backside.

"Do you think you can sleep?" Syler whispered in her ear and she gave Megan the softest kiss on one lobe.

"I wasn't sure before, but now I think so," Megan said. She interrupted herself with a yawn. She snuggled back and molded her body more firmly against Syler's. The arm around her middle tightened just a fraction.

Through her happy, sleepy haze, Megan reached out and picked up her cell phone. "I'll set the alarm. Is four hours good for you?"

"Perfect. I still want to sleep tonight."

"Done." Megan set her phone down and burrowed under the covers. She was conscious of Syler against her and loved the feeling of being held safe and warm in her arms.

"Good night, Meg."

"Meirav," Megan whispered on the edge of slumber. "That's my Hebrew name."

"It's lovely," Syler said. "Just like you."

"Ppft, sweet talker," Megan replied, but she was secretly pleased at the compliment.

"*Laila tov, Meirav,*" Syler said softly. Megan was intrigued by the fact Syler knew goodnight in Hebrew. The language sounded beautiful in Syler's low voice.

Megan wanted to say more, but just replied, *"Oyasumi, Saira."*

THE RATTAN BLINDS barely moved even though all the windows were wide open. Megan brushed her hair with both hands and raked it back into a messy bunch, which she stuffed into the fake-tortoiseshell clip. The fan in the middle of the room only stirred the tepid air that was thick with the smoky, slightly fishy haze Megan had been breathing for the past year.

"When did the symptoms start?" Megan asked the elderly woman on the battered exam table. She was holding her belly, which looked swollen.

"One week ago, maybe two. Since the rains finished," she said. Megan stifled a groan. She had to remember time moved differently there. With a reassuring word or two of comfort, Megan reached out and picked up her go-to book of illustrated medical terms she used to help her explain things to her patients. She crossed her sandaled feet, barely hidden under the long hem of her cotton skirt as her fingers flipped through the well-worn pages until she found the one she wanted purely by instinct. A racket started up outside, most likely a truck passing by, and Megan pitched her voice to carry over it.

"Have you been eating—" Megan looked up, annoyed as the roar of an engine drowned out her words. Through the window, she saw a battered pickup barrel into the small dirt yard that fronted the clinic. Megan was about to say something in exasperation but was interrupted by shouting and honking. The door to the exam room slammed open and Sister Tilda ran in. Her watery blue eyes were bright with worry behind her thick glasses. Megan's heart gave a great lurch. Sister Tilda never bothered her unless it was truly an emergency, and she never hurried.

"Doctor Maier, I think you'd better come out here." she said. She bowed her grey-clothed head toward the patient with a word of apology.

"What is it?" Megan asked. A sick chill trickled down her spine.

"Just come. Now."

Worry choked her as Megan dashed through the dusty,

cluttered lobby. She took the three steps from the porch at a dead run. Her white coat flapped around her legs, hampering her. She was greeted by a bunch of guys from the village. They huddled around the bed of the truck. Megan sucked in a breath at the blood spattered on the sides of the truck and streaked over the tailgate.

"Three of them crashed," one of the men said. "I'm sorry, I'm so sorry, Doctor ma'am. We tried to warn them but they couldn't stop in time. Please forgive us."

Megan shouldered through the small crowd and the words drifted around her.

Sorry.

We're so sorry.

They were going too fast.

The dust was too thick.

She clambered up onto the rear tailgate and looked into the bed of the truck that held three long bundles of red-stained canvas tarps. Two of them moved slightly and groaned in pain. The other one was completely covered and, even as Sister Tilda raised her voice in prayer, Megan reached out and pulled the covering back. The broken, bloodied face that looked back at her wasn't the one she'd been silently expecting.

It was Syler.

Her hands lost their grip and Megan fell back. Her scream split the air. She was falling into a black pit and reached desperately for anything to stop her. Someone grabbed her and Megan fought them with every bit of strength she had. Through her panicked breaths, Megan became aware of a calm voice repeating the same thing over and over.

"Wake up, Meg. It's just a dream."

Finally she broke free from the thrall. Her eyes snapped open. Megan was twisted up in the futon cover. Her body shook and her clothes were soaked with sweat. As soon as she stopped struggling, the arms that were restraining her settled her into a firm hug. Even as she gasped in panic, Megan reached out blindly, seeking Syler's face with her hands.

"You're all right," Megan whimpered. She needed to see and touch the unbroken, unblemished skin in front of her, still half in the dream. "You're not hurt."

"Of course not," Syler said. She submitted to Megan's frantic examination without question. "I'm fine. See, everything's all right."

Gentle hands stroked Megan's hair and held her head.

"It's all right. Ssh, it was just a dream," Syler said. "Slow down. Breathe Meg. I'm here."

Even though her lungs begged for air as if she was drowning, Megan took a breath and held it for five seconds before letting it out. She'd counseled herself through this more than once and the familiar routine took the edge off her panic. The tremors wracking her body calmed and her breathing went from ragged gasps to choked sniffles.

When Megan calmed down, Syler's arms fell away from her. Somewhat sheepishly, Megan straightened her T-shirt and dragged her damp hair out of her face with both hands.

"Sorry about that," Megan said.

"Don't apologize," Syler said. She paused, then reached out and touched Megan on the shoulder. "Do you want to talk about it?"

Megan nodded. She took a breath before she said, "I dreamed about the accident. I haven't done that for a while, but I guess tonight kind of brought the memories back."

"Sweetheart," Syler breathed. "I'm so sorry. You thought it was me, didn't you."

"My brain likes to torture me like that," Megan said in what she hoped was a joking tone. "It's happened with just about everyone I'm close to. This was one of the first things I worked out with my therapist. I'll be okay," Megan added quickly. "I just want to know you're here with me."

"Of course. I'm not leaving you," Syler said in a soft voice that told Megan she understood more than what she was saying. "Dreams are just your mind clearing out junk. They don't mean anything."

"I know," Megan said. "Thanks."

"No need to thank me." Syler got a grin on her face and said, "Here's one for you. The most intense sex dream I ever had starred me and one of my brothers. I won't tell you which one so you don't get a mental image when you meet him."

"Seriously?" Megan asked.

"Yup. It was incredibly detailed and massively real. But it's cool, though, in the dream I was a guy too."

"Okay, you win," Megan said. She put a hand over her mouth to hide the smile.

"Yeah," Syler replied with a shrug. She stroked a hand up and down Megan's back and said, "How about I get you another T-shirt? This one's soaked through."

"Thanks," Megan said. Syler stood and Megan shivered alone for a moment before Syler put a new T-shirt in her hands. As Megan peeled off her sweaty clothing, Syler casually draped herself on the futon. She faced the wall to give Megan privacy.

As soon as Megan was in clean, dry nightwear, Syler rolled over and looked at her.

"Come here, Meg."

She needed no more convincing than the soft, husky tone in Syler's voice. Megan lay down and Syler snuggled up to her back once more. Strong arms came around her and Megan relaxed into the embrace. However, the last image of the bloody ruin of Syler's face haunted her for a long time. Megan stared into the darkness and listened to Syler's regular breathing until she at last fell into an exhausted, dreamless sleep.

Chapter Nine

FOR THE REST of the week, preparations for Passover gripped the hospital and Megan threw herself into them. She enjoyed the rituals even as the anxiety of having to brave the Seder with Charles gnawed at her. He called her once to tell her the brand, exact size, and price of the box of Passover chocolates she was to bring to the dinner. After he ended the call, Megan wanted to scrub her phone with disinfectant wipes.

Even though they were both rushed and busy, Megan saw Syler almost every day. She loved catching glimpses of her in the hallways and felt a secret, happy thrill when they shared glances as they passed each other. They managed to behave and kept their interaction in the hospital decent, although Megan often dreamed of Syler's kisses and ached to feel Syler's arms around her.

Due to their heavy schedules, they didn't really get much alone-time with each other, save for one evening Megan invited Syler over to watch a movie. Syler showed up in her tux with a chilled bottle of sparkling juice and the movie ended up being nothing more than background noise for a marathon makeout session on the sofa that left Megan breathless and hovering on the edge of reason.

Thursday morning at the hospital, the office and hallways were eerily silent. Tension sang through the air. Megan was hyperaware of the passage of time, her mind occupied only with wondering how Sakura's operation would proceed. She used the cover of doing her early morning rounds to prowl around the operating rooms and caught a glimpse of Syler. She was standing at one of the long sinks, head down and already masked, her long body swathed in the blue-green scrub suit and her hair tucked up under the close-fitting cap. The scrub brush was in her hand and water droplets sparkled in the fluorescent lights as they tracked down over her strong wrists. Her movements were practiced, hypnotic, almost meditative.

Another troubling development was that Nikky didn't show

up for her appointment that day, and Megan was on edge with worry. She didn't have much time between appointments and a few walk-ins that needed to be squeezed in. She was certain she heard the child's characteristic voice a few times from the waiting room. Halfway during her morning examination hours, Megan had the opportunity to speak to Luka while retrieving some antibiotics for an elementary student with an ear infection.

"Did Nikky Okamoto come in today? She was supposed to have an appointment with me."

"Really?" Luka raised his eyebrows. "Doctor Bleaker saw her."

"What?" Megan growled. She clenched her fists inside her pockets, then forced herself to relax. Breathe, she counseled herself. There had to be an explanation. She couldn't take her anger out on Luka. She grabbed the request form from the pile and started filing it out. "Anyway, have you heard   anything about Sakura-chan's operation?" Megan asked in a quiet voice, not looking up from the form.

With a shake of his head, Luka said, "It's too early to tell." He reached out and gave Megan's hand a squeeze. "Hang in there, Megu. Whatever the outcome, Syler's going to need you to be strong for her."

Megan replied with a nod. On her way back, she swung by the storage cabinet as her stock of speculums was getting low. With an impatient motion, Megan sorted through them until she found a bunch of Teitel ones and shoved them into a pocket of her lab coat. She pulled on a fresh hygienic mask before she ducked back into her exam room. She manufactured a smile as she did so and hoped it reached her eyes.

Public examination hours ended and Megan was too preoccupied to even think about either lunch or her reports. As soon as she could get away from the examination room, Megan stormed into Charles's office. She didn't bother to knock and he looked up from his computer without changing expression.

"What a pleasure," he said in a dry tone. "What brings you here today, Megan?"

"I think you know," Megan said. She put both hands on the desk and loomed over Charles. For once she felt in control of the situation. "Why did you take me off Nikky Okamoto's case?"

Charles leaned back in his chair and steepled his fingers. He took his time before he answered. "You were becoming too involved in the case. I reassigned the patient before you did something to damage the hospital's reputation and relationship with the Okamoto family."

Megan started to spit out an angry retort, but he cut her off.

"Stop this now," Charles said. He stood and Megan lost whatever ground she'd had. "It would be to your benefit to desist before anything worse happens because of your misguided persistence. Now, this is not a threat and I do not wish to antagonize you, but if you do not wish to be reassigned, you will give up your actions right now. I don't think I have to remind you that with your history and reputation, you will have a very difficult time finding a position elsewhere. Remember, I am doing this for your own good."

"For my good?" Megan snapped. "You'd better be right about nothing going on in that home, or else it's you who is going to be *reassigned*. I don't want to threaten you either, but the Okamotos aren't the only family who hold sway in the medical community. You and the rest of the Brockmans are nothing more than *machers*." With that, Megan turned and stormed out, seething.

With her mind full of both anger at Charles and concern for Sakura, Megan couldn't sit still. She made several unnecessary trips from her desk to the washrooms near the OR where Syler and her team were working. Instead of ringing with the usual strains of "Living on a Prayer" or another of the songs Syler usually played during operations, the hallway was quiet. On the tenth trip, Megan saw Syler standing in the hallway with Sakura's parents. Syler looked tired and her scrubs were soaked with sweat.

Megan kept a respectful distance. Both Chiho and Toshi bowed deeply in front of Syler, who shook her head and reached out to them, urging the young couple to straighten up. In turn, they took her hands and, against her protests, bowed again. They spoke for a few moments more and Megan hung back, pressed against the wall. Her heart beat fast and she wondered if she was overstepping the bounds of their new relationship. As the two sets of footsteps faded off into the distance, Megan drew up her courage and stepped around the corner. Just like the first time Megan had seen her, Syler stood tall and gracefully lanky with her arms crossed over her chest. This time her head was bowed in defeat. The eyes that met Megan's as she approached were haunted and empty. The impassive expression Syler wore looked brittle.

"Hey, are you okay?" Megan asked softly. She stopped a prudent distance away. Hard-won instinct kicked in before she could stop it.

Slowly, heartbreakingly slowly, Syler shook her head. She rubbed a hand over her face and raised her eyes to the ceiling as she let out a long breath.

"Syler, do you want me here?" Megan asked. She didn't move forward, but took a leaf from Syler's book. "Tell me if you do. If not, it's all right. I'm not going to make this about me."

She'd already turned to leave when the answer came, a whispered, "Please stay, Meg," that was almost below her hearing.

A note in Syler's voice spurred Megan into action. She moved quickly and opened the door to one of the private consult rooms. She took a quick look over her shoulder before she slid the sign on the wall from vacant to occupied. Across from the consultation desk, a padded bench was pushed against the wall and Syler sank down onto it. Her head fell into her hands. Megan watched with a searing pain in her chest but didn't dare to reach out. She was about to say something when Syler began to speak.

"There's nothing more we can do," she said, her voice muffled. "Nothing left to do but wait for the end." Syler raised her face and Megan bit her lip at the tears she saw shining in her eyes. Syler's hands shook and she clenched her fists. "Meg, I told them their little girl is going to die and I can't do anything to stop it. And they thanked me." Syler's shoulders slumped and she scrubbed a hand across her face.

The raw pain in her words unfroze Megan and she crossed the narrow distance separating them until she stood directly in front of Syler. In one quick, decisive motion, Syler reached out and wrapped long arms around Megan. She pressed her face to Megan's blouse. Megan let her instincts take over and cradled Syler's head against her. She rubbed a hand over Syler's back in an attempt to smooth the knotted tension in her muscles.

"I shouldn't have let myself get this involved. I shouldn't care this much."

"It's all right to care," Megan said. "We can't be automatons in this job. That's what pushes us to do our best. It's perfectly all right to be sad and angry, but never feel guilty. You did all you could."

"It wasn't enough. I couldn't fix what was wrong. I couldn't make her better. And now my hands are tied."

Syler trembled against her. The arms around Megan were almost uncomfortably tight, but she didn't mind. She lowered her head and pressed a quick kiss to Syler's temple. The skin against her lips was damp with sweat.

"You gave Sakura-chan more years than anyone could have predicted," Megan said. "You gave her family the chance to see her through four birthdays and get to know the precious little girl they brought into this world. Four years of baseball debates and hugs and dressing up as laundry for Purim. That's why they're thanking you. You gave them a miracle. It's more than enough."

"I know, but I can't make myself believe it." Syler's voice broke as she said, "Why does this have to be so hard? She's just a baby, just a tiny little angel who never had a chance." Her words tumbled out, rough and harsh. "I don't want to let her go, Meg."

Her shoulders shook as the tears came. Megan held Syler when the deep sobs wracked her. She stroked back Syler's hair and whispered words of comfort. The storm passed and Syler dabbed somewhat sheepishly at her face with the handful of tissues Megan pulled from her pocket.

"You're going to get through this," Megan said. She sat down on the bench and busied herself straightening her lab coat over her lap to give Syler a bit of time and privacy to get herself back in order. Even though they were separated by a judicious distance, Megan never felt closer to Syler, as if she'd been allowed to see a part of Syler that very few people had. Megan was glad she was able to repay the support Syler had shown her after her own post-op breakdown. It was a vulnerable time for anyone. The fierce concentration and stress played havoc with emotions after the crisis was over and the pressure-seals came off.

"Look at me, I'm a mess," Syler said. She slouched back against the wall and gave a weak laugh that nonetheless sent a spear of hope through Megan. "I'm gross and sweaty and stink like disinfectant. I can't believe you still hugged me."

"None of that matters. You always smell good," Megan said.

"And you're beautiful."

Syler's head came up and she looked at Megan with wonder in her eyes. "Huh? Really?"

"You don't think so?"

"I don't know," Syler said and shoved a handful of hair out of her face. "I never thought of myself like that."

"How can you not know how beautiful you are?" Megan gave Syler a gentle nudge with her elbow. "We do have access to mirrors six days a week. You, Syler Terada, are the most beautiful person I have ever met. Outside and inside. Believe it."

With a crooked grin, Syler said, "I really like hearing you say that."

"I'll say it anytime you want and it will be just as true." Megan reached out and wrapped her fingers around Syler's. "Are you going to be all right?"

"Yeah, I think so," Syler said with a slow smile that radiated warmth. Syler gave her hand a squeeze. "Thanks, Meg, for putting up with me and letting me blubber all over your shirt."

"That's what girlfriends are for," Megan said with a proud tilt of her head.

"You're the best girlfriend I ever had," Syler told her. "And the best one I ever will have."

The simple candor of the words hit Megan hard and she felt the sting of tears as a fist of guilt clenched in her gut. While she scuffed her sleeve over her face, Megan held out a hand and accepted a tissue from Syler. An arm came around Megan's shoulders and she let her body relax against Syler's.

"Sorry, I guess blubber-monster syndrome is contagious," Syler said.

"We need to quarantine you," Megan joked weakly.

"Sure, just give me a bunch of takenoko and crossword puzzles and I'll stay put for as long as you want." Syler glanced at the clock on the wall, then got to her feet with an apologetic look. "Sorry, I have to go and finish up my reports. Me and my team are going out for something to eat tonight. It's going to be pretty grim, but you're welcome to join us."

"Thanks, but you go ahead," Megan said, awed that she'd even been asked. "You need your team-time, and I don't want to mess that up."

"Nah, they see me enough anyway," Syler replied. She

crossed her arms over her chest and leaned back with her usual careless grace. "We'll probably end up back at my place for de-stressing, so how about coming over then? You've only personally met Atsuko and Taka-chan so far and the rest of them really want to meet you, too. Since that night at the clinic, they've become fans of yours, it seems."

"That's good to hear." Megan said, shyly pleased about that step in their relationship.

"So you're coming tonight?"

Megan hesitated before she said, "If you're sure it's not an imposition."

"No way, it'll be great to have you there." Syler's face broke into a wide smile that Megan had no choice but to return as her body filled with a happy light in response. "We'll get back to my place at about eight I think, but I'll shoot you a text when we know our exact ETA."

"I'll be waiting," Megan said. She closed her eyes as Syler leaned down and gave her a sweet, lingering kiss that had Megan wanting more before it was even finished.

The rest of the day passed slowly. Megan fought her own sadness at the news about Sakura with every ounce of her professional mettle. She found Jayco and commiserated about life in general over cups of lukewarm machine coffee until Luka pounced on them and sang annoyingly happy songs at them until they escaped to their respective desks.

After she finished her paperwork, Megan swung by the grocery on her way home to get some snacks to bring over to Syler's that night. She ate some leftover pasta and lounged around her apartment. After darkness fell, she changed into her Audrey Hepburn outfit. She looked at her washing machine and pondered the feasibility of putting a load in that evening when her phone chirped with the message inviting her up to the roof of Syler's apartment. With her phone cradled in one hand, Megan picked up the snack-filled shopping bag and let herself out.

Megan couldn't stop the happy smile as she pattered down the stairs to street level. The evening was still warm from the day's sunlight and the wind was quiet for once. That would be the first time she went to Syler's apartment. They always hung out at her place and Megan wondered if there was a reason for that. Maybe Syler didn't want Megan to feel ashamed at the huge gap in the value of their apartments, or maybe she just liked the big sofa in Megan's living room. Megan had to admit she had a certain fondness for it, helped quite a bit by the many good memories she had of things that happened on that sofa lately.

Syler's apartment was in a clean and stylish five-story building that boasted a glassed-in lobby with an intercom system and black marble floors. Megan uneasily thought of the ancient cracked linoleum and security-free openness of her own building. There was a button marked "R" and Megan pressed it. She guessed there was a camera, because a moment later Syler's voice said, "Come on up!" The door lock buzzed, and Megan let herself in. As she took the elevator up to the fifth floor, Megan wondered what she should do if she was ever invited over on Shabbos, given the restrictions on using electronic switches like the ones at the front door.

The sounds of talking and laughter led her up the short stair-case to the roof. She was met by strings of lights and potted plants that were big enough to be trees. Someone had their phone in a speaker holder and Indian trap music filled the air. A few low tables were scattered about the perimeter of the roof, all of them held clusters of candles and bowls of smoking incense. The effect was relaxing and magical.

A squat out-building took up one corner. Megan later found out it housed a storage shed and a small but hospitable washroom. On a thick rug in the middle of the roof, Syler and the rest of her team sprawled out, either sitting or lying across plump floor cushions. As Megan hesitated in the doorway, Syler glanced over and got up immediately with a big smile. She twined their hands together and pulled her close for a kiss on the cheek, which Megan shyly enjoyed, peripherally aware of the other people nearby.

"Thanks for coming," Syler said. She looked relaxed and casually gorgeous in a body-hugging T-shirt emblazoned with the Wonder Woman logo, and faded jeans. Under the T-shirt, she wore a ribbed grey top that was long enough in the arms it was either menswear or bought overseas. She led Megan over to sit with the group.

"I hope you don't mind me gate-crashing your party," Megan said. She lifted the bag and said, "I brought snacks. Nothing special, just some cheese and fruit from the supermarket plus crackers."

"Hey, anyone with snacks of any kind is always welcome on Terada Terrace," Taka-chan said. He lifted the lid of the cooler. "What'll you have? We've got beer, Chu-Hi, some of those cocktail partner thingies plus soft drinks if you'd rather."

"I'd love a beer, thanks."

Megan exchanged the bag for a can and settled down on a cushion with Syler on one side of her and Dani the scrub tech on the other. Atsuko was lying down across from them but she got up and helped Taka-chan add Megan's snacks to the laden table next to the cooler. Atsuko had her hair in braids and looked comfortable in a loose cotton dress. She'd layered it with a woolen shawl that looked handmade.

Megan glanced around. She didn't see the surgical assistant Nobuhiko Ohta, but before she could even ask the question, a cheerful clatter from the stairway ushered the final member of the group onto the roof.

"Hey Nobu!" a few people called out in greeting.

"Sorry to keep you all waiting," Nobu said. "I'm here, now the party can start!"

Megan noticed a significant question-like glance passed between him and Syler, which he answered with a nod.

He caught sight of Megan and gave her an abbreviated bow before he plopped down cross-legged on the rug. Nobu had always seemed like the most reticent member of the group, but his eyes were bright and intelligent behind his glasses and out of the hospital, he was more chatty than Megan had ever seen. From listening to the surgical nurses, Megan knew he supported Syler flawlessly. He was her assistant for his entire professional career. They'd worked together since Syler hand-picked him during his internship.

Taka-chan handed the newest addition a can of beer and the roof resounded with *kampai!* as the collection of drink cans met in a happy clunk in the middle of the group. After he swigged from his drink, Nobu put his can aside and held up his satchel with a mysterious look on his face.

"All right, who's for a bit of feel-good and relaxation?"

Megan felt the other members of the group's eyes on her as Nobu withdrew a plastic bag that contained a number of white sticks. After a moment of incomprehension, Megan realized what they were. The incense and candles suddenly made sense.

"You're not going to call the cops?" Daniela asked. She peered at Megan over the top of her can of cassis orange.

"Of course not," Megan said.

"Good," Dani said. She looked over at Syler and said, "Megan one, ex-bitch zero."

"What?" Megan asked, appalled. "Yukina called the cops on you?"

"She threatened to if we brought the stuff here," Syler said with a sour look.

"Well at least the landlord here seems pretty cool," Megan said. "Letting you have parties on the roof and all that."

"Oh yeah, she is," Taka-chan said. He aimed his gaze over at Syler, who accepted a rolled joint from Nobu.

Megan choked on her beer. "Syler owns this whole building?"

"She didn't tell you?" Taka-chan asked. His eyebrows rose to meet the silver waves of hair.

"It has always been my dream," Syler said as she came back over and took her place on the cushion next to Megan, "To pay an inordinate amount in fixed-asset tax. Plus, if this surgeon thing doesn't work out, I always have something to fall back on. I hope you're not upset that I didn't mention this. It tends to freak people out when they find out I own this money-pit. Well, me and my brothers, but they're officially hands-off."

"I don't mind, I think it's great." Megan tilted her head and looked at Syler with new respect. "Does anyone I know live here?"

"Ken-mama's on the third floor," Syler said. "Other than him, I don't think there's anyone else you might know, but most people living here are *seku-mai*." Syler used the abbreviation for sexual minority with practiced ease. "I have an agency take care of most things around here so I actually didn't even know he lived here until we happened to meet in the elevator one day a few months ago. His partner's the nicest guy and they've got the cutest little mini dax called Maron."

Megan clasped her hands as she pictured the domestic scene. "It must be nice to live here. After all, the owner's an amazing person and the view from the roof is not to be missed."

With her usual quicksilver grin, Syler took out a Zippo and flicked it into life before she lit up. She took a long drag and let out the pungent smoke in a slow, lazy stream.

"Nice one, Nobu, this is good stuff," Syler said to Nobu, who was busy nursing his own joint. He merely nodded in return.

Nobody gave Megan any pressure either way but she had to admit being more than a little curious. Syler was halfway through her next puff when Megan decided to move. She put down her beer and plunked herself down in front of Syler. Megan fixed her with an expectant expression. Wordlessly, Syler held out the joint and Megan took it. She drew in a slow lungful, just as Syler had done.

"Hold it for a while," Syler told her. "Don't let the magic out too soon. There you go."

"Thanks, I needed a bit of de-stressing," Megan said. She rolled her shoulders and finished her long exhale. "I had a bit of a *discussion* with Charles today."

"Oh? About what?" Syler asked as she passed the joint back to Megan.

Through a cloud of smoke, Megan angrily retold the day's events and the not-threat Charles had given her.

"That man," Syler said and shook her head. "Look, if Mrs. Okamoto needs someplace safe to go, I've got a room here that's furnished and empty. I was thinking of renting it out on a weekly basis, you know, to people here on business or something. It's been professionally cleaned and everything, but I haven't gotten around to listing it yet. She and Nikky are welcome to stay there."

"That's very kind. I'll be sure to let her know." Megan blinked as emotion welled up in her throat. Syler just smiled and put an arm around her.

They passed the joint back and forth until it was about halfway done. As the glowing embers got closer to their fingers, Nobu produced a bunch of hemostats from his bag of wonders and handed them around. At that point, Megan felt she'd had enough and let Syler have the rest.

The scent of incense surrounded her and Megan watched as a lazy, mellow mood settled over the group. She didn't feel any different. Megan took a quick self-inventory to confirm that the herbal relaxant didn't have any effect on her except for the fact that she'd just realized what the question was.

"I know it!" Megan declared. She stood up and spread her arms wide. "I know the question! The question to the answer of life!"

As the rest of the group more-or-less paid attention to her, Megan decided to tell everyone what the question was. Unfortunately, she got distracted by the snack tray and forgot what she was going to say. Megan decided to make the best of the situation so she helped herself to a tangerine and some cheese. She plopped down on the carpet and offered a piece of the fruit to Syler, who leaned over and ate it directly from her fingers.

"Thanks," Syler said. She laughed as Megan looked around and blushed. She scooted her cushion closer to Megan and said, "Don't worry about those lowlifes. They're cool. Besides, they don't even date women."

"I do!" Taka-chan piped up.

"Yes, but in your case, you *also* date women."

He just grinned and passed over a small bunch of grapes to Syler. She pulled one off and held it out to Megan, who didn't hesitate before she bit into the firm fruit. Juice spurted into her mouth and a drop ran down into Syler's palm.

"Sorry about that," Megan said. She delicately licked the juice from her bottom lip before she took Syler's hand in hers and kissed the drop from her skin.

"No problem," Syler said and fell over sideways with a euphoric expression on her face.

The team chatted for a while and Megan joined in and enjoyed trading insults with Taka-chan before he got roped into refereeing a heated debate that began between Syler and Dani.

For some reason, Syler piled three cushions on top of each other and perched on the perilous tower of them. She slapped her hand down on one knee and declared, "Squares because the top and bottom edges are equally distributed among the pieces. That way, if you're sharing with someone, the ratio of top crust, which is arguably the best part, is equal among the participants. In addition, it ensures the symmetry of any corner-based toppings."

"Oh pu-leeze," Dani said as she gestured with the glowing tip of her joint. "Triangles because you can stand the pieces on their sides and it looks pretty, also it's easier to shove into your mouth that way."

"What are we talking about?" Megan asked Atsuko out of the corner of her mouth.

"The great, the endless, Sandwich Debate," she said.

"Oh," Megan replied, blinking.

After a long-winded speech by Syler where she included a made-up fact and was promptly smacked down by Dani, the debate petered out. Syler spread her cushions out and made a kind of sofa for herself with them. She sat cross-legged on the middle one and looked like the ruler of a very small and furniture-deficient country. The group members drifted off to their own pursuits. Atsuko danced by herself to the music while the guys and Dani piled crackers and cheese on top of each other and played a game with them that required the loser to feed the winners.

Megan leaned back on her hands and stared up into the night sky.

"What are you thinking about?" Syler's low voice brought Megan back to earth.

"Nothing really," Megan said. She noticed Syler had a fresh bunch of grapes in her hand and she scooted closer until her knees touched Syler's. "Just how yummy those grapes look."

With a slow smile spreading over her face, Syler picked a grape and held it out for Megan. Syler's eyes flicked down to her fingertips and her smile got wider and naughtier before she put the fruit between her teeth and leaned forward, presenting it with an air of challenge.

A quick glance around assured Megan the others were otherwise occupied and she and Syler were, for the most part, alone in their own world. She put her hands on Syler's knees for balance and rose up to meet the softest lips she'd ever tasted. Megan swallowed her half of the grape and looked up to meet Syler's gaze. The fire in the depths of her eyes called Megan and she pushed Syler back to lie down on her cushions. The sudden action drew a peep of surprise from Syler that Megan thought was adorable. She put both hands on either side of Syler's head and looked down at her for a moment in indecision. Megan saw nothing other than raw need so she bent her elbows and lowered herself until her lips touched Syler's. She closed her eyes and gave herself to the kiss. She let it deepen as Syler's arms came around her.

After only a minute, Megan broke the kiss and sat up to a round of applause. The entire group gathered around them, hooting and clapping madly.

"Good one," Dani said. She gave Megan a thumbs up.

"I didn't think you were paying attention," Megan said by way of explanation. She sat back on her heels and failed to feel anything other than awesome.

Syler tossed a stray cushion toward the group. "Those pervs all have eyes on the backs of their heads. Not paying attention, my ass."

"I don't care if you think I'm a perv," Nobu said. "That was super hot! Aw man, I wish I hadn't broken up with Yuichi-kun!"

"Sorry, can't help you there," Syler said with an unconcerned shrug.

Atsuko piped up, "How about growing a personality?"

"Oooh," the other members of the group said in unison.

Dani said, "And that's a ten-point bump for Atchan on the Burn-o-meter!"

They chortled and joked for a while more, but Megan was focused on one thing only. She wanted to get Syler alone. Soon. No, not soon. Now.

Megan reached over and tapped Syler gently on the thigh. Syler instantly dropped the debate she and Dani were having about fire extinguishers and turned to Megan with her eyebrows raised in a questioning expression. "What is it Meg?"

"Could you walk me home?"

"Sure," Syler said. She got to her feet in a graceful motion and helped Megan up. She held out her arm and Megan happily took it. "Do you want to grab some snacks for the road or anything?"

"That's okay, I have plenty already, and *Pesach* starts tomorrow so I won't be able to eat most of them," Megan said. She looked back at the rest of Syler's team, who were in various degrees of groovy. "Thanks for letting me crash your party. It was a lot of fun."

"No worries," Taka-chan said. He gave a broad wave and said, "Oh and Syler, take your time. We can amuse ourselves fine without you."

"If you're sure," Syler said. She tossed a casual salute to her team before she escorted Megan down the stairs and to the elevator, which already waited at their floor. "Your chariot awaits, my lady," she said with a sweeping gesture.

"You know, I've never been to your room," Megan said as the elevator made its smooth descent. "Maybe you could show it to me? Not tonight, but sometime in the future, if that's okay."

Syler shifted her weight and awkwardly stuffed her hands in her pockets before she said, "Sure. It's not really all that nice, but I wouldn't mind having you over sometime. Honestly, I like your place better."

"Really? It's so small and grungy. I haven't even finished unpacking, the kitchen is more like a galley, and there's no elevator or auto-lock."

"Who cares about all that?" Syler leaned close to her and said in an intimate voice, "It's got that great sofa. And you."

"Hmm," Megan said and tapped her finger on her lower lip. "Well then, how about you come up and give your regards to my sofa?"

"I'd love to," Syler said.

The security doors opened and they stepped out into the cool night. Megan reached out and took Syler's hand as they crossed over the bridge. Underneath them, the river was black and sprinkled with starlight. It was nice hanging out with Syler's team and being free to just be herself. Maybe a bit too free. Megan remembered the show she'd given everyone and the resulting standing ovation.

"I hope they don't mind having me around," Megan said. "Your team, I mean."

"Of course they don't," Syler said. She gave Megan a sideways glance. "You're special to me and that counts for a lot with them. Plus you brought good snacks and provided entertainment and had a fun time without calling the cops even once. What's not to like?"

Megan was glad for the darkness as her ears felt rather radiant. Only a minute later, Megan unlocked the door to her apartment. Instead of the clinically-bright overhead light, Megan switched on her bamboo-shaded floor lamp. Even with the soft glow of the lamp, after the ethereal atmosphere of the rooftop terrace, Megan's own room seemed very mundane. However, the sofa looked inviting and she didn't hesitate to curl up next to Syler who had sprawled down on it.

"Are you feeling okay?" Syler asked. "Tonight was your first taste of the herb, after all."

"I feel good," Megan said. Syler slung her arm over the back of the sofa and Megan snuggled under it. Her heart gave a kick as she leaned in close to Syler and whispered, "But I could be better."

"Oh really? And how can we accomplish that?" Syler sat up and gently traced Megan's lower lip. The contact sent a thrill through Megan's body and zeroed in on the spot between her legs. She shifted her weight as the pressure grew, not helped at all by the lingering herbal buzz.

"Like this," Megan said.

She rose onto her knees and swept Syler up into a kiss that continued right where they'd left off on the rooftop. Megan arched her back in pleasure as Syler's arms came around her and molded their bodies together. Without breaking the kiss, Syler guided Megan down to lie on top of her, their legs intertwined. The hands on Megan's back stroked down to hold her hips in a move Syler favored, both to give and receive. Megan responded to the gentle guidance. She bore down as Syler moved beneath her. Syler's heat pressed against her own where their bodies met.

"I want you to tell me something." Syler pulled away just enough to pant against Megan's lips, "Tell me again what you said back there. In the hospital."

Megan put her hands down and levered herself up enough so she could gaze down into Syler's face. She'd said a lot of things, but one particularly came to mind. "You are beautiful. Your body, your heart, and your soul."

Syler reached up and held Megan's hair back from her face with both hands. "Thank you," she breathed.

Spurred by the emotion in Syler's eyes, Megan drew the tip of her tongue over her lower lip and was rewarded with a long, appreciative look. Megan said, "But I may have forgotten to add a few things. You are also respectful and brave and funny and too damned sexy for your own good."

Syler laughed low in her throat and pulled Megan against her once more. "You don't say."

"Yes, and did I also mention I love your shirt? I think it's the best thing ever. I get to make out with Wonder Woman."

"This is my disguise," Syler said. She bent her head and pressed her lips to Megan's neck in a heated line of kisses, pausing to say, "I'm actually Black Canary."

"Well whoever you are, keep doing what you're doing because I really like it." As she spoke, Megan let her hand drift up the side of Syler's hip and skim under the hem of her T-shirt. She caught her breath and held still, silently asking for permission to continue.

It came in the form of Syler's whispered, "Please, Meg."

Long fingers came down and guided Megan's hands to brush over the sleek skin of Syler's belly and up over the soft ridges of her ribs. Megan let out a whimper of need as Syler shifted so Megan once more cupped the unbelievable softness of her breasts. Megan's body was on fire. Tension rippled through her. She needed more. Syler's kisses on her neck only added to the thick heat that gathered deep inside herself. The T-shirt rode up over Megan's arms and she struggled to keep it at a decent level as she didn't want to expose Syler. Long fingers came up to grasp the hem of the T-shirt.

"Do you want me to take it off?" Syler's voice hummed through Megan's chest.

Her heart gave a great thump. Megan swallowed and said, "Would you really?"

"Yes."

"Then please, Syler," Megan said in a strained voice. "Show me. I want to see you."

She barely had time to draw in a breath before Syler whipped the shirt and undershirt over her head in a single sweeping movement. Megan was greeted by the view of Syler, nearly bare before her, chest heaving under the black sports bra. Megan swallowed hard, unable to take her eyes from the sight. Syler hooked her thumbs under the band of her bra and Megan could barely control the wave of desire that swept through her as Syler pulled it off as well, freeing her breasts. Megan caught her breath at the beauty of her form. Syler's shoulders were slender but mus-cled, her body sleek and graceful. Her breasts were firm and small, the wide, dark aureoles topped with nipples that stood proud and already hard. Megan ached to hold that fullness in her hands, her mouth watered to taste those tempting buds. On the verge of surrendering herself to her desire, Megan froze in indecision. Could she really do something like that? Would Syler let her?

"Meg," Syler groaned as she shifted under Megan. Her breath came harder and she gazed up, her eyes bright with need. "It's okay to touch me. I want to feel you on me. God, I need it."

That was enough. Megan put both hands on Syler's waist and moved up to cup her in one smooth motion. As Megan's hands came around her, Syler's head went back and she gave a deep moan. Megan lowered her head to press a kiss into the valley between Syler's breasts. Her heart and body thrummed. Her thumbs found the taut nipples and heard the hiss of Syler's indrawn breath. Megan reveled in the sensation and stroked Syler until she was rock-hard. With each breath, Syler's hips thrust against her. Megan shivered with building tension as she let her lips trail lower. The supple flesh pebbled and rose as she reached the aureole. Experimentally, Megan brushed the darker skin with her lips. The resulting gasp from Syler resonated through her.

"Yes, that's so good, Meg. I love what you do to me," Syler said in a strained voice. She threw her hands over her head and arched back, presenting herself to Megan. Syler's voice was low and urgent as she said, "I want your mouth on me. Could you do that? Like you're licking cream off a cherry."

Megan got a jolt of arousal as she readied herself to do as Syler asked. Her tongue found the swollen nub and, after giving it a slow, sensual caress, she couldn't hold herself back any more and drew the nipple fully into her mouth. She let out a breath that wanted to be a moan of desire at the wonderful feeling of Syler within herself.

"Oh God, yes Meg."

The words were enough to give Megan the will to continue. She opened her mouth and took Syler in deeper. Megan gave herself to the task and reveled in the feeling. She nearly lost herself to the taste of Syler. Her world narrowed to only that hard bud in her mouth and Megan closed her eyes and let her tongue play with Syler as much as she desired. Her lips made wet sounds as she teased and tasted. A hand stroked gently through her hair as Syler said, "I've got two of them, baby girl."

Megan understood. She released the nipple she'd been concentrating on and switched sides. She wasted no time on teasing before she sucked hard at the firm nub. Megan reeled from both the fact that she had another woman's breast in her mouth as well as how much she enjoyed it—how much they both were. Underneath her, Syler's breathing got ragged and desperate, the movement of her hips more urgent. The tension gripping Syler rose to a dangerous level.

"Okay, okay, that's enough, Meg," Syler said. Startled, Megan released Syler and raised her head. Syler had a hand over her face and her chest heaved. "Oh fuck, if you keep doing that, I'm going to come."

"Sorry, I got carried away," Megan said. She twisted her fingers together, worried that she'd pushed Syler too far.

"Oh no, sweetie," Syler sat up and grabbed both of Megan's hands in hers. She was half-naked, fully erect nipples glistened in the lamplight, but Syler looked just as comfortable and brash as she did in scrubs and a white coat. "You are amazing. It's um, been a while for me and I'm a bit hair-triggered. I just need to go home and finish up before I spontaneously combust in your face."

The words evoked a dangerously compelling image. Megan slipped down to kneel on the floor at Syler's side. Her own need throbbed painfully and she could only imagine the torment Syler was in at that moment.

An impulse born of pure hunger came to Megan and she said. "You could do that here." She shifted and the deep, thrumming tension in her thighs reminded Megan of her own perilous state. She swallowed and said, "Or I could do it for you."

"Meg, I couldn't ask you to do that." Syler paused and Megan could see she was wavering.

"I don't mind," Megan said and cringed at her words. Was there really a polite way to tell a person you'd love to jerk them off? "I can't in good conscience let you just walk around outside like that."

"Are you sure?" Syler asked as her eyes searched Megan's face. "I mean, I don't want you to do anything while you're buzzed that you'll regret later."

"I'm absolutely sure I want to do this," Megan said. "And I'm not that buzzed. Syler, I need to touch you. If you're all right with that."

"Yeah, I am. You sweet thing, you really are the best girlfriend ever," Syler murmured.

Syler let out a breath and reclined back against the pile of cushions. Still focused on Megan, Syler reached down and pulled her jeans open with a quick tug. She lifted her hips to slide them down a fraction. The movement exposed the wide elastic waistband of her underwear. That alone brought a humming thrill of arousal to Megan and she bit down hard on her lip to control herself. Megan edged forward on her knees until she was pressed up against Syler. Megan trembled with nerves and anticipation, but the look of trust and need in Syler's expression gave her the courage to continue. Syler reached out and drew Megan down to meet her in a slow, searching kiss. Megan's body grew warm and electric as Syler's tongue filled her mouth. Megan was extremely aware of Syler's bare skin, separated from her only by a single layer of clothing. Megan put her hand on Syler's thigh and the motion was met by a low moan against her lips. Encouraged, Megan trailed up Syler's leg. Her fingers skimmed lightly over the crotch of Syler's jeans and Syler bucked against her, silently begging for more, but Megan just continued her slow, upward journey until her fingers were resting on the firm skin of Syler's belly.

The waistband of Syler's underwear was beneath Megan's fingers when Syler broke the kiss. She touched her forehead to Megan's and whispered, "I have one rule."

"All right, just say it."

"Outside only," Syler said between heaving breaths. "I've never had anything inside me and I'd like to keep it that way."

A strange jolt fluttered through her chest as Megan realized that meant Syler was a virgin. Technically, anyway. However, Megan just nodded and said, "That's fine, you can trust me." She bit her lip and glanced down, suddenly overwhelmed with the reality of the situation as she saw Syler's jean-clad legs spread over the cushions of her sofa. Syler's body trembled. She was supine in surrender.

With a burst of uncertainty, Megan cleared her throat and said, "I've never done this before. Um, well, not to anyone else. Just let me know if I'm not doing anything right."

"Sweetie," Syler gasped, "I'm so fucking close right now there's pretty much nothing you could do to stop me."

"Okay then," Megan said in a soft voice. "Lay back and I'll take care of you."

She was very aware of Syler's eyes on her as she put two fingers into her mouth and wet them thoroughly before she put her hand flat on Syler's belly. With that, she eased her hand down. Her fingers delved under the waistband and stroked through the coarse patch of hair. The instant Megan's fingers met slick flesh, Syler let out an inarticulate cry and her hands clutched at the back of Megan's shirt. Megan could barely believe the feelings that flamed through her as she felt the resilient softness of Syler's outer lips against her fingers. Megan parted them and drew in a breath of wonder. Syler was so wet, Megan needn't have bothered with licking her fingers, although she had to admit the act had been quite sexy in itself. Her fingers slid over the delicate skin until she found Syler's hardness within the velvet folds.

"Oh yeah, right there," Syler gasped. She reached up and took Megan's face in her hands. "Kiss me, Meg. Hard and deep."

Megan's belly gave a jolt at the request. She pressed Syler back into the cushions with a fierce kiss, letting her tongue telegraph the motion of her fingers. Their bodies rocked together as Megan delved into the slick heat. Her fingers stroked in quick circles. Syler was right, it only took a few swift caresses of the engorged flesh before Syler's body was gripped by an intense tension. She broke away from Megan's lips and drew in fast, shuddering breaths.

"Keep going hard and steady like that Meg," she gritted in Megan's ear. "Oh fuck, I'm gone."

The tremors started up and Megan held herself still as Syler's climax ripped through her. The peak was so strong and Syler's arms were so tight around her that all Megan could do was suck in a few breaths and hold herself still as Syler arched against her.

Slowly, the waves ebbed and Syler buried her face against Megan's shoulder. Her body went limp and her breaths came in great heaves. Megan withdrew from the sultry heat, which caused a few more jolts to rock Syler's hips. Her fingertips were sticky with Syler's essence and Megan was seized by the desire to taste it. Startled at the sudden, intense impulse, Megan surreptitiously grabbed a tissue before she slipped her arms around Syler.

With Syler's body nestled against her own, Megan dropped a few kisses to Syler's sweat-damp brow and whispered, "I've got you."

Megan held Syler to her. The last aftershocks faded from Syler and left her body soft and limp. What they had just done wasn't only about having fun or even releasing tension. Syler put herself in a very vulnerable position, both physically and emotionally. She trusted Megan to respect her in that moment of complete surrender. Megan could only hope she'd managed to rise to the occasion. Her lingering doubts vanished as Syler flopped back against the cushions and gave a catlike stretch. She opened her eyes and looked straight into Megan's soul.

"Megan Maier," Syler said in a weak voice, "You just fucking blew my mind. That was actually a first for me. Sorry I went off so fast but you were just so fucking good."

"Really? I'm glad to hear that," Megan said with a flash of surprise before she understood. Of course. Syler had been a *bari-tachi*. It was the first time for someone to please her, dear God. The thought left Megan breathless. However she was feeling too happy and relaxed to let things get serious. She got a wicked impulse and purred, "Maybe next time I won't let you finish so quickly. I think I'd like to draw things out, tease you until you're just begging for me. And then maybe you'll tell me your favorite baseball team."

"Oh God, Meg that would probably kill me. You are just as evil as you are sexy." Syler reached out and took Megan's hand. Slowly and deliberately, she kissed the fingers that had just taken part in the previously mentioned blowing of her mind. "You really are the best," Syler said. She dropped another kiss onto the palm of Megan's hand before she glanced up and asked, "Are you sure you're all right? I wouldn't be opposed to returning the favor, if that's okay with you."

"Actually, I'm on my period," Megan admitted. "It's day two and I was feeling a bit crampy before, but I seem to have been magically cured. It must be something in the air."

"I'm glad you're feeling all right now," Syler said. She leaned close and whispered, "But think about it, baby girl. I know it's kind of against the rules for you, but I have access to gloves and you know I don't have a problem with blood."

"Another time and I'd consider it," Megan said. "But I just don't feel right, and you have to get back to your guests. I'm sorry—"

"No don't apologize, Meg. I'm fine with going at whatever pace you feel comfortable with. I was half-joking anyway."

"Okay, thanks for understanding," Megan said. "How about I get us some tea? It'll be a few minutes if you want to freshen up."

"Thanks, I think I will," Syler said.

Syler heaved herself off the sofa and pulled her discarded sports bra over her head as she wandered toward the washroom.

By the time Megan returned with cups of cold wheat tea, Syler was dressed again and looked extremely relaxed.

Megan sipped her tea and said, "I'm sure everyone will be wondering about why it took you so long to walk me home. Well, okay, I guess it's pretty obvious. I hope nobody gives you a hard time when you go back." She nudged Syler and gave her a little smirk. "You're glowing."

"Don't worry about it," Syler said. "Taka-chan and Nobu will be jealous, Atsuko won't care, and Dani will give me a high five, try to get me to spill the details—which I won't—and then go home and jump her husband."

"That's...good?"

"It is," Syler said. She stood and pulled Megan into a hug. She stroked a hand up and down Megan's back and murmured, "Thank you, Meg."

A happy flush filled her and Megan returned the hug. She wished for a kiss, but knew that in the state she was in that could easily lead to Syler being even later, and she didn't want to keep Syler away from her team any longer. After Syler left, Megan sat in her empty room with the TV on in the background, her heart full of new emotions and her body aching from thwarted arousal.

Chapter Ten

ON FRIDAY AFTERNOON, when Megan went home to change for that evening's Seder, she stood, stumped and fuming in front of her closet. Charles's order for her to cover her knees rankled her and the contrary American in her raised its head. Megan was seized with the urge to follow the letter but not the spirit of the imperative. She nearly grabbed the unopened Singapore Airlines hostess uniform she'd won in a raffle on her way back from Thailand, but calmed down enough to text Syler for her opinion. The brief text conversation resulted in Syler lying on Megan's futon while Megan, in only her slip and camisole, held up various outfits and debated their appropriateness. Syler enjoyed Megan's state of undress far too much and wasn't really much help, but Megan liked her being there anyway.

After she decided on a plain and modest dress and jacket combination, Megan draped the outfit over a nearby pile of boxes. She slouched back against the wall.

"I wish I was going with you," Megan said with her eyes on the ceiling.

"Maybe someday," Syler said in a soft voice.

"Actually I wish I was staying here with you." Megan gazed at Syler who was spread out in a most unselfconscious sprawl, comfortable and handsome in her worn jeans and the Wonder Woman T-shirt Megan regarded as her favorite thing in the world. Syler's long-sleeved undershirt was a deep red and increased her overall aura of superhero-ness.

Syler shook her head and grinned before she said, "You wouldn't want to deny Charles the pleasure of your company. I'm sure it's the closest he's ever going to get to actually having a date with a willing human. And not just any human, he's getting a date with an intelligent, accomplished person of impeccable class who also happens to be foxy as hell."

"Don't even think that," Megan said with an internal wince even as she flushed at the words Syler used to describe her. "Tonight is so not anything even resembling a date." She let her gaze rest on Syler for a moment before she said in a low, sultry voice, "The only person who's allowed to date me is you."

"Good," Syler said.

The heady feeling from the compliments inflamed Megan's desire and she got an absolutely wicked idea. With a carefully impassive expression, Megan stepped over the end of the futon and propped her foot up on her dresser.

"There's one more thing I have to decide," Megan said, "And that's the issue of leg-wear."

With that, she ran both hands from her ankle to her thigh. She allowed the lacy hem of her slip to slide up to a dangerous degree and was treated to Syler falling back onto the crumpled-up quilt with an expression of surprise. That quickly turned into one of frank appreciation as Megan pulled out a pair of black, lace-topped stockings. While Megan usually wore thigh-highs out of necessity, given the fact that even the largest size of Japan-made pantyhose was too short for her, the pair in her hand was much fancier and sexier than her usual ones.

"Yes, these will do nicely." With her eyes modestly lowered, Megan took her time pulling on the first stocking. She drew the delicate material over her foot and ankle and took care to smooth any potential wrinkles out by trailing her fingers over the sheer stocking. Slowly she followed the gentle curves of her knee and thigh. Finally, she stroked her hands over the wide lace band and repeated the action with the other one. Satisfied, Megan put her foot down and clasped her hands in front of herself.

"Meg, you're killing me," Syler said in a choked voice. "That's the sexiest thing I've ever seen in my entire fucking life."

"Really? I had no idea," Megan said and blinked innocently. "I was simply putting on my stockings."

She dropped to her knees on the futon and made a happy sound as Syler's arms came around her and pulled Megan against her chest.

"By the way, you can call me anytime you need wardrobe advice. Like when you're putting on your stockings," Syler said. First she kissed Megan lightly on the temple, then slowly worked down to the side of her neck. "Or taking them off."

Syler gave Megan a light nip on one shoulder. Her hands lingered on Megan's back before they stroked down to hold her around the waist. Megan rolled onto her back and Syler followed.

She ended up lying on her side with her head propped up on her hand. Megan took Syler's free hand in hers and laced their fingers together briefly before she brushed a light kiss across Syler's knuckles. Once Megan released her, Syler pressed her palm very gently against Megan's belly. The warmth of her hand filled Megan and she arched her back in pleasure.

"How are the cramps today?" Syler asked.

"Better," Megan said. She let out a purr and said, "Much better, especially with you here. Syler, Don't move your hand."

"I won't," Syler said in a low voice. She shifted closer and pressed their bodies together. She slipped her arm under Megan's head and made a pillow for her. "Is this okay?" Syler asked.

"Yes, but let me know if your arm's going to fall asleep."

"Nothing on me is going to fall asleep, not when you're this close to me," Syler told her as she lowered her head to drop a line of soft kisses on the side of Megan's neck. She trailed down to where Megan's cleavage peeked out of the lacy neckline of her camisole. With one last kiss, Syler whispered, "God, you're so sweet and sexy, Meg. I'm never going to get tired of this." She paused and asked in a sultry voice, "Are you sure I can't move my hand?"

"That depends," Megan answered as her heart gave a pleasant jump. "Where do you want to put it?"

"I was thinking," Syler whispered against the softness of Megan's breast, "Up a bit. Maybe ending up around here." The tip of her tongue darted out and Syler traced the line of Megan's cleavage.

That broke the dam of Megan's control and Megan responded by pushing Syler down and kissing her thoroughly. She welcomed the wandering hands with a hungry moan. It was quite some time before Megan had been able to get dressed for the dinner.

BACK IN THE office, Megan sat at her desk and listened to the muted sounds of the other people in the room. The nurses were having some kind of meeting in the tea corner and the other occupant, one of the junior doctors who regularly worked in after-hours admissions, tapped away at his computer. Megan had a number of reports spread out in front of her, but she wasn't paying attention to them. She was thinking only of Syler.

Megan pursed her lips and balanced her pencil under her nose. She thought about the way Syler would look at her without wavering, which made Megan feel as if she was the only person in the universe. She loved the way she felt when she was in Syler's arms. Megan let out a sigh as a bubble of giddiness filled her. It wasn't only the physical things that she loved. Megan loved the way Syler spoke to her and treated her with such tenderness and respect, how Syler gave herself, both body and heart, so freely and never pressured Megan, or even acted like she expected anything in return.

She loved Syler's unconventional approach to life and how she gave absolutely zero fucks about anybody who disapproved of her. Megan loved how Syler would blast Bon Jovi and Aerosmith during surgery, how she always got into the oddest arguments with random people and didn't mind if she won or lost as long as she could work a good monologue in there somewhere. Megan loved — she drew in a quick breath.

She loved Syler.

The pencil fell onto the desk and rolled off the edge, but Megan didn't notice. Her hands clutched at the scattered papers as Megan faced the knowledge squarely for the first time. She had fallen in love with Syler. She felt wonderful and terrified at the same time.

Her thoughts were interrupted by Charles's voice, which was even more grating and annoying than usual.

"I trust you are able to set aside your very important tasks in favor of accompanying me to only the most sacred event in our faith," he said with what Megan judged to be a definite sneer. "As well, I'm sure I don't have to remind you that Shabbos begins at sundown."

"Oh yes, of course," Megan said. Clumsy with haste and aggravation, she swept the offending papers and pen into one of the desk drawers. All of it ended up in a jumbled heap and she slammed the drawer shut. She swallowed her annoyance and put on a fake smile before she turned around and stood. "I was just finishing up here."

"All right, then. Shall we?"

Megan didn't miss the calculating way Charles gave her a quick inspection from head to foot and back up again. She submitted to the scrutiny with her head up and was very glad he didn't have x-ray vision as she was sure the stockings that Syler had appreciated so much were not on the list of Charles-approved Shabbos dinner wear. His elbow suddenly jutted out at an odd angle and Megan stared at it for a beat until she realized with an unpleasant jolt she was meant to take it and allow Charles to parade her through the hallways of the hospital like a prize trout.

That was not on the list of things Megan was going to allow to happen. She faked a joking expression and poked at him with a finger. She was very aware that a few of the nurses turned from their meeting to glance at her.

"Come on, now Charles," she said. "It's not the nineteen fifties anymore. I can walk perfectly well by myself."

She picked up her bag and slung it over her shoulder. The chocolates she'd been instructed to get were still in the plastic bag from the grocery. She didn't miss the scathing look Charles gave her.

"I should inform you, Megan," he said, incidentally pronouncing her name exactly the opposite to what Megan preferred, "There is no eruv set up here to allow for public carrying." Charles paused as if waiting for Megan to put her bag down. She didn't.

While Megan had been careful to observe the Shabbos prohibitions as best she could, her pockets were full of tampons and she didn't feel quite ready to face the world outside without her pill bottle. She noticed Charles wore a tie clip made out of his own key, which allowed him to keep it with him even on the Sabbath. Megan didn't feel like explaining and she didn't think she'd win if she tried to argue her case, so she just stood still.

When Megan didn't move or speak, Charles took a step back and turned to head for the door. As he walked, he said, "A small group has been trying to set one up, though, I oppose the idea."

"Why?" Megan said. She hurried to keep up with Charles. "Wouldn't it make things easier for everyone if there was an eruv here?"

"I think having a loophole area is detrimental to self-discipline. It leads to carelessness and ill-observance. What if the barrier wasn't properly maintained? That could lead to an unwitting breach of the rules and I do not wish to risk that."

As they walked, Charles went on at great length about his ideas about observance, and Megan felt that each word was a jab at herself. None too pleased to be with the Shabbos-police, Megan had a hard time staying neutral. By the time they got to the parking lot, Megan already deeply regretted allowing herself to be put into that situation. She sat in the lemon-scented car and on the short drive from the hospital, entertained a fantasy about getting out of the dinner by faking an illness and inviting Syler over to "take care" of her. Those pleasant, bordering on naughty, thoughts kept Megan entertained until Charles parked in a coin parking lot near the tall, three-story house where Rabbi Sharon and her husband Peter lived. Charles put on a superior air and suggested that Megan leave her bag in the car so she would not disgrace herself by disrespecting the Sabbath in the presence of their rabbi. Megan stifled her sigh as she stashed her purse under the seat.

The setting sun cast their shadows in front of them as they walked the short distance to the stately, red-brick house. Rabbi Sharon answered the door at Charles's knock. The entrance hall was full of shoes and the house rang with talking and laughter.

"*Gut yontif,*" Rabbi Sharon greeted them.

"*Chag Sareach, Rev Kleiner,*" Charles answered in a pompous way.

The rabbi hugged Megan and shook Charles's hand while Peter beamed at them from the hallway. He carried a basket of yarmulkes and squeezed by to put it down on the shoe cupboard. Megan covered her hair with a small lace cap and Charles always wore his own, so Megan assumed the basket was for any gentile guests who joined the festive dinner.

"I'm glad you could come, Meirav," Rabbi Sharon said. Megan passed her the gift of chocolates that Charles was so insistent she get, relieved to be rid of it. As they followed the men into the living room, Rabbi Sharon leaned close to Megan and said, "It's lovely to see you've come with Chanoch. He's never brought anyone before and I have to say, you make a wonderful couple."

Startled and dismayed, Megan shook her head. "No, it's not like that. Not at all."

"Oh really? Well, I wouldn't rule it out too quickly. I know your parents would be pleased to know you weren't alone anymore. And I think anyone would agree you two would make a fine match, and not only because of your family connections."

Megan resisted rolling her eyes and was saved from having to think of a response by their arrival in the living room. Most of the other guests either sat on various chairs or reclined on floor cushions. The air was full of conversations in various languages. Children ran around and giggled. In the other room, Megan caught a glimpse of two long white-covered tables where they would have their dinner. Already the tables were set with candles and the round dishes that held the symbolic foods. Next to each place setting were small prayer books. The bundles of matzo were also on the tables, ready to be broken, and one piece hidden for the children to find. Megan relaxed into the jovial atmosphere as she remembered her own many Passovers with her parents and relatives over the years. It had been a while, but Megan felt like she was coming home.

Megan ducked away from Charles and found Jayco, who graciously offered her his spot on the floor. He scooted over and Megan smoothed her skirt over her knees as she sank down onto the cushion.

"Happy payday!" Jayco announced and held up a hand for Megan to high-five. "I am so ready for it."

"Me too," Megan said. "I can't wait to actually get some things for my place. Starting with dishes from the pottery festival. I hope they've got some nice pieces."

"They should have," Jayco said. "I looked up the sellers online and there's this one studio I'm really interested in. They make dragon-themed dishes and stuff."

"Really?" Megan tucked her feet up underneath herself and listened intently as Jayco told her about the various studios he'd discovered. The Millers came over and Megan enjoyed a brief conversation with them and awed over numerous photos of a pair of beagles Edie proudly called her grand-pups.

After a while, the party moved to the dining room. Resigned, but not surprised, Megan took her assigned seat next to Charles. She was already more than ready for the dinner to be over.

The evening started off with the ritual hand washing. A woman Megan had met only in passing at the synagogue came over to them carrying a filled cup with a bowl in her other hand and a towel slung over her arm. Megan waited for Charles to go first, then slipped her ring off and placed it next to her plate as the water was poured over her hands. Megan dried her hands on the towel and the woman moved onto the next person. She reached down and got a jolt. Her ring was gone.

She knew exactly what had happened. Megan stabbed Charles with the iciest glare she could muster.

"Give it back," Megan hissed. She didn't care if people looked at her.

Charles returned her glare with his own, obviously not pleased with her sudden anger. Wordlessly, he tossed the ring onto the table and Megan snatched it up. Her skin was hot and felt too tight. Distraction came as Rabbi Sharon stood and gave the blessing, even though Megan felt anything but blessed. The meal progressed with a lively mix of ritual, prayers, talking, eating, and drinking. Megan was almost back to her usual good cheer when Charles put his wine glass down with a significant thump.

He addressed the general area."Passover is a time for us to celebrate freedom. Not only the obvious, the freeing of the Jews from slavery, but also it is a time for us to free ourselves from the shackles of the past."

Megan didn't like the direction Charles was going with his lecture. Her hackles rose. She didn't speak and Charles continued. He glanced at her at significant points.

"The past is dead. Holding onto what has gone before is not only unhealthy, but it is also harmful for the life of the person mired in it. This obsession with something that has logically ended is, quite frankly, embarrassing. Memories are a cold companion and moving on is the only healthy course of action."

"So we have to just throw away all our memories?" Megan asked. "What if they are precious and comforting? What if they're all a person has left?" The couple across the table from them had listened with polite interest, but with Megan's outburst, they looked at each other with unease.

"I find that hard to believe," Charles said. He folded his hands and looked superior. "When memories interfere with the will to continue living in a proactive way, then it is beneficial for everyone to move past them. To put the past where it belongs, in the past."

Megan seethed, but she knew she would lose her temper if the discussion progressed any further. She hated herself for capitulating, but she just nodded and said, "I can see where that might be appropriate." She tiled her head and faked a smile as she directed her next question to the couple across from them, "So, Nobuko, you were saying that you and Yoshihiro were thinking of spending your Golden Week vacation in Nagano? That sounds wonderful. What were you planning to do there?"

The discussion drifted to safer topics and Megan was relieved, although she felt Charles looking at her a few times throughout the evening. As soon as she could, Megan escaped from the table and played with the children, glad for their boisterous buffer zone.

When the Seder ended, everyone bid each other cheerful goodnights and Megan slipped out of the warm house with a guilty feeling of relief. However, her penance was not over yet as Charles decided it was his duty to walk her home. Megan's purse was being held hostage in his car, so she had no choice but to start the journey home with him. Except she did not want to suffer through his plodding conversation any more than she had to.

"It's not far," Megan protested as soon she she'd gotten her bag. "And it's out of your way."

"It is dangerous for a woman to walk alone at night," he said. "I am assuming you do not wish to be attacked, dragged into the bushes, and raped?"

"What?" Megan's face froze in an expression of disgust.

Charles fell into step with her. "If you would *like* your body and dignity to be defiled, then be my guest and go wherever you like all by yourself."

Megan just shook her head and tolerated his stolid presence. She walked as fast as she could without making it obvious she wanted to be rid of him.

"Did you enjoy the dinner?"

"Yes, it was lovely," Megan said automatically. She started to dredge up a semi-honest thanks but Charles interrupted.

"I noticed you did seem to enjoy spending time with the children. You do have a way with them."

"They're all good kids," Megan said with a smile. That was the one fun part of the evening and she was determined to keep that as her main memory of the event.

"Yet you don't want any of your own? It seems hypocritical."

Megan gave a fake laugh even though she didn't want to

have that discussion again. "Well, I get to play with them and get them all riled up and then hand them back to their parents and go home to my quiet, non-childproofed home."

"Don't you think it's selfish to deny your children their chance to be alive?"

"No, I don't think that's selfish," Megan said. "It's more selfish to have children with the intention of making them take care of you when you're older, or to magically fix some problem in your marriage. And I think it's also selfish to bring more people into this world when there are existing ones who need a secure home and loving care." She'd had this discussion a number of times before with different people and she wanted to cover as many bases as she could before Charles could get to them.

"What if everybody thought like you do? The human race would die out. Do you want that? What if your parents had thought like that?"

Megan let out a long breath that wasn't a sigh. If her parents had not wanted children, then Megan would not care because she wouldn't exist and she would have been spared from suffering through the discussion she was currently having with Charles. The argument was endless and Megan had no hope of winning. She just said, "At any rate, it's not an option for me right now. I'm actually—" She nearly said too much and bit her lip to quell the compulsion. That man really did bring out the worst in her.

"You owe it to your faith and your bloodline to carry on to the next generation. Besides, all women want to have babies," Charles barreled on. "You will too, one day."

"Uh huh," Megan grunted. At long last, her building came into view and Megan picked up the pace. "Thanks for walking me home, Charles," she said. They arrived at the front steps and Megan turned to him with a smile that was born of relief more than anything else. "I'll see you at work."

Megan's heart gave a leap of alarm as Charles resolutely followed her into the lobby.

"I will bid you goodnight then," he said.

Charles reached out and Megan looked down in alarm as his hands closed over her shoulders. She was trapped in his clammy grip. Before she registered what was happening, Charles bent his head and came at her. With a yelp of panic, Megan shoved him away and jerked herself back a step. White pain exploded behind her eyes as the back of Megan's head impacted with the mailboxes.

Her bag fell to the floor and she went down to her knees. She grabbed the back of her head and hissed out a curse.

"What language, Megan. It is unbecoming a woman of your upbringing. You really do have a number of vile habits, don't you?"

Through tear-filled eyes, Megan looked up. Charles held her bag in one hand with her pill bottle in the other. He read the label with a clinically disinterested expression. Megan lunged for the bottle, missed, and staggered into the middle of the lobby. She dearly wanted to let loose with a few more choice words.

"Don't touch me," Megan said. She tried to control the volume of her voice. "And do not touch my things."

"Excuse me," Charles said in a bland way. "Would you like me to put everything back on the floor where it was?"

Megan just fixed him with a withering glare.

"How are you dealing with the side effects?" he asked and gave the bottle a shake. "Loss of sexual function and decline in libido are the most common I've heard. This particular medication has been found to cause anorgasmia in some patients."

"That is none of your business," Megan said through gritted teeth. She shook with the urge to lash out, to slam Charles back into the wall and let him know how it felt to have someone invade his personal space. "Now give that back."

"It looks like you're due for a refill," Charles said and passed Megan her bottle and bag. Megan grabbed both and hung onto them. "You really shouldn't let your prescription run out. I will take care of it for you."

"I don't need your pills," Megan said. "And I think you should go now."

Charles looked at her for a long moment before he turned to go. "Thank you for a lovely evening, Megan," he said with a smile that did not reach his eyes. "Hopefully the first of many. Goodnight and sweet dreams."

Megan could only shake her head in disbelief. As the front door swung shut behind Charles, Megan grabbed her key from her mailbox and bolted for the stairwell. Her mind whirled.

Charles had tried to kiss her! He acted like he had some claim on her! Megan slammed and locked the door behind herself and collapsed onto her sofa. Bathed in the warm light of the lamp Megan turned on before she left, she crushed a cushion to her chest as she pondered how the hell she was going to get out of that situation.

After a while, Megan got up and paced around her room, too full of anger-fueled energy to sit still. She wished she could text Syler, or even plug in her lights to call her over, but Megan dismissed the notions. That evening she'd flaunted the Shabbos restrictions too much already and she wanted to at least make the effort to keep them, for her own pride if nothing else.

The events of the day simmered. Megan scowled at various things in her room to distract herself. She couldn't turn on the TV or listen to music on her phone. She couldn't play any video games, and neither could she even unpack her boxes as they were taped shut. At least she remembered to pre-tear a bunch of toilet paper, she thought with dark humor. Megan knew the limitations on various activities was to encourage people to spend time with each other and have freedom from daily drudgery to rest and pray, but Megan was bored and lonely.

It was no use to fret over the things she couldn't do. She needed to focus on what she could do.

At any rate, she didn't want to be stuck in her room anymore. After changing into comfortable and warmer clothing, Megan trotted out to the little park across from her apartment. She wasn't afraid of anybody bothering her. The area was quite safe and the cheerfully dilapidated shops that flanked the park were still open. The street was awash in the leaked light from their windows. A few cars were in the empty lot next to the park. Megan assumed they belonged either to customers of the little pub on the corner or the closing staff of the shops.

At that hour, the park was deserted and Megan idly sat on one of the swings. Her feet skimmed lightly over the hard-packed dirt as she gently swung back and forth. She raised her face to the night sky and looked at the stars. For a while, Megan amused herself by picking out the constellations she recognized. The hum of the passing cars was the only sound and Megan felt the tension and anger of the day leaving her. While the whole business with Charles was odious, she enjoyed the evening otherwise.

Megan pondered the turn her life had taken recently. She never thought she'd feel the way she did now. She never thought she would fall in love again, but she had. And with all of her heart and soul. She closed her eyes and drank in the fragrant night breeze. Even as she wondered at her own emotions, Megan was aware of a gnawing worry at the back of her mind. There were things she'd never told anyone, secrets she had not even dared to breathe aloud. What if she bared all of herself to Syler, let her see who Megan truly was? Could Syler forgive her—could anyone?

It was a long shot. Megan couldn't even forgive herself. Her eyes popped open and she stared into the sky as tears blurred the stars into sparkling rainbows. A moment later, she heard footsteps and sat upright when a familiar lanky body came into view.

"Syler!" Megan called out. Her heart gave a happy jump and her morose mood lifted as Syler loped into the little park and slung herself down on the swing next to Megan.

"Fancy running into you here," Syler said with a grin. She kicked both feet out in front of herself. "Luka just took me out for a drink at Ken-mama's in exchange for listening to his troubles."

"Is he all right?" Megan asked.

"He will be, I think. Poor Lukie's a bit hung up about Jayco," Syler said with a sideways glance at Megan. "They've been talking a lot and flirting a bit so Luka asked him a few questions. Apparently Jayco's never had a boyfriend, but he's never had a girlfriend either. He seems a bit ambivalent either way. For the moment, Luka's playing it cool, and I agreed it was the best thing to do in this case."

"I don't have any advice but I hope we can all still be friends," Megan said. "No matter what happens or doesn't happen between them."

"I'm sure it'll be all right," Syler said. "Luka and Jayco are both reasonable people. Anyway, how was your evening?"

"Oh, dear God above," Megan put her head in her hands. "Is it okay if I don't talk about it yet? I just want to enjoy being here with you."

"Of course," Syler said. She got to her feet and came over to stand behind Megan.

As Syler's arms came around her, Megan straightened up and

leaned back with a happy sigh.

"Is this all right?" Syler whispered in her ear.

"Yes, it is," Megan replied. She drew in a quick breath and tilted her head back as Syler's lips pressed against the side of her neck in a soft kiss. Her body thrilled from the contact and she ached for more. "But it's a bit cold out here. Do you want to come up for a minute?"

"That sounds nice." Syler's voice was warm, her lips brushed Megan's skin as she spoke.

The arms around Megan dropped and Syler stepped forward and held out a hand, which Megan took. Together they walked out of the park and Megan was seized by a giddy urge, spurred by the light touch of Syler's fingers on hers. Megan raised their clasped hands as they reached the orange circle of streetlight and gave a pirouette like a ballroom dancer. Her feet caught on each other and she let out a squeak as she lurched forward.

Before Megan could even register what was happening, Syler scooped her up and held her in a strong yet gentle embrace.

"Easy there, Meg," Syler said. "I've got you."

"Sorry," Megan said with a quick laugh. She didn't move to break Syler's hold on her. "It looks like those four glasses of Passover wine caught up with me," she said and with a reluctant sigh, took a step back.

"Don't worry about it," Syler said. She bent close to Megan and spoke in her ear, "How about I show you some more dance moves when we get back to your place?"

"Hmm, maybe—yes!" Megan blurted out. She felt as if she was electrified, her fingers and toes tingled as she and Syler crossed the street and entered the familiar scruffiness of the lobby.

Chapter Eleven

"DOCTOR TERADA, IF I may have a few minutes of your time," Megan said in a clipped voice. She shifted the bulky pile of x-rays and files in her arms as she caught up with Syler, who was just finishing her morning rounds. The evening before ended quite pleasantly with Syler's "dance lesson" being performed mostly horizontally. Megan hadn't wanted to mar it with the nasty events that had happened at the Seder as well as after it, but she couldn't keep silent about it much longer.

Syler turned and gave Megan a smile that melted her knees and reminded Megan that she had more on her mind than just talking. The previous evening ended far too soon for her liking, and a few days ago she made an interesting discovery she wanted to share.

"Of course, Doctor Maier. I assume this is about the matter we were collaborating on earlier?"

"That's correct. I have a few items of utmost importance I need to discuss with you. This way please," Megan said. She swallowed the jolt of adrenaline as she ushered Syler up the stairs and down the hall of the quietest part of the hospital. Megan came to a stop in front of an unmarked door and shouldered it open.

Once they were inside, Syler raised both eyebrows and looked around at the interior, which was illuminated by a single overhead bulb.

"You realize this is a linen closet," Syler said with humor in her voice and a wicked spark dancing in her eyes. She had her hands loosely buried in the pockets of her lab coat and looked singularly striking that morning.

"Is it really? How careless of me. I happened to come across this room in my exploration of the hospital, and I merely thought it was a small and rather oddly-equipped meeting room," Megan said. She dropped her files and backed Syler up against the door. "A meeting room, that for some reason locks from the inside," Megan purred as she pressed up against the supple strength of

Syler's body. "With your permission?"

"God, yes, do it."

Megan reached behind Syler and slid the deadbolt shut.

"You are amazing," Syler murmured. She reached out and cupped Megan's face in her hands. Megan didn't need any more encouragement and she surged forward, catching Syler full on the mouth in a long, deep kiss that left both of them gasping.

Megan closed her eyes and snuggled into Syler's embrace as Syler's heartbeat thundered in her ears. Spurred to speak, Megan took a deep breath and said, "Syler, I need to tell you something. I think Charles really believed we were on a date. He tried to kiss me last night." Megan shuddered at the memory. Syler's body stiffened against hers. Syler dropped her arms and moved away from Megan a fraction.

Megan hastened to add, "I didn't let him."

"That's good," Syler said. She faced the wall. No emotion showed on her face.

With a sick jolt in her gut, Megan reached out and caught Syler's hands. "Look at me," she said. "Syler, this is not going to be history repeating itself. First, I would rather stick hot needles in my eyeballs than actually spend time voluntarily with that pompous, obnoxious *paskudnik*. The only reason he even got a chance was he took me by surprise. He crossed the line and I'm not going to let it happen again. Ever. Second, I have you." Megan was grateful for the look of relief and trust Syler gave her. "You are my one and only. I promise you. You do believe me, right?"

"Of course," Syler said. Her shoulders sagged and her expression softened. "It's difficult to forget the past sometimes."

"I'm not her," Megan said. She took a step back and pulled her stethoscope from where she'd slung it around her neck and stuffed it into a pocket of her lab coat. The neatly folded rows of hospital linens were firm and unyielding at her back. She lowered her head and gazed up through her lashes at Syler. Megan purred, "Come over here and I'll prove it."

Megan basked in Syler's heated gaze as she raised a hand to her own collar. Her fingers deftly undid the top button of her blouse and worked down until she felt a cool draft caress her bare skin under the sheer lace of her bra, much different from the usual domestically-made garments, which tended to be thick, over-decorated, and padded. Megan was very aware of the low murmur of appreciation as she bared herself to Syler's inspection. The imported and somewhat pricey front-opening bra Megan discovered in the local department store proved itself a very worthy investment. She opted against a camisole that day, harboring a few naughty inklings of what its absence might provoke that seemed not to be unfounded.

Slowly, reverently, Syler came forward and took Megan's face in her hands. Their lips met in a soft kiss that was not nearly enough for Megan. With a quick motion that was answered by an appreciative groan from deep in Syler's throat, Megan took Syler by the hips and pulled their bodies together. As she ground herself against the slender thigh that slipped between her own, Megan opened her mouth to Syler. She needed Syler with a harsh desperation that only drove Megan to press hard against her.

"Touch me," Megan panted when she finally tore herself from the kiss. By that time, she'd gotten her blouse completely unbuttoned and the cotton of Syler's shirt was rough against her bare skin. It wasn't enough.

Syler didn't reply in words, but instead captured her mouth once more in a deep kiss. Megan arched against her. She wanted Syler's hands on her more than anything. The hands that held her head lowered to her shoulders and Megan's breath hitched in anticipation. Syler dropped her lips to Megan's neck.

"You are so beautiful," Syler said in a harsh whisper. "My God, Meg. Sweet Meirav."

Her hands found Megan's fullness and cupped her. Megan gave a soft moan, aware that they were still technically in public as well as at work, but was unable to hold back. The warmth from Syler's hands drove her wild. A deep thrumming started up in Megan's belly and she arched her body, pleased that Syler took the hint and increased the pressure between her legs, encouraging Megan to rub up against her. For the first time in her life, Megan was free from the shyness and uncertainty of acceptance that had always held her back, and she was drunk with that freedom. Her skirt rode up wantonly but Megan was beyond caring. She was on fire with need. The attention Syler paid her filled her with desire and she didn't want it to stop. Syler's breath was hot on Megan's skin as she kissed the softness of Megan's breasts that spilled from her bra. Thumbs found her taut nipples and stroked them through the sheer lace.

Megan's chest heaved with her panting breaths. Her breasts swelled against their lace confines. She looked down to where Syler held her, reveled in how those long fingers touched her. Megan drew in a deep breath as she watched Syler's lips tease her. She wanted more. Megan was on fire with the need to have Syler's mouth on her directly.

"It undoes in the front," Megan gasped.

For an instant, Megan had a flash of unease. Maybe she was pushing things. However the reverent murmur of Syler's assent reassured her that Megan's request was most welcome. The sudden release of tension around her chest was followed by the unbelievable heat of Syler's skin on her own. Megan couldn't hold back the whimper of need as she held Syler's shoulders, then moved to cup her head. Megan's breath came hard as she directed those teasing lips to her aching nipples.

The first contact was gentle. A slick tongue brushed over her skin and Megan bit back the cry that welled up in her throat.

"Please Syler," Megan whispered.

She lifted her chin and leaned her head back. She pressed into the folded sheets behind her as Syler took her into her mouth, one hand held Megan on her other side. The tongue and deft fingers worked on her achingly hard nipples and increased in speed as Megan's breathing kicked into high gear. She was dizzy with pleasure and the feeling of Syler against her. It was almost too much. She drew Syler to her once more and welcomed her lips with a searing kiss as she let her teased-hard nipples rub against Syler's shirt. Megan didn't care about how tousled they both became.

Syler was the first to pull away. Gentle hands refastened Megan's bra and resettled her with an expert touch. Megan fought the groan of disappointment but accepted the decision.

"Wow," Syler said. She let out a breath and sagged back beside Megan. She leaned against the folded linens. Her long fingers wrapped around Megan's. "That was just, wow. Sorry, I'm not thinking very clearly right now."

"Neither am I," Megan said. Her legs shook and her knees felt like they were on the verge of giving out. While Megan knew she shouldn't, she couldn't help but slowly run her tongue over her lower lip, imagining she could taste the lingering sweetness of Syler's kiss.

"Keep looking at me like that," Syler told her in a heated whisper, "And I'm gonna need CPR."

"That's fine," Megan said. Her lips quirked into a little smile as she slowly buttoned up her blouse. "I think there may be a few people around here who are qualified to administer that. Including me. I assure you, my mouth-to-mouth technique is beyond reproach."

"It certainly is."

As much as Megan enjoyed their little hideout, she knew the two of them couldn't just vanish for an extended period of time without arousing suspicion. Megan finished tucking in her blouse and stepped into the middle of the small room.

She held her arms out and asked, "Am I decent?"

"Looking good," Syler told her. She reached out and smoothed back Megan's hair with both hands. She tucked the loose strands behind her ears and straightened her butterfly barrette. "Perfect. Okay, how about me?"

Megan gave Syler a long once-over, from the toes of her smart loafers, up the long legs encased in charcoal dress slacks, to the slender curves of the body under the cotton shirt that Megan's bare breasts were pressed against only moments before. Her heart pounded and Megan swallowed a gush of desire as she let her gaze rest on Syler's lips, deep pink and swollen from the hungry kisses they'd shared, finally meeting Syler's eyes.

"You pass," Megan said, her voice tight with emotion.

"Good," Syler answered with a rakish grin.

"Do you have any idea," Megan said in a carefully casual voice as she bent down to retrieve her dropped files, "how wild you make me?"

"Hmm, I don't think I do. Maybe you'll have to show me sometime," Syler said. She pulled the deadbolt back and eased the door open. "Okay, the coast is clear."

As Megan followed Syler into the hallway, she blew back the wavy strands of hair that fell into her face. The push and pull between them, the anticipation and sweet stress of unspent sexual tension was dizzying. Megan felt like she was going to explode if she had to keep stopping just as things were getting good, but at the same time she cherished the low ache within herself, the simmering desire that sang through her veins. Syler called that out from somewhere inside her, and Megan was willing to bet she did the same to Syler in return.

All Megan had to do was make sure Charles never came near her again.

With some effort, Megan was able to put herself back into business mode and fell into her normal work routine. Even her daily paperwork was completed fairly quickly. Only one small upset marred the overall pleasant feeling of the day. After she came back from her afternoon rounds, Megan found an envelope from the hospital's in-house pharmacy on her desk, full of the exact medication she'd spent the past several months withdrawing from. Scowling, Megan shoved it into her increasingly-cluttered desk drawer and locked it without another thought before she turned back to the draft of her latest journal article.

"I see you are working very hard," the dry voice came from behind Megan and startled her so her hand jumped and crumpled the paper she was reading.

Megan hunched her shoulders in defense. She took her time turning around in her chair.

"Charles, what a surprise," she said, not even trying to hide her annoyance. Megan shook off her usual deferential posture and faced Charles squarely. "That's close enough. I don't want a replay of last night."

"It seems you would like me to apologize for something," he said. In blatant disregard of Megan's words, he came over to lean against the side of Megan's desk and she forced herself not to recoil from him. "This is exactly what I had hoped to avoid. I believe you may have misunderstood my intentions. I was merely thanking you for your time and presence at a special event. However, it seems that you have once again cast my welcoming and innocent gesture in a sleazy light, which I believe says more about the state of your mentality than mine."

He stopped talking and looked down at her with an expectant expression. Megan could barely keep her mouth from dropping open at his attempt to gaslight her once again.

"As long as it doesn't happen again, then I'm prepared to let the matter go without further comment." Megan clenched her hands and rested them on top of the report she was working on, very aware of her ring shining in the overhead lights. Even as a wave of guilt welled up inside her, Megan decided to play her trump card and said, "I would hope you respect the fact that I am in mourning."

"One year is considered a sufficient amount of time to mourn. Any longer and the practice becomes unhealthy," Charles said in his bland way that infuriated Megan to no end. "I'm sure your late husband would not appreciate the hostile attitude you have taken toward what is nothing more than a friendly overture. I simply wish to share some of your time and help you to adjust to your new life and circumstances."

"I appreciate that," Megan said, although she didn't at all. "However, I assure you I am adjusting quite well and have no need for additional assistance."

At the dismissive tone in Megan's voice, Charles stood. He loomed over Megan and she edged her chair slowly away, alarmed at the dark look on his face.

"I am a patient man," he said. "But not everyone is. With your breeding and background, I assure you the vultures are circling. It is time for you to realize who can be beneficial to you and who is simply taking advantage of a woman in a delicate and vulnerable state."

The silence stretched out. Megan was angry and short of breath. A lifetime of being trained to defer to authority warred with her natural instinct to tell Charles to go fuck himself.

"Thank you for your concern. Is that all?" Megan asked. She wanted the discussion to be over and Charles away from her.

"Actually, I wanted to discuss the matter of your medication."

"I'm not taking it," Megan said. "And you shouldn't just be giving people meds like that without proper supervision."

"Exactly," he said. He reached into his blazer and withdrew a business card holder. He placed a neatly printed card on the desk. "Which is why I have arranged an appointment with one of our therapists, who I feel will be very helpful in managing your treatment."

"I have a therapist," Megan muttered.

"That's good to hear. However I hope you realize you can't simply quit taking your medication because you are feeling better. That's an indication it's working."

"I know that," Megan said. She didn't want to explain the long, hard road that led her to that point in her life. Megan knew people with clinical depression genuinely benefitted from those types of drugs. Megan hadn't. Her chemicals weren't unbalanced and the meds just messed up what little control she had over her own life and emotions.

"Don't worry about the exam fees," Charles told her. "It will be covered by the hospital."

Which meant he would know if she went or not. Megan got a sick chill. She didn't look up as Charles left. Seized by a fit of anger, Megan yanked her pill bottle out of her bag. She opened it on her way to the ladies' room and didn't hesitate before she flushed the remaining pills. The empty bottle got tossed unceremoniously into the garbage. As Megan walked down the hallway back to her desk, she felt as if she was walking out of a prison cell.

THE REST OF the week passed in a blur. Sakura was put into isolation in order to keep the risk of infection down and most of Syler's extra time was taken up checking on her. Megan didn't begrudge the time they missed spending together. That was Syler's chosen life work and it took priority. Between her usual duties and the Angel Hand Clinic, Megan's schedule was full as well. She managed to dodge Charles and the looming threat of a forced visit with the hospital's therapist by allowing him to assume she was back on the medication. He still seemed to find almost daily excuses to either come by her desk or corner her in the hallway. His constant presence and insistence she take the depression meds worried her.

Megan worried about Nikky as well and came up with a plan, glad at least in that area she was able to act.

On Friday, she finished her morning rounds and examinations and went home to change into her best outfit. It was a cream Chanel suit with a slim-fitting skirt and gently tailored jacket. Megan put her hair up in a twist and dug out her much-hated beige high heels. Megan didn't have much jewelry and settled for her usual necklace and the Larsson & Jennings watch her parents gave her when she was accepted into med school.

Suitably outfitted, Megan transferred her wallet and phone to a slim pocketbook and took a last look in the mirror. She paused with a grimace. She would have to put on makeup to really look the part. With a resigned sigh, Megan dug through one of the opened boxes in her room and came out with a battered and ancient pouch, which yielded lipstick and mascara. After a few tries and a lot of swearing, Megan managed to get herself painted in a way that didn't make her look like a cross between a panda and a clown.

She took the bus and once she got off at her stop, Megan checked the map on the back of the card Fabia gave her. She ended up in a small cluster of shops. Megan didn't hesitate as she trotted into the one with rows of brand-name bags and accessories.

"May I help you?" A perfectly made-up model-like saleswoman slipped out from behind the counter and Megan immediately felt like a scruffy teenager playing dress-up in her mother's clothes.

"Yes," Megan said. She studied the saleswoman and tried to imitate her elevator-girl stance. "Would Fabia-*tencho* be in today?"

"Of course, one moment please."

She ducked into the back room and Megan studied the wares on display. The counter was full of watches and jewelry and the walls were lined with bags. Although she let Fabia assume otherwise, Megan had never been a big one for brand-names and the appeal of having a super expensive handbag that everybody recognized was beyond her.

"Are you looking for something?" Fabia came over to her. Megan could see the accusation in her eyes.

"Actually yes," Megan said. She tittered as if the high-class and somewhat prissy atmosphere infected her. "I need to buy a birthday present for my—" Megan choked. She couldn't say girlfriend, but as they were speaking Japanese, Megan fell back on the gender neutral and casually familiar phrase people used for their partner, *uchi no hito*. My person.

"Really?" Fabia's expression brightened and her eyes flicked to Megan's hands and Megan knew she was looking for the ring. "Did you have anything in mind? We have a nice selection of watches and wallets. What is your budget?" She bustled over to a glass counter that apparently held their men's section.

Megan passed over a Breightling watch that, while she knew it would look gorgeous on Syler's wrist, Syler already had a Tag she favored. As Fabia showed her a number of items, Megan chatted about harmless topics and felt like her brain was falling asleep.

The inane chatter put Fabia at ease and she joined the conversation quite willingly. As the talk meandered, Megan browsed and one piece in particular caught her eye.

"Oh, I like those," Megan said as she spotted a pair of tiger-eye cufflinks nestled in a velvet box toward the back of the display. Obligingly, Fabia took them out and Megan studied them. The stones were square and set in platinum, with two brilliant cut diamonds sunk into a corner of each. They reminded Megan of Syler's eyes in the sunlight. For someone who owned a tux, they were a perfect complement. Megan recognized the brand as an old, well-established one that she respected for their refusal to use anything other than fair-trade gems. The price was fitting for such a well-made set, which set it far above and beyond what Megan felt comfortable giving Syler for her birthday. At least for the first one. Even as her inner voice scolded her for splurging on a gift she would most likely never be able to give, Megan couldn't leave without the cufflinks.

"I'll take them," Megan said.

"Very good choice," Fabia said. Her calm and businesslike tone belied the fact that Megan had just dropped the equivalent of a month's salary into her shop's coffers. She nodded over to the sales assistant, who rang the purchase up. She didn't even bat an eye at the white and silver card Megan handed over.

While the saleswoman was busy wrapping the box, Megan said, "I haven't had so much fun shopping before." She felt fake and didn't regret it. Megan took a chance. She leaned forward and placed a hand on Fabia's suit-covered arm. "Why don't you let me take you out for a cup of tea?"

"I don't know," Fabia said. She gave Megan a suspicious look.

"Come on, your shop assistant won't let the place fall apart," Megan said. She opened her eyes wide as the mascara decided to stick her lashes together. "And I never get to have girls' talks being stuck in the hospital all day."

"You work in a hospital?" Suddenly the salesgirl was back and focused on Megan. She pressed the gift bag into Megan's hand and said, "Introduce me to a single doctor."

Megan took the bag and stepped away from the counter. "Um, no," she said. Megan turned and gave Fabia her best smile. "Shall we go, then?"

"All right, just let me get my bag," Fabia said.

Megan had noticed a few coffee shops along the way and directed Fabia into the one that looked the most discreet. While the probability was low, the last thing she wanted was for Charles to spot her with Fabia. The café was also a bakery and the entire front window was full of decorated cakes, truffles, and little cups of custard pudding that were made on-site.

They were seated at one of the inner tables and Megan was pleased to see they were surrounded by plants that served to hide them from not only passers-by outside, but also the other customers. The cakes they selected from the front window arrived. Fabia whipped out her phone and took several photos of the exquisite dessert.

"It's so pretty," Fabia said. She changed the angle and snapped a few more. "It's almost a shame to eat it."

"Umph," Megan said with her mouth full of cake. She swallowed and chugged her iced latte before she said, "I, uh, didn't have lunch today."

They'd both switched to English after leaving the shop, and Megan wondered if it was on purpose on Fabia's part in order to conceal their conversation. As Megan scrubbed at her face with a napkin, incidentally taking off half of her lipstick, Fabia ignored her cake. Instead, she dug into her purse and came up with her gold case. She offered a cigarette to Megan in an automatic way before taking one for herself. Fabia lit herself up then held out her lighter for Megan.

"Oh my," Megan said as she blew out a stream of smoke. "I didn't just ask you out here to bum a ciggy, but I have to admit it's one of the reasons." She took a drag and let it out slowly. "For some reason they get uppity at the hospital if they catch the doctors puffing away all the time. Go figure, huh?"

"So are you gonna ask me about my family?" Fabia studied her nails.

"Not unless you have something you'd like to tell me," Megan answered. She placed her cigarette on the edge of the ashtray where it streamed a noxious thread of smoke into the air. "How's Nikky?"

Fabia sucked hard at her cigarette before she answered, "Fine." She shook her head and scowled at her nails. "The same as always. He wants to wear a pink tutu and he's telling everyone stuff like he's going be a princess when he grows up. I tell him if Papa found out he'd be in trouble, but he doesn't listen. I try to get him to stop, tell him the other children would bully him and he would have no friends, but he just keeps on doing it."

Nikky was one strong kid. Megan had to admire that.

"What's wrong with letting Nikky wear pink and be a princess?" Megan asked in a gentle voice.

"It's prissy and wrong," Fabia snapped. "Papa wants a real boy."

A few things started to make sense. Megan realized she would have to tread carefully.

"Have you ever thought about having Nikky assessed?"

"For what? To make him normal?"

"To confirm that you actually have a daughter," Megan said. Fabia gave her an alarmed look and Megan continued, "There's no reason to pressure Nikky either way, but there are signs that you shouldn't ignore. For your child's sake, and for the rest of your family, I can't stress enough that this is normal. Nikky *is* normal, and needs your love and support."

"I don't want a gay kid."

"Whether Nikky is gay or not is not relevant, not to mention it's too early for anyone to know that," Megan said. "This is about gender, not sexuality." Fabia didn't reply and Megan pressed on. "If it turns out your child is actually transgender, it's wonderful you're finding out so early when you have so many options. Think of it this way, you've got a special, unique person in your life. Not everybody gets such an extraordinary child. Just look at Haruna Ai, Laverne Cox, and Jazz Jennings and the beautiful people they are as well as the great things they're doing."

Fabia just shook her head. Megan placed a small card onto the table and slid it across to her.

"If you and Nikky need a place to go, someplace safe, you can go here. My number's on the back."

Fabia stared at the card with undisguised alarm. "If Papa finds out about this—"

"He won't," Megan said with calm resolution. "Trust me, Fabia. I want to help you and Nikky. You don't have to say anything, just put the card in your purse."

With thinned lips, Fabia did. Then she stood and with a quiet and cultured *gochiso sama*, she thanked Megan before she swept out and left Megan with the check. The meeting went better than she had expected. Megan took one last drag of her cigarette before stubbing it out. With a shrug, Megan reached across the table and pulled the cake toward herself. If she was paying for it, she might as well eat it. Megan snapped down the cake in two bites and washed it down with the rest of her drink.

SUNDAY BROUGHT A long-awaited day off. Megan had a debate with herself over the day's wardrobe and eventually chose a pair of jeans that flattered her butt and a body-hugging top with short, puffy sleeves and a square neckline that showed just a hint of cleavage. She locked her door with a song in her heart and pattered down the stairs. She burst from the building just as Syler pulled up to her building in a classic-looking Suzuki Jimny. Luka and Jayco were in the backseat already. They looked eager and frolicked around like a pair of Labrador puppies.

"Hang on," Syler said as Megan opened the door. "Sorry about the mess." Syler leaned over and pitched a squashed tissue box and a few faded felt anime character dolls into the backset, which resulted in a volley of complaints from Luka.

"You're shotgun," Jayco told Megan as she buckled herself up. "So you're also in charge of the tunes."

"All right, if it's okay with the driver," Megan said. She glanced over to Syler, who was scruffy and gorgeous in her jeans and long-sleeved T-shirt, and got a brilliant grin and nod in return. Megan turned her attention to the stereo system and scrolled through Syler's playlist. "How about some oldies for the road?"

"Whatever you want," Luka said. He held up one of the dolls. "Hey Syler, can I have this? I love Liberation Executive."

"Sure." Syler aimed a grin at Luka through the rearview mirror, which sported a pair of fuzzy pink dice. "I only like winning those in the UFO catcher games. I usually just give them away anyway."

The car filled with the rousing rock tunes. Luka burst into song and danced in his seat with his new felt friend.

At around the halfway point on the way to Tokobe, they stopped at a parking area for a bathroom break and a stretch.

"Who's going on the Ferris Wheel with me?" Luka asked as they reconvened in front of the main building. He twirled and pointed to the towering ride behind them. "You can choose the audio program as you go around. "Last time I was here we chose the 'adventure' one and it had lions and stuff in it."

"We?" Syler raised a brow.

"My last boyfriend. Oh, and the boy before him too," Luka said without guile. "What can I say? I'm a boy-magnet."

Megan noticed Jayco looked uncomfortable at that, but she just said, "That sounds fun. How about we all go on it?"

"Okay!" Luka jumped up. He grabbed Megan's hand and tugged her toward the ride. "Come on, folks! Last one there has to buy everyone a coffee!"

Syler and Jayco scrambled to join them and they ended up in a single carriage, facing each other. The horror soundtrack filled the air with popping bolts and the sound of scratching and eerie wind-noises. Luka shrieked theatrically and jumped with every new sound. He clutched at Jayco who tolerated the attacks with patience.

While the parking area sprawled out underneath them, Megan enjoyed the lively, joking discussion going on around her. She tried not to share too many covert glances with Syler or give into her body's urgings and lean against her in the close confines of the molded plastic bench, but it was difficult. To make matters worse, Syler casually draped her arm over the back of the seat and Megan hoped Luka wouldn't notice when he piped up.

"Okay girls," Luka said in a mock-stern tone. He leaned across the narrow space that separated them. "You two have been finishing each other's sentences and giving each other a ton of flirty nudges and glances the entire time we've been here plus that sassy top Megan's got on just screams 'date' so out with it." Luka leveled a finger at first Syler, then Megan. "You two are going out, aren't you?"

Megan drew in a breath. She didn't know what to say. A shared look with Syler elicited an almost imperceptible nod. A pleasant flutter of nervous excitement woke up in her chest.

"Yes, we are," Megan said. A weight Megan hadn't realized she'd been carrying lifted. She met Syler's brilliant grin and was freed. Syler's arm came around her shoulders and this time Megan didn't fight the soft pull as she nestled against Syler's body in the way she'd been aching to for the entire ride.

"I knew it!" Luka said. His joyous but piercing voice filled the small space. He whirled to look at Jayco, who was holding one ear and wincing. "See that! I was right and you were wrong!"

"Wrong about what?" Syler asked. She drew her brows together and didn't look pleased at all. "That we were together?"

"Oh no, that wasn't an option," Luka said. He waved Syler's glare off with a flourish. "I predicted Megu-chan would be the one to spill it! You're way too stoic, sweetie. So there, Jayco!"

With his usual humble manner, Jayco just shrugged and said, "It doesn't matter who said what." He looked over to where Megan lounged in Syler's loose hold. "I'm just glad you felt you could tell us. Mazel tov!"

"Thanks," Syler said. "And I'm sure you guys will be discreet about this."

"Of course," Jayco said.

"But you're such a cute couple," Luka whined. "And all the nurses know how Megan helped fix your 'dislocated shoulder' that one time." He used his fingers to make quotations marks in the air.

"Hey, that's the official story, and you are not going to question it," Syler said. She gave Megan a glance that was full of mischief. "Besides, in case of any future medical emergencies, we've found a room that locks, and there are always the private shower stalls on the fourth floor."

"Oh, you are so bad!" Luka clapped his hands to his mouth. "I shouldn't even be hanging out with you. I'm going to be corrupted!"

"Uh huh," Syler said. She didn't look moved in the slightest by Luka's plight. She leaned back and shook her hair out of her face.

The recording made some kind of *woo-woo* noise, but Luka's bright voice drowned it out.

"We're almost at the top, people! And you know what that means!"

"The ride is halfway over?" Syler said in a bored voice.

"No, silly," Luka huffed. "It means you have to kiss! The couples who kiss at the top stay together forever!"

"Not doing it," Syler told him.

"You're no fun."

"If you wanted to let us fool around, you guys should have gotten a separate carriage." Syler clasped her hands behind her head and said in a lazy way, "And if that really worked, Lukie, you'd be sitting here with at least two more boyfriends than you have now."

"Maybe we didn't kiss and that's why they're not here," Luka said. He puffed his cheeks out and slouched in his chair.

"Besides, we're too classy to put on a show for you all," Syler said.

"Yes, that's right," Megan said with her head held high. She pointedly didn't think about the incident on Syler's rooftop, but she did allow herself to entertain the brief fantasy of what might have occurred if the guys weren't sitting just across from them.

They crested the ride without incident and soon disembarked at the bottom.

The rest of the drive went quickly. The pottery festival was held on either side of a small river, with the different studios in their own little booths. Cheerful awnings and tents lined both banks and the air was filled with the voices of the sellers as they called out for people to look at their particular wares. The scent of grease and burnt sugar wafted over from a herd of food stalls toward the middle of the festival. A makeshift stage was set up to one side of the parking area and it held a cluster of mesh vest-clad seniors who appeared to be some kind of neighborhood committee, accompanied by a person wearing the improbable costume of a giant plush soup tureen.

Jayco gazed out over the scene, his face radiant with interest. He said, "Let's split up and meet back here in an hour or so?"

"How about two," Syler said with a glance at her watch. "There's a lot to see here and you don't want to miss anything."

"Sounds good," Jayco said. He looked over at Luka and held out a hand, "Want to come around with me?"

"Of course!"

Megan covered her mouth to hide the surprised smile as Luka clasped Jayco's hand with a cute, shy look. They walked off, hand-in-hand.

"How about we start on the other side," Syler said. "Give the guys their space."

"I wonder if this means they've come to some kind of understanding," Megan said as they waded into the crowd.

"Maybe," Syler said. "If so, then at least it will cut down on the late-night advice sessions with Lukie."

She put a gentle hand on Megan's lower back and guided her through the crowd. Syler was excellent at navigating through the throngs of people and kept a good pace until they got to the first in the long line of sellers. Megan enjoyed looking at all the different dishes and had a great time selecting the items that caught her eye. She found out Syler's taste ran to simple items, and she favored striking designs and bold colors. Syler bought a large number of everything. The canvas bag she brought with her strained with the load. Megan's own bag got heavy even though she'd only bought a few things. She limited herself to essential items and passed over silly or tacky ones that were amusing but ultimately would end up being clutter.

"Do you want to take a rest?" Megan asked as they came to a small clearing where a number of tables and benches were set up.

"Sure," Syler said. She nodded over to one table. "It looks like that one's free."

"I'll get it." Megan, being less loaded down, scrambled through the milling crowd to claim the table. She turned around and signaled to Syler with a triumphant wave.

"Nice," Syler said as she came over. She set her bag down on the ground and sprawled into the plastic lawn chair with a happy sigh. "I can't believe how many deals I got today."

"I found a lot of nice things too," Megan said. "Jayco scouted out a good place."

"He sure did." Syler straightened in her seat and said, "Want to get something from one of those stalls?"

"Okay," Megan said. She jumped up. "But I'm going. You have to sit here and guard our table. What would you like?"

"Thanks Meg." Syler took a slow survey of the offerings and said, "The crepes look nice. I'll have a strawberry one."

"Oh, me too! Be right back," Megan said and took off on her mission. As she stood in line, she glanced back over her shoulder to where Syler lounged at their table. She had her elbows propped up on the table and leaned her chin on her clasped hands. She was beautiful, casual, and striking all at once. A wave of warmth seeped through Megan.

"*Oi, mite are,*" a male voice called attention to look at something and interrupted her thoughts. Megan turned to a lanky mid-twentyish guy who stood with his friend. They were just close enough for Megan to overhear them and she wondered if that was intentional. The guy pointed rudely at Syler. Megan frowned as the guy asked, "*Osu ka, mesu ka?*" which caused both of the guys to erupt into juvenile snickering.

Bristling, Megan wanted to stomp over to them and shout that whether a person was male or female was none of their goddamned business. So what if a person didn't conform to what someone had arbitrarily decided was proper for their gender? *Pishers,* she seethed to herself and had to fight to put on a civil face as she got to the head of the line and placed her order. The two guys had moved on but Megan still felt put out. The fellow manning the stall wore his T-shirt with the sleeves rolled up, which showed off his tattoos. He gave Megan a knowing look as he expertly flipped the freshly made crepe off the circular griddle.

"Don't mind them," he said. "Your friend's beautiful."

While Megan was a bit embarrassed he'd heard the exchange, she gave him her best smile.

"Yes, I think so too," Megan replied.

She paid and took her order back to the table. As Megan slid into her chair, she was unable to resist the temptation and asked, "Hey beautiful, did you miss me?"

"I was inconsolable," Syler said. She scooted her chair closer to Megan and nudged her. "Want to come over to my place tonight and help me put all my new dishes away?"

"I'd love to," Megan said with a happy thrill. She took a bite of her crepe. It was still warm from the griddle. The whipped cream mixed with the strawberry jam and made a sweet avalanche of flavor in her mouth. Megan groaned pleasure and said, "This is sooo good! Why does everything taste so much better outside, I wonder?"

"Yeah, I know what you mean. Maybe it's the air or something," Syler said. "Oops, you've got a bit of jam on your mouth there." She started to reach over to Megan but stopped before she completed the gesture. Syler got a wicked gleam in her eye and leaned close enough to whisper, "How about I lick it off?"

"Syler! You are evil!" Megan said. With the hand that wasn't busy holding her crepe, she grabbed Syler's shoulder and was about to give her a shove when she got an idea. Megan brought one finger up to touch Syler on the cheek and said in a low, sly voice, "How about you do that tonight?"

Syler caught her breath and returned Megan's sultry look with her own. "Why yes, I believe I could. So I guess that means you're going to go around with jam on your face all day?"

"Sure. I think it's a nice fashion statement," Megan said. She withdrew her hand and idly scooped a bit of cream from her crepe with her finger and put it into her mouth. She enjoyed how Syler's eyes fixed on her. "Maybe I'll put jam some other places too."

"Oh, I'm not the only evil one here," Syler collapsed onto the tabletop. "Meg, why do you have to be so fucking hot? It's not even noon yet and already you've got me going crazy."

"Sorry," Megan said, although she was not.

They finished their snack and picked up their bags once more. Megan actually did wipe the jam off as she didn't want to attract either unsolicited comments from passers-by or ants.

"Do you need to get anything else?" Syler asked as they headed in the direction of the car.

"No, I think I've gotten enough," Megan said. She mentally catalogued her purchases with satisfaction. "How about you?"

"There's just one more place I want to go," Syler said and turned to Megan with a conspiratorial look. "And I need your help. Come on, the seller's over here. I saw her shop when we first came in and knew I'd make this my last stop."

Intrigued, Megan followed Syler and ended up in front of a booth that was staffed by a woman of around fifty. She had let her hair grow long and free, and it was streaked with white. Her clothing was layered and eclectic. She called out a cheerful welcome when they came over. Megan looked at the wares displayed. Apart from a few odd knickknacks, the entire table was filled with rice bowls. Each one was different, from tiny pink bowls painted with cherry blossoms to delicate white and blue speckled ones, even including a massive, deep green one that looked like it would overwhelm all but the largest hands.

"Pick one you like," Syler said. "And it can be yours when you come over to my place."

Megan bit her lip as a rush of emotion nearly overwhelmed

her. She couldn't speak and simply nodded instead. She wished she had the nerve to reach out and take Syler's hand.

"Actually, pick two," Syler said.

"Why?"

"Well, I've been thinking," Syler said with a flash of shyness that Megan found adorable, "when I actually got my butt in gear and got dishes, I wanted to make a kosher kitchen. It's kind of been a dream of mine for a while. You know, maybe one day inviting people over for a meal or whatever." She stopped and looked a bit nervous.

"That's great," Megan said. This time she did reach out and gave Syler's hand a quick squeeze. "I wondered why you bought so many of each thing."

Syler returned her squeeze. Then they both bent over the selection with serious faces as they studied the various rice bowls. Megan picked up a few to weigh them and check their size and feeling. One in particular fit perfectly in her hand. It was painted a delicate green with subtle variations in the color here and there. Another one Megan liked was a similar size but splashed in brown and orange.

Megan turned to Syler, who had a simple dark blue bowl in her own hands. "These two," Megan said.

"Good choice," Syler said. She picked up a matte black one and nestled it into the blue bowl. "I'm going with these, I think."

She gathered up the four rice bowls and paid for them. While the artist wrapped them, Megan shifted her bag from one shoulder to the other and idly wondered what Syler's apartment was like. If it was anything like the rooftop area, it would be richly decorated, unassuming, and homey. Maybe she had lots of candles and cushions there too. Megan wondered if Syler had a sofa they could get comfy on. She certainly seemed to enjoy spending time on Megan's. Megan came back to the present as Syler tucked the last purchase of the day into her bag, and once more they drifted into the crowd.

Back in the parking lot, Syler opened the trunk and they piled their shopping bags into the car. After everything was put away, Syler leaned back against the driver's side door with her arms crossed loosely and waited for Luka and Jayco to come back. As Megan rounded the car to join Syler, she caught sight of the rude guy from outside the crepe stall and his friend. They hovered over the barrel in the makeshift smoking corner and the rude guy earned his name once more as he stared then spat on the ground. Megan swallowed the brief jolt of anger. She had an idea. She stood in front of Syler and took both of her hands.

"Kiss me," Megan said.

"Here?"

"Yes. Right here and right now." Megan's heart thundered and her body buzzed just from being so close to Syler. She leaned in close and murmured, "So I can flaunt my gorgeous, sexy girlfriend in the face of a couple of *schmendricks* who are probably drowning in jealousy right about now."

With a shrug, Syler said, "That's a good enough reason for me."

Syler reached out and put her hands lightly on Megan's waist. She guided Megan to step closer and nestle against her. Megan took Syler's face in her hands and drew Syler down to meet her in a kiss that started sweetly but soon got hot. She leaned into the kiss and held Syler tightly to her. Megan's body responded in a dangerous way as she opened her mouth and welcomed Syler. The softness of Syler's breasts pressed against hers as Megan urged their bodies closer together. Syler's hands were hot on her waist and drifted lower before they slid into the back pockets of Megan's jeans and cupped her backside through the denim. A deep heat started up in the pit of Megan's stomach as she gave herself fully to the kiss. Her body molded itself to Syler's. She knew people were watching and she didn't care. Megan had never felt so exposed or so free.

"Oh just lovely!" A sarcastic voice broke Megan's blissful mood. With a guilty cringe, she turned in Syler's embrace. Luka and Jayco stood a few meters away. Luka had his hands on his hips and heaved an annoyed sigh, while Jayco just gave them a thumbs up gesture. Luka continued, "You won't kiss at the top of a private Ferris Wheel but have no problem with a massive lesbian PDA right in the middle of a crowded parking lot? Who's too classy for what now, hmm?"

"That's because it was Megan who suggested it," Syler said, "And not you."

"Oh you!" Luka threw his hands into the air. "I give up!" He puffed his cheeks out for a moment, then deflated and said, "At least Megu-chan didn't waste her money on those jeans. They make her butt look super cute."

Megan's mouth fell open.

"I wholeheartedly agree," Syler said.

"Stop that," Megan said. She pressed her hands to her face. "You're making me blush."

"So now you're suddenly shy?" Luka asked archly. He let out a squawk and scampered around the car with Megan in hot pursuit. The merry chase ended as Syler reached out and intercepted Megan. Her long arms pulled Megan into a loose hug.

"So how about getting something to eat and then heading back?" Syler asked before she dropped a kiss onto Megan's temple.

"Sounds good," Jayco answered as Luka was busy sulking.

Syler released Megan and unlocked the car. Everyone got buckled up and Syler pulled into traffic.

"I want to eat soba," Luka piped up as the market fell behind them. "It's famous here and I know a—"

"No!" Syler and Megan said at the same time.

"What? Is it pick on Luka day?"

"It's not personal," Megan said. She glanced back over her shoulder. "How about something less noodly?"

Jayco popped up from the back seat and said, "There's a place I found online that looks good. It's vegan and the place is run by monks. The restaurant is actually inside the temple. I just checked their site and they've got a couple tables open. How about I make a reservation for us?"

"That sounds great," Megan said.

The other two members of the group added their own agreements. Jayco and his phone leaned into the front seat. He conferred with Syler for a while and she set the navigation according to his instructions.

Chapter Twelve

THE DRIVE HOME was quiet as the guys passed out in the back seat and slept most of the way. Syler kept the volume of the music low and at stoplights often reached over and took Megan's hand. They shared a number of long, telling looks that had Megan buzzed and breathless. Syler dropped Luka and Jayco off at Suito Station and made a short detour to let Megan bring her bag of dishes up to her room before they pulled into the parking lot behind Syler's building. Megan caught her breath, excited to see the place where Syler lived.

The elevator doors opened on the fifth floor and Syler took Megan over to the entrance of the corner apartment. Unlike Megan's building, there were only four apartments on each floor. The corner ones took up the length of the entire building and sported balconies on both the north and south-facing sides.

With her hand on the doorknob, Syler paused and Megan saw the indecision on her face.

Syler took a deep breath and said, "Um, just so you know, the place is pretty bare. I'm not really one for home decorating. Anyway, come on in."

Curiosity warred with unease as Megan stepped into the entrance hall that was easily triple the size of her own. She was grateful to be allowed into the place where Syler lived, her own private space and sanctuary. Megan slipped off her shoes and walked down a long hallway before she finally came to the large central room.

She looked around and sucked in an involuntary breath. Syler hadn't been exaggerating when she'd said the place was bare. The classy lamp Megan had gotten used to seeing from the outside was the only furniture in the entire long living room. The walls were devoid of photos or any kind of personal touches and the vast empty floor echoed with their soft footsteps. The kitchen was open-plan with an island and at least had a shadow of life in the form of a single red mug that sat in the drain board on one side of the double sink. A tall folding chair was pulled up to the island and Megan imagined Syler eating her meals there, maybe playing with her phone or watching the small TV that was mounted on the wall of the kitchen.

"Sorry it's not very hospitable," Syler said. For the first time she looked unsure of herself, with her hands stuffed into her pockets and her head bowed so her face was obscured by the fall of hair. She blurted out, "I can go up to the roof and get some cushions and stuff if you want."

"No that's fine," Megan said. She put her handbag down on the wide open expanse of floor and gave Syler her best smile. "I'm just glad you let me come over."

"It's no problem. Nobody's seen my place besides my team, but I really like having you here. *I'm* glad you came over," Syler said. "How about I get us some tea?"

"Thanks," Megan said. She followed Syler over to the kitchen area and perched on the tall chair. As Syler puttered around in the kitchen, Megan looked over the bare living room that almost ached with emptiness. She sipped cool tea from the cup Syler passed her and wondered why Syler left it that way. It occurred to her that maybe Yukina took everything with her when she left, because Megan couldn't imagine a couple living in that empty room for long. Then it hit her.

"The furnished room," Megan breathed. At the sudden words, Syler turned to look at her. Megan said, "You lived there, didn't you? What happened? I mean, if it's all right to ask. I don't want to bring up anything that isn't my business."

"No, you're right. I—we used to live downstairs." Syler paused and said, "When someone breaks your heart, it feels like taking a javelin to the chest. The only cure is space and time." Syler put both hands on the counter and looked down at them. Her shoulders sagged and she said, "After she told me she was done with me and why, I couldn't even stay in the same place, it was too painful. I came up here and let Yukina live there until she could get her new place sorted. I told her to take anything she wanted, but she only took her personal things, which left me with an apartment full of stuff I couldn't even bear to look at. All the memories had turned to poison."

The bleak expression on Syler's face undid Megan's resolve and she slipped around the counter to wrap her arms around Syler, who didn't hesitate before returning the embrace. The tension left Syler's body as she let out a long breath and nestled her face against Megan's hair.

"That was very generous of you," Megan said without rancor. "You must have loved her very much."

"At the time I thought I did," Syler said. Her voice took on a lighter tone as she continued, "Besides, I've got a whole building. I could live on a different floor every week if I wanted. Having no furniture's actually pretty convenient. Sometimes I put on some good tunes and have a one-person dance party in that big open space. Plus, cleaning's a breeze."

"That's true," Megan said. She sank into the feeling of Syler's arms around her. Just being close to Syler made Megan feel at peace and quieted the nagging guilt that never quite left her. "But you should think about investing in a sofa one of these days."

"Why?" Syler asked. She moved back and looked at Megan with a glint of humor in her eyes. "Then I'd be out an excuse to go over and hang out on yours."

"You don't need an excuse for that. You're more than welcome to visit my sofa any time you like. We both are rather fond of you."

"Glad to hear it. Anyway, how about we get started? Do you want to wash or dry?" She heaved the large canvas bag onto the counter.

"I'll wash, since I don't know where anything goes," Megan said as she stepped up to the big double sink. She noticed Syler had set up two washing-up bowls and two sets of sponges.

"That's okay, I don't know either," Syler said. She piled the dishes on the counter and Megan unwrapped them. "I was thinking," Syler said as she looked up at the cupboards, "meat dishes will be the warm-colored ones and dairy the cool ones. Good idea?"

"Great idea," Megan said. She already felt at home in Syler's place, bare as it was. The feeling increased as she unearthed their rice bowls. Megan paused to stuff the discarded wrapping paper into a plastic bag Syler produced from under the sink. After she gathered up the few original dishes, Syler put them into a cardboard box and stationed herself beside Megan at the sink.

As they worked, Megan felt her heart grow heavy with guilt. Syler had invited Megan into her life and made sure she had a place in it. She even gave Megan her own rice bowl, which was a significant admission of intimacy. Syler had shown Megan her scars, trusted her with her weaknesses, her insecurities, and her failures. The trust and openness Syler gave her made Megan feel blessed and grateful, and sick with disgust at herself that she hadn't returned that gift. She fell silent as she thought about what she was hiding. She needed to say something soon, before more time passed. Megan could only pray that Syler would understand and not hate her for the deception.

"Hey, are you all right?" Syler's gentle voice cut into Megan's thoughts.

"Yeah, I was just thinking," Megan said. Her throat got tight and she had to force the words out. "Today was really nice. I don't want it to end."

Syler put down the dish she was holding and faced Megan with her hands stuffed into her pockets. "Look, Meg, I wanted to ask, did those guys at the market give you a hard time because you were with me?"

"I don't care what some random *prostak* has to say about me or who I choose to spend time with," Megan said in a tight voice. She blew back the hair that fell into her face.

Megan put the last dish into the rack before she rinsed her hands and quickly patted them dry on the towel. She almost pulled away as Syler took both of her hands and drew Megan to her. Megan settled into Syler's arms even though she felt like she shouldn't enjoy the warmth and softness so much.

"Sometimes I forget, this is all new to you," Syler said in a quiet voice. She pressed a kiss into Megan's hair. "Don't let it get to you. It takes a while, but you'll learn to tune out the static."

The words hit Megan hard and she pulled herself from Syler's arms. She hugged her arms to her chest in an attempt to gain a bit of control. "Syler I need to tell you something."

"What is it, Meg," Syler's voice had a note of fear that further cut Megan's soul. "You're not having second thoughts about us?"

"No, never," Megan said. She bit her lip and willed the tears gathering in her eyes to stop. She didn't want Syler to think she was fishing for sympathy. She took several deep breaths but couldn't summon the courage to speak.

"Talk to me, please. You're freaking me out here." Syler gave her a half-grin as she spoke, but the pain in her eyes remained.

"I'm not having second thoughts," Megan whispered,

"But you might."

"Let me decide that," Syler said. She reached out as if to touch Megan on the shoulder but stopped before she completed the gesture.

"Can we," Megan's voice cracked and she stopped for an instant before plowing ahead, "Can we go up to the roof?"

"Sure," Syler said. She darted into the entrance hall and shuffled into a pair of rubber sandals. She indicated one of the other pairs of sandals lying scattered around and said, "You don't have to bother with shoes if you don't want."

Megan didn't reply. She couldn't. She just picked up her bag and draped the strap over her shoulder before she slipped on the ballet flats she'd come in. If Syler asked her to leave, Megan wanted to do so as smoothly and quickly as possible. When they got to the roof, Syler went into the shed and came back with her arms full. She unrolled the thick rug and tossed a bunch of cushions down. The tables were still scattered around the rooftop, but they were bare of the candles that had helped to create such a warm atmosphere the last time Megan was there. It was still too early for candles, at any rate. The days were getting longer and sunset was still a few hours away. The lazy evening sun cast the entire rooftop into a golden glow and Megan studied the sky for a moment to gather her thoughts. Syler sat across from her on her own cushion and the silence stretched out between them.

Megan rubbed a hand over her face to dash off the sheen of sweat that cooled in the breeze. She couldn't let the moment drag out any longer. Waiting was agony for both of them. Syler's gaze rested on her. Megan took a deep breath and tugged her ring off. The air was cool against the newly exposed skin.

She held the ring in her hand and said, "I never had a husband. I've never been with a man." Megan couldn't bear to look up. "I was with a woman before you."

Now that the first step was taken, the words flowed from her mouth, falling over themselves as she desperately tried to fill the gaping void of uncertainty that opened up within herself.

"It's true we were matched up online." Her hands clenched around the ring. Megan hated the tears that trickled into her nose and made her sniffle. "I had never been in a relationship and I felt that I needed to take that step, be proud, and take an active part in the lifestyle. It was my duty as a lesbian."

It was strange and surreal to be coming out to Syler at that late time, after all that had passed between them. At last, Megan raised her head and looked at Syler. She sat perfectly still, her face pale with shock.

It was a shock to Megan as well. She had never actually called herself a lesbian out loud to anyone before. True, she had come out to her parents, but instead of saying the actual word, she had simply introduced her partner Yasu as Yasuko, using the feminine suffix "ko" so they knew. Megan looked down at her newly-bared left hand. As she continued, her voice was strained and broke in places.

"We were only together for about half a year before I got the go-ahead for my clinic and she agreed to give up her life here and move with me." Megan scrubbed at her eyes with shaking hands and she paused to collect herself. "In Thailand, we were living as roommates. It hurt me to deny what I was and what we were to each other, but I got used to it. Then when she was taken from me," Megan had to stop there and swallow a few breaths before she could continue. "I still had to deny my grief for the six months I was there, cleaning up my mess. I mean, she was only my roommate after all.

"When I came here the rumors started, and I let them continue. It was such a relief to show my feelings, let people know about what I'd had and what I'd lost, even though people were saying husband instead of wife." She raised her face to the sky. Megan couldn't stop the tears and forced herself to talk through them. "It would be so easy for me to say Yasu was transgender or intersex, but she wasn't. Nonconforming, yes, but the deception was all mine. I wasn't ready to deal with the fallout and rejection from letting people know I'd been with a woman but at the same time, I couldn't deny her existence. Syler, I couldn't let her die twice."

Megan lowered her gaze and hugged herself. Syler had both hands clenched in her lap. Her brow was knit and she gnawed her lower lip with her teeth.

Pain overcame her. Megan bowed her head and said, "I understand if you can't trust me anymore. If you don't want to be with me anymore, that's fine. I'll leave quietly." Megan drew in a shaking breath and said, "I just want you to know that what we had really was all new to me. I never lied about that." Megan fell silent and waited for judgment.

After a long, agonizing moment, Syler said, "So that's why I never got my free toaster oven. Here I was thinking it was stuck in customs." She rose and came over to Megan, who let out a squeak as Syler pulled her into a tight hug. She buried her face in Megan's hair and said, "Meg, I knew from the start that there was something you weren't telling me. Something maybe you couldn't." Her hand rubbed up and down Megan's back as she spoke, and the words filled Megan with a warm rumble. "This is actually a lot better than what I was afraid of. If you think I'm going to dump you because you had a girlfriend instead of a husband, you're sadly mistaken. I've got history, but honestly I don't mind either way. You chose to be with me, and that's enough."

"But," Megan gasped, her mind still stalled in disaster mode, "I lied to you and everyone else."

"You never lied to me," Syler said. "Okay, I'll give you non-disclosure, but everybody does that to a certain degree. I simply believed what I heard from the rumor-mill without questioning any of it, and you are not responsible for that." She paused and said, "And I know you would have told me if I had only asked."

"Yes, I would have." Megan knew in an instant that it was true. Stung by the reality of her situation, she added, "But I didn't. You're not angry that I didn't tell you sooner?"

"I'm sorry we live in a place and at a time where you have to deny who you are just to get basic recognition," Syler said. Her hand didn't stop its slow passage over Megan's back. "But I'm not angry. God, I couldn't be angry with you, Meg." Syler drew back and took Megan's face in her hands. She paused and seemed to be gathering her nerve before she spoke in a soft but sincere voice. "I'm in love with you."

"You are?" Megan squeaked in disbelief.

"Yes, I am," Syler said. "I love you, Meg. With all my heart and my soul." She dropped her hands and worried at the hem of her T-shirt as she added, "Just because I blabbed it doesn't mean you're under pressure to say it back. But I needed to say it. I decided I was going to tell you today. I couldn't keep the words in anymore. I hope this doesn't freak you out, because I don't mean it that way."

A wave of joy broke over her. Megan squeezed her eyes shut

as she tried to calm the roaring emotions. Syler loved her. Her heart felt like it was going to jump out of her chest. She opened her eyes once more and looked at Syler. There was nothing more than love and understanding in her gaze. Megan wondered how she could ever have doubted her.

"You mean it," Megan said even as emotion choked her. "How did I get so lucky?"

"I'm the lucky one," Syler said. She brushed a gentle hand over Megan's cheek. "I just want to be with you. You're not going to get rid of me that easily. Don't cry, okay Meg?"

"I'm not crying," Megan said through her tears. She sniffled and leaned into Syler's caress. "I'm actually happy. I feel like I could just float away or explode or something like that. I wish I had told you earlier. I'm such an idiot."

"No you aren't," Syler said. "Our journey together started the day we met. You don't owe me any explanation about what you did or who you were before that. Only if you want to share, then I'm here. I want to be your safe place too, Meg. Will you let me?"

Megan nodded. Syler reached out and gathered her up in a warm hug.

"Sweetheart," Syler said in a low, hesitant voice. "Was one reason you felt you had to hide this from me because you felt that if I knew, I wouldn't respect your boundaries?"

"No, of course not." Megan drew back and ached for the hurt look on Syler's face. "That didn't even occur to me." She bowed her head and gathered her resolve before she spoke again. "More than anything, I was ashamed to tell you." Megan buried her face against Syler's shoulder. Her next words came out muffled. "There is so much I don't know and so much I've never experienced. I felt—inadequate. I've never come out to anyone other than my family. I've never gone to the bars or pride festivals or anything I should have. I've never even—" Megan stopped as her nerve gave out. She pressed her palms to her eyes, unable to continue.

"Meg, sweetie," Syler said. "I don't care if you've done everything there is to do with a hundred people or dated exclusively trees or nobody at all. It doesn't matter if you can name all the gay bars from here to Shinjuku ni-cho complete with who the mama-san is and their signature drink, or if you have no clue. This isn't a test you have to study for." She stroked a hand up and down Megan's back in a gesture that reassured Megan to no end. "Take me. I've only had three girlfriends in my entire life, including you, a handful of awkward first-and-last dates and a bunch more that never got past the texting stage. In high school I wasn't ready and in university I was too busy. And now, let's just say this neck of the woods isn't exactly a hopping gay paradise, even for someone as out as me. Never be ashamed of what you are, Meg. You don't know how proud I am of you, how much I admire your strength."

"I'm not that strong. I was scared and worried," Megan said. She closed her eyes in silent gratitude. Syler was so forgiving. But even the most forgiving person had their limit. Megan just hadn't found it yet and a cold, hard fist of ice within her clenched in her gut the more she thought about what else Syler would have to forgive if there were to be no secrets between them.

"Do you want to talk a bit more?"

"No," Megan said, she pulled away slightly and met Syler's eyes. Megan nearly drowned in the love she saw in them. The cold feeling faded and Megan only thought about what was right before her. "I want you to show me how much you love me. And I want to show you that I—" Megan's courage gave out just before she said the words. Instead she finished with, "I need you so much I barely know what to do with myself."

With that, Megan reached up and brushed a finger over Syler's lower lip. She hovered for an instant on the silken skin. Then she surged up and caught Syler with a deep kiss. Syler's arms came around her and crushed them together. Megan pulled Syler back onto the cushions with her and let Syler's entire length come down over her.

Even though she hadn't been able to say what she ached to, nevertheless a barrier that stood between them fell. Their connection resonated like never before. A slender thigh slipped between hers and Megan gave a moan against Syler's hungry lips. She opened her legs to the insistent pressure between them. Megan ran her hands down the sleek lines of Syler's back and found their home on her hips. She gave herself completely over to the demanding kiss and pulled Syler hard against her. The action was met by Syler's groan. She rocked her hips against Megan's. Thrilling waves of pleasure shot through Megan with the hungry, intimate contact. Overcome by the sensations, Megan broke the kiss and threw her head back. She pressed into the cushions beneath her. Syler's lips were hot on her neck and Megan's eyes fluttered closed. She wanted to touch all of Syler, and be touched in return. She wanted to spend the night safe in Syler's arms and wake up next to her.

"Take me to your room," Megan said between gasping breaths. "I want you to make love to me."

"Meirav," Syler whispered Megan's name in a reverent hush. She put her hands down and levered herself up off Megan's body. "Are you sure?"

"Absolutely," Megan said. "As long as you are."

Syler just answered with a slow smile. She stood and held out a hand to help Megan to her feet. A deep trembling started up in her knees and travelled upward as Megan went down the short flight of stairs to Syler's room.

They made it as far as the entrance hall before Megan couldn't wait any longer. She grabbed Syler and pressed her back against the wall. The kiss took her breath away. Syler's body was fully against hers and Megan felt the strength of Syler's need as her hands travelled up from Megan's hips to her back.

"Syler," Megan whispered as Syler moved her lips to kiss the side of Megan's neck.

"What is it Meg?" Syler asked between hot, wet kisses.

"I, um, I don't really know how to say this," Megan said then stopped. She mentally cursed herself for not being able to say what she needed. She pulled away and looked up at Syler.

She was flushed and breathing hard. Megan had to fight the wave of desire that threatened to sweep her feet out from under her. With a gentle touch, Syler reached out and tucked a strand of hair behind Megan's ear. "Hey, I love you. You can tell me anything. I'm pretty sure you're not an alien shape shifter or three dogs wearing a coat, but heck, even if you were, that's cool. I'm up for a new experience."

Megan stifled the nervous giggle that welled up in her throat. She took a deep breath and said, "I just don't want you to use a toy on me. Not tonight."

"That's it?" Syler said. "Thank God. I was a bit worried about that because I couldn't give you that even if you wanted it. See, a year ago I chucked the strap on I had and never bothered to get a replacement. Toys are fun, but there's plenty of other things to do that are just as good. Still, if the mood ever strikes you, just let me know. I'm always happy to oblige and I know a good shop in the city that can help us out."

"Thanks for understanding," Megan said.

"I want to know everything you like and everything you desire."

"All right," Megan replied with a happy flush. She couldn't believe how simple and straightforward things were. She said, "My main desire right now is to get naked with you."

Syler leaned close and murmured, "God, that's such a fucking turn-on. How about we move to the bedroom, then?" Her eyes danced as she said, "It's warm and comfy and much more conducive to getting naked."

"Okay," Megan said. "Lead the way."

Megan let go of Syler and stepped back. Syler very gently took Megan's hand in hers and led her through the bare living room and through a doorway. Megan glanced around as Syler stepped away from her and pulled the curtains closed against the glowing sky. In contrast to the spare apartment, that room felt lived-in with a small computer desk and a wooden dresser. The top acted as home to a row of comic books and novels plus two small, battered volumes that Megan could have sworn were prayer books. A small cluster of weights in the corner were likely the reason for Syler's toned arms and back.

One entire wall was taken up by the glass French doors that led to the balcony. In the middle of the floor was a thick double mattress, which sported a number of pillows and a blue and white patterned bedspread. A corner was rumpled and the sheet underneath looked suspiciously like the cape Syler had worn for her Purim costume. Megan caught her breath in the instant she surveyed the room. She was so close to falling into those soft cotton depths with Syler.

Megan's heart thundered in her ears. She sank down to perch on the mattress. It was a good one, firm and comfortable underneath herself. Not squeaky either, which was a very good thing. She looked up at Syler, who gazed back at her. Megan didn't break the contact as she pulled her top from her waistband.

"If things ever get stale between us," Megan said in a husky whisper, "I want you to remember this moment. How you felt seeing me here, on your bed for the first time, knowing what we're about to do."

"Stale or not," Syler said, "I'm going to remember it forever."

Syler's gaze never left her as Megan pulled her top over her head and reached down to unbutton her jeans. Her fingers trembled with nerves and need. She had just gotten her zipper lowered when she decided she wanted Syler to do the honors for the rest of her clothing. Megan edged backward until she lay fully on the bed.

She draped herself over the pile of pillows and purred, "Are you going to come over here and help me?"

With a quirk of her lips, Syler crossed the small distance and knelt down next to Megan. She reached out and took Megan's face in her hands. One gentle thumb brushed over her bottom lip and Megan's body came alive once more. A fierce heat grew within her belly, electric tingles trickled downward to gather between her thighs.

"I love you so much, Megan," Syler murmured.

"I love you too," Megan replied. The words were inadequate to express what she felt for Syler, but she still got a deep surge of joy as she was finally able to speak them.

"Hearing you say that to me," Syler said in a heated whisper, "You don't know how good that is."

With bright eyes, Syler leaned forward. Megan drew a breath as their lips met in a soft kiss. Syler held her lightly at first, but as the kiss deepened, the strength in Syler's touch also increased. Megan opened her mouth as a gentle tongue quested to find hers. From there, the kiss got hot and hungry, fast and wet. A jolt of desire raced through Megan and ended right between her legs. As their lips devoured one another, Syler stroked her hands down Megan's face and over her shoulders. She trailed down Megan's back and came up to cup her breasts. Megan gasped with need as Syler's thumbs teased her nipples through her bra. In an instant, Megan was hard and thrilled with the touch. Megan shifted and drew Syler to lay down on her.

They came together in a frenzied clash. Megan pressed her body against Syler's. As Syler kissed a line down the side of her neck, Megan canted her hips in wanton pleasure and stroked her hands down from Syler's shoulders. She ghosted over her long body until she was holding Syler's hips. Syler yielded to her and at once Megan knew they belonged together, that Syler craved what was happening between them just as much as Megan did.

The softness of the pillows at her back contrasted with the resilient strength of Syler's body on her front. Megan closed her eyes and moaned in anticipation as Syler found the clasp of her bra.

Syler hesitated for an instant. Megan gasped out, "Please Syler, take it off. I want you to see me. I want to feel you on me."

Syler sat up and pulled Megan up as well. With a quick twist, Syler opened the clasp and the bra fell into Megan's lap. Her skin was already hot and tingling, and being exposed to Syler's eyes and hands, inflamed her. Megan tossed the garment aside and hungrily reached for Syler. She tugged Syler's belt open and yanked out her undershirt.

"Slow down sweetie." Syler's hands were gentle on hers. "We have all night."

"I just want you so much," Megan said. Her thighs trembled with need and Megan couldn't stop from shifting around as arousal clamped down on her. She was so wet, her panties stuck to her. The cool air of the room on her bare breasts was not helping at all. "And I don't want to wait. I want all of you, right now."

"God, I want you too," Syler breathed. She reached down and in one clean motion, pulled off both T-shirt and undershirt as well as her sports bra. She tossed them aside and rose to her knees. As she drew Megan's hands to her once more, Syler said, "How about you finish up here."

With her fingers resting on the waistband of Syler's jeans, Megan edged forward. She was on level with Syler's breasts and decided to make the best of the position. As she fumbled with the button, Megan leaned forward and took a taut nipple into her mouth. A sharp intake of breath followed by strong hands cradling her head told Megan she was doing something right. Megan soared with the freedom to touch, to reach out and claim Syler's body with her hands and mouth. A hunger lit up within her and only burned hotter as the seconds slipped by.

Megan slowly released the hard nub from her mouth as she pulled the zipper open and felt the familiar wide waistband of Syler's boxer briefs under her fingers. Instead of dragging Syler's jeans off at once, Megan gave into a wicked urge and slipped her hand into the opened fly. She delved between Syler's thighs to hold her over her underwear. Megan's fingers cupped the resilient softness and she felt the heat and dampness of Syler's arousal through the sturdy cotton.

"Oh God, Meg," Syler gasped. Syler reached down and grabbed Megan's wrist. Instead of pulling her away, as Megan expected, Syler held her against the firm swelling between her legs and rocked with the pressure as she did so. "Fuck, that's good. I'm so fucking wet, I can hardly stand it. What are you doing to me?"

Megan wasn't sure how to answer that, but she figured it was a rhetorical question anyway. With a sigh of longing, Megan dropped a quick last kiss to each taut bud before she moved away. She placed a hand on Syler's chest and gave a light shove. Syler obligingly sprawled backward onto the pile of pillows. She lay there, tousled and panting. Her nipples stood erect and wet from Megan's kisses.

Still sitting up, Megan looked down at the woman who had fallen in love with her, who had accepted her deception with grace and who was on the verge of sharing the most intimate action two people could.

"You are so beautiful," Megan whispered in awe.

"That's my line," Syler said as a crooked grin broke over her face.

With the knowledge Syler was drinking her in, Megan rose up and slipped her own jeans over her hips. She wriggled to help get them off. Her panties went along with them. She kicked the last of her clothing over the side of the mattress without a care where it landed. The instant she was completely bare, she wasted no time and reached out to urge Syler's jeans down and off, where they joined Megan's discarded clothes on the floor. Megan caught her breath at the graceful lines of Syler's body. Her eyes devoured the long legs with their slender muscles and the slim hips.

Megan froze, unable to tear her attention from the dark, short-trimmed patch of hair between Syler's legs, which did nothing to conceal the tantalizing view of swollen flesh. The outer lips were flushed and parted slightly, showing the hint of glistening inner lips as the erect bud peeked out from between them. Megan's entire body trembled with the desire to touch Syler, worship her body and bring her to the peak of pleasure. Her heart pounded in her ears and resonated all the way through her. At that instant, Megan had no doubts that she could finish what they'd started.

"I hope you're not going to just look," Syler said. She drew up one knee, which incidentally gave Megan a spectacular view. Megan gulped as a fist of arousal hit her hard. "It's a huge turn-on, but I need more. I need you on me, Meg." Syler hoisted herself up and held out her arms. "Come here."

With that, Megan reached out and settled over Syler. For the first time their bodies came together with nothing between them. Hard nipples teased the soft flesh of breasts, bellies slipped against each other, legs intertwined. With a groan, Syler reached up and drew Megan down to meet her in a kiss that seemed to reach the bottom of her soul. Megan clamped her hands down on Syler's hips. She opened her legs and allowed Syler to push a strong thigh between hers. Not breaking the kiss, Megan whimpered in need and followed the frantic thrust of Syler against her. A gush of wetness slicked her thighs and she rolled her hips into Syler with a fluid grace she'd never dreamed of. The rushing, roaring need was overwhelming. The first deep tremors of climax sparked into life and she tore herself from the kiss.

"Syler, I can't stop it, I'm coming."

"Not yet, Meg," Syler said in a harsh whisper against Megan's mouth. She sucked in a breath. "Hang on, sweetie."

After the ravenous kiss, Megan's breath came in short, desperate gasps. Her body begged for more, but she forced herself to lay still. The throb of need between her legs drove Megan crazy. She didn't know how long she'd be able to hold out. Syler's wetness and resilient flesh was spread against her thigh. Syler let out a shuddering groan as Megan moved just enough to shift her weight so she wasn't directly on top of her.

"Sorry," Megan said. "I didn't mean to do that."

"That's okay. I can't believe how good you feel on me," Syler said. Her eyes searched Megan's face. Syler dropped one hand from Megan's face and trailed down her back, causing Megan to arch with the gentle contact. Syler moved against her and Megan had to bite her lip as the wave of arousal hit her once more. "You're really close, aren't you?"

Megan sucked in a lungful of air and said, "Yeah, I am. Syler, please don't stop."

"How do you want me to take you over?" Syler rose up and

pressed her lips to the side of Megan's neck. Between kisses, she whispered, "Anything you want, I'll do it. Do you want me to get you off just like we are now? Rub your sweet pussy over me until you can't take it anymore?" Her voice was low and urgent. Hearing the raw, sexy words drove spikes of need through Megan and she struggled to contain herself as Syler said, "Do you want my mouth on you? Do you want me in you? Do you want me on your clit until you come?"

Megan swallowed the rush of raw need. She trembled on the precipice with her body aching for Syler. She knew exactly what she craved. As Syler moved underneath her, careful not to press against her directly, Megan gasped out the words, "Yes, God yes. Syler. I want to feel you inside me."

The hand on her back moved down and trailed over her hip. Megan lifted herself just enough to let Syler's fingers delve between her legs. The first brush against her sent a shiver through Megan and she bit off a strangled moan of need. Desperate for more, Megan pulled up one knee and opened herself fully to Syler. Gentle fingers stroked up her entire length and paused just shy of entering her.

"Meg, you're so ready for me, my God," Syler whispered against Megan's skin.

"Please," Megan said, only able to get out those words. She threw her head back, breaths ragged as her body sang in anticipation.

"Open your eyes, Meg. Look at me."

Megan did and nearly fell into Syler's sun-flecked gaze. She had never felt so desired, so loved and so treasured. Their breaths mingled. Still Syler didn't make the final move and Megan knew what she had to do. With a deep groan of longing, Megan lowered herself down and felt Syler sliding into her. She held still for a long moment as she adjusted to the novel sensation of someone actually within her, something alive and not just a silicon-sheathed plastic thing—of Syler in her.

"That's it Meg," Syler breathed. Underneath Megan, she shifted and said, "You feel so good, you're so soft and so tight. Come on sweetie, you can do this."

Megan's mind was blank. As much as she wanted to speak and try to convey an ounce of the feelings that gripped her, she couldn't. However, her body urged her to move. Megan rocked her hips back and forth, pumping Syler in and out. Megan had never been on top before. She had never moved like that and she loved it. She knew Syler could see her and she didn't care. She needed every inch of Syler. Every movement drove Megan closer to the edge. Her hips started to jerk. Her movements got harsh and erratic as her body shivered with the need to explode.

"Yes, Meg," Syler's eyes were half-closed. Her breath hitched. "You are so fucking sweet. God, that's so hot. Take all of me, bury me deep."

Megan pumped hard and did as Syler asked until she couldn't take any more. She held her body still. Only her breasts moved with each heaving breath. A slick, wet thumb worked her clit and Megan let out a cry as something came loose inside of her. The pressure peaked, a sharp twinge gripped Megan and she threw her head back, needing one last push to get to the edge. Her hips worked madly as she drove Syler deep inside. Even as her body moved in sharp thrusts, Megan panted like a bitch in heat, desperate for release. Syler's free arm came around her hips and held her close. Syler pressed into her, circling her hardness as she buried herself deep within Megan. A shock of fire lanced through her and Megan bore down, pleading for more with every gasping breath.

"That's it, Meg," Syler's voice, husky and breathless, filled her mind. "Come for me, sweet Meirav. Give me everything you have."

She didn't have a choice but to comply. The wracking spasms came down over her and exploded into a white wave of sheer ecstasy. She had never given herself over to anyone like that, but she felt safe in Syler's embrace and Megan let her body go. She was vaguely aware of Syler's soft words urging her on, but she had no comprehension. The waves didn't seem to want to end. The arm around her hips tightened and the fingers deep within her twitched and curled slightly. The pressure set off another blinding chain-reaction of fireworks that threatened to knock Megan over completely.

After the storm passed, Megan collapsed in a limp, trembling pile on top of Syler, sucking in deep breaths. Syler withdrew from her and that alone sent a new series of jolts through her hips.

Strong arms came around her and Megan snuggled into the embrace.

"Are you okay?" Syler asked. She dropped a tender kiss onto her temple.

"Perfect," Megan purred. She wriggled a bit and gave a long stretch, very aware of Syler's naked body against hers. A glowing, golden wave of contentment enveloped her. "I never knew I could come like that. Syler, you aren't a doctor, you're a magician."

"I'm glad you approve," Syler said with a self-satisfied look. She met Megan's lips in a slow, soft kiss that spoke of longing and tenderness. The brimming feeling of completion that had started when Syler touched her didn't leave.

After she drifted away from the kiss, Megan hoisted herself up onto her elbows and slowly drew one leg over Syler's body. The tension in the muscles under her told Megan that Syler was still holding onto her own climax, but just barely.

Megan bent low and let her breasts brush lightly over Syler's. Zings of pleasure sparkled through her as the swollen tips trailed over Syler's skin. She lowered her head and kissed Syler's neck before she moved up to her favorite place, just under her ear. It was time for Megan to give back what she'd received. She placed one finger in the hollow of Syler's collarbones and drew it down her chest. Syler shivered at the first contact and Megan paused, unsure if her touch was welcome.

Syler closed her eyes and whispered, "Keep going, love. I usually don't need this, but fuck me Meg. I really fucking need to come."

"What should I do?"

"Whatever you want." Syler's voice was strained. "God, this is so good. You are so good, baby girl."

The words gave Megan a shot of pure joy. She gently teased Syler's earlobe with a light kiss before she moved slowly down the side of Syler's neck. She followed the course of her fingers with her lips as she trailed kisses down to the smooth valley between her breasts. Megan savored every inch. She stroked her fingers over the tight muscles of Syler's belly and ended just shy of the patch of hair between her thighs. Her fingertips brushed the wiry curls. Megan heard the catch in Syler's breath and felt the thudding of her pulse pick up in speed. Under her hand, Syler's body was taut and shivering with need. Her breaths were fast and harsh.

"Meg, sweetie," Syler's voice was tight, "I need you so bad. You make me hotter than I've ever been in my life."

Emboldened by the knowledge, Megan slid her hand lower. This time nothing blocked Megan from feeling the thick, velvet softness and damp heat.

"Is this okay?" Megan asked. As she held Syler, she very lightly ground the heel of her palm into the slick folds and felt the firmness of Syler's arousal, sheathed in the delicate hood.

"What you're doing right now is really getting me going," Syler said. "But it's not enough. I need something else from you." Megan didn't miss the glint of fire and love that burned in Syler's eyes as she took Megan's hand from her. "I want you to trib me. Open your legs for me, Meg."

Megan moved to do as Syler had asked and straddled her thigh once more. Syler was even wetter than before and Megan slid as they settled together. Syler arched back and gave a deep moan.

"Right there," Syler said. She put both hands on Megan's hips and guided them together. "Yes Meg, right there."

Deep in her belly, arousal fluttered and woke again as Syler's spread open sex met hers. Megan leaned into the caress and dropped her weight, happy to hear an appreciative hiss from Syler. Megan kissed Syler's neck and stroked down from her shoulders to tease her nipples with her fingers, all the while moving in slow waves against her. Syler's hands were on her hips, urging her on. The wetness between them grew as Megan's engorged clit slid against Syler's. They were both breathing hard, chests heaving against each other.

"Faster, Meg," Syler said into her ear. "Harder. Oh fuck, yes, that's good."

Inspired, Megan reached down, slid her fingers over Syler's hip, and trailed down the back of her leg to urge Syler to bend her knee up, which she did. The sudden increased contact had Syler panting out Megan's name.

"Meg, sweetie, I'm nearly there," Syler said.

"I'm here, Syler," Megan breathed. She wished she was better at bedroom talk.

Syler's fingers tightened reflexively on Megan's hips. Megan fought her own new rush of arousal as Syler's head went back into the pillows. Her eyes fluttered closed as the first wave of release hit her. The experience of witnessing her lover's climax was no less powerful than the first time she'd touched Syler. In the throes of ecstasy, Syler radiated pleasure with her entire body, lithe limbs tensed and muscles shuddered as she let go. It was so erotic. Simply watching had Megan's body humming once more with unfulfilled tension. The impact of sharing that intimate moment hit Megan. For an instant, she quailed. She was not worthy of such a gift.

Megan banished the thought and concentrated on holding Syler to her. She drew out the last shivers of Syler's climax with a fast twitch of her hips. Between Megan's legs, wetness gushed anew. Tension twisted deep in her belly and an undeniable rush of arousal filled her once more.

"Syler, I need to come one more time," she gasped out. Megan clamped her teeth over her lip to keep from whimpering aloud.

"I'll give it to you, baby girl," Syler said in a breathless voice. Her hands gripped Megan's hips and started a slow grind against her. "Like that, yeah do it to me, Meg."

A thrumming heat rose up within Megan. She could only ride it out. She shifted away from direct contact with Syler's spent clit and pumped hard against Syler's thigh, guided by the hands on her hips. She gritted her teeth as her body shuddered with the first waves of her climax. She was wetter than she'd ever been in her life and unashamedly painted Syler's skin with her slickness. Megan was vaguely aware of Syler's whispered words of encouragement as her thighs clenched. The first ripples of her orgasm jolted through her body and Megan was aware of nothing else. Her hips bucked and shook and Megan threw her head back in pleasure. She gave a cry as she climaxed.

Her movements slowed as the tremors died down and Megan caught her breath. Strong arms came around her. Megan burrowed into Syler's embrace, exhausted and glowing. The waves of release ebbed. The lingering sticky wetness between her legs was a testament to what they'd shared. Megan savored the act of simply having Syler hold her.

After a while, Megan drew back and lay down on the crumpled comforter, bare as the day she was born. She was warm and limp, her belly still buzzed. Megan had never thought she was capable of multiples — before that day, even one had been a challenge. She rested her cheek on her folded arm and looked across the small distance to where Syler lay in a boneless sprawl.

"I feel like a sponge someone squeezed all the soap out of," Syler said. She reached over and brushed a sweat-damp tendril of hair from Megan's forehead. "The things you do to me, Meg. You should come with a warning label."

"I believe someone once said it takes two to tango."

"Someone very wise, no doubt," Syler said. She paused and studied Megan deeply for a moment. Megan felt very pleasant and sleepy as she melted into Syler's gaze. Even though they weren't touching, she still felt the connection between them, strong and true like a river of light.

"You know," Syler said in a soft voice. "I can't decide if your eyes are blue or grey."

"Does it matter?" Megan asked.

"Not really," Syler said. "The only thing that matters is what I see in them."

"And what do you see?"

Syler went still for a moment before she suddenly sat up. She got up and went over to her dresser as she said, "Now that would be a conversation for another day." She opened the top drawer and rummaged around in it while Megan enjoyed the view of her trim rear and sculpted back. Syler glanced over her shoulder and caught Megan ogling but answered with only an arch of her brow. Without haste, Syler stepped into a pair of drawstring shorts and pulled a T-shirt over her head before she said, "It's still early, how about I make you some dinner?"

The idea of Syler cooking for her made Megan irrationally happy.

"That sounds wonderful, thank you."

"Great." Syler came back with a T-shirt and cutoff sweats in her hands and sat down next to Megan. "Here are some clothes for lounging around in. Nothing glamorous, but you look smoking hot in anything." She got a wicked gleam in her eye and purred, "Or nothing at all"

"*Etchi!*" Megan playfully called Syler out, whose eyes lingered with evident enjoyment on Megan's bare form. Syler made no attempt to hide what she was doing. The intensity of her look sent a shock of arousal through Megan. Immediately, her skin flushed and her nipples tensed and hardened.

"Guilty as charged," Syler said. "You'll have to look pretty far to find anyone more perverted than me. But it's all for you, Meg."

Fighting a smile and blush at the same time, Megan sat up and accepted the pile Syler passed her with a word of thanks.

"I'll give you a bit of privacy," Syler said.

She turned away and sat down on the side of the mattress. Megan couldn't help but come up behind her and press her bare breasts to Syler's back. Syler froze and drew in a breath, which Megan replied to by kissing her on the neck. With a hungry growl, Syler whirled and tackled her. Megan let out an undignified squeak as she landed on her back.

"Now that's—" Megan's protest died as Syler claimed her mouth in a greedy kiss.

The kiss ended with both of them breathing hard. Megan gazed up at Syler. A deep hunger flickered into life within her, one that dinner was not going to satisfy.

"Would you stay with me tonight?" Syler asked in a soft voice. "You're more than welcome here. But I completely understand if you'd rather go home. I mean, this wasn't exactly planned and I'm sure you have—"

Megan reached up and this time it was Syler who was interrupted by a hungry kiss.

"I'd love to stay the night with you," Megan said as she tried to catch her breath.

"Good," Syler said.

She leaned down and pressed her lips to Megan's once more, and their exit from the bedroom was delayed for several eventful minutes. Megan finally managed to get dressed. They wandered into the kitchen as the last embers of the setting sun streamed in through the living room curtains.

"How about a tofu and broccoli stir fry?" Syler's head poked out from the opened refrigerator door. "I've got a bunch of bean sprouts I can chuck in too, sound good?"

"Sure, that sounds great," Megan said. As Syler piled ingredients on the counter, Megan jumped up. "I'll get the dishes. I guess it's pareve, which counts as dairy?"

"That's right," Syler said with a grin. She pulled a cutting board from under the sink and started chopping. The handle sported a piece of blue tape around the handle, indicating Syler had already divided her cooking implements according to kosher directives. As she cut the veggies with the ease and grip of a professional, Syler continued, "I really like cooking, but it's so depressing to do it for one."

"I know what you mean," Megan said. She pulled their rice bowls down from the cupboard. Her hip brushed Syler's as they stood in the confines of the kitchen. While it was larger than the tiny galley-like cubby in Megan's apartment, it was still quite cozy with the two of them standing in it. However Megan didn't mind the close quarters at all.

As Syler swept the ingredients for their dinner into a frying pan that also had a line of blue tape on the handle, Megan set out the dishes. When she finished, Megan stood at the island and wondered what they were going to do as there was only one chair.

Syler was apparently thinking along the same lines because she said, "Sorry about the whole lack of chairs situation. Why don't we have a roof picnic? After all, the cushions and stuff are still out."

"That's a great idea," Megan said. She leaned against the counter beside Syler. Her body glowed with pleasure and her mind filled with the memory of Syler's skin on hers, the completion she'd found within the circle of Syler's arms.

"What are you thinking, Meg?"

"Just how much I love you and how happy I am to be with you," Megan said with a contented sigh. She was being sappy, but she couldn't help it. She reached out and caught Syler's hand in hers. She cherished the freedom to touch her lover as much as she wanted. Megan gave a gentle tug and Syler abandoned her task to come over and fold her into a hug. Megan closed her eyes and murmured, "This is so nice."

"It really is. I want to hold you forever," Syler said. Suddenly the frying pan on the stove gave an angry sizzle. Syler jerked back with a quick expletive and hurriedly resumed her stirring. "Okay, forever is a relative term, given I don't want to burn your dinner."

"That's fine," Megan said. She stifled a giggle at the rare moment of Syler's lack of poise.

The stir-fry smelled delicious as Syler added a number of different spices and sauces to it. She paused with a fiery red jar of

Korean *gochujang* in one hand.

"How spicy do you like?"

"Very," Megan said. The words came out easily for once, without any sting. "I've always liked spice, but when I was in Thailand, people were always bringing home-cooked dishes to the overworked village doctor, like real authentic burn-your-face-off curries and soups that I'm sure used kerosene as a base, so I got to the point where I'm pretty sure I can eat a live blowtorch. So hot, but oh so good." Megan got a sly look on her face and purred, "Kind of like you."

"Spicy-hot it is!" Syler laughed and added a generous dollop.

While Syler cooked, Megan filled their rice bowls and put them on a tray. Syler dished up the stir-fry onto a platter and passed it over. Megan finished the arrangement with two sets of chopsticks.

"If you want real beer, I think there's some in the mini-fridge upstairs," Syler said. She held up a can of non-alcohol beer. "I'm on call tonight, so I'm just going with this."

"That's all right," Megan said. "I'm so relaxed I'll probably go to sleep if I drink." She lowered her voice and said, "And I don't want tonight to end too soon."

"Okay then, two Asahi Dry Zeros coming right up." Syler answered Megan's sultry look with one of her own that sent a zing of fire through Megan.

They moved upstairs and got settled. Megan held her rice bowl in one hand as she helped herself to the fragrant and steaming veggie mixture on the low table between them. They ate in comfortable silence. Megan enjoyed the cool breeze of the evening and the companionship. The sky darkened and Syler plugged in a few strings of lights which hung like stars over them. When she was full, Megan put down her chopsticks and leaned back with her can of beer in her hand. Across the table, Syler fixed her with a long, wondering look.

"So you're out to your family? When did you tell them? When did you know?" Syler asked. She leaned forward as she spoke. Her eyes never left Megan's face. "Is it okay for me to ask about that? I just want to know everything about you and what brought you to this point in your life. You don't know how much I thought about this, why you were with me. I mean, I told myself there are people who are bi and that's fine. I thought maybe after what you had and lost, you couldn't be with another guy and I was a safe option. I thought about a whole lot of scenarios, but I had no idea what was going on inside your mind and your heart. I want to know." She put her empty bowl down and clasped her hands. "If you'll let me."

"It's all right," Megan answered. A spur of guilt dug into her at the rawness of Syler's expression and the need in her voice. The time to hide was over. Megan took a sip of her beer before she said, "There's not a lot to tell. I'm not straight or bi, but it's not like I woke up one day with the epiphany that I was a lesbian. I was never really interested in dating when I was younger, but I always liked Takarazuka." She shrugged and shared a grin with Syler.

"Yeah, I should have known," Syler said. "Straight women don't read *Graph*."

"That's true. I have a weakness for women in tuxedoes." Megan took a moment to remember Syler in her tux and how gorgeous she'd been. "I never had anyone in my life, so coming out wasn't an issue for me until I was with Yasu. I went home one Friday night and told my parents during Seder."

"Were they okay with it?"

"They were actually very relaxed about the whole situation," Megan said. "After all, I was a fully licensed physician by that time and living on my own, there's not much they could have done to me. I'm pretty sure they were more relieved than anything, you know, that I finally had someone in my life."

"They seem like good people," Syler said. "Acceptance is always good."

"That's true. I think they're still hoping I'll find myself a nice Jewish girl one of these days, though," Megan said with a small laugh. She shifted and fixed Syler with a searching look of her own. "How about you? I can't imagine you'd need convincing to come out, especially if you were in the States."

"You're right about that," Syler said with her usual easy manner. "I was eighteen when I told my family, they were like, we know, and?" She grinned. "These days, when we're all hanging out at our dad's place, me and my brothers sit out on the porch with beers and talk about women we think are hot until my dad gets exasperated with us and makes us play basketball with him." She paused to take a swig of beer before continuing, "I've never regretted choosing to live openly, but I've had a long time to get comfortable with myself. Own my identity, so to speak. People can be pretty narrow-minded and conservative, but in the end, this is my life. I'm not going to change myself to fit into society. And society is changing, Meg. Some places faster than others, but it is changing."

"I hope so," Megan said.

"I don't want you to think I expect you to be as open as me," Syler said. "Sometimes it's not safe to come out and I trust you to make that decision for yourself."

Megan looked deep into Syler's eyes and saw the trust and respect in their depths. Warmth billowed up in her chest. Megan reached across the table to take Syler's hand in hers.

"I am proud of what I have with you, and I want to be more open where I can," Megan said. She felt a cold brush of worry even as she said the words. While Megan wasn't worried about other peoples' opinions of her, Charles finding out would be professional suicide for both of them. Someone more understanding would let their relationship slide under the radar rather than lose two valuable members of the staff, but Megan couldn't see a rulemonger like Charles giving them an inch, especially if it let him get rid of Syler.

"You know I'll support you and I'll be there for you no matter what," Syler said. She let go of Megan's hand and gathered up the dishes. "How about a bath? Are you okay with reheated water? I can refill it if you want."

"No, that's fine," Megan said. She glowed at the thought of a nice, luxurious bath, perhaps one she wouldn't have to take alone. "I reheat mine too. It's a waste to use it only once."

"Great, I'll run the cycle while we clean up."

"Okay, but while *I* clean up," Megan told her. She reached out and stilled Syler's industrious stacking. "You cooked so I'll do the dishes. Besides, I already know where everything goes."

"No argument from me there," Syler said.

Together they put away the cushions and rolled up the rug. Once the roof was tidy again, Syler hefted the tray and headed down the stairs. While Syler was busy with the bath, Megan washed the dishes and put them away. As she moved through the room, Megan discovered Syler's scent still clung to her skin. She basked in the memory of what they'd done and dreamed about what was yet to come.

"Okay, bath's ready," Syler said as she came into the kitchen. She stood behind Megan and lightly wrapped her arms around Megan's waist. She dropped a quick kiss into her hair and said, "You're the guest of honor so you go first."

"Why don't you join me?" Megan asked.

"Really? Are you serious?"

"Of course," Megan said. She leaned back into Syler's embrace. "I can wash your back."

"Now that's an offer I can't refuse." Syler let go of Megan and propped her elbows on the island. "The washing-up area's not huge so I'll give you a head start and come in when you're in the bath. You'll find towels on the shelf and soap and shampoo inside, so help yourself to anything you want."

"Okay," Megan said.

The bathroom was clean and modern, the big bath full of fragrant green water. Under the spray of the shower, Megan perched on the bathing stool and luxuriated in the lightly scented body soap before she bent over to wash her hair. She rinsed off and sank into the depths of the bath. A Syler-shaped shadow appeared on the other side of the frosted glass door.

"Is it all right if I come in?"

"Sure," Megan said. "I've finished washing and I'm just relaxing now."

She lay in the scented water and closed her eyes as Syler took her place in the washing-up area. The steam from the shower filled the room. Megan drifted on happy thoughts, which were interrupted by Syler offering her the soaped-up sponge. Megan got up on her knees in the tub and leaned over the side to give Syler's back a good scrubbing.

"This is one thing I missed while I was in Thailand," Megan said. "Although it was so hot all the time I think even if I'd had the option of a hot bath, I wouldn't have taken it."

"Me too. God, that's nice," Syler said as Megan swept the rich suds over her skin. "In Michigan we had the standard American-style bath, so I never really understood the whole co-bathing thing." She turned and glanced over her shoulder, "But you know what? I think I get it now."

Megan's already warm skin tingled with the heat of Syler's words and gaze. She lowered her gaze and replied, "It is nice, isn't it?"

"Certainly is. Oh, down a bit? Yes, right there." Syler's wet hair parted over her nape. As she lowered her chin with a sound of pleasure, the allure of the unbroken expanse of skin was too great and Megan abandoned the sponge in favor of sliding her bare fingers down Syler's back to her slim waist. She was about to pull away when Syler's voice stopped her.

"I think you missed a spot."

"Where?" Megan asked. She let out a gasp of pleasure as Syler took her soapy hands and slid them around to cup her breasts. The feeling of Syler's nipples hardening under her slippery fingers sent happy jolts from her fingertips directly to between her legs. Megan couldn't stop the moan of longing that welled up from her throat.

"That feels so good," Syler said. Her head was still tilted forward and Megan gave into the urge to press her lips to the exposed nape of Syler's neck. Syler leaned into the caress and said, "My God Meg, I think I'm done and then you set me off again. You must think I'm a total sex maniac." She gave a low chuckle and pressed back so Megan's breasts were against her.

"Not at all," Megan said. Her breathing got heavier as she moved ever so slowly against Syler, eased by the slickness of the soap between them. "Not any more than I am, which is actually quite a lot so, um, what was the question?"

"I forget," Syler said. "Just don't stop what you're doing."

Now that Syler was flush with her, she had more room to maneuver. As she rained kisses over Syler's neck and shoulders, Megan heard the catch in Syler's breath and continued to tease the hard nubs with her fingertips. Syler pressed back into the caress. Megan was once more in awe at how well they fit together, how Syler responded to her.

"I'm loving you touching me," Syler purred. "But I need to get this soap off me and I really want to join you in that tub."

Megan retrieved her hands and Syler grabbed the showerhead, which she used to hose the suds off first Megan, then herself. Once she was free of bubbles, Megan scooted over to one side of the deep bath as Syler climbed in.

"It's a bit cozy in here," Syler said. She settled down and sent a green tidal wave cascading over the side of the deep tub.

"I don't mind," Megan said. She turned around to nestle back against Syler as long legs settled on either side of Megan's body.

"Me neither. Is this all right? Not squashed?"

"Not at all," Megan said. Syler put her arms around Megan and held her close. With a small wiggle that sent a thrill through her entire body, Megan said, "I liked watching you, but being held by you is much better."

Syler's laugh echoed through her.

"I like being with you like this. I really do," Megan said. She picked up a double handful of hot water and let it trail through her fingers. "I've never been so...naked with anyone like this before."

"Neither have I," Syler said.

That surprised Megan, but she let it go without comment as she didn't want to break the deep harmony she was feeling with Syler's limbs wrapped around her. Although it did make sense, considering the role Syler mentioned she'd been asked to play in her previous relationships. A certain amount of detachment was necessary to be a *bari-tachi*, Megan knew that much from her own experience.

Megan settled back into Syler's embrace and closed her eyes, content to simply exist in the moment with Syler's entire length against her. Megan surrendered herself to the supple arms that held her with such strength and trust. She didn't allow herself to dwell on how much she would miss Syler's presence when she left, how empty and meaningless Megan's life would be without her. What Megan had done could not be forgiven. She did not deserve a happy ending. Even in the hot, fragrant water, Megan shivered.

"Are you okay, Meg?"

"Fine. I'm just getting a bit sleepy."

"Me too." Syler held up a hand and said, "And I'm pruning up, so how about we get out?"

Megan agreed. She put all other thoughts from her mind. The floating, euphoric feeling returned as she dried off in one of Syler's big, fluffy towels and stayed with her as she dressed for sleeping. In the big comfy bed, Megan snuggled into Syler's arms, certain no nightmares would take her that night, no matter what the future held for her.

About the Author

Mildred Gail Digby has a BSc in geology, however Takarazuka, pachinko, and no laws against drinking beer outside lured her to teach in Japan. Her favorite thing to do is add lesbians to any situation and make a novel about it. She dreams one day of working as a professional beer taster and devotes a good deal of her time honing her skills in that area which, to an uninformed outsider, appears to be simply drinking a lot of beer.

She shares her non-angst-filled life with her wife of nearly ten years where the most excitement they have is deciding where to eat and forgetting where they parked their bicycles. Mildred is a sucker for oddball characters, opposites attract, and women getting what (and who) they want. She will squeeze a happy ending out of anything and still blushes when she writes love scenes.

Another Mildred J. Digby title to look for:

Phoenix

What would it take to make you ditch your career, your pride, and run from everything you believe in? In private investigator Ashe Devon's case, it's the fact that her client ended up dead while under her protection. Out of the P.I. business, Ashe is just trying to survive the daily grind of her boring, vanilla life when her former boss calls her out of retirement for one last job: protect a local DJ from a violent stalker. Ashe is fully prepared to turn down the case until she meets the client.

Mystral Galbraith, aka Phoenix, is unashamedly gay, just a tad awkward and musically brilliant. Ashe is instantly captivated by her and can't ignore the fierce young woman's plea for help. Neither can Ashe ignore the stirrings of long-forgotten emotions that set both her heart and her boxer briefs on fire. While Ashe struggles to keep her relationship with Mystral professional, the tension between them simmers just beneath the surface.

More than Ashe's pride is involved — failure could cost Mystral her life. But is Ashe the right person for the job? If she doesn't get her hormones under control, the undeniable pull between them could compromise her judgment and open the door for history to repeat its tragic lesson.

ISBN 978-1-61929-394-6
eISBN 978-1-61929-395-3

MORE REGAL CREST PUBLICATIONS

Melissa Good	Tropical Convergence	978-1-935053-18-7
Melissa Good	Winds of Change Book One	978-1-61929-194-2
Melissa Good	Winds of Change Book Two	978-1-61929-232-1
Melissa Good	Southern Stars	978-1-61929-348-9
Jeanine Hoffman	Lights & Sirens	978-1-61929-115-7
Jeanine Hoffman	Strength in Numbers	978-1-61929-109-6
Jeanine Hoffman	Back Swing	978-1-61929-137-9
K. E. Lane	And, Playing the Role of Herself	978-1-932300-72-7
Jennifer McCormick	Tears of the Sun	978-1-61929-396-0
Kate McLachlan	Christmas Crush	978-1-61929-195-9
Kate McLachlan	Hearts, Dead and Alive	978-1-61929-017-4
Kate McLachlan	Murder and the Hurdy Gurdy Girl	978-1-61929-125-6
Kate McLachlan	Rescue At Inspiration Point	978-1-61929-005-1
Kate McLachlan	Return Of An Impetuous Pilot	978-1-61929-152-2
Kate McLachlan	Rip Van Dyke	978-1-935053-29-3
Kate McLachlan	Ten Little Lesbians	978-1-61929-236-9
Kate McLachlan	Alias Mrs. Jones	978-1-61929-282-6
Lynne Norris	One Promise	978-1-932300-92-5
Lynne Norris	Sanctuary	978-1-61929-248-2
Lynne Norris	The Light of Day	978-1-61929-338-0
Nita Round	A Touch of Truth Book One: Raven, Fire and Ice	978-1-61929-372-4
Nita Round	A Touch of Truth Book Two: Raven, Sand and Sun	978-1-61929-404-2
Nita Round	Fresh Start	978-1-61929-340-3
Nita Round	Knight's Sacrifice	978-1-61929-314-4
Nita Round	The Ghost of Emily Tapper	978-1-61929-328-1
Kelly Sinclair	Getting Back	978-1-61929-242-0
Kelly Sinclair	Accidental Rebels	978-1-61929-260-4
Schramm and Dunne	Love Is In the Air	978-1-61929-362-8
Rae Theodore	Leaving Normal: Adventures in Gender	978-1-61929-320-5
Rae Theodore	My Mother Says Drums Are for Boys: True Stories for Gender Rebels	978-1-61929-378-6
Barbara Valletto	Pulse Points	978-1-61929-254-3
Barbara Valletto	Everlong	978-1-61929-266-6
Barbara Valletto	Limbo	978-1-61929-358-8
Barbara Valletto	Diver Blues	978-1-61929-384-7
Lisa Young	Out and Proud	978-1-61929-392-2

Be sure to check out our other imprints,
Blue Beacon Books, Carnelian Books, Mystic Books, Quest Books,
Silver Dragon Books, Troubadour Books,
and Young Adult Books.

VISIT US ONLINE AT
www.regalcrest.biz

At the Regal Crest Website You'll Find

~ The latest news about forthcoming titles and
new releases

~ Our complete backlist of titles

~ Information about your favorite authors

Regal Crest print titles are available from all
progressive booksellers including numerous sources
online. Our distributors are Bella Distribution and
Ingram.

www.ingramcontent.com/pod-product-compliance
Lightning Source LLC
Chambersburg PA
CBHW071834020726
47502CB00004B/1350